Obsession

by

Nigel Lampard

Enjoy!
Nigel
20th May 2015

Also by Nigel Lampard

Naked Slaughter
Subliminal
The Loser Has To Fall
Pooh Bridge
In Denial

Published by Bardel 2015
© Nigel Lampard 2005

Second Edition

No part of this book may be reproduced or transmitted in any form or by any means, electronic or mechanical, including photocopying, recording, or by any information storage and retrieval system, without permission in writing from the publisher
This is a work of fiction. Names, places, businesses, characters, and incidents, are either the product of the author's imagination or are used fictitiously and any resemblance to any actual persons, living or dead, organisations, events or locales, or any other entity, is entirely coincidental.

The unauthorised reproduction or distribution of this copyrighted work is illegal.

Cover designed by Bardel
Image provided by www.123RF.com

Dedication

I would like to dedicate this novel to my wife, Jane, who over the years has been extremely patient as I tapped away on my laptop at all times of the day and night

Acknowledgements

I am grateful to Clare and Billy who very kindly allowed me to use their cottage in Westerham, Kent as the main setting for this novel.

Chapter One

Now that the White Cliffs of Dover were a good deal closer it meant the cross-channel ferry was coming to the end of its hellish passage.

During Matthew Ryan's road trip from Germany through Holland and Belgium to France, the rain lashed down. Even when on full speed the windscreen wipers on his car had difficulty in giving a clear view ahead. He stopped twice for his own safety, pulling off the motorway so that he could regain the courage and composure to continue his testing journey.

He was sure the awful weather would guarantee the cancellation of all crossings – a night in a decent hotel was definitely preferable, although it would mean getting home a day later than planned.

However, as he approached the last stage of his journey to Calais the rain abated slightly and, looking towards the north, he saw there was a definite line in the grey scudding sky and the brighter weather was heading his way. Maybe he would get home on time after all. Unfortunately, the wind did not ease off as much as the rain and just before boarding the ferry's instability was evident even when tied to the dock in Calais.

Among the other passengers, there were the stalwarts with asbestos stomachs who had something to prove as they tucked into every manner of fast food, washing it down with copious quantities of lager. Others, knowing their limitations, were less adventurous and stuck with water and crisps. At the other end of the scale, there were those who, regardless of when they had last eaten or drunk something and with all the will in the world, could not keep anything down. Some of these unfortunates made it to the toilets, but others did not.

This final group were the ones who forced Matthew – who was in the water and crisp grouping – up on deck to get some fresh air.

He swayed his way down the aisle among the other passengers and then crawled up the stairs, trying his hardest to look like an accustomed sailor, which he wasn't. The outer door proved difficult to open but once outside on deck the gale brought with it the fresh air he needed. It also brought a feeling of power as he forced his way to the railing to gaze down at the grey mysterious water surging past thirty feet below where he stood.

Initially he thought he was alone but he wasn't.

Further along the deck, beyond the lifeboats, was a woman.

She was holding her coat tight against her body and her long dark hair billowed horizontally as she looked across the water towards the white cliffs that indicated their journey's end. The woman had not seen Matthew, or if she had she wasn't showing any awareness of his presence.

Her face was in shadow, and she was standing perfectly still, but her posture made him look in her direction every few seconds.

Something was not quite right.

She seemed oblivious to the howling gale that was buffeting her, biting into her face and twanging the ropes on the lifeboat above her head.

It was mid-March and the temperature had not crept above five or six degrees all day, the wind chill must have dropped the temperature to below zero. The ferry was pitching and rolling to such an extent that Matthew clung to the railings in front of him for his own safety, his eyes still on the woman. She was resting her chest against the top rail, her arms still clutching the coat about her, but rather than looking at the horizon now she was staring at the rushing water.

There was a crash and Matthew tightened his grip on the rail, his attention diverted for a few seconds from the woman. When he looked back, she had taken off her coat and thrown it on the deck. She seemed to move in slow motion as she lifted one foot then the other onto the bottom railing, her thighs resting against the top support.

Suddenly, it was obvious what she intended doing.

Instinctively Matthew rushed towards her, slipping on the wet deck as he tried to cover the short distance between them. She had already swung one leg over the top rail by the time he reached her.

He grabbed at her as she launched herself.

Her arm was wet and slippery but luckily she was small and slim. She hadn't managed to get her other leg over the railing before he stopped her.

"Let go!" she screamed as he pulled her back from a certain death. "Let me fucking go!"

She started to struggle, her strength amazing for somebody her size. He hadn't noticed before but she had kicked off her shoes. One of her bare feet caught him in the stomach making him lose his grip on her arm. She frantically crawled towards the railing again and started heaving herself up. This time he put his arms round her waist so that he could drag her as far away from the side as possible.

The woman became subdued, the fight having left her as quickly as it started. He set her down on the wet deck with her back to the cabin wall. She was a mess and he was a mess. Her head was on her chest, and she was crying: no, she wasn't crying, she was sobbing.

"Why ... why didn't you let me do it? Why couldn't you ... you simply let me jump?" she pleaded through her tears.

Having acted impulsively, he didn't know what to say. "I couldn't just stand by and watch you do that," he told her.

"Do what and why not?" she asked, her tone suggesting his actions were illogical. "You don't know me. My loss would have meant nothing to you." There were no intonations in her voice, but she was almost certainly English.

As she stared at her hands in her lap, she looked like a wet rag doll. Matthew didn't doubt that he had done the right thing, he couldn't have remained a bystander while somebody tried to commit suicide.

"If I hadn't helped, my conscience would never have allowed me to rest because –"

"Help? Help?" she spat at him from under the bedraggled hair covering her face. "You could have helped by pushing me over the side not pulling me back from it."

"Look," he said, ignoring her. "Can I get you inside? What may have seemed good reason to kill yourself –"

"Don't you dare start psychoanalysing and patronising me. You don't want to know and there's no reason why you need to know. Just fuck off and leave me here. Pretend you never fucking saw me," she said, her expletives seeming out of place.

She began to get up so he put a restraining hand on her

shoulder, forcing her to sit down.

She started crying again.

"Look, whoever you are, why can't you just mind your own fucking business? It's taken me ages to pluck up the courage and then you have to poke your nose in. Just fuck off!" she shouted.

"I can't."

"Fuck off!"

"No."

The ship must have hit a particularly large wave because there was a loud crash and they both lurched to one side. Matthew reached for the woman again to stop her from falling over.

"You're bloody determined that I shouldn't hurt myself, aren't you?"

She lifted her head and he saw her face properly for the first time. Her make-up had run and her eyes looked very sore. Soaking wet hair clung to the sides of her face, but nothing could hide her prettiness. She was younger than he originally thought, maybe late twenties or early thirties. She reminded him of somebody but he dismissed the notion straight away – now was not the time to try to think who she looked like.

Her lips parted as she began to speak, her white teeth were small and even, but then she changed her mind and instead she lifted one hand to cover her mouth. What he saw was a face that had everything to live for – not one, if he hadn't acted, that should be lifeless and floating in the English Channel.

"Who are you?" he asked before she could say anything further.

She took her hand away from her mouth and lifted her head as her eyes narrowed. "There's no need for you to know."

"If you say so, but I'm afraid I am not leaving you here to try again. You need help," he said.

"Do I? What if I tell them you attacked me? What then? What if I tell them that you sexually assaulted me, put your hands on me, and I had to fight you off?" Something in her eyes told Matthew that her proposed accusations were insincere.

He reached for her coat and attempted to put it round her shoulders because she had started shaking uncontrollably. It was either shock or cold or both.

"Nothing would be gained by doing that. We both know the

truth," he said.

Initially she resisted his efforts but then she leant forward and let him put the coat round her shoulders.

"You really ought to let me get you inside," Matthew said, picking up her shoes before handing them to her, he was surprised when she took them from him. After putting on her wet shoes, she lifted her hands to her hair and pushed some loose strands behind her ears. She was still shaking.

"Why are you doing this?" she asked.

"Because you need help,' he said again.

"I bet you wouldn't be doing it if I were a man."

Her comment brought an ironic smile to his lips, and he shook his head. "I would like to think it wouldn't make any difference."

Turning to face him, she looked directly into his eyes for the first time. "If I agree to go inside will you promise that you won't tell anybody what I tried to do?"

It was progress.

"You do need help but no, I won't tell anybody what happened. Are you alone? I mean did you come on board with anybody?"

She shook her head slightly. "No, I'm on my own. I'm on my own big time."

"Is that why ...?"

He didn't finish his question ... it was none of his business. Taking hold of her elbow he helped her get up.

"I suppose I ought to thank you," she said as they walked back towards the door.

In the short space of time in which the whole incident had taken, Matthew hadn't noticed that the ferry was making progress towards the port of Dover, but he guessed they were still about five miles out. The wind had dropped significantly. He held the door open for her and then followed her into the relative calm. Just inside there were toilets, males to the left and females to the right.

She stopped by the door.

"I'm going to tidy myself up before going back down." When she saw him hesitate, she added, "Don't worry I'm not going to do anything silly but I would like you to wait for me, please."

He did as she asked but quickly decided the sensible thing to do would be to walk away. They were close to Dover and it would be easy to make sure they did not see each other again before the ship docked. Then he would be on the M20 heading for London, the incident behind him but almost certainly not forgotten.

He stayed where he was.

It wasn't a feeling of responsibility that stopped him from walking away, it was more a nagging need to find out why somebody like her could be so brave and yet so foolish as to contemplate throwing herself into the icy Channel. There was no doubt that if he had not been there she would have done it. Not knowing whether she was a foot passenger, part of a coach party or whether she had her own car, didn't help.

She said she had come on board alone, if she were telling him the truth that would discount her being on a coach. If she were a foot passenger, and her disappearance never reported, her death would only be discovered when the tide washed her white and bloated body up on some beach, or it was spotted floating in the Channel.

Had she been right to ask him whether he would have done the same thing for a man? He would have tried to stop a man from jumping over the side but if he had succeeded and the man had come to his senses, there would have been a quick handshake, a little embarrassment and a story to tell his grandchildren, if he ever had any.

So why was he now waiting outside the female toilets for a complete stranger? It may be because she was a woman. In fact, it was because she was a woman, but he was also inquisitive.

He wanted to know why … his thoughts were interrupted as the woman re-appeared.

She looked at him and there was a trace of a grim smile on her face. She hadn't had a bag with her but she had used something to brush her hair, and washed her face which was now free of make-up. He revised his opinion about her age again: she was probably nearer thirty-five than thirty. Her eyes were a dark brown, her hair thick, long and naturally jet-black. She was about five and a half feet tall with a slim figure. His eyes dropped to her hands in search of a telltale wedding or engagement ring, but there was neither.

"Thank you for waiting," she said. "Do you think they are still serving drinks, I could do with something very strong?"

"Possibly but there's only one way of finding out," he said.

The bar was still open. He bought a soft drink for himself and a double brandy for her. She gulped half of the brandy down immediately.

"Do you have a bag somewhere?" he asked.

"I left it in the car," she replied. "People who want to kill themselves don't need handbags. Do you have any cigarettes?"

He went and bought a packet from the bar, which was then in the process of closing. She ripped off the cellophane wrapping before pulling out a cigarette and putting it between her lips. He had forgotten to buy matches but a man sitting at the next table was quick on the uptake and leant over with his lighter.

She exhaled towards the ceiling as she picked up her brandy, her eyes on Matthew. "So who are you?"

He shrugged. "Does it really matter who I am?"

"At least give me your first name … on second thoughts I'm not sure I want to thank you for what you did … but at least I'll know the name of the person who kept me on this earth for a little longer."

He smiled. "All right, my name is Matthew."

"And mine is Francesca."

She finished her brandy.

"You mentioned a car. Are you going to be all right to drive?" he asked.

She tapped the glass. "It takes more than this to make me incapable of driving."

"No, that's not what I meant. You've just been through a pretty traumatic experience," he said noticing that the man who had lent her his cigarette lighter was taking more than just a passing interest in what they were saying. "You could be in shock."

"Matthew, I've been in a state of shock for a good deal longer than you appreciate. What do you think made me try and …" Matthew indicated their inquisitive neighbour with a slight nod of his head. She looked at the man and said, "do what I did?"

"An unfair question because I don't know. It's just that a combination of that drink and –"

"Anyway," she said, interrupting him, "why should you worry? When we drive off this boat we'll never see each other again."

"True but I'd hate what happened up there to have been for nothing."

She shrugged. "You'll never know, will you?"

"That's also true."

Although he wanted to ask what had caused her to be so unhappy, it was evident that she was not going to reveal anything else about herself.

As he looked at her and wondered, a rather guttural male voice announced over the ship's tannoy that the ferry was approaching Dover, and would car drivers and passengers please return to their cars. Francesca was fiddling nervously with a paper napkin she had picked up from the table.

"Are you sure you'll be all right?" She nodded in reply. "Which deck is your car on?" he asked.

She shook her head. "I haven't the faintest idea. I didn't think I'd ever be returning to it, so what was the point in ..." Lifting the now mutilated napkin to her eyes she wiped a tear away.

"Look, Francesca, I can't let you wander aimlessly round looking for your car and what's more, I'm not very happy about you being on your own once we do find it ..." Matthew closed his eyes and took a deep breath, knowing that if he didn't walk away he was going to be dragged into something that he would regret "... I will help you find your car and then I want you to promise me that you'll meet me once we are through Customs."

The tears were still in her eyes. "Why are you doing this? Why can't you just leave me alone?"

"I don't know but I can't."

People were milling around them, all trying to find the right stairs that would lead to their cars.

Francesca stood up. "All right I agree, and I'm sorry for swearing at you earlier."

"Not a problem," he said, smiling. "Do you remember roughly where you were when you came up from the car deck?" he asked, taking her by the arm.

She looked around her. "Opposite the Purser's office, I think."

"Come on, then, I know where that is."

They found her car remarkably easily.

It was a silver-metallic Audi S3 with what could only be

personalised number plate – FRA 1 N – which surprised Matthew for some reason. She had not struck him as being the sort of person who would go in for such things. Her handbag was still on the front passenger's seat and the keys were in the ignition.

His car was on the same deck but on the opposite side of the ferry to hers.

Once she was behind the wheel, he squatted down by the open door.

"Have you driven into Dover before?" he asked.

"Yes."

"There's a garage soon after Customs. Will you wait for me there?"

"Yes."

He closed the door and she lowered the window. "If I get there first I'll be at the far end by the shop,' he said.

She closed her eyes and nodded. "I'll be there."

Matthew went back to his own car.

Fortunately, as the stream of traffic approached Customs, he was only five cars behind Francesca. She seemed to be edging forward perfectly normally so he had no reason to doubt that she wasn't going to stick to their agreement. Both cars passed the watchful customs officers without incident so Francesca's car was in full view as she approached the garage.

She did not stop.

Suddenly she accelerated and steered left from the slow moving line of traffic, and as she reached the roundabout at the entrance to the Port, she took the first left onto the link road for the A2.

Matthew attempted to follow but a car coming up the outside lane blocked him in. The last he saw of Francesca was a fleeting glimpse of her car in the door mirror as she sped back across the bridge over the Port and out of his life.

Chapter Two

The first three months of the year had not generated the anticipated progress with his consultancy that the previous seven months had supposedly guaranteed. Financially Matthew was in a break-even situation but he thought with the number of promising contracts that had materialised towards the end of the previous year things were going to improve significantly.

However, the cancellation of the most lucrative contract due to a lack of funding, and at the last moment, jolted his confidence significantly. He often wondered why when funding became difficult, the training budget was the first to be cut. Because of this cancellation, he made a mental note to change the contract-break clause in future dealings with European companies.

Any misgivings he might have had regarding this temporary blip he was experiencing in business, was more than adequately compensated for by what he knew was waiting for him an hour and half's drive away … at the end of his journey.

The incident on the ferry – if incident was the right word – was going to be the cause of an interesting conversation or three when he got home. Although Laura would only have what he told her to go on, she would no doubt psychoanalyse the woman and his actions too. In some ways he looked forward to the conclusions she might draw.

Once through the A20 Roundhill Tunnel and just before the M20 started at Folkestone, and with little traffic about, his thoughts drifted away from what he regarded as home and back to his ex-wife, Emily. It was always the same – soon after agreeing they were a couple they had gone to Folkestone for an illicit weekend to 'cement their relationship' as Emily had put it, for him it was forty-eight hours of wonderful exploration, and not of the sights Folkestone had to offer. As they drove away after lunch on the Sunday, Emily had asked why they had gone all the way to Folkestone – and why Folkestone – when they could have achieved the same outcome by staying in her bed in her flat all weekend.

It was always Emily.

He couldn't rid his mind of his memories.

Whenever he started to be grateful for the happiness Laura had brought into his life, Emily was always there in the background and her presence, albeit imaginary, made him feel guilty. He felt guilty because he shouldn't allow her to still be affecting him in this way, and then because he had found happiness with another woman after all. He told himself repeatedly that she had no right to play on his mind so much after so long. She was the cause of the break-up of their marriage, not him.

Nevertheless, each time he began to blame her he only added to his own guilt. Emily did not control his thoughts so he had no right to try to pass his guilt onto her.

So why didn't he just forget about the whole miserable episode, and move on? Emily was history, he had his and Laura's future to consider now.

It was because his thoughts and memories were not only with his ex-wife but also with Sarah. He didn't want to remember what Emily had told him, Sarah was as much part of him as she was of Emily.

They had married twelve years earlier in 1989, after what friends referred to as, unfashionably, a whirlwind romance.

Having met in the March they walked down the aisle the following August. Surprisingly, when they first saw each other at a party – neither knew the host as she was a friend of their respective partners – they were both in long-term relationships. The attraction was mutual and Matthew's girlfriend – Lisa – didn't appreciate what she saw, whereas Emily's boyfriend – Chris – was oblivious until Lisa pointed out what she had sensed out to him. Ironically, Chris and Lisa married six months after Matthew and Emily.

When they met, Matthew had recently started a second career, having decided that teaching was not for him. The constant changes in curriculum and the more radical changes in discipline in the classroom plus political correctness, forced him to look elsewhere. He loved his subjects – history and psychology – and he loved the opportunity to share his knowledge and experiences, but the constant interference by outside agencies drove him out of what he thought was his true vocation.

He moved away from teaching to lecturing and joined Xanadu

International Limited, a team of management consultants that made use of various facilitators throughout the UK. Imparting the theories and practices of management (and leadership) techniques on junior managers was new to him, but fortunately what he – and the others in Xanadu – told them was new to the students too. Matthew spent eleven happy and lucrative years with Xanadu after which he had built up sufficient confidence and capital to try to go it alone as a consultant.

He decided he would describe himself as an Organisational Development Consultant, and offer his services to any company or organisation that wanted an external change agent to help with its growth and management of subsequent change. He often reflected on the irony (bordering on hypocrisy) of the fact that the facilitators of his departure from teaching were the very body of people he had now joined.

At first, he and Emily were very happy.

Having honeymooned in Malaysia they returned home and to their individual careers: Matthew to Xanadu and Emily to her investment consultancy. Before they married, they bought a house in Stratford-upon-Avon, which suited her as she was based in Leamington Spa and him because Xanadu didn't really have a base. It went wherever the work took it. Being in central England gave Matthew access to the motorway network, a mainline railway station and an international airport in Birmingham.

Probably because he was the one who did the travelling, he coped with their short separations far better than Emily did. He was never away for more than two weeks at a time but after a couple of years, Emily became rather disenchanted with his absences. The arguments were more frequent and what was worse, they became quite personal.

When Emily fell pregnant in 1994, and although her pregnancy wasn't planned, it seemed to inject a modicum of rationale into what could have become a failing relationship. Although Emily suffered from severe morning sickness during the early months, she coped well but as the bump grew in size and she became more uncomfortable, the inevitable changes that a child would bring also began to tell.

Regardless of biological fact, she accused Matthew of being selfish because he did not seem to accept she still had her own career to follow. He counter-argued that she was still going to work, whether he agreed with it or not, and if Emily wanted their lifestyle maintaining he had little choice but to carry on as he was.

Sarah was born on 30th November 1994 and Emily returned to work on 5th January 1995. They employed a child-minder – Amanda was the third of three, the first two having been given their marching orders for various reasons – who looked after Sarah during weekdays from eight o'clock in the morning until six in the evening.

Nevertheless, due to Matthew's continued absences and sleepless nights for both of them when he was at home, the marriage began to suffer once again. There were fewer arguments but more silences.

The other directors of Xanadu understood when he told them he was going to have to restrict his availability both in time and to contracts that were available closer to home. Initially the changed schedules worked well, but after a few months, the patience of the other directors was wearing a little thin. That is when Matthew decided to set himself up as an independent consultant. The theory was that if he were in control then Emily might have less of a reason to find fault. His salary might drop a little initially, but he hoped it would pick up as he became more established.

Unfortunately, and at the time unbeknown to him, the eventual seeds of the breakdown of their relationship, and their marriage, had already been sown before Sarah was born ... in more ways than one.

One mid-week evening in July 1995 when Emily and Matthew had actually managed to find time to be with each other, a simple misunderstanding led to a particularly virulent disagreement. Her work had been taking her out – not away but out locally – in the evenings more and more over the previous six months, and there were a few times when she needed to go to weekday conferences/seminars that resulted in overnight stays.

On this occasion, he had forgotten she was out the following Friday evening, which meant they were double-booked. He was due at a quarterly assessment conference with Xanadu at which he also wanted to tell the other directors about his decision to start up on his own.

Either he was extremely naïve or he walked around with his eyes closed: he didn't know which it was – maybe both – but it didn't really matter because the result was the same.

When Sarah was born, both he and Emily were thirty-five years old. The preceding years had been stormy but containable and the same description applied to their sex life. More often than not, when they did argue, they did not allow the resultant resentment to fester until the following morning. Usually if there was any lingering animosity, going to bed was a good way of bringing them to their senses, albeit temporarily.

However, after Sarah was born there was more festering than lovemaking. It appeared as though Emily had lost interest in sex and seemed more than happy to lie in bed and brood. If Matthew attempted to return to their old ways, he was left in little doubt that it wasn't an option. He put the reduction in Emily's libido down to post-natal depression: his research on the Internet told him that it could go on for years. As a result he threw himself into his work and, when they were together, he was determined that their relationship was going to come out of whatever she was in, stronger than when she had entered it.

Naivety or blindness apart, he was not prepared for what Emily threw at him on this particular evening. The misunderstanding over the Friday engagements led to another period of silence, which remained even after he had given one of the more on-side directors a call to ask him to cover for his absence with the others.

When Matthew went back into the living room after the call and told Emily, all she could say was, "I should think so too." Then she went back to the magazine she was supposedly reading.

During dinner and before he made the phone call their conversation was non-existent once the clash was realised. He did the washing up then rang Charles Rickman.

Emily's attitude and general demeanour was testing his patience anyway, but her comment made him really want to find the underlying cause of whatever was behind her mood change.

"What's happened, Em? Why are we like this?"

Without looking up, she said, "Don't call me Em, I've never

liked it. My name's Emily."

"I'm well aware what your name is."

He went over to the CD player and turned the music down.

"I was listening to that," she said, like a spoilt child.

"And you still can but, to be quite honest with you, I think you and I are just a little more important than music at the moment."

He sat down in the chair opposite his wife.

"You and I?" she repeated, appearing indifferent to what Matthew was saying, and still without taking her nose out of the magazine.

In her mid-thirties, Emily could pass for somebody ten years younger but since Sarah's birth what she looked like did not seem to bother her as much as it used to, except when she went to work. In retrospect, Matthew supposed he should have read the signs but, as he did not want to admit what he believed was happening, he chose to ignore them instead.

Her short blonde hair was as immaculate as it always was, but she wore no make-up and her eyes lacked the sparkle they once had. He couldn't have cared less about whether she wore make-up but, until Sarah was born, Emily rarely let him see her in the morning until she put her face on – her words not his. She was quite tall and she often complained about her boyish figure, but he had always regarded her as being perfect in every way. He felt like that when they met and, even to this day, he still thought the same.

"You know exactly what I am saying, so don't try to play the innocent with me," he said as he took a sip of the whisky he had poured before phoning Richard. He needed courage then in the same way he needed it now.

At last, she lowered the magazine.

"Don't play the innocent, Matthew? Are you implying I'm guilty of something?"

"Emily, for God's sake, we've got to do something. I can't go on the way we are."

"The way we –"

"Stop bloody well repeating everything I say and talk to me. It's been going on for too long and it's crucifying me."

She threw the magazine onto the coffee table before reaching for her glass of white wine. Leaning back in the chair, she let her eyes rest on his. There wasn't a hint of affection. Her body language was defensive, her expression critical.

"I'm sorry if I'm repeating what you have already said once again," she said sarcastically, "but what has been going on for too long?"

"You know damn well what I'm referring to," he replied through clenched teeth. "It's been seven months since Sarah was born –"

"And you will wake her up if you don't keep your voice down."

"For Christ's sake, Emily, don't shut me out. Tell me what is wrong. Tell me how I can help."

A few moments silence followed while Emily pondered her reply. She stared at him and her expression went from being critical to being defiant. Her eyes then narrowed and she started to speak a couple of times but obviously thought what she was going to say wasn't right. Matthew remained silent because there was nothing he wanted to add.

He wondered why it had taken eighteen months of heartache and nastiness to get to this point. Sarah, bless her, had to be the catalyst. He never doubted either his or Emily's love for Sarah and he knew that, regardless of how depressed Emily might be, she could never harm Sarah. He watched her going into their daughter every evening to make sure she was all right before settling down for the night herself, and she could not disguise the look of love and devotion – there were even times when her eyes brimmed with tears of happiness, but not because she was with him.

Although he may not have understood what was happening, he had accepted the changes in Emily, but things had now come to a head – and all because of a bloody misunderstanding – and enough was enough.

"It's because I don't love you anymore, Matthew."

He was still musing over what was happening when Emily spoke so, at first, her words did not register.

Looking up he frowned.

"I'm sorry?" he said.

"I said, it's because I don't love you anymore. I'm not in love with you and I don't love you."

She did not move.

The glass of wine was in her hand and, after hitting him with such a devastating blow, she took a sip almost as though they were discussing the weather.

She was waiting for his reaction.

"What do you mean you don't love me?" he heard himself ask but not believing the question should be necessary.

Emily shook her head slightly. "I would have thought that was obvious, Matthew. I no longer want to be with you or want you anywhere near me." Her eyes remained defiant, testing him.

She took another sip of her wine.

"And how long have you felt like this?" he asked in a monotone, the true meaning her words slowly permeating its way into his brain ... his body was numb

He imagined it was like knowing you had been shot, you knew you were either severely injured or dying but the pain had yet to reach the brain.

"Does it matter? It's the way I feel now that matters,' she said.

"But what have I done to make you feel this way?"

She shrugged. "You've done nothing really, I suppose. I didn't just wake up one morning and decide that I didn't love you."

"I must have done something. I'm the same person you married."

Regardless of how he felt inside, he was not going to let her feel as though he was crawling. He was determined that they were going to get through this crisis and they were going to do it together and like adults.

"Then perhaps I'm not the person you married ... not any more. Maybe I'm the one who has changed."

He wanted to say, "You're dead bloody right you're the one who has changed," but he did not want to antagonise her. They were going to get nowhere if he provoked an even more bitter argument, so one of them had to remain in control. "Are you telling me that you want to leave, is that what you're saying?" he asked.

She looked genuinely shocked. "Leave? Where on earth could I take Sarah? I can't go to my mother's, not with a young child."

Her mother had early onset dementia, and on an almost daily basis, she was becoming a greater danger to herself and maybe others. She was destined for a nursing home and in the not too distant future.

"So under the circumstances, I don't think asking any of my friends to put Sarah and me up while I find somewhere else would be at all practical."

"Are you saying that you want me to move out?" he asked.

This time there was no hesitation. "Yes, I think that would be the most sensible solution."

"And where, pray, do you expect me to go?" He couldn't believe what he was asking.

Matthew had driven down from Newcastle this afternoon fully aware of the fact that there was a problem. Nevertheless, any thought of it being so serious was furthermost from his mind. He was convinced it was temporary but he hadn't the faintest idea how long temporary was – given the slightest inkling of what was going on in Emily's mind, he would have done something about it far sooner. Her criticism that she had always hated him calling her 'Em' was hurtful, but what went with the criticism was devastating. He had always called her 'Em' and she always called him 'Matt'.

"It will be easier for you than it would be for me," she said.

"Easier? What do you mean easier? And what makes you think that you have any more right to keep Sarah than I have?"

"I'm her mother."

"And that simple piece of logic is supposed to provide all the answers, is it?" He downed the remnants of the whisky and started to get up, glass in hand.

"You're not going to get drunk, are you?"

He glared down at her. "No, I do not intend getting drunk but would it make any difference? After the bombshell you've just hit me with, I would have thought I'd be free to do anything as long as it doesn't affect you."

For the first time since he arrived home, he saw a slight sign of affection in Emily's eyes.

Perhaps there was still hope.

"Would you like another glass of wine?"

"Yes, please," she replied, her voice softening a little.

"I think we need to discuss Sarah," he suggested as he put her glass of wine on the coffee table before resuming his seat opposite her.

Emily picked up the glass, held it in both hands and gazed at the liquid as though it was a crystal ball.

"Matt, I'm sorry," she said slowly. "It's not that I don't love you, I didn't mean that, that was very unkind of me." She was speaking to the glass, her head bowed so he couldn't see her eyes. "I do love you," she said, the anger having left her voice, but there was an emotional undertone. "There's someone else," she added very quietly.

"There's someone else?" he repeated.

It wasn't meant as a question because her admission was an explanation. Not wanting to be with him because she no longer loved him was one thing, but loving somebody else more than she loved him was another. In some ways, it was more final – if it was just the two of them he would fight to keep her, the introduction of another man could put her beyond his reach.

"I see," he added.

Suddenly his blindness and naivety hit him like a sledgehammer. The late evenings, the nights away – why had he never suspected?

She had never given him a reason to suspect. There had been no looks, no mistakes, no giveaways and no marks on her body that hadn't been there the last time he looked at her.

If you love someone and you believe she loves you, then there is that magic ingredient in any credible relationship and it is called trust. He trusted Emily to tell him the truth, so when he thought she had, obviously he believed her. Maybe if he had asked the right question he might have detected her hesitation, but he believed there was no need – in fact it had never entered his head.

Emily wasn't the sort of female who had extra marital affairs, even if they were going through a bad phase, she would never need to find solace in another man's arms, in another man's bed.

He had been a bloody fool, a blind naïve idiot.

"Is that all you're going to say – I see?" she said.

"What else can I say? I don't want to know who he is but I would like to know how long it has been going on."

Emily was focussing on her glass of wine again and something told him there was about to be another admission, another revelation. Closing his eyes in anticipation, he tried to control his anger before the truth hit him.

"Sarah isn't your daughter," she said.

Knowing what was coming, he could have spoken those words for her.

If the whisky glass had not been such good quality it would have shattered in his hand, his grip was so tight.

Even then, he tried to find an explanation.

Losing Emily, which he obviously had, was devastating but being told the other person in his world, for whom he would gladly lay down his life, wasn't his, was earth-shattering. The little bundle of warmth tucked-up in her cot upstairs surrounded by her teddy bears, dolls, and pictures, but more importantly the all-consuming love he had for her, was not his. He had not fathered her, she wasn't part of him.

He opened his eyes and Emily was looking at him, tears falling down her cheeks.

"I'm so sorry. It just happened," she said.

"Just happened? It just happened over two years ago and it's been just happening ever since? Have you any idea what it's like to have been living a lie for so long?" Matthew held up his hand as she tried to speak. "But of course you do, you've been living the same lie, in fact, you are the liar, aren't you?"

"I never lied to you, Matt."

"Isn't not telling me the truth the same as lying? The fact that you conceived our child with another man, isn't that lying? The fact that you walked round this house as Sarah grew inside you and pretended it was my baby, is that not lying?"

Her head dropped and she nodded, it was her admission of guilt.

"I'm so sorry," she said again.

"You can stop saying that because if you were in the slightest bit sorry you would never have done it in the first place. Maybe getting pregnant was a mistake but what's been going on ever since has been one big lie. You have lied to me and you even lied to Sarah when you called me daddy in front of her. How are you going to tell Sarah one day that not only was she a mistake, but also that the person she thought was her daddy isn't her daddy after all?"

It was nearly nine in the evening and Matthew wondered what was going to happen that night. He was beginning to think quite dispassionately and even then, he was asking himself – why?

In less than an hour his entire world had collapsed and yet he was thinking of something as pragmatic as where he would spend the night.

Regardless of the atmosphere that had existed between the two of them for eighteen months – for her over two years – they had always shared the same bed and they had always kissed good night. Maybe one thing was in her favour: as soon as she discovered she was pregnant, Emily had switched off and they hadn't made love – 'not had sex' would now be more appropriate – except on one occasion when they went to a party in a neighbour's house and they both got very drunk. Matthew presumed that she was moralistic enough not to jump out of their bed, having had sex with him, into her lover's ... or vice-versa.

Why was he allowing her to have standards?

The woman he loved was the same flesh and blood she had always been, and she was sitting opposite him. However, he was now so withdrawn, so emotionally shattered, he did not recognise her anymore.

Her hair, her face, the little scar on her right cheek that happened when she fell off her bike when she was five years old; he long slender neck, slim shoulders, the thrust of her breasts under her shirt, he rounded hips, shapely thighs, knees and calves, and her small delicate feet, were now all foreign to him.

It was as though she was a ghost or just an illusion. He would look back on this evening and regret the way he had handled his emotions and the situation and he knew he would end up blaming himself.

"Perhaps she is young enough not to realise –" Emily said.

"Don't you dare tell me that you're going to introduce further lies into her life. When she is ready, she will deserve to know the truth, she will deserve to know what sort of person her mother really is. I presume her father is already married?" Before letting her answer, Matthew added, "I also presume that you've got your acts together and that his wife – I am still presuming he is married

– is being told the same facts of life as I am?"

"Yes, he is married," Emily said quietly, "but, no, tonight wasn't planned. He will be telling his wife but I don't know when."

"You're sure of that, are you? You are sure that he isn't going to run a mile when he finds out your expectations of him are more than he's willing to give? Is that why you can't run to him instead of forcing me out of my own house?"

He finished the second glass of whisky, deciding not to have another because he needed to find somewhere to sleep that night. If stopped and breathalysed, it would really make his day.

"I don't know." Emily reached forward so that she could put the wine glass on the table. The tears had stopped but the traces were still on her cheeks.

He wanted to cross the room and hug her, to tell her that it would all be better in the morning. Regardless of what he'd thought earlier, he couldn't just fall out of love with her because of what had been said. It would take time and he hadn't had time to even start thinking about it, let alone do it. He was still in love with the woman, his wife, sitting opposite him and she was hurting, as he was hurting, and he wanted to do something about the pain they were both suffering.

"Matt, you've got to believe me when I say I didn't want any of this to happen. I've wanted to tell you ever since I found out I was pregnant but... but," she shrugged, "it sounds a bit facile to say that the opportunity never arose."

"There was obviously no pressure on you from Sarah's father?"

Matthew didn't know why he chose to say Sarah's father rather than *him*. Whether it was to hurt himself or out of spite, he didn't know, but the words were there before he could choose any others.

"We didn't know what to do," she said.

Matthew's eyes narrowed as he heard Emily refer to them as *we*. As far as he was concerned, he and Emily had always been a *we* and no one else had any right to look on their relationship with her as being a *we*.

"He's married and has two children. We thought," there it was again, "that we," and again, "could manage and hold our marriages together at the same time –"

"– leap in and out of bed with each other whenever the fancy took you," Matthew said, finishing the sentence for her.

Emily held his look.

He realised he was making her relationship with her lover sound dirty and she didn't like it.

"It isn't like that. It's not just sex. If it were I wouldn't have allowed it to go as far as it has. I'm in love with him, Matt, and I want to be with him. I want to spend the rest of my life with him."

"You said the same to me all those years ago."

"Don't, please don't. I'm not proud of what I've done and am doing to you."

"And to Sarah, but she's a little young to understand, isn't she?"

"What will you do?" Emily asked, her eyes telling him that he was being unfair to use Sarah in that way.

"What? Do you mean right now or for the rest of my life?"

Her eyes rolled in obvious muted exasperation. "You're not making this very easy."

"You think I ought to make it easy for you? What do you want me to say, Em? Do you want me to say how thrilled I am that you have found someone to replace me and that I hope you'll both be very happy? Come off it, you have just completely shattered my – no, not my, our world – and our world includes that little bundle upstairs. Why couldn't you just have let things run?"

"I've told you why. I can't go on being with you when I want to be with him. I …"

"You've managed that for over two years, why the sudden need to change?"

"Stop it, Matt. Nothing you say is going to change things." She took a deep breath. "I go back to my question and I meant short term."

"By short term you mean tonight?"

"Yes, tonight and however long it takes for –"

"For you to get a divorce so that you can marry Sarah's father? If he's ever free that is."

"Yes."

"I know what society expects of me because, after all, I earn my living telling others how stereotypical we all are. Society would tell me to do the honourable thing and pack a few belongings in an overnight bag, find some sleazy motel for a few nights and then come back for my other possessions later, preferably when you and Sarah aren't here. I must then be a good boy and stay out of your life while we become strangers. Solicitors will start acting as intermediaries arguing over who gets what and how much. Suddenly lives are shattered and people who once loved each other learn to hate instead. They learn to communicate through strangers. We must meet our friends in pubs or restaurants and tell them how we haven't loved each other for years, and what a bastard the other has been, but in my case that would be a lie I wouldn't be willing to tell." He paused. "Oh, and as compensation, I would normally get access to my daughter so that we can go for a McDonald's and a play in the park every alternate Saturday or Sunday. I would fill her up with ice cream so that I can ruin her evening meal, and you can tell her what an awful person her daddy really is, but that's not the way it is, is it? You'll be able to tell her that you want to be with her daddy. You can tell her that the man you have been living with ever since she was born was just somebody you met and stayed with for a while until you found somebody better. Oh, and I guess because the little girl I thought was my daughter when I left yesterday morning isn't, then I won't be allowed to have access. After all, she isn't even a blood relative, is she?"

The tears were back in Emily's eyes and she lifted a hand to her face to wipe one away as it started running down her cheek, but Matthew couldn't stop himself.

"This morning I was a family man, with a simply gorgeous seven-month old daughter and a wife whom I adored, regardless of the temporary lack of a physical relationship. I had a house, a mortgage, a fast car and lots of money to spend. What more could any man ask for? Tonight, I would willingly give up everything else simply to be told that the daughter I believed was mine this morning is still mine, and that the wife whom I love tonight as much as I loved her this morning, loves me. If I do pack that society-recommended bag, what difference will it make to you?"

Emily's tears had turned to sobs and, for the first time Matthew could feel his own eyes beginning to water as true realisation hit home.

"I'll tell you the difference it'll make, you'll be free. You can go to bed tonight and not have to wonder what I'm thinking, not have to put up with me lying next to you feeling frustrated but happy in the knowledge that the woman I love is only a few inches away from me. She is there for me to touch but no more. You are half of me, Emily. If I leave then that half will leave with me and stay with me, but I don't want you as a memory, I want you to be with me and I want to be with you. You'll also have everything around you, secure in the knowledge that you still have somewhere to live and that gullible bastard of an almost ex-husband will still pay the mortgage, still provide for you and somebody else's daughter until he can, maybe, do the providing.

"And if Sarah's father proves to be as big a bastard as I think he is, you'll also know that I still won't cut you out of my life. Why? I'll tell you why, because you and Sarah mean so much to me that I don't care what you have told me tonight. All you have to say is that you will stay with me and we'll put it behind us, we'll start again. I really don't think you realise just what you mean to me. Another man might have fathered Sarah but she is still my daughter, our daughter. You can't bring what we had to a complete halt simply by telling me to go and spend the night in a strange room somewhere."

Matthew realised he was doing exactly what he had told himself he wouldn't do. He was pleading for the relationship, the marriage, he knew in reality was over. He was pleading with Emily to give them another chance, to pull something out of what remained. It did not matter that she had been having an affair for over two years, that their daughter wasn't theirs: nothing mattered other than stopping the unbelievable foolishness. He wanted to take Emily by the hand and go to bed. He wanted to lie in their bed and hold her, and listen to the baby alarm, to their daughter breathing, snuffling, and turning over in her cot.

He wanted them to be a family again.

Emily just sat quietly looking at him, her hands clasped in her lap, with tears rolling down her cheeks.

Suddenly she stood up and, through the tears, she spat, "You bastard," at him, before rushing out of the room.

He heard her go up the stairs and then the floorboards above him creaked as she moved round the room to her side of the bed.

There was silence.

Matthew just sat and stared at where she had been, his own tears blurring his vision.

He had lost her, lost everything.

His world – their world – had simply fallen apart and he could do nothing about it. He had not wanted to plead and now he knew why. By pleading, he had made her feel guiltier than she already felt. The guilt had become too much for her so, if it were possible, he had actually made the situation worse. If he had distanced himself from his emotions, he might have been able to make her see sense, but by telling her how she would feel if he were to leave, he had played straight into her hands. He had given her what she wanted. He had committed himself to the inevitability of losing her and Sarah to another man, another world.

Matthew, whether he wanted it or not, was on his own.

Before leaving the house that evening – his overnight bag was still in the car – he could not even go into Sarah's room and say goodbye. If he did, he knew it could be the last time he ever kissed her, the last time he ever touched her, the last time he ever told his daughter how much he really loved her. Each time he told Sarah how much he loved her, he also told her how much he loved her Mummy.

Sarah was still his daughter so there mustn't be a last time.

As he closed the front door as quietly as he could, he knew that no matter what happened to him or her, he would always be in love with Emily.

He would always love Sarah, his daughter.

Chapter Three

Since he moved out of the marital home nearly five years ago, Matthew had only seen Emily once and, as he expected, Sarah stayed well in the background. His solicitor agreed that access could be difficult because Matthew wasn't Sarah's biological father. He still didn't know, nor did he ever want to know, who Sarah's biological father was. The whole episode had broken his heart and he vowed never to get involved with another woman in the same way again.

That was why he was now on his way up the M20 to be with his live-in girlfriend. That was not what he called her in private but it was how she, Laura, liked people to think of her. In her words, she certainly wasn't his wife ... yet, and the term 'partner' conveyed for her mere association, or a co-worker and certainly not somebody who shared his bed, sometimes his bath, and lots of other things.

When he saw Emily across the courtroom in the December after they separated in the July of 1995, she could not make eye contact, whereas he could not stop looking at her. He simply couldn't believe that two people who had once declared their undying love for each other could be so distant.

Their respective solicitors insisted that they settle the proceeds of their marriage before the divorce reached the courts. Matthew had agreed with this approach to an extent but he was determined, much to his solicitor's chagrin, not to break the promise to himself that Emily and Sarah would not want for anything. He could afford it, and regardless of what she had done to him, he couldn't bear the thought of her ever worrying as to where the next meal was going to come from.

Emily had insisted, via her solicitor, that Matthew should sue her for divorce on the grounds of her adultery although she refused to name the co-respondent and he believed this was for his benefit. If he had ever discovered his name Matthew would have found him, and ... well, he wasn't sure what he would have done, but the co-respondent, as they called him, wouldn't have walked away undamaged.

Dates, times and places where adultery took place remained undisclosed – her admission appeared sufficient. Acknowledging in public that his wife had preferred to have sex with another man, was quite enough for Matthew, and having a baby with him was going too far.

Clinging onto the hope that right up to the day of the divorce Emily would change her mind and agree to him going home, was preferable to the hearing the sordid details.

However, the first stage of the divorce was finished quickly, which he guessed pleased Emily. The Absolute followed the Nisi within a matter of weeks and Matthew, without wanting to be, was a free man by the end of January 1996.

He no longer had a wife and he had never had a daughter.

Matthew stayed with Xanadu for longer than expected. His newfound freedom, albeit under such devastating circumstances, allowed him to give back a lot of what the other directors had patiently given to him before that awful evening in July 1995.

Staying where he was meant some of the financial aspects of the divorce were quickly recouped. By the end of 1996, after living in a rented flat in Oxford for the preceding eleven months, Matthew bought a cottage in Westerham, in Kent, just south of the M25. He had no links with the area, so that is why he chose it.

He wanted to distance himself from the Midlands. When living in Oxford and although forty-five miles from Leamington Spa and Stratford, there was always an outside chance of bumping into Emily or one of her friends/work colleagues.

He kept women out of his life until he moved to Westerham but he then met a divorcee at one of the seminars Xanadu ran in Esher, Surrey. Matthew and Cassie – she hated Cassandra – struck up a relationship that showed promise. They never actually lived together but the friendship lasted for six months before they mutually agreed that each had taken what they needed from it. They parted friends, vowing to stay that way, but they had not seen each other nor spoken since.

Another three months passed which included six weeks in the Far East where Matthew brought The Royal Brunei Armed Forces up to speed with how to introduce, maintain and reap the benefits of Continuous Improvement – late 20th Century management speak for improving effectiveness and efficiency. On his return, a few more work commitments took him to Scotland, Northern Ireland and Holland.

The trip to Holland gave new energy his original plan of years ago to launch his own consultancy. He was convinced that he was ready and, more importantly, his contacts were ready for him. He spent a year – during which he had three casual and brief relationships – dedicating his spare time to learning German and French to an acceptable standard, before he felt completely ready to launch Ryan Enterprises Ltd (Organisational Development Consultant).

After so long, Matthew was sorry to leave Xanadu. If what the other directors said at his farewell were true, they too were sorry to see him go especially as they added he could return at any time. He wasn't sure whether their offer was down to their belief in him succeeding or not on his own, or whether they would truly want him back!

Both 1999 and 2000 proved to be good years in more ways than one. As well as adding to his bank balance and paying off a considerable amount of the mortgage on the cottage in Westerham, in the millennium Matthew also met Laura.

As he passed Junction 4 on the M20, Laura was now in Matthew's thoughts, his ex-wife, Emily, and the rather disturbing incident with Francesca on the ferry pushed, perhaps temporarily, to the back of his mind.

In a roundabout way, Emily had actually brought Laura and Matthew together. His murderous intent towards 'whoever-he-was' decreased with time, although he did appear in Matthew's dreams every now and again. The man who had stolen his wife and 'daughter' was faceless and, by the time Matthew had finished with him, he was also, to Matthew's great delight, lifeless. In reality, he would have been incapable of such an act, but in his dreams, he could do whatever he liked – which included murder.

Although time had passed, Emily and Sarah were always in his thoughts but then, one day in the spring of 2000, he had a sudden urge to find out whether they were all right. He had probably left it so long because, previously, he would not have felt he could cope with even remote contact without getting himself upset.

In 1998, his solicitors informed him that the monthly allowance he was paying to Emily and Sarah could stop so he assumed Emily's lover had kept his promise and that the three of them were now living together. Charles Borthwick, the senior partner in the firm of solicitors Matthew employed, had always implied that Matthew was unwise (an idiot) to pay so much for somebody else's daughter and to an ex-wife whose behaviour had been inexcusable.

Matthew had told him to mind his own business.

Nevertheless, five years down the line, security bursting from his bank balance, a nice home, and most importantly Ryan Enterprises Ltd launched and doing very well, he felt ready.

He spent an hour on the Internet looking for what he believed was a suitable firm that would guarantee discretion. Eventually he found one he thought might be suitable and, by coincidence, their offices were in Sevenoaks, just over six miles from Westerham. They were not cheap, and as soon as Matthew walked into the front office, he could tell that he was dealing with a professional organisation. The receptionist was polite, offering him coffee before he was ushered into an equally impressive office. The name plaque on the door and on the desk told him that Laura Stanhope, whose post-nominal qualifications were as impressive as her office, would be looking after him. The only thing that put him off slightly was Laura Stanhope's age.

The woman who came out from behind her desk to greet him was medium height, with professionally shaped shoulder-length auburn hair, and a very pretty almost childlike face with a small nose, full lips and large blue-green eyes. She was wearing a tailored grey business suit that made the most of her slim figure. Matthew took her proffered hand, noticing her manicured nails. Her hands were small and soft, as was her touch.

"Won't you sit down, Mr Ryan?" she said, indicating a chair in front of her desk. "Janie will bring your coffee through shortly." She smiled before resuming her seat behind her rosewood desk. "I apologise for the rather impersonal barrier," she added, putting her hands on the desk, "but I will need to take some notes and I do hate resting a pad on my knees."

"That's not a problem," Matthew told her.

The door opened behind him and the receptionist, who he now knew was Janie, came in with the coffee. On the tray with the cups and saucers were a coffeepot, a sugar bowl and cream jug, all of which appeared to be silver.

Having poured the coffee, Laura Stanhope picked up her fountain pen, unscrewed the top and looked at him. "Now, Mr Ryan, how can I help?"

"I think you'll consider it to be pretty straightforward," he said after tasting the coffee. It was excellent. "I want you to find my ex-wife and let me know that she and her daughter are all right."

"I see," Laura Stanhope said with a slight lifting of her eyebrows. "I would agree that it sounds straightforward, Mr Ryan, but I'll reserve judgement until after you've given me a few details. When did you last see your ex-wife?"

"Nearly five years ago, in the divorce court."

"And where was that?" Laura asked, her expression not revealing her thoughts.

"Leamington Spa." Matthew saw Laura write 'L/Spa' on the pad in front of her.

"Were you living in Leamington Spa at the time?"

"No, my wife was in our house in Stratford-upon-Avon and I was in a flat in Oxford."

She wrote 'S-on-A' and 'Ox' next to 'L/Spa'.

"You haven't seen her since?"

"No."

"Have you been in contact with her in any other way?"

"The house was sold four years ago but, as I'd given it to her, all her solicitors needed from me were a few signatures."

Laura Stanhope's eyebrows lifted again. "You gave the house to your wife as part of the settlement?" she asked.

"Yes."

"May I ask who divorced whom and why?" When she saw Matthew's surprised look, she added, "Mr Ryan, I can assure you of our total prudence in all matters. Discretion is our middle name."

"Yes, I saw that on your web page." She made another note on the top right hand corner of her pad, 'I-net'. "Well I suppose I divorced her and the grounds were because of her adultery."

"She did the dirty on you?"

Matthew was a little surprised by her choice of words. "Yes," he said.

"And you gave her your house?"

"Yes, and an allowance." Matthew didn't feel the need to expand on his reasons, not yet.

"An allowance and the house, I see," Laura commented. Her voice, as well as her eyebrows, gave her away this time. "Do you know …?" and then she corrected herself. "But of course you wouldn't know where she is living now. If you did, you probably wouldn't be here."

Matthew shrugged. "Yes, I would still be here because I would want an independent third party to discover what I would like to know."

"I understand," she said, "or I think I do. Were there any children?"

He hesitated, which caused Laura Stanhope to look up from her pad, frowning slightly. "Yes, as I said, there was one, a daughter. She will be coming up six now."

"What's your daughter's name? And you may as well give me your wife's details at the same time."

"Sarah," Matthew said. He couldn't bring himself to say she wasn't his daughter. "My ex-wife's name is Emily, Emily Elizabeth."

"Has she remarried?"

"I assume so, yes, or she is living with a man."

"Do you know his name?"

"No," Matthew said straightaway, "and at no time during your investigation or in any report you may produce, do I want his name mentioning."

Laura Stanhope made a few more notes. The top sheet of her pad was beginning to fill up. "I will make sure your instruction is followed, Mr Ryan, but obviously she may have changed her surname."

Matthew nodded. "Yes, of course."

"Do you happen to know the name of the solicitors she used during the divorce?"

"Macarthur, Creighton and Smailes," Matthew told her. "They have offices above a travel agent at the top of The Parade in Leamington Spa."

"Why, when you lived in Stratford, did she use solicitors in Leamington?"

"That's where she worked. She was an independent financial advisor and she too had an office in The Parade, but it was down with all the estate agents near the park."

"Did she use her married name or maiden name for her office?"

He let a slight smile creep onto my lips. "Her maiden name, but only because it seemed more appropriate. Her maiden name was Sterling."

"I see what you mean," Laura said with a hint of a smile. "That will certainly help and could make things easier. What about her parents and does she have any brothers and sisters? Do you have any of their details?"

"Her mother was very ill before the divorce. I would guess that she is either dead or in a nursing home somewhere by now. Her father died about ten years ago. Emily was an only child and I know that there were some aunts and uncles on the scene somewhere but I didn't meet any of them, except at the wedding. I think they all originated in the West Country."

"Right," Laura Stanhope said, making a few more notes in the remaining gaps on the sheet of paper in front of her. "I think I've got everything I need." She ran the pen over her notes. "Oh, yes, there was one other question – your daughter, Mr Ryan, don't you have access?"

Matthew had not been able to admit it to himself at the time and he certainly was not going to admit it to a complete stranger now. He understood the significance of the question but it didn't need more than a yes or no answer. "No, I don't have access." Laura Stanhope looked up and he could see in her eyes the conclusion she had drawn. "And the answer is no to what you are thinking. I don't have access because I didn't ask for access."

Laura Stanhope had the decency to blush slightly. "I didn't mean to imply anything, Mr Ryan."

"There's no need to apologise, Mrs Stanhope. It was a logical conclusion to draw but, on this occasion, an inaccurate one."

Laura Stanhope smiled. "Thank you, Mr Ryan, but I'm still sorry." She put down her pen. "And it's Ms Stanhope, Mr Ryan. Rather pretentious, I know, but I don't really want to call myself Miss and I would prefer not to be called Mrs. I am also divorced. Stanhope is my maiden name and, as I am in the process of reverting to Stanhope legally, I invite my clients to call me Laura."

"Laura it is," Matthew said, but as a client he wasn't ready to be called Matthew.

"Now, Mr Ryan," Laura said quite pointedly, "what precisely do you want me to find out?"

"I simply want to know that Emily and Sarah are well and happy. I don't want any other details. As I mentioned earlier, I certainly don't want to know to whom Emily is married, if indeed she is married. It might be worth knowing where she is living so that, if I am ever in the area, I can make sure I don't accidentally bump into her but, unless it's really necessary, I don't see the need to know her address."

"How should I judge whether they are well and happy?" Laura asked, looking slightly concerned.

Matthew thought for a moment. "I was pleased when I saw that you were female, Laura. I thought that a woman's intuition would be better than a man's in a situation like this."

"I don't normally get paid for my intuition, Mr Ryan. I usually get paid for the facts I discover."

"On this occasion, your intuition will be just fine."

"I'm afraid I have to charge the same whether it's facts or intuitive guesswork you want, Mr Ryan."

"And that is?"

"It's four hundred pounds a day, plus expenses." It was Matthew's turn to raise his eyebrows. "I'm good, Mr Ryan, but if you would like to set an upper limit, then I will achieve what I can in the time allowed."

Matthew let his breath out slowly. "All right, four hundred pounds plus expenses it is, but I would ask for an interim report once we've reached two thousand pounds and then I'll decide whether you should continue."

"That's a fair proposal, Mr Ryan. Shall we go into the outer office and Janie will draw up the contract."

"Before we do," he said, "Emily must not know who you are, what you do, and why you are doing it."

Laura nodded. "I understand,' she said, inclining her head.

Chapter Four

Laura Stanhope contacted Matthew three days later.

Before he left her office after his initial visit, she told him that she normally did not try to run more than four investigations concurrently and he was her fifth, but for him she would make an exception.

"I've found her," she informed him just a little solicitously.

"I'm impressed," he told her.

"It wasn't that difficult. People who don't want to be found cover their tracks. Those who don't even know they are being sought leave trails a mile wide."

"And?"

"I'd prefer not to give you my interim report, if that's what it is, on the phone, Mr Ryan. Are you available to have a drink together somewhere?"

When the phone had rung at seven o'clock in the evening, he was surprised that it was Laura Stanhope. He rather expected any contact from her to be during office hours.

"Well, yes, of course. Actually I haven't eaten yet, have you?"

"No, Mr Ryan, I haven't. I'll come through to Westerham. There's a nice pub by the village green. It's called The Grasshopper, I think, but you'll know that. Say eight o'clock?"

"If we are going to have dinner together, it's Matthew, Laura, and I'll be there at eight o'clock."

As he put the receiver down, the reason for her call generated a feeling he had not experienced for a long time. He felt excited and just a little apprehensive. If Laura Stanhope normally operated in this way, he was more than willing to oblige.

When he walked into The Grasshopper an hour later, Laura was already there and, whether he was a client or not, she wasn't dressed for the office. It was a warm evening, so quite a few people were outside watching the world go by, but Laura was sitting in a corner in the bar, a tall stemmed glass of red wine in front her. She stood up as she saw Matthew and joined him at the bar. She was wearing white calf length cotton cut-offs below a casual pink shirt. Her business suit hadn't needed to do her any favours but, seeing her dressed casually for the first time, it crossed his mind that she could wear anything and look exactly as she was ... rather lovely.

"Hello, Matthew," she greeted him without hesitation. "What would you like to drink?"

"Hello, Laura," he replied, taking her hand and shaking it gently. "I was going to ask you the same thing."

"Don't stand on protocol. It'll all go on your bill anyway," she added with a mischievous grin.

"A pint of lager then, please," he said.

Sitting down at the table, Laura reached into her bag for a packet of cigarettes. "Oh, sorry, I didn't offer you one."

"No, thanks, I gave up a long time ago."

"Yes, so did I," she said. "You don't mind if I do?"

"Not at all."

After a few puffs of her cigarette, Laura put it out and picked up her wine. "I've asked for a table in about half an hour."

"Does the meal go on my bill as well?"

"No," she said smiling, "only the alcohol." Her expression became serious. "As I told you on the phone, Matthew, I found Emily and Sarah. In fact I found them a couple of days ago but I needed the extra time so that I was able to tell you what you needed to know, what you are paying me for."

"And?"

"I don't think she's remarried or, if she did remarry, I don't think they are still together." She saw Matthew frown. "Yes, my comment does require an explanation. They are living in quite a nice area of Leamington Spa. Emily is driving a relatively new Renault Clio and, from what I saw, she wears very expensive clothes. Sarah is going to a school about a mile from the house and Emily drops her off and collects her. There was no obvious sign of a man in her life and this was confirmed when I went into the house."

"What? You went into the house? I thought –"

"I met Emily and talked to her."

"You did what?" Matthew asked a little too loudly.

"It's all part of the service, Matthew." Laura finished her wine before reaching for another cigarette. "You can't tell whether somebody is happy or not by simply watching them. You have to speak to them and look at the immediate environment in which they live."

"But how did you do that without alerting her?"

"Professional and trade secret, I'm afraid, but I spent about an hour with her yesterday evening."

He had spent the best part of five years thinking, wondering, imagining, even fantasising about somebody who had been his life, and yet he had not had the strength of character to fight for her. However, in a matter of seventy-two hours, a complete stranger had gone into Emily's house and spoken to her for an hour. He would have given up the unimaginable to talk to Emily for five minutes, to see Sarah playing with her friends for a minute, but an hour?

He was just about to ask a couple of direct questions, one of which would include the phrase 'contrary to instructions', when a waiter appeared and informed them that, if they were ready, they could go through to the dining room.

It wasn't until after the first course had been served that Laura resumed her account of what had happened. Matthew decided to give her the benefit of doubt before challenging her methods.

"Emily gave me the impression that, although materialistically she was perfectly all right, her tone and the general way in which she moved gave a different impression," Laura paused while she put some pâté on a piece of crisp-bread. "While we were talking, Sarah was in the other room watching a video. When Emily invited me in, Sarah also came to the door. She was a polite little girl and looked as though she didn't have a care in the world. But Emily was different."

"In what way?"

Laura stopped eating and looked at him. "She seemed terribly despondent, very down. Almost as though she was grieving but was doing her best not to show it."

"You said there was no evidence of a man in her life. Perhaps that was the reason," he suggested.

"Normally I would answer that statement with a very feminist remark," Laura told him with a hint of a smile, "but it's not appropriate. No, when I say there was no evidence, I mean literally no evidence. No photographs, there was nothing male hanging in the cloakroom and no telltale signs of a man being around in the kitchen. I'm trained to look for such things Matthew, and there was nothing. I think I can almost guarantee that she isn't married, regardless of the fact that she was wearing a wedding and engagement ring, and nor does she have a man living in the house with her."

"But that doesn't mean to say there isn't anybody."

"No, of course it doesn't, but as far as boyfriends in that context are concerned, I would only suggest this time that there isn't one of those either." Laura resumed eating but she was watching Matthew closely.

"You suggested she might have been grieving. Could that be the explanation? Do you think she might have lost someone recently?"

"That wouldn't explain why there was no evidence that I could see of a man having been around. There was nothing."

"The rings she was wearing, can you describe them?" Matthew put his soupspoon down and picked up the last piece of his bread roll.

"I can because I thought you might ask, and I'm a woman." She smiled. "The wedding ring was a simple band of gold but the engagement ring was an unusual diamond cluster. It was square with what I think was an emerald in the centre."

Matthew stopped chewing.

Laura had just described the engagement ring he had bought Emily twelve years ago. They bought the engagement ring and both wedding rings at the same time in a shop in York, and almost on the spur of the moment. It would be too much of a coincidence if anybody else had bought her an identical ring and, even if someone had, Matthew believed Emily would have exchanged it straightaway. So why was she still wearing the ring he had bought her?

"So you don't think she's happy?" Matthew asked, hoping the shock of hearing about the engagement ring, didn't show.

"No, Matthew, I don't think she is and I'm sorry. I'm not sure what you wanted to hear but if I'd been able to report that she was obviously deliriously happy and very much in love, then," she shrugged, "maybe that would also have been something you wouldn't have wanted to hear."

"I suppose for rather selfish reasons you could be right, but what you have told me is simply confusing."

"She was still wearing the rings she wore when you were married, wasn't she?" He hadn't hidden his reaction.

"The engagement ring, yes, but the wedding ring was like so many others."

The waiter cleared away their plates before returning almost immediately with the main courses. Matthew found that his appetite had disappeared with Laura's news, but he was still enjoying her company.

They moved away from what Laura had discovered and onto what were in her opinion, quite personal subjects. She was thirty-one and had been divorced for six months. Her husband, Patrick Schofield, had treated her pretty badly. She implied that she there was physical as well as verbal abuse and that their parting was rather acrimonious. They were only married eighteen months before they separated.

It was after the separation she decided to try her hand at private investigation. She had a law degree but wanted to be her own boss, and although relative early days, things were going well. While studying for her law degree she was in the Surrey Police and, after doing an 'A' Level in law at school, she found sufficient self-discipline to go that one stage further via the Open University.

As she talked, Matthew began to find her more and more interesting. There was no doubting her prettiness – he had seen other men's heads turning – but she could have proven to be a complete bore. The restaurant was quite crowded but Matthew noted that she didn't look about her when she was talking. Instead she made him feel as though she too was enjoying his company and quite happy to give him all of her attention.

"So do you normally wine and dine with your clients?" Matthew asked as the waiter brought their coffees and a couple of very generous brandies.

"Good Lord, no," she replied feigning surprise. "You're the first but then again, nobody has ever asked me to do what you asked me to do before. I wanted to find out what you are really like."

"And?"

"Now you're fishing but you come across as the sort of man

who would want to know if an ex-wife who had done the dirty on him, and he hadn't seen for five years, was happy."

"What does that mean?"

"It means that I like you and, having said that, it means that I am being completely unprofessional and will probably hate myself tomorrow for having said so." Laura sipped her brandy, her eyes not leaving his.

"Aren't private investigators allowed to have feelings?" he asked, amused by her slight embarrassment.

"Of course they are but, as I said, it's unprofessional with clients."

"Who says so?"

"I do."

"I see. I'd better leave, then."

She put her hand on his arm. "Don't you dare, and anyway, if you don't need me to investigate your ex-wife any further, then you are no longer my client."

"Surely I'm your client until I've paid the bill."

"Now you're splitting hairs."

"Would you like another brandy or coffee, or both?"

"I think I would like both, please."

He beckoned the waiter over but managed to steal a look at his watch at the same time. It was just after ten o'clock.

"Are you working tomorrow?"

She looked surprised. "What, on a Saturday? I am shelf, oops sorry, self-employed." She picked up the brandy glass. "I'm not sure I ought to drink this but, then again, I'm not sure why I shouldn't." She took a sip before reaching for her cigarettes. "Do you approve of me smoking?"

Her question surprised him. "It's really none of my business what you do."

"Don't be so evasive. Do you or do you not approve of women who smoke?"

"I don't think 'approve' is necessarily the right word. I don't disapprove but I do think they are being a little silly, especially when there is so much anti-smoking campaigning going on."

"Isn't that why some people smoke? They don't like being told what they should and shouldn't do, but I am not saying that's why

I smoke."

"Would you step out in front of a car that was speeding towards you? Road safety experts suggest it's not a very safe practice."

"Of course I wouldn't."

"I rest my case for the defence."

It was nearly midnight when they left The Grasshopper and they had both drunk more than they were used to.

Earlier when Laura asked Matthew where in Westerham he lived, he started describing the location of the cottage but then suggested that as it was within walking distance, why didn't she go with him and see for herself.

"Why not? It sounds lovely. I'm sure my car will be all right out there," she said, indicating the car park with a tipsy wave of her hand. "I presume the experts would say that I am in perfectly safe company?"

"Of course, and I think the fresh air will do us both good."

The evening was still quite warm.

They left The Grasshopper and walked down the London Road until they came to Southbank. The single-track private road was a cul-de-sac that ran parallel to a stream on one side and a mixture of terraced and semi-detached houses on the other. Matthew's semi-detached cottage was at the very end of the road. They talked about the weather, the way tourists thronged to Westerham throughout the year, and a little about its history and its connection with Winston Churchill. As they moved into Southbank, the street lighting was not so good and Laura linked her hand into the crook of his arm.

"Spooky!" she said, gripping his arm tightly.

"I think it's one of the more pleasant aspects of where I live. As it's a dead end, the only people who usually drive to the very end are those that live there but, of course, there are those who are simply inquisitive. ... or lost."

"Inquisitive like me, you mean?" she asked.

"You're invited," he told her.

Once inside the cottage, Matthew showed Laura into the kitchen.

"This is lovely," she commented, looking round the room.

"You've made it look very homely. Oh, and I love AGAs."

"You sound surprised," he said, plugging in the kettle.

"No, I didn't mean that to be the way it must have come across," she said, taking off her coat and throwing it over the back of a chair. "I suppose it's not what I would have expected from a man living on his own."

He smiled. "I'll take that as a compliment. Do you want to see the rest of the cottage before we have a coffee?"

"Please."

"I said so downstairs but it really is lovely," Laura commented a few minutes later as they went from room to room. "Was it like this when you moved in?"

"I have to admit that I haven't changed it too much. The previous owners had good taste."

Laura hesitated as she entered his bedroom. "This is more male," she commented. "It's sort of ..."

"Sort of what?"

"Well, functional, if you see what I mean." She moved further into the room, taking in every detail. "It's tidy, clean and, yes, functional."

He stayed by the door. "What exactly do you mean by 'functional'? That's the second time you've used that word."

She went across to the window so that she could peer into the darkness beyond. "Are the neighbours friendly?" she asked without turning round.

"Yes," he responded, smiling to himself.

Suddenly he felt a little nervous. He had found Laura attractive from the moment he met her but, up until only a few hours ago, their relationship was purely professional but now she was in his bedroom.

"As friendly as any neighbours will be towards a man living on his own," he said.

Laura turned round, resting her hands on the deep sill as she looked at him.

"I think I ought to be going," she said.

"Why? You haven't had the coffee I promised you." He shrugged. "And anyway, you've had a little too much to drink to think about driving. Do you want me to call you a taxi?"

Laura kept her eyes on his. "Do you want to call me a taxi?"

"No. I just thought –"

"Well, stop thinking and start doing what we know we both want."

Chapter Five

Just two weeks later Laura moved in with Matthew.

He agreed as they discussed the suggestion – which was made by him – that they were both being impetuous, but his logic was quite simple, why wait until recklessness became measured awareness? The thrill of the unknown, they decided, was part of the gamble and they were both adult enough to retrace their steps if they concluded that they were making a dreadful mistake. The only stipulation Laura made was that Matthew paid her what he owed before she unpacked any of her suitcases.

That was now nearly a year ago and, although by applying a cliché it was perhaps understating what he and Laura had found in each other, they never looked back. They quickly discovered that they liked the same things, whether it was music, the theatre, sport, books or even TV programmes. They found an unbelievable contentment in their relationship, often asking each other whether a supreme effort was being made so as not to upset what they had: the answer was always, no.

So why didn't they just enjoy it?

Regardless of him influencing Laura's decision to move in with him, as Matthew lolled in a chair watching Laura unpack her cases, a feeling of unmitigated guilt overwhelmed him. He had no reason to feel guilty and Emily had no right to be the source of that guilt … but it was still there.

Moreover, nothing ever changed.

Although there were only another thirty miles to go and he was getting ever closer to home, he felt worse than he had for the preceding fifty miles. It was always the same: the overriding feeling of guilt subsumed all the longing, the need and the excitement.

Laura was responsible for turning his life round and giving him a happiness that he thought he would never find again, but he could not forget, no matter how long ago it was, that Laura had believed Emily was so unhappy. If she were unhappy at the time Laura conducted her investigation, then she could be even unhappier now. Whether Emily had been the cause of their marriage breaking down or not, he still thought that he had no right to be feeling the way he did, even if she didn't feel the same.

Such feelings always reached a peak just before he got to Westerham. Fortunately for both Laura and him, the guilt lessened significantly when he drove down Rysted Lane towards Southbank and its access to the double garage to the side of the cottage. As the headlights of his car lit up the wisteria and clematis that covered most of the west wall, he knew he was home, and home meant that Laura would be waiting for him.

She always wanted him to ring her when he was about an hour away so that she could make sure she was not in the middle of something when he let himself in through the front door. There had been a couple of occasions when she too was away conducting some investigation or other, but careful planning ensured such times were kept to a minimum.

This time she was waiting for him on the path between the garage and the front door. She was beaming with outstretched arms as he approached.

"Lovely to have you home," she told him before they hugged each other.

"I've only been away for a week," he said just before they kissed under the arch that in a few months' time would be a mass of red roses.

"It's quite long enough."

She picked up his laptop, he lifted his case and they trooped into the house with an arm round the other's waist.

The extra large corner bath they had installed in the main bathroom about three months after Laura moved in, allowed them both to wallow in the scented water. Laura had lit a dozen candles that were scattered haphazardly around suitable surfaces. Matthew had a long and very cold gin and tonic within easy reach, Laura a whisky lemonade.

"So, tell me about your trip," Laura suggested, her arms stretched down the side of the bath, the suds just below her small breasts.

"Your hair looks nice, it's shorter," Matthew said.

She lifted a soapy hand automatically but then thought better of it. "I had it done the day before yesterday. I didn't like it at first but now I'm happier. I had it lightened a little as well."

"It's lovely."

"Thank you," she said, lifting one foot so that she could rest it on Matthew's chest.

"I have some good news and some bad news. Which do you want first?"

Laura pouted. "The good news, please."

"All right, the good news is that my five days with 'Sappro' in Maastricht went well but, while I was there, I heard that the week I was due to have in Koblenz had fallen through."

"That's bad news?" Her toes were rubbing his chest gently. "You'll be at home."

"We need the money," he told her but not too seriously.

"I want to talk about that later." Her foot moved slowly down towards his stomach.

"I may be able to get a couple of days work here and there in this country. There's time."

She put her foot back in the water and carefully drew her legs under her as she knelt in front of him, the suds slowly sliding down her body.

"Shall we try and keep the water in the bath this time?"

"You're not listening."

"And neither are you."

An hour or so later, sitting in the conservatory with plates of pasta and salad on their laps, and dressed in white towelling bathrobes, they resumed the conversation they started in the bathroom.

Matthew began by telling Laura about the woman on the ferry. He told her every detail of what had happened.

"Didn't you report it?" she asked him. She listened intently to what he had to say, her expressions ranging from amazement to bewilderment.

Matthew shrugged. "It's not that I didn't think about it but I did sort of promise her that I wouldn't. It was the only way of getting her inside and out of danger, or so I thought."

"What did you say her name was?"

"Francesca."

"Nice name," she commented with a slightly sarcastic undertone. "And her car had a personalised number plate?"

"Yes, FRA 1 N."

The pasta was good. He tried once to stand over Laura while she cooked the same dish in an attempt to see what she did with it, but she ushered him away and told him it was another of her trade secrets.

The Rioja he selected for that evening was equally good.

"That should be pretty easy to trace," Laura commented.

"There's no need," he said, smiling as Laura's need to find answers to everything. "She's long gone."

"Call it professional interest, but why would somebody intent on committing suicide like that, knowingly leave a car with personalised numbers plates to give the game away?"

"Sorry, I don't follow."

"Well," Laura said, frowning slightly, "it just doesn't add up. It seems almost as though she wanted to advertise who she was as quickly as possible."

"Do people who are contemplating suicide think logically? She couldn't exactly take her car with her, could she?"

"No, of course not but … Matthew, you'd be surprised. You hear about notes left behind, letters of explanation or salvation, whatever you want to call them. That's nothing compared with what some people do, though. The washing, the ironing, even housework, everything has to be neat and tidy. Some suicides must think that they'll be judged differently if they leave their personal life in order. I'm not sure where they think the judgement will take place, in this life or the next. Yes, Matthew, people who are contemplating suicide can become the most calculating, devious people when, before, they were candid and openly straightforward."

"So what do you make of Francesca?"

Laura thought for a moment before giving Matthew her verdict. Shaking her head, she said, "She wouldn't have gone through with it. Almost certainly she knew you were there, and if she didn't think you were going to react she wouldn't have gone ahead with it."

"What on earth did I say that allows you to draw a conclusion like that? She was nearly over the rail when I got to her, a second or two later and there would have been nothing I could have done to save her. If I'd slipped again I would never have reached her."

Laura gave him one of those 'men are so naïve' looks.

"The trouble with you, Matthew, is that you think every woman you meet wants protecting. The female of the species is cunning and more than capable of taking care of herself. More often than not, making a man feel powerful and in control is all part of the game. It's amazing what you can achieve by using such tactics."

"We'll come back to that," he said smiling at her obvious challenge, "but you haven't answered my question. What I hear from you is that the entire episode was the result of a calculating female mind rather than a suicidal one. Am I right?"

Laura nodded. "You catch on quite quickly … for a man."

He threw a cushion at her but missed, hitting her empty plate instead, and it, together with the knife and fork, clattered to the floor.

Picking up the plate, Laura said, "See, now you feel threatened, and resorting to violence is your way of coping with it."

"But you provoked me."

"Did I? You are supposed to be the amateur psychologist. You taught the subject for long enough. Work it out for yourself. And I'm not referring to man's inability to accept defeat peacefully."

"I have never professed to being a psychologist," he said, smiling at her. "I simply studied the subject at university to a sufficient level to be able to teach it. But I still can't see from what I have told you how you can draw such conclusions."

Laura sat forward, this time placing her plate on the conservatory floor.

"Fact one: she knew you were there. Fact –"

"But –"

"Hear me out. Fact two: she wouldn't have contemplated launching herself over the side if you hadn't been there."

"How can you say that's a fact?"

"Because I'm a female and only females understand members of their own sex."

"A specious argument!"

"Not at all., it's an obvious fact."

Matthew shook his head. "You've lost me."

"Fact three: the swearing and struggling were done deliberately to make you, the male, feel responsible. If you had walked away at that point, it would all have stopped. If you had left the deck and waited on the other side of the door, I guarantee she would have followed you only seconds later."

"Conjecture!"

"Fact! Fact four: the need for a drink and a cigarette, both provided by you, moved you away from being responsible to being the bringer, the hunter. Fact five: little girl lost not knowing where she'd left her car, dependability becomes duality …"

"There's no such word."

"Yes, there is. It means you were now doing something together, sharing: you were both involved. She was beginning to reel you in."

He shook his head again. "You're about to defeat your own logic. Even if these manufactured facts were real facts, how do you explain the 'fact' that she drove off at high speed at the first opportunity."

"Matthew, you were hooked and, once hooked, she played with you for as long as she needed. When she tired of you, she reeled you in completely, made you make a commitment, and then threw you back into the water. The game was over."

Laura leant back into her chair, a satisfied smile on her face, and reached for her cigarettes.

"So, according to you, it was all a set-up. She was bored and wanted a bit of excitement to while away the last part of the crossing from France."

Laura drew on her cigarette and nodded, the smile still on her lips, her eyes defying him to come up with an alternative explanation.

"I was there, Laura. I saw the way she was and it wasn't an act. I genuinely believed she wanted to kill herself and –"

"And the nearest man, in fact the only man, leapt to her rescue. No, Matthew, I'm sorry, I can't believe you really accept that as the truth." Laura drew on her cigarette again as she picked up her wine. "You were meant to believe her intent. If you hadn't, you wouldn't have reacted the way you did."

He took a deep breath, a feeling of defeat evident as he shook his head. "The point is I have no way of turning back time to prove you wrong."

Laura shrugged. "It wouldn't prove anything, Matthew. It's so obvious."

"All right, I'm not saying I agree with you, but do I detect just a small amount of jealousy in your reasoning?" He sat back and waited for her answer.

Laura had been stubbing out her cigarette as he asked his question and she used this to delay looking at him. Once out, she then used the cigarette butt to move the ash around until it was all in one corner. Only then did she look at him.

"What makes you think I'd be jealous?"

"It's rude to answer a question with a question but, in this case, you're simply using it as a delaying tactic."

He took the bottle of wine from the windowsill and filled his glass, then leant forward so that he could also fill Laura's. Taking the full glass, Laura sat back in the chair and curled her legs under her.

"I'm not delaying anything, only wondering why you feel the need to ask the question." She narrowed her eyes. "Is there something that perhaps I should feel jealous about? Something you are not telling me?"

Matthew smiled. "Another question and this time I admit it's a tricky one. You have managed to turn my question into an accusation that I did something, which, if it were true, it would give you, a reason to be jealous." He paused when he saw Laura's expression. "Actually, I was only asking whether the fact that I helped this woman in the first place generated in you, for whatever reason, a feeling of jealousy."

She cocked her head to one side. "Would you have done the same if she had been a man?"

This time Matthew shook his head. "She asked me the same thing." He paused again. The conversation was taking a turn he hadn't expected. "Look, Laura, a lot of what you said about protecting and feeling responsible was, I admit, accurate. And no, I probably wouldn't have felt the same way if she had been a man, but I defy you to tell me that other men wouldn't have reacted in exactly the same way."

"I'm not saying they wouldn't, but tell me, what would you have done if, rather than ending her game when she did, she had pulled into the garage as you asked her to?" Laura lit another cigarette and waited

She didn't normally smoke more than four or five cigarettes a day but when she was feeling argumentative, or threatened, she sometimes smoked one after the other. Matthew seemed to have touched a nerve with something he had said. Previous experience told him he ought to leave things where they were and change the subject, but this time he wanted to know where she was coming from.

"I suppose the honest answer would be, I don't know," he said.

"And the dishonest one?" she asked, her head still cocked to one side.

He closed his eyes as the answer to his question dawned.

Leaning forward he spread his hands in front of him. "Laura, I really don't know what you want me to say. It's obvious that, for some reason, you have gone from telling me, quite light-heartedly, that you believe I was duped by a very calculating female, to wanting an argument about my underlying intentions. Why?"

"I don't want an argument, I want an explanation."

"An explanation of what?"

Laura stubbed out her half-smoked cigarette, this time quite forcefully.

"All right, Matthew, if you want to play games, tell me what was going through your mind when you thought she was going to be waiting for you on the other side of Customs, or, and perhaps more importantly, you had been waiting for her."

She lifted her head, her eyes staring as she waited for his reply.

He was beginning to feel just a little annoyed. Since she moved in with him of course they had argued, or perhaps had disagreements would be a better description, but they never doubted each other. It was obvious now, though, and for some illogical reason, she thought that during his brief encounter with Francesca he had designs on the bloody woman: a woman, who in his opinion, he saved from a certain death, but if he understood her correctly, this temptress had merely been playing with him.

"Regardless of what I tell you, I suppose you're going to come up with another fact to twist the truth into to what you want it to be," he said. "I saved a woman's life, and, all right, I felt responsible for her welfare, but that's all it was. I wanted to see her on the other side of Customs just to make sure she was, under the circumstances, fit to drive to wherever she might be going, that's all."

"I have no intention of twisting the truth and thank you for putting it that way," Laura said through clenched teeth before adding, "If she had decided to carry on with her little game, I wonder what would have happened."

"I really don't believe this, Laura. What are you getting at now?"

"What I am getting at, as you put it, is that if she'd extended the game to, let's say, wanting your company for a little longer, and for 'your company', yes, you can substitute the word 'sex', would you have obliged?"

Exasperation had now taken over from his annoyance.

Matthew picked up his plate before bending down and collecting hers from the floor. After straightening up, he looked down at her.

"I really don't know why you suddenly feel the need to do this, Laura. I told you what I told you because, in my line of work, it's not every day you get to do somebody else a good turn, male or female. I guess with what you do, you think there has to be an ulterior motive for every action. I'm sorry you feel the need to group me in with some of your less desirable clients. I have told you what happened and why it happened. If you really want to know what I was thinking about as I waited to go through Customs, it was that I sincerely hoped I wasn't going to be delayed too long because I wanted to get home to you as soon as possible."

Laura was looking up at him, her face expressionless, but he could see that her eyes were beginning to water.

"I'm now going into the kitchen," he said, "to do the washing up. I then fancy an early night. If you think I'd have preferred to spend the night and have sex with some nutty female who was hell bent on drowning herself, rather than spending it with you, then no doubt I'll see you in the morning. If not, I would be very happy if you were to join me and we can perhaps, a little later, talk about money. It's what you wanted to discuss earlier, remember?"

With his words hanging in the air her left the conservatory.

Chapter Six

It was ten minutes before Laura joined Matthew in the kitchen.

After apologising and using worry as the reason for her unexpected hostility, she explained that because the woman Matthew met and saved on the ferry was undoubtedly unhinged, he, being the sort of person he was, could so easily have found himself drawn into something that could have resulted in a more dangerous situation.

She then went on to describe a couple of the undesirables she had investigated, the results of which made her a lot more sceptical and circumspect about human behaviour, and in particular their motives ... especially for some women.

Later, as she lay with her head on Matthew's chest, his arm round her shoulders, Laura said, "I hope you accepted what I said earlier."

"Of course I did, and I'm sorry for storming out, but ... no, let's forget about what happened on the ferry, and downstairs ... I think you said you wanted to talk money."

"Yes," she said. "I pay myself a good salary and I know I've got a pretty hefty mortgage on the flat but, now it's rented, that's almost covered. You pick up all the bills here. I want to do more."

"You already do your bit," he told her. He couldn't overstate his own situation but he did admit that he would be reluctant to break into his investments if he were unable to find work to replace the Koblenz contract, and therefore what Laura was offering him was quite timely.

"I don't call paying for the weekly shop doing my bit. I want to do more than that. Two people can't live as cheaply as one, not the way we live anyway, and your bills have gone up since I moved in."

"What do you suggest?"

"Actually it's more than a suggestion," she said, turning her head so that she could see his face. "I went to the bank today and opened a joint account. I've arranged to have five hundred a month transferred into it, so if you do the same and we pay all the household bills from that account, then I'll consider that I'm doing my bit. What do you think?"

Matthew hugged her. "Sounds as though you've got it all arranged, so I'm happy if you are."

She kissed his shoulder. "That's sorted, then," she said in an East London drawl. "There's something else I want to ask you."

"Go on."

"Next Monday, I'm due to go to Warwick on a case I picked up last week. It's pretty uncomplicated by the sound of it. A client, who is paying through the nose for child support, is convinced his ex-wife is cohabiting but he needs corroboration."

"Shouldn't he go to the authorities with what he thinks his wife's up to?"

"He will once I confirm, if I can, his suspicions. But I don't think it would do any good because cohabiting isn't justification for them to authorise withdrawal of support."

"And he's still willing to fork out your daily rate just to find out?"

"You make it sound as though I'm ripping people off," Laura said.

"Not if you're paying some of it into this joint account you've opened." He squeezed her arm to let her know he was only joking.

"Anyway," she said, "back to Warwick. I wondered if while I'm up there you wanted me to go and see Emily again to see if there is anything new I can tell you."

Matthew's mood changed immediately.

During the preceding year, Laura had brought him what he could only describe as a new lease of life and a reason for going on. It hadn't been that bad before she arrived on the scene but companionship counts for an awful lot and she had boosted his self-esteem in more ways than one.

Although very different to Emily, she had the same self-contained feel about her. Emily had always given Matthew the impression that, if he were to die in whatever circumstances, she would mourn his loss but life would go on. She had never given him the impression that he needed to do anything else other than insure himself appropriately. Even now, Emily was the only beneficiary in his will should something ghastly happen to him, but each time he thought about it, he knew that he must revise where his loyalties really ought to be, and therefore where his money should go in the event of his premature death.

With Emily, it had been the little things she was good at that made him realise the bigger things would come to her as a matter of course. She used to check the oil in her car and chastise him when he didn't check the tyre pressures on his car. If he were away for only a few days, she would mow the lawn, trim the hedges, change electric plugs and do things that were normally in the man's domain.

Comparison between Emily and Laura was to be expected. Laura was the same as Emily as far as interdependence and independence were concerned. Although she gave the impression that she needed the interdependency, he also knew that she was quite capable of existing on her own. He guessed he was being rather patronising towards both Emily and Laura, but he also believed his thought processes were perfectly normal.

His current thoughts took him back to what had caused the argument earlier and Laura's comment that *the female of the species is cunning and more than capable of taking care of herself. More often than not, making a man feel powerful and in control is all part of the game. It is amazing what can be achieved by using such tactics.*

Matthew wondered if men really were so gullible or was it just him … and maybe a handful of others?

Interdependence and independence apart, Laura differed from Emily in nearly every other way.

Although she dressed formally for work, around the house, and when they went out, she always preferred to be very casual – joggers and T-shirts for the house, jeans and casual tops for evenings in The Grasshopper, which had become their local, and when they went to restaurants. She did dress up if they were going anywhere special, the theatre for example. They made a point of going to London at least once a month and then she dressed for the occasion. Emily had never liked being too casual. Matthew had very rarely seen her wearing trousers even round the house.

Emily had also been conservative where cooking was concerned. She had eaten, but sometimes reluctantly, Matthew's experiments and tolerated pasta, which he loved. She had been very much into healthy eating. Laura, though, adored anything Mediterranean, closely followed by Thai, Malaysian and Indian cuisine. Eating Laura's hot spicy food on a Sunday after Emily's traditional roast took some getting used to.

Emily had been equally unimaginative where decorating was concerned – walls were magnolia, carpets subdued, pictures conventional and curtains functional. In contrast, Laura's personality was as abstract as her preferences for décor. With bright, but acceptable, coloured walls and strange metal objects on surfaces, plus outlandish pictures with hidden messages that Matthew, after looking at them from every angle, could not understand, summed up Laura's individuality quite accurately. She hadn't exactly taken over the cottage, merely stamped her personality on it – where appropriate.

From the beginning, Emily's attitude towards sex had fallen neatly into line with her conventional and traditional approaches towards the rest of her life. Matthew had respected how established her beliefs and needs had been, but whenever he thought about her, and that was often, his memories only added to his disbelief that she had been carrying on with somebody else for so long before they eventually separated.

It made him question his own attitude and wondered whether he had been the one at fault and not her. She had never, as far as he could remember, initiated sex because that was, in her opinion, the man's province. Although, until she fell pregnant with Sarah, she had never refused Matthew, it was obvious on occasions that she was reacting as a duty rather than because of her own needs.

After he and Emily separated, the short affairs that occurred before he met Laura were mirror images of what he experienced with Emily … except with Cassie that is, because she was a little more adventuress. The conclusion he drew was inevitable, deciding he was the one who was boring.

Laura changed all that.

The first time they had sex – after the initial meeting in The Grasshopper – she introduced him to something he had not previously experienced. For a start she made him feel as though she wanted him as much as he wanted her and that is the way it stayed.

Matthew no longer needed to judge when the time was right; Laura never left him in any doubt that the time was always right. She was either a damn good actor or he had struck gold.

Laura took the initiative as often as he did, her needs sometimes surpassing his own. She was unconventional, experimental whenever the fancy took her, and she always managed to make him feel as though he was the answer to all of her desires. There were even occasions when he was the reluctant one. Very early on in the relationship Laura revealed that she liked to take risks, whereas he thought that a man of forty and a woman in her early thirties should perhaps behave a little more decorously. Sometimes the places in which Laura chose to make love were both adventurous and just a little risqué but, fortunately, they went undisturbed and after a while, Matthew began to relax and Laura's somewhat bizarre behaviour became an exciting expectation rather than a concern.

Laura was pretty and sensual, whereas Emily had been handsome and accommodating. Laura dressed to attract; Emily had dressed to go with the occasion but nearly always conservatively. Laura took Matthew with her to buy her underwear and expected to be surprised every now and again with something he bought her while abroad. Emily had always gone shopping alone to buy what she needed and, early on in their relationship, made him only too aware that his choices – which he thought were an expectation – and hers, were entirely different.

He often told himself that it was wrong to compare but he did because it was necessary. With Laura, he had everything most men would crave for, in Emily he had had someone he loved. He had fallen in love with Emily the first time he met her. He had never fallen out of love with her. His thoughts, whenever he was driving home to Westerham and to Laura, confirmed that. Emily's infidelity had dented his self-esteem but not his deep feelings for her.

He blamed himself for what had happened, telling himself that if he had been a better husband she would not have needed anybody else.

With Laura, the same feelings were not there, not to the same intensity. She was a wonderful and considerate person and they were very happy together, but he did not love her, not in the same way he loved Emily.

Maybe he felt he could not love two women at the same time.

So did he want Laura to go and see how Emily was?

It had been a year since the last visit and he wasn't sure he wanted there to be another one. For all of their sakes, he had to keep the past as the past and not try to live in it as well as in the present ... and plan the future.

He wasn't being fair to Laura.

She *was* his future.

Emily was his past, regardless of how he felt.

He had to move on.

"I'm not sure it would be wise," he told Laura, trying not to let the tone of his voice tell her why.

She sat up in bed and looked at him. "Oh! I thought it an ideal opportunity."

"For what? You told me a year ago that she wasn't happy and I did nothing about it, there was nothing I could do about it. If you were to come back and tell me the same, or worse, nothing would change."

Laura's eyes didn't leave Matthew's but, for a few seconds, she didn't say anything. She was obviously mulling over what he had said, he just hoped it had been the right thing.

"She's still there, isn't she? She's still very much part of you, isn't she?" Laura said.

"Don't, Laura, please, don't even go there. There really is no point in discussing it. It leads us nowhere."

He covered her hand with his and he could see in her eyes exactly why they had to move on.

"I'm sorry," she said. "You're right. It was silly of me. It's been too long."

She settled back down in bed, her head once again on his chest.

After about ten minutes, her breathing became slower and rhythmic. She was asleep. Matthew lay awake reliving his years with Emily and, regardless of what he had said to Laura, longing to know whether she and Sarah were all right, that they were now happy and hoping that she missed him just a little. He knew he was being stupid, weak and introspective but, as always, he concluded that although it is reasonably easy to recognise one's failings and weaknesses, it is something else to try and do what you know ought to be done.

He spent hours on his feet lecturing others about coping with change: its inception, communication, being reactive to feedback, redesigning change as a result, its re-introduction, feedback, further change and feedback, and then communicating the results of the change. Because of his wisdom, he expected others to handle change far better than they had done previously. As he stared at the greyness outside the bedroom window, he could hear himself – "But changes in the workplace and in one's personal life are very different. In the former you are usually among a group that is managing the change, in the latter it's, more often than not, down to one person, and that person is you. Handling personal change is a lot more difficult than handling corporate change."

Emily had imposed change into his life.

There was no prior communication, no discussion about handling it together, no reviews, no alternatives, and no reaction to feedback. It was a change he did not want then and still didn't want now. He had simply done what he could to exaggerate the benefits of the status quo and to play down the drawbacks of the imposed change.

He thought he acted quite reasonably under the circumstances. If he had walked in unexpectedly and told Emily that he was having an affair, that he had a child by his mistress and that he was leaving, there would most certainly have been change. Although it would have been his decision in the first place to wander, Emily would have used just two words to explain – quite succinctly – his immediate and long-term future. He would have been out on his ear and financially 'taken to the cleaners' – an appropriate cliché.

He wasn't being retrospective.

One evening he and Emily had discussed the remote possibility of such a thing happening when, for once, she had consumed a little too much alcohol and become morose. She had wanted to know if he would be able to live without her, if anything were to happen, be it an accident or if ... God forbid!

She had not wanted to go there.

Only now did he realise that she had been telling him indirectly what she would expect from him when she declared her infidelity. She was already having the affair and she was already pregnant with what he naively assumed was their baby. Unfortunately for both of them, he didn't get the message and, when the time came, he didn't react in the way he was supposed to.

Even when he allowed his imagination to take over and he pictured her in bed with her faceless lover, he could not stop feeling about her the way he did. Even when he could picture her smile and grimace as she enjoyed with her lover what she obviously had not enjoyed with him, he couldn't stop loving her. There were certain sexual acts he couldn't bring himself to imagine her doing ... maybe because she had always been reluctant ... no, he wouldn't go there.

Ironically it wasn't the physical side of their relationship that upset him the most, it was the little things, the looks, the one-word exchanges that meant so much, going in to check on Sarah together late at night, and the completeness that only a man and a woman in love can share.

She had told him she loved him, so she must have felt that unity at one time or another. How can someone be totally and utterly devoted to another human being one minute and then, a short while later, discard them as unwanted?

Laura's suggestion that she should see Emily again had surprised him for another reason. The first time had been in her professional capacity and they had known each other for only five minutes. Even so, in the last twelve months any conversation about their previous marriages was one-sided. Laura had told him every detail about the abuse she suffered, explaining that he was the first person she was able to talk to about it since her divorce. She had a brother and a younger sister but, for different reasons, she was not able to confide in them.

Her brother, Simon, was on a long-term contract in Australia with a company that dealt with health and safety, and, although they wrote, e-mailed and phoned each other, he had not been back to the UK for them to talk. As far as her brother was concerned, Laura had made a mistake and had done something about it. Lisa, her sister, who was twenty-eight and living in Hounslow, had problems of her own. Little sisters shared confidences with big sisters but not vice-versa, not according to Lisa anyway. Her problems were marital also but, in Matthew's opinion, they were nothing compared to Laura's experiences.

Although that didn't stop Laura telling Matthew that Lisa's husband expected her to give up her career, have a family and become a loving wife and mother rather than an advertising executive. Lisa wanted to be a wife but not a mother, and as for giving up her career, well … that was not an option.

Laura told Matthew that if her problems had been as simple as Lisa's, she may have said something, but the abuse she suffered wasn't the sort of thing you necessarily wanted to discuss. Laura's parents, who were in their early seventies and lived in Nottingham, never liked her husband and were pleased the marriage ended.

Matthew had never met either of Laura's siblings, or her parents, because she said she wanted her relationship with Matthew to stay just between them; she didn't want her family's problems interfering. He accepted her reasoning but hoped in the not-too-distant future the opportunity would arise for him to meet Laura's parents in particular.

One evening, when she had recounted almost everything, Matthew told her that he was surprised she ever contemplated trusting another man again.

Smiling, she said, "Even after what I experienced, Matthew, I needed to have my prejudices proven wrong."

"And you reckoned I was a reasonable bet, did you?"

They were sitting in the kitchen having a simple candlelit evening meal. He was used to Laura's love for candles. He tried to come up with an explanation and decided it was her way of blanking out everything that wasn't immediate. The candles, even in the kitchen, created just the right ambience for an intimate conversation, albeit Laura's memories were painful and it showed.

"There was something about you when you walked into the office for the first time," she said. "I don't know what it was, but I knew that our relationship was going to develop." Her brow furrowed as she tried to think of something that might satisfy his curiosity. Shaking her head she suggested, "It was a gentleness, a tenderness – you seemed to care."

"How could you tell that after knowing me for only a few minutes?" he asked.

Laura shrugged. "Female intuition."

"Oh that! That's a woman's response to any question a man asks but she doesn't want to answer."

"If you say so," she said.

Laura dropped her smiling eyes to her plate so that she could chase a few grains of rice round its rim.

She had made a simple but delicious curry.

"I can't believe any man could treat a woman the way you were treated," Matthew said. He could see that Laura felt the pain and humiliation again as she related the many incidents she experienced and put up with for so long.

"He was a sadist it's as simple as that. He enjoyed forcing me to commit acts that I found degrading and humiliating, and he didn't care how much pain he caused, in fact he took pleasure from it. But I knew if I didn't comply I was in for a beating." Laura winced once again as the memories flooded back. "The depravity was more acceptable than the pain he could inflict elsewhere. When he hit me, he was always careful to make sure that the bruises weren't visible." She paused, but only for a few seconds. "He was an animal, Matthew, an absolute animal."

"Did you ever suspect anything before you got married?"

She raised her eyebrows. "If only. No, he was too clever. He was kind, considerate and I suppose subdued sexually. After we married though, he changed almost overnight. It was as though I'd become his possession and he could do with me what he wanted."

"Wasn't there anybody you could turn to? You were in the police, after all." As he poured more wine into their glasses, Matthew wondered what had happened to her female intuition before she got married. Perhaps nobody asked the right question.

"Who was there to turn to? Outwardly, he was perfectly normal. He had a good job, and according to people I met who knew him, he was always the life and soul of the party. The women adored him and the men envied him. Who would believe me? I'd have been labelled a paranoid woman who lacked imagination." After taking a sip of her wine, Laura added, "As for the police, it's not the sort of thing you share with colleagues when you're in a male-dominated workforce, most of whom don't want you there in the first place."

"Where is he now?"

Laura shrugged again. "We lived in Kensington and, as far as I know, he's still there."

"Has there been any contact at all ... since I mean?"

"There was at first. He was full of remorse, wanting me to take him back and promising that he would treat me properly if I did."

She continued to sip her wine, her eyes telling Matthew that she was, even then, still reliving what her ex-husband had done to her.

"But there's been nothing recently?"

"The promises turned to threats," she said. "He told me that if he couldn't have me, nobody would."

"How long ago was that?"

"About three months before the divorce came through, but I was on the point of taking legal advice when it all stopped. Suddenly there was nothing."

"And there's been nothing since?"

"No, thank God."

"I hear what you say about women in the police but you were still a battered wife. Surely you had sufficient reason to go to the police, officially that is, before the threats started?"

Laura reached for her cigarettes and lighter, which she had put next to the microwave. After retrieving the ashtray from the windowsill, she emptied it before she sat down again.

"As I said, the pain he inflicted didn't leave visible bruising," she said, "and I can assure you that you don't want me to go into detail. As far as his sexual perversions were concerned, it was either that or ..." She stopped and Matthew reached across the table, covering her hand with his.

"There's no need," he told her reassuringly. "You're free of him now."

"I'll never be free of the memories."

Matthew thought it best if he tried to move on. "You've got me now and, as you've discovered, I'm pretty unimaginative where, well, you-know-what is concerned."

She stretched out her arm and ruffled his hair. "You-know-what? If you mean sex, then say it," she told him mockingly.

"You're learning," she added, smiling.

"I'm still surprised that you can let a man anywhere near you."

"I can understand that but, as I said, you're different, as I am sure are so many others. I just picked the wrong one to marry."

"Didn't we all."

"The difference is that you loved Emily and still do."

It always went that way.

Laura would tell him all about the ghastly things she experienced, but as soon as he tried to introduce his own recent past into the conversation, she would block whatever he wanted to say with a statement or observation.

If he denied what Laura said about him still loving Emily, they both knew he would be lying, but the alternative was unacceptable. By not denying what she said, he was not lying to himself or to her, and therefore they both knew that it was wise to change the subject. Whether by doing so he was making Laura feel more insecure he didn't know, but she hadn't ever said or done anything further that gave him any clue as to what was really going on inside her head.

However, he did know what was going on in his own head.

He wanted to be able to discuss how he felt about Emily, to try to get her out of his system, because as long as she was on his mind, the place in his life that Laura deserved was not there, and that was slowly breaking him in two.

Needing Laura to understand and accept how he felt, was paramount, because it was the only way they would ever move onto something more than they had already found.

Chapter Seven

The police knocked on the door at precisely eleven minutes after seven. Matthew could be that precise because he had been clock-watching for the previous three hours. He had last spoken to Laura at just after one o'clock this afternoon. She had finished the job she had set out to do and was leaving Warwick imminently, or so she said. She had been away for only one night, having left the cottage early the previous morning.

She wanted Matthew to go with her.

"I could claim for you on expenses," she told him as she busied herself in the kitchen. She had mislaid a comb and she was sure she was in the kitchen when she last used it.

"Expenses?"

She stopped what she was doing and looked at him. "Entertainment," she said, innocently. "I'd put you down as entertainment, but only if you came up to expectations." She put her tongue out and then carried on searching for her comb.

"I don't know what sort of company you run but claims for entertainment are supposed to be in connection with prospective clients, actual clients and the competition," he mocked her.

"As I said, if you're good enough you would satisfy the first two and hopefully me," she said and added, "Ah!" as a large black comb appeared in her hand as if by magic.

"You're incorrigible," he said, taking her coat from the back of a kitchen chair and holding it out to her.

She put the comb between her teeth as she slipped her arms into the coat. "No, I'm not. I'm gentle, kind and very considerate but you'll also see that I can be extremely threatening unless you change your mind and come to Warwick with me."

"I'd love to but I really have to be in Newmarket by midday."

"Can't you put them off?" Laura asked, pouting.

"A day's work is a day's work. With the future in mind, it's also a day's money."

"All right, I'll just have to find some younger man in Warwick to take your place. I'll check out his credentials beforehand though, he'll need to rise to the occasion."

Laura flounced into the hall, deliberately swinging her hips seductively.

"Harlot," Matthew said to her retreating backside.

"What happened to Jezebel?" Laura asked over her shoulder as she picked up her laptop. "Bring my bag, boy," she ordered.

Matthew collected her overnight bag from the bottom of the stairs and followed her out through the front door.

It was a lovely crisp morning.

The rising sun shining through the trees was already causing the ripples on the nearby stream to shimmer and sparkle. The birds were singing and he heard the church clock chime eight.

Laura opened the boot of her car, deposited the laptop and reached for her bag as Matthew held it out.

"I asked you a question," she reminded him, trying to hide the smile on her face.

"Jezebel?" he asked. "When did I ever call you a Jezebel?"

"The other morning, when I disturbed you a little too early because I felt frustrated …" She looked up and noticed the milkman standing on the other side of her car, a beaming smile on his face.

"Mornin', Mr Ryan, Mrs Ryan," he greeted them. "Lovely mornin'."

They had never bothered to tell Tim Collins, the milkman, they weren't married – there was no point.

"Morning," Laura and Matthew chorused.

Tim handed Matthew two pints of cold milk and touched his cap before going back through the gate.

"You'll be getting us a bad reputation," Matthew told Laura.

"Getting?" she asked, as she left her car and crossed the few feet between them.

Still holding the bottles of milk, Matthew put his arms round Laura's waist as they kissed goodbye.

"Behave yourself," he whispered in her ear, the fragrance of her perfume having its usual effect.

"I will." Laura kissed him on the lips. "Right, I must fly. See you tomorrow afternoon, I won't be late." She twirled round and got into her car, lowering the window once settled.

"I'll miss you," Matthew told her, bending down by the door.

"And I you," Laura replied with the sort of smile that told them both that they should be saying more.

Then she was gone.

The car's exhaust smoked a little in the cold air as she pulled away. She manoeuvred round the road works fifty yards away up Rysted lane and then with a wave of her hand, she was beyond the corner and out of sight.

"Mr Ryan?" the male police officer asked.

There was a female police officer at his shoulder who looked as though she was hardly old enough to be out of school, let alone in the police service.

"Yes," Matthew said, tentatively. "My name is Ryan. How can I help?"

The man reached up and took off his cap before he asked the question Matthew knew what would follow. "I'm Police Constable Richards and this is Woman Police Constable Phillips. We are from the station in Sevenoaks. May we come in, Sir?"

The silly thoughts that go through people's minds when trying to think of an explanation for an unexpected occurrence often appear so stupid in retrospect. Matthew found himself wondering why in this day and age of political correctness, policewomen were still referred to as *woman* this and *woman* that, when in the majority of cases it was pretty bloody obvious you were talking to a woman.

Even without his cap – under which was a shock of very red hair – the male police officer was a couple of inches taller than Matthew. He was probably about thirty and Matthew thought, incongruously, that he appeared to be a little thin for a police officer.

"Of course," Matthew said, standing to one side. They both walked past him, hesitating once they were a few feet into the hall.

"Straight through," Matthew suggested. "I've just boiled the kettle. You could probably do with a cup of tea."

Why they might want a cup of tea when he knew what they were going to tell him, he had no idea – another incongruity. Maybe he just needed to say something so that he could delay what they had to say.

They stood by the breakfast bar.

WPC Phillips, who could not have been more than five and a half feet tall, took off her hat to reveal a striking young face but one that convinced Matthew she really was far too young to be fighting crime. Her natural dark brown hair tied back into a severe bun, didn't help. He noticed three hairgrips equally spaced above each ear.

"Would you like a cup of tea?" Matthew asked again, moving across to the kettle.

"Mr Ryan," WPC Phillips said, speaking for the first time. "I'm –"

"I know what you are going to tell me," Matthew informed her. "So let me make it a little easier for you. There's been an accident, hasn't there?"

He flipped on the kettle and then made himself turn round and look at them. They were both staring at the floor.

The girl nodded as she lifted her head. "Yes, Sir, we think so. I'm afraid it's Mrs Stanhope –"

"*Miss* Stanhope," Matthew informed her, waving his hand, dismissively. Laura had given up calling herself 'Ms', deciding it made her sound pretentious. "What do you mean you think there has been an accident?"

"Don't you want to know how Miss Stanhope is, Sir?" asked PC Richards, in a tone that suggested Matthew's priorities were slightly wrong.

"Of course, Constable," Matthew apologised. "I'm sorry. I think I'd already imagined the worst."

"Not quite, Sir," said WPC Phillips, "but she is badly injured."

As he slumped against the draining board, Matthew took a deep breath

The kettle clicked off.

"Would you like a cup of tea?" WPC Phillips added, moving towards him.

"Please," he replied, absent-mindedly. "The tea is in this cupboard and the fridge is behind that door."

He walked past the female police officer, through to the far end of the kitchen. Pulling out the chair on which Laura's coat had hung the previous morning, he sat down. He could hear WPC Phillips opening and closing the other cupboards, probably looking for mugs, but the noise was like an echo. Although he had assumed the worst, the reason why the police were in his cottage hit him like a sledgehammer.

The woman whom he would not admit he loved was lying in hospital badly injured many miles away when she should have been at home with him. He had only started worrying when she hadn't arrived home by four o'clock, and that hadn't given her much leeway for traffic and road works. The accident could have happened at any time after she phoned him but, even so, the police had, he thought, done extremely well to track him down so quickly.

As PC Richards pulled out the chair opposite Matthew, it scraped on the floor. "Do you mind, Sir?"

Matthew looked up. "No, please, sit down and tell me what happened."

"We don't know all of the details, Sir. The Warwickshire police phoned about an hour ago."

WPC Phillips crossed the kitchen clutching three mugs of steaming tea. "Hope you take milk, Sir. I've put two sugars in because you need them."

Matthew smiled up at her. "Thank you. If you'd like a biscuit, they are in that cupboard over there."

"No, thanks, Sir," said PC Richards, speaking for both of them.

"Look, can we drop this 'Sir' business? You are not here to arrest me, I hope. Can we be a little less formal? My name is Matthew." Matthew offered to shake hands with WPC Phillips who stole a furtive look at her partner.

"Gillian, Sir, but ..." she started to say.

Matthew switched to PC Richards. "Peter, Sir," he said, taking Matthew's hand.

Matthew decided to let the *Gillian, Sir*, and *Peter, Sir*, pass because he had probably already overstepped the mark with his informality.

"So who is going to tell me what you do know and, more importantly, the quickest way I can be with Laura?"

His imagination was working overtime.

When he first opened the front door and saw the police officers, he immediately imagined that Laura was lying on a mortician's slab, her pale dead face expressionless. He even saw the pathologist, scalpel poised, as he prepared to slice into Laura's body. The police could have been there for any number of other reasons but, no, Laura had to be the only reason. When WPC Phillips – Gillian – had described Laura's condition as badly injured, he had then imagined Laura connected to a myriad of bleeping machines, her head bandaged, and her face pale and impassive.

Peter Richards sipped his tea before taking the initiative. "As we said, Sir, the details are a bit limited but as far as we can gather Miss Stanhope was crossing a road in Warwick when she was hit by a car."

The scene flashed into Matthew's mind.

As she fell forcibly against the bonnet of the car, he could hear Laura screaming and then he saw her being tossed like a rag doll over its roof to the hardness of the road behind. He saw broken bones, arms and legs twisted at strange angles.

He closed his eyes, shuddered and shook his head.

"But ... but earlier one of you implied it wasn't an accident," he said slowly.

"It was me, Sir," Gillian said, looking across the table at Peter. "Perhaps I shouldn't have suggested that at this stage –"

"Gillian, I have no wish to get you into trouble but you must have had good reason to say what you did. All I want to know is what happened, where Laura is and how soon I can get to see her."

Peter spoke for Gillian. "It's just that there were witnesses to the incident and some of them have said that they think it was deliberate."

"Deliberate? You mean somebody drove into her on purpose?"

It was Peter's turn to look at Gillian. "That's what we were able to glean from the Warwickshire police, Sir," he said, without making eye contact.

"I see." Matthew had not delayed asking his next question for any other reason than he was scared of what the answer might be. "And how serious are her injuries?"

"This time I will use the Warwickshire's exact words," Gillian said. "They implied ... no, sorry they said she was one very lucky lady. She hadn't regained consciousness when they phoned, but they did say she's broken an arm and her body is very badly bruised but, other than that, there are no really serious injuries."

"Thank God. She is a very fit lady," Matthew informed them, trying to think of any reason why she had been so lucky. "Was the driver of the car caught?"

The fact that Laura was probably in a coma had not washed over him but there was little point in asking either of his guests to elaborate.

"Not at the time of the call, Sir, no. The Warwickshire police have a description of the car but nothing else. It must have happened so quickly."

"And where is Laura?"

"In Warwick General, Sir," Peter volunteered.

"Thank you. How did you find me so quickly?" Matthew asked as he finished his tea.

"Miss Stanhope was carrying her passport, Sir, and your name, address and telephone number were given under the 'who should be contacted in the event of an emergency' bit, Sir." Peter had pulled his hat towards him across the table, indicating that he thought it was time they left

"What happens now?" Matthew asked.

"What do you mean, Sir?"

"Well, is there a procedure to follow, or can I just go to Warwick General Hospital and see her?"

"We don't really know what they've done, Sir, but because there's a possibility that it was deliberate, there could be a police presence."

"But that wouldn't stop me from seeing her?" Matthew asked.

"No, Sir," suggested Gillian. "We'll phone ahead and tell them we've seen you and that you're on your way." She had taken the cue from Peter. She stood up and popped her hat back on.

"Well, thank you for coming round so quickly," Matthew said as he followed them to the front door.

"We're sorry we had to come at all," Peter said over his shoulder. "We hope when you see her that she's regained consciousness. The Warwickshire police will want to question her."

"I understand, but thank you again."

"Good evening, Sir," Gillian said politely as they went down the path towards their car.

Matthew watched them until they were out of sight behind the garage before closing the door. The enormity of what he thought he was going to be told had hit him the moment he first saw them at the door, but for some reason he thought it wasn't right to show his emotions in front of strangers. He had reached the kitchen and was reaching for the bottle of whisky, when the tears arrived.

He hadn't cried since that first night after he left Emily and Sarah, then it was the loss, this time it had to be the shock.

When Emily had told him that she was leaving him for someone else, he hadn't cried straight away, not in front of her. The tears were there but he hadn't cried.

He was angry.

Even when Emily told him that Sarah was this other man's child, he didn't cry.

He felt cheated.

When his father died, and then his mother only six months later, he hadn't cried then either.

He felt empty.

Although he wanted to cry on each occasion, after that first night alone there weren't any more tears. Instead he resorted to the bottle and his work: the former in moderation and the latter very, very heavily.

So why now, when he was reaching for the whisky bottle, was he suddenly weeping like a child? The tears blurred his vision and his first attempt to pour the whisky into the glass resulted in wet fingers and a wet worktop. He gulped down the neat liquid but it did not stop his mind working overtime.

Was he in denial?

Could it be that he felt more for Laura than he allowed himself to admit? The thought of her lying alone in a strange hospital bed, surrounded by strangers and with the police waiting to speak to her, was too much for him.

Reaching out to pour another whisky he suddenly stopped. He had to get to her as quickly as possible. She may have already regained consciousness as Peter had hoped but, if she hadn't, he wanted to be there when she did.

He threw a few overnight things into a bag and was out of the house less than ten minutes later. There were things he should have done before leaving but he would worry about those once he knew Laura was going to be all right. Although the seriousness of the situation had hit him almost immediately, the fact that the police thought what had happened was not an accident had yet to register.

Leaving Westerham on the A25 and bypassing Oxted, he headed for the M25. As he drove, he began to think for the first time about what the police had implied ... it wasn't an accident.

He had always been worried that Laura was never very far from danger. She often admitted that a few of her clients were no more than low life with money. If some of her clients were that bad, then the people she investigated on their behalf were probably a good deal worse. It must be an undesirable by-product of her profession that she upset people, either those to whom she gave the results of her investigations or, and probably more relevantly, those who were being investigated. A stranger prying into your personal life was not always welcome.

Laura told him repeatedly not to worry. She tried to convince him that the vast majority of the cases she took on were simple – mainly marital problems where either partner thought their trustworthy other half was playing away from home. When Matthew tried to indicate that when found out the wayward might plan retribution on her, she told him not to try applying his psychology training to her profession, and, anyway, it was more sociology than psychology.

That simple and questionable statement – like female intuition – was her answer to his worries and she never allowed him to take it any further.

In reality, Laura's explanation merely added to his worries. Well, perhaps now she would listen to him and perhaps he would listen to himself as well.

It was a few hours after the rush hour so the M25 was not particularly busy for a Friday evening. Matthew was following a couple of cars in the outside lane that were being held up by what looked like a Renault which had overtaken a slower car in the middle lane, but was refusing to pull in. Looking in the mirror, he could see a queue of about ten cars behind him. After a good deal of flashing and weaving from lane to lane from the car directly behind the Renault, its driver took the hint and moved into the middle lane. The pack behind it, including Matthew, showed how macho they were by roaring past the Renault at a good twenty miles per hour over the speed limit.

Turning off the M25 and onto the M40, Matthew estimated that he would be in Warwick by about ten that evening. As he accelerated down the slip road, he noticed that the dark-blue VW Golf, which had been in his rear view mirror almost all the way since he had joined the M25, was about fifty yards behind him. It was never close enough for him to see the driver, but it had always been there. Matthew shrugged, put it down to coincidence, and moved into the middle lane to overtake a posse of army vehicles that were sauntering along in the inside lane.

Once settled, his thoughts went straight back to Laura. If somebody accused him of taking her for granted and not giving a lot in return, he would have to plead guilty as charged. The speed with which they got together after their first meeting surprised them both. Nevertheless, it was mutual and unforced. Although during that first evening in The Grasshopper, neither thought their relationship would progress into anything else, they decided afterwards all the signs were there. Finishing up in bed a matter of an hour after they left the restaurant, certainly wasn't planned.

Matthew had repeatedly asked himself why it had happened and so quickly. He put it all down to the fact that they were two lonely and available people who took an instant liking to each other. He tried to explain it away by telling himself that they met when they were both feeling particularly vulnerable and then, after further thought and a little unwillingly, put it down to simple lust … or if he were being kind, chemistry.

He shrugged and smiled as he thought about that first night, his hands gripping the steering wheel as he slowed for some road works at Beaconsfield.

Perhaps he was loathe to accept his own explanation because he did not want to admit it to himself or to Laura, that he had needed her for nothing more than sex initially. The physical attraction, as far as he was concerned, had been mutual and spontaneous. However, if lust were the answer then, a proper relationship came out of it, a relationship that they both wanted and needed. Why, then, if it was a relationship they both wanted, was he ignoring his true feelings for her and had been doing so for such a long time?

Why had it taken a tragedy to bring him to his senses and for him to admit how he really felt?

The answer, once again, had to be Emily.

His psyche had not allowed him to believe that he could be in love with two women at the same time. If Emily and he were still together then the situation would not have existed: he and Laura would never have met. It had been years since he saw Emily: was he going to go through the rest of his life resisting his own feelings, telling himself that he could never feel for somebody else the way he had always felt, and still did feel, about Emily?

When he and Emily parted, he promised himself that he would never get deeply involved again.

It had not taken much for him to break that promise.

Perhaps it was now time he took responsibility for his own actions.

The hospital was well signposted and, in view of the time, parking was easy. Matthew went to the main reception area and asked for directions to A&E. The nurse behind a smaller reception desk in A&E gave him the once-over when he asked for Laura Stanhope.

"And may I ask who you are, Sir?" she enquired, looking over his shoulder. He hadn't seen any police but he guessed that's what she was looking for.

"Yes," he replied patiently, "my name is Matthew Ryan."

He knew what was coming next.

"Are you a relative, Sir?"

"Not in the sense you mean it, no, but Miss Stanhope lives with me and has done so for quite a while. I presume that qualifies me to see her."

The nurse, a large, formidable, but not unattractive female in her late twenties eyed him warily. "Not necessarily, Mr Ryan.

Would you excuse me for a moment?"

She didn't wait for Matthew to reply before withdrawing to the back of Reception. Picking up a phone, she mumbled something unintelligible into the receiver.

Returning to the desk, she said, "Take a seat over there, Mr Ryan," indicating a row of plastic chairs behind him. "Somebody will be with you shortly."

"Who will this somebody be?" Matthew asked.

She looked quite shocked at his impertinence. "Shortly, Mr Ryan," she replied, glaring at him.

Matthew reluctantly did as he was told, joining about half a dozen others who were either waiting to be seen or were waiting for those who were being seen. It was a long time since he had been in a hospital and he did not remember ever having been in an A&E department, although in his childhood he must have broken bones and been rushed somewhere.

Looking around at the exits from the reception area, he wondered where Laura would be. The extra-large nurse kept on glancing in his direction, appearing certain that he was going to do something untoward. The flippancy of his thoughts, he decided, was due to tiredness and worry.

He tried to control his thoughts, but with no one to talk to, it was difficult. Fortunately, only a matter of minutes later another rather officious looking nurse came through one of the doors and, after conferring at Reception, crossed the floor in his direction.

"Mr Ryan?"

"Yes," Matthew said, standing up.

"Would you care to come with me, please?"

He followed the nurse back through the door after which she led him to an area that appeared to be the hub of a number of sidewards. It was very quiet, except for the odd cough.

"Mr Ryan," the nurse said quietly, turning to face him. "I'm going to let you see Miss Stanhope but only for a few minutes. She's comfortable but shaken."

The nurse began to move away.

Matthew wondered what she meant by 'shaken'. "I was told she'd been unconscious," he said, touching her arm.

The nurse reacted as though he had molested her.

She snatched her arm away, turned, and glared at him, staring at the spot on her uniform that he had touched. She then took a deep breath and rested her eyes on his.

"She was," she said, almost indignantly. "She regained consciousness about an hour ago. There doesn't appear to be any damage but we'll have to wait to be sure."

"Is her arm badly broken?"

Her expression changed from indignation to surprise. "We thought it was broken but the x-ray told us otherwise: a badly sprained wrist and a bruised elbow."

"I see, thank you."

The nurse moved away again. "May I ask who told you about her condition?" she enquired over her shoulder.

"The police." He said. "The police in Westerham told me when they came to tell me about the accident."

That seemed to satisfy her, so Matthew assumed he had just saved the nurse in Reception from a carpeting.

"The police were here but they left about twenty minutes ago."

"They've questioned her already?"

The nurse stopped again.

"They most certainly have not," she said. "I told them to come back in the morning. Miss Stanhope is in a state of shock and in no condition to be cross-examined by the police."

She reached for the door-handle to a sideward and slowly opened the door. Matthew equally slowly followed her into the room as he tried to peer round her.

The nurse went to the other side of the bed and picked up one of Laura's wrists to check her pulse, which caused Laura to open her eyes. When Matthew and the nurse had entered the ward, Laura had looked – as he so often found her late on a Sunday morning – fast asleep. It wasn't until she moved her head to look at the nurse that he saw the cut on her forehead, and bruising on her cheek and neck.

"Mr Ryan is here to see you, Miss Stanhope," the nurse informed Laura. "He can have five minutes."

Laura hadn't realised that Matthew was in the room and the speed with which she turned her head made her wince with pain, but even that did not stop her face breaking out into a broad smile.

"Matthew!" she whispered huskily.

The nurse moved away from the bed.

"Her neck is bruised which means there is probably internal swelling as well, so don't make her talk too much," she ordered. "Five minutes, Mr Ryan, no more," she reminded him as she left the ward.

"Can't leave you on your own for a second," Matthew said as he took Laura's proffered hand in his, at the same time bending down and kissing her lightly on the lips.

He sat on the edge of the bed holding her hand. "What on earth happened?" She tried to shrug but winced instead. "I'm sorry," he apologised. "I'm doing exactly what the nurse told me not to do."

"That's ... that's all right," Laura croaked, her sore throat making her eyes squint. "In answer to your ... your question, I don't know. One minute ... one minute I was crossing the road, the next thing I know I'm waking up in hospital."

"Don't you remember anything?"

"If I did I'd immediately try and forget it," she said, smiling. "All ... all I remember is being lifted off the ground and thumping my head against something. It all happened so quickly."

Her voice was so quiet Matthew had to lean forward to hear her.

"The police ..." he began to say but then stopped. There was little point in repeating what he knew. If Laura thought it was an accident, then that is how it ought to remain for the time being. "Well, thank God your injuries aren't as bad as they might have been. You could have been killed."

"I ... I feel as though I've been hit by a tank but the nurse told me that I ... I was very lucky." She grimaced as she swallowed.

"You can say that again. I would guess that once they've checked you over completely, they will probably let you out in a day or two."

Matthew thought the nurse had returned to order him out of the ward but she only glanced at them before carrying on down the corridor.

"What's the time?"

"Nearly eleven."

"Thank ... thank you for coming," she said, clutching his hand tightly, her eyes watering.

"What on earth did you expect me to do?" He lifted her hand and kissed her fingers.

"I should have looked where I was going."

"So perhaps should the driver of the car that hit you. Are you in a lot of pain?"

"No," she lied. "Un … uncomfortable, that's all. You're not driving back tonight, are you?"

"Back? I'll be going back when I can take you with me."

She smiled, her eyes now brimming with tears. "Matthew, I –"

"Don't," he told her. "It's me who should be telling you."

"What?"

"That I love you."

Chapter Eight

Much to Matthew's surprise, Laura's discharge was earlier than he expected. He thought she needed keeping under observation for longer, but the hospital was adamant – there was nothing seriously wrong with her and they needed the bed for a more serious case.

They left just before one o'clock.

The police, again much to Matthew's surprise, turned up this morning just after the doctor did his rounds during which he pronounced Laura fit for her return home on the condition that she got as much bed rest as possible for the next week or so.

The police, a uniformed sergeant and a woman police constable, asked Matthew to leave the ward while they spoke to Laura. About twenty minutes later they found him in the reception area from where they went into what was called the Families' Room.

After sitting down and establishing Matthew's exact relationship with Laura, the sergeant looked at Matthew and shrugged.

"There's not a lot we can do," the sergeant said a little sheepishly.

The WPC was standing by the window.

"Why?" Matthew did not know whether the police knew that he was aware of their suspicions.

"A simple hit and run," the police sergeant said, clasping his hands together in front of him.

"Simple? It could have resulted in a woman's death."

The police sergeant looked up.

"That's not what I meant," he said apologetically. "It happens more often than people realise. I meant the circumstances were no different to other incidents. Lots of witnesses but everybody concentrates on the victim and can very rarely describe the perpetrator."

"You've got nothing?"

Matthew sipped the coffee he bought from the drinks machine when the police had re-appeared from Laura's ward. He was unhappy about the sergeant's conclusion but there wasn't anything he could do about it.

The sergeant shrugged. "How many dark-blue or black VW Golfs are there in this country?"

The description immediately triggered Matthew's memory. The police sergeant saw his reaction and frowned.

"A dark-blue VW Golf?" Matthew repeated. "I was followed by a dark-blue VW Golf yesterday."

The sergeant and the WPC exchanged looks. "What do you mean by 'followed'?" the sergeant asked.

"When I was on the way here yesterday evening, a dark-blue VW Golf was sitting behind me for a lot of the way."

"May I ask where you came from and which route you took?"

"From Westerham in Kent and then the M25 and the M40," Matthew said.

"So this VW was behind you on the motorway?"

"Yes."

The WPC replaced the unopened notebook back in her pocket. The sergeant's head dropped and he shook it slightly.

"As I said, how many dark-blue VW Golfs are there in the country? I don't suppose you saw the number plate?" the sergeant said.

"No, sorry."

"There we are then."

"What time did the accident happen?" Matthew asked.

"About three yesterday afternoon."

"I was told just after seven o'clock. If there is a connection, the driver who hit Laura would have had ample time to get from Warwick to Westerham." Matthew knew he was clutching at straws.

"Agreed, but the connection I'm afraid is rather tenuous."

The sergeant began to get up.

Matthew moved in front of him.

"The police officers that came to see me suggested your lot had told them that it wasn't an accident," he said.

The sergeant hesitated before saying, "A couple of the eye witnesses we spoke to did think that the driver deliberately swerved to hit Miss Stanhope, yes, but it's not the first time we've heard that. If the driver in an accident is wearing sunglasses, a back-to-front baseball cap and is under twenty-five, then he has to be guilty. You'd be surprised at the stories people come out with in support of their own prejudices."

He began to move past Matthew.

"So you can do nothing?" Matthew asked.

"What can we do?" The sergeant said, turning round. "We've got nothing to go on and we certainly don't have the resources to speak the owners of every dark-blue VW Golf in the country."

"What if she had been killed?"

The sergeant stared at Matthew for a few seconds.

"We may have followed through a little more but, from my experience, we wouldn't have got anywhere," he said.

"So it's the degree of injury that determines the allocation of resources?" Matthew suggested. It was a genuine question but he could feel the anger building up in him.

Again, the sergeant stared at Matthew before answering. "There are degrees in everything, Mr Ryan."

He picked up his cap from the table and indicated to the WPC to leave the room.

When they were alone, the sergeant closed the door.

"Look, Mr Ryan," he said, "I know how pissed off you are, but my hands are tied. I take orders as well as give them. Off the record, if Miss Stanhope had been seriously injured or killed then, yes, we would have spent longer on the case and probably still got nowhere, but she wasn't. She is no worse off than a lot of people would be if they'd tripped over and fallen. She's a very lucky lady but her luck means that we can move on to something else. I'm sorry but that's the way it is."

The sergeant held out his hand.

"I think I understand," Matthew said, "but you're right, I am pissed off and there's nothing you can do about that either."

He shook the sergeant's hand.

Arriving back at the cottage just after four o'clock in the afternoon, Matthew helped Laura up the stairs and put her straight to bed as ordered. The journey down from Warwick had been reasonable but, although Laura was stretched out on the back seat and he'd made her as comfortable as possible, every bump in the road caused her to cry out. Matthew had taken the hospital authorities to task about her indecently hasty release but they had not relented. They needed the bed. Laura also tried bravely to tell Matthew that she was all right and that they would manage, but he could tell that she would have much preferred to have stayed a day or two longer with professional twenty-four hour care overseeing her.

As Matthew helped her undress, the full impact of her accident was apparent. She was an absolute mass of bruises. Her chest, abdomen and thighs looked as though somebody had beaten her with a cricket bat. The right-hand side of her face was also very discoloured, as was her throat. How she got away without breaking any bones and without serious internal injuries was nothing short of a miracle. There were strict instructions on how to remove and replace the bandages on her left wrist and arm, as well as when to administer painkillers. When told to contact her GP on arrival home, Matthew wanted to say he wasn't stupid, but he didn't.

Sitting on the side of the bed, slowly spoon-feeding Laura with some chicken soup – soup was the only food that didn't hurt her throat too much – he thought about what had happened, not that many other things had been on his mind since just after seven o'clock the previous evening.

He could not dismiss, or even start to dismiss, the fact that the police had thought it had not been an accident. If they were right, once she had recovered, Laura was in for a hard time from him to find another job. He had been toying with the idea that they could work together, as lecturing on 'Continuous Improvement' was definitely a good deal safer than delving, perhaps a little too deeply, into people's private lives. He realised he was being sexist when he concluded that if Laura stood up and gave a lecture on 'change in the workplace' she would have the undivided attention of the males in the audience. They would make a good team

"What ... what are you thinking?" Laura asked as he wiped away a smudge of soup from the corner of her mouth. "It's lovely to be pampered," she added as he inspected his work, "but I am quite capable of feeding myself."

Her voice was even huskier as the bruising in her throat was still coming out. The hospital told Matthew that she would probably get worse before she got better, but she was in no danger.

"Just how lucky we were," he said.

Now was not the time to start talking beyond today. He had decided that he would be cancelling the three days' work planned for the following week. Laura was going to need all the attention he could give her, whether she wanted it or not.

She shook her head slightly, the pain the movement caused obvious in her eyes. "I ... I think lucky is an in ... inadequate word. 'Godsend' or 'blessing' are probably better."

"Whatever, you're here that's the main thing, and as for pampering you, you'd better get used to it. If the NHS can't provide the care you need, then I will."

She lifted her right hand and ran her fingers down Matthew's cheek. "Thank you," she said, smiling. "And although I didn't say anything at the time, I love you too. I think I was in shock!"

"I'm sorry –"

"Don't you dare ... dare apologise. As long as you said it because you meant ... meant it rather than out of sympathy ..."

"I should have told you ages ago but –"

"Stop ... stop apologising."

"Look, talking is hurting you. I'll take these things downstairs. You try to get some sleep. Do you want another pain killer?"

"No," Laura replied, resting her head back on the pillows. "It's not a ... as bad as I make out. I ... I'm only doing it to ... to make you feel I need loving."

"You don't need to be in pain for me to do that."

Laura's condition worsened and by the Sunday afternoon, Matthew was so worried that he called out her doctor. His main concern was her breathing. There was a rattle in her throat and she could not take any liquids, let alone food. He was also aware that although the hospital had told him to contact Laura's doctor on their return home, his decision to leave it until Monday did suggest he was stupid after all.

Dr Brian Smith did not complain in the slightest at having his day of rest disturbed. He was knocking at the front door of the cottage fifteen minutes after Matthew's phone call. Matthew explained to him what had happened before handing over the envelope the hospital had given him.

Taking his reading glasses off, Brian Smith looked at Matthew sternly. "I think, Matthew, you ought to have contacted me before you left Warwick Hospital, not twenty-four hours after your return."

Brian Smith and Matthew were both members of Westerham Golf Club and they had played together once or twice. The doctor was in his mid-fifties, short, about five and half feet tall, almost completely bald and, on his own admission, a couple of stones overweight, but he could hit a golf ball further than anyone else Matthew knew.

"I should have, Brian, I'm sorry. Shall we go up?" Matthew said.

"I think we'd better," the doctor said, still annoyed.

Laura was asleep but they could hear her troubled breathing before they went into the bedroom. Brian's concerned expression mirrored the way Matthew felt. Crossing the room hurriedly, Brian picked up Laura's wrist and took her pulse straight away. She moved as he did so.

"Hello, Laura," he said, smiling. "Had a bit of an accident, I hear." Laura tried to reply but only succeeded in screwing up her face in pain. "Best if you leave the talking to me, I think. But if you can nod or shake your head in answer to my questions, it would help."

The doctor lowered her arm onto the bed, still smiling. He opened his bag and took something that looked like a small shoehorn and an even smaller torch.

"Can you open your mouth as far as possible?" Laura looked frightened. "I see," he said quietly. He felt gently around the side and then the back of her neck. "I would like to look at the rest of the bruising, Laura. Would you like Matthew to stay?"

Laura nodded.

"I'll go if you want me to, Brian."

Matthew was standing on the other side of the bed holding Laura's hand.

"No, no, Laura wants you here, so you must stay. Can I wash my hands in your bathroom?"

"Yes, of course," Matthew told him, "it's through that arch over there." Once Brian had disappeared, Matthew squeezed Laura's hand and said, "Don't worry, he'll sort you out. I'm in trouble for not calling him yesterday."

Laura tried unsuccessfully to look relaxed.

Dr Brian Smith gave Laura a thorough examination, shaking his head a couple of times when he saw the multi-coloured bruising on her thighs and abdomen.

"You're a very fortunate young lady," he said, confirming everyone else's beliefs. He pulled the duvet back over her. "How you managed to get away without breaking anything defies everything I know about the human body." He shook his head. "Yes, a very fortunate young lady."

He looked at Matthew and indicated with his eyes that he wanted to speak to him but not in front of Laura. Putting his equipment back in his bag, the doctor took hold of Laura's hand.

"Your throat is badly bruised and that is causing the difficulty with your breathing, but you know that already. It's time something was done to really help you."

On the landing, with the bedroom door closed, Brian Smith undid his collar as his shoulders slumped.

"Matthew, Laura should never have been released from hospital and you are assured I will be representing my case to Warwick General in no uncertain terms. I understand that beds are at a premium but Laura was a priority in my opinion. We have a choice, either you can take her through to the hospital in Sevenoaks or I can call for an ambulance."

"I'll take her."

"Fine and in that case I will phone ahead and tell them that you are on your way. A few days should see her through the worst but she does need twenty-four hour medical care. With all the enthusiasm in the world you can't provide her with that."

An hour later, Laura was under the care of the Sevenoaks hospital. Although she had tried to tell Matthew that she was all right and did not need to go back to hospital, she had to admit that her inability to complete a pain-free sentence did suggest that perhaps medical care was necessary.

Brian Smith's estimate had been remarkably accurate because Laura was allowed home the following Wednesday. Her voice was far from being back to normal but the rasping in her throat every time she took a breath had gone, and the colour was returning to her cheeks. She was able to use the sofa in the living room for further convalescence but doing anything other than reacting to the calls of nature was out of the question.

"God, it's good to be almost back with the land of the living," she said.

"I bet it is," Matthew said, handing her a cup of coffee. "You had me and others very worried for a time."

She sipped the coffee as a look of utter delight crossed her face. "I didn't think anything could taste so wonderful. Was I an absolute pain?" she asked.

"Why on earth do you think you were a pain? Brian Smith rang yesterday and he had already had a call from the Registrar in Warwick General in response to his complaint. Evidently, according to him, heads will roll."

"Oh, I hope not," Laura said. "They did their best."

"That's a matter of opinion. Would you like some lunch?"

The colour was returning to Laura's face but she still looked, not surprisingly, very drawn. "It's a lovely day. We'll go out later and get some fresh air."

"A sandwich would be nice," she suggested, smiling and stretching her legs out on the sofa. "It's good to feel half normal again."

As Matthew went towards the kitchen, he remembered the mail he had collected for Laura over the previous few days. He took the assortment of envelopes in to her.

"Anything to do with work doesn't even get opened," he told her before going back to the kitchen.

He was slicing some cheese when he heard her cry out.

"Matthew!"

He stopped what he was doing and rushed back into the living room. The little colour that had been in Laura's cheeks had disappeared and she was staring at a piece of paper in her hand.

"What is it?" he asked, moving across to her.

Laura handed him the piece of paper with tears in her eyes.

It was a standard sized sheet of writing paper but the message on it appeared to be cut out letters from a newspaper or magazine. Matthew stared at it, not wanting to believe what he was reading, but in his sub-conscious, something told him that he ought not to have been surprised. The police had implied that what happened in Warwick was not an accident. He was now looking at something that supported their belief.

FUcKinG BItcH

YOU SHoulD be FuCKinG DEAD. YOU wiLL be tHe nEXt time. I wOn't fUcKing FAil agAIn. YoUR reMAINing daYS on thIS eARTh aRE FUCKing nUMbeRED.

I aM YoUr fuckInG dESTinY

Matthew stared at the piece of paper and the words became blurred. Slowly he sat down on the sofa, his eyes glued to the product of a very perverted mind.

Why?

He turned the paper over but there was nothing on the other side. Reaching down he picked up what he thought was the envelope – Laura had dropped it on the floor, probably in shock. He had obviously looked at all of the letters addressed to her, but he remembered nothing that particularly caught his eye.

The address was typed and looked like any other routine letter.

Laura Stanhope
The Old Forge Cottage
56 South Bank
WESTERHAM
Kent TN16 1EN

The stamp was first class and the postmark Royal Tunbridge Wells. The franking told him the letter was posted the previous Monday. There were no other marks on either side of the envelope.

"What does it mean?" Laura asked her voice full of emotion.

Matthew reached for her hand as she leant forward, burying her head in his shoulder.

"It's probably nothing," he said quietly, trying to reassure her but realising how stupid he must have sounded. "It'll be some freak who saw the reports in the papers. It happens all the time."

"Papers? What … what reports in the papers?" Laura lifted her head slightly from his shoulder and looked at him, the tears still brimming in her eyes.

"Your accident got coverage in some of the local papers. I wasn't going to let you see them until you had completely recovered." He stared at the piece of paper again.

"But why didn't they say anything at the hospital? They must have seen them."

"I don't know, Laura. Maybe they thought you didn't need reminding."

She lifted her fingers to her eyes so that she could wipe away the tears. "If it is a freak, how did they know where I live? How did they get this address?"

"Some of the articles said that you were from Westerham. It wouldn't have been that difficult to obtain the rest if the right questions were asked of the right people. You only have to catch some minion off guard and tell them you are a well-wisher and want to send a card."

Again, and although Matthew did not believe a word he was saying, he was trying to reduce his own worry as well as Laura's. From her expression, he hadn't convinced either of them.

Somebody wanted Laura dead.

People, and especially people with perverted minds, do not make that kind of threat unless they fully intended carrying it out.

Chapter Nine

The police arrived within an hour of Matthew calling them.

The sergeant had done her homework. She had not only checked her station's log entries but also she had spoken to the Warwickshire police. Whether it was by design or coincidence, Gillian Phillips was with her, but Matthew was relieved to see an official face he recognised.

The sergeant introduced herself as Wendy Carter. She was quite tall, probably in her mid-thirties, with a severe look about her. Her eyes were a dark brown with jet-black eyebrows and there was no evidence of any make-up. Her slightly hooked nose and thin lips added to the severity of her appearance, as did the netted bun.

Standing next to her at the front door, Gillian looked frail and still very, very young by comparison but – and Matthew was pleased to see it – not the slightest bit intimidated by her superior. Before the sergeant could say anything, Gillian had chipped in with am "Good evening, Mr Ryan."

"Hello, WPC Phillips," Matthew responded, deciding, regardless of the seriousness of the situation that had brought them to the house, it would be better if he kept things formal. He didn't want to get her into trouble and Gillian's understanding smile told him that she was grateful.

They went into the living room and when offered a drink, he was surprised Sergeant Carter said that she would like a cup of coffee. Having asked what everybody wanted, Gillian suggested she made the drinks and headed for the kitchen. Matthew's respect for her increased but he did notice Laura's frown that said, "How does she know where my kitchen is?"

Sergeant Carter sat in the chair nearest to Laura and listened intently as Laura described the little she could remember about what happened in Warwick. Once she had finished, Sergeant Carter asked to see the letter. She handled it very carefully holding it by one corner as she read it. She then examined the envelope, equally carefully, before putting both into a plastic bag she extracted from her uniform pocket.

"We'll take these away for some tests," Sergeant Carter

informed them. "Now, Miss Stanhope, do you mind answering a few questions?"

"That's why you are here," Laura told her, smiling politely as Gillian handed her a cup of coffee. "Thank you."

"Miss Stanhope, it may seem rather a strange question to start with but do you know anybody who has reason to make the sort of threat contained within that letter?" Sergeant Carter asked as she sipped her coffee.

Having handed out the drinks, which occasioned another frown from Laura, Gillian sat down next to Matthew on the second sofa. She seemed perfectly relaxed as she eyed Laura cautiously.

Laura stole a glance at Matthew before answering Sergeant Carter's question. "Matthew thought it was probably some freak, Sergeant," she said hopefully.

"Mr Ryan could well be right, but in such situations it would be best if we explore all possibilities, even if it is only to dismiss them."

Matthew smiled a thank you at Sergeant Carter. Her voice did not match her appearance: it was soft and melodious, with a hint of a Welsh accent.

"No, there is nobody. I have already been through the list of clients in my mind, and no, there isn't anybody."

"Laura is a private investigator," Matthew volunteered. "She was also in the police for six years."

He thought he was being helpful, but the sideways glance Sergeant Carter gave him suggested that she would prefer Laura to answer her questions herself, so he sat back with his coffee but he did see Gillian raise her eyebrows slightly.

"Miss Stanhope, WPC Phillips made me aware of what you do and I have to say that, from my experience, it is as easy to make enemies in your profession as it is in mine. Are you sure there's nobody you can think of?"

Laura shook her head. "No. I can be that certain. Of course some people might be a little upset with what I discover but not upset enough to want me dead." She hesitated. "Surely?"

"There are some strange people out there," Sergeant Carter informed them, echoing Matthew's own concerns. "Would you mind if at some stage we had a look through your files? I fully appreciate that their contents will be confidential but, if this threat is not a hoax, then we really do have to investigate all possibilities."

"I understand but …"

"I think –" Matthew started to say that the request was a sensible one but Laura interrupted him.

"Matthew, it has taken me quite a while to build up my business and if my clients became aware that their personal files had been shown to the police I may as well close the business down now. Confidential means confidential, and I am sorry, I am not willing to break confidences and divulge details of my clients."

"But …"

"No buts, Matthew," Laura said, glaring at him.

He knew what the look meant: there was something he didn't know and, if he did, he wouldn't be saying what he was saying.

"All right," said Sergeant Carter, reassuming control. "Obviously we could make access to the files official, if it were ever to come to that, but without wishing to frighten you any more than you already are, Miss Stanhope, the Warwickshire police did conclude that what happened in Warwick was probably a deliberate act rather than it being an accident."

They all heard Laura's sharp intake of breath and she shifted uncomfortably on the sofa.

"I …" she began to say but stopped as she closed her eyes and slowly shook her head.

"I'm sorry but it does mean that this threat must be taken seriously. I do not think the confidentiality between you and your clients is more important than your life."

Laura opened her eyes slowly and Matthew expected to see tears but there weren't any. Instead, she looked at all three of them, her eyes, after lingering on Matthew's, finally resting on Sergeant Carter.

"I understand, Sergeant," Laura said, "but I think we ought to look at other possibilities before assuming that whoever sent me that letter is either a client or maybe somebody I'm investigating. I understand that it is the obvious area to look into but not the only one."

Laura had spoken confidently and Sergeant Carter's reaction

was to sit back in the chair, an expression of acquiescence on her face.

"We are assuming," Laura continued, "that if what happened in Warwick was deliberate, it has to be connected to that letter. The two incidents could be totally unrelated." She held up her hand as both Sergeant Carter and Matthew tried to interrupt her at the same time. "I fully appreciate that it is the most logical deduction but, if there's one thing I learnt from my time in the police and from my current job, it's that assumptions have to be proven before being taken any further."

"But, Laura," Matthew said, "that letter referred quite blatantly to the expected outcome of the Warwick incident. Whoever it was, was trying to kill you. Please don't let semantics place you in greater danger than you're already in."

Laura was still trying to send him a message with her eyes and he shook his head slightly, trying to tell her that he didn't understand. The initial shock after discovering it may not have been an accident had disappeared, and Matthew assumed her police training had kicked in.

"I'm not," she told him in a very controlled manner.

Matthew decided to change tack. "Sergeant, I agree we must take the threat to Laura's life very seriously. What can we do now?"

Sergeant Carter sat forward, clasping her hands together. "Until we have something really tangible to go on, I would recommend that Miss Stanhope is never left alone and especially in a place where what happened in Warwick could be repeated."

"I understand. Do you think the threat could include me?" he asked.

Matthew felt Gillian move next to him as she too sat forward. She coughed nervously before she spoke and Sergeant Carter looked at her, willing to let her obvious protégé have some input into the discussion.

"It doesn't appear that you are a target, Mr Ryan, but that does not mean to say that you are not expendable if the person responsible for that letter really means to do what was said."

A supportive smile crossed Sergeant Carter's lips accompanied by a slight nod of her head.

"WPC Phillips is right, Mr Ryan," she said. "You must not assume anything in a situation such as this, but, unless Miss Stanhope is happy to stay here and never go out, you have little choice. Unfortunately, we do not have the resources to give either of you twenty-four hour protection, not based on what we have so far, that is."

"And what do you need to allocate resources?" Matthew asked. Her comment had annoyed him. "A dead body?"

Sergeant Carter spread her hands in apology. "It would be a bit late then, Sir, wouldn't it? No, Mr Ryan, but we do need a motive and a lead as to who it might be."

"I'm sorry, Sergeant, that was uncalled for. Laura and I will take every precaution and, if we come up with anything, we will come straight to the station."

"A phone call will do," Sergeant Carter said.

The two police officers stayed for another thirty minutes, most of which was used to advise Matthew and Laura as to how they should be vigilant and never be isolated. Laura was very good and listened to the advice given. Matthew wondered whether she had ever been in a similar situation where she had given similar guidance.

As they moved away from the door, having checked the road outside once the police officers had left, Laura suddenly turned and buried herself against Matthew.

"I'm so scared," she said.

He put his hand against the back of her head and held her against him. "I promise I won't let anything else happen to you." He kissed her hair, wondering if he would be able to keep his promise. "Come on, let's have a drink."

Sitting in the living room, Laura cupped the whisky glass, staring at it as though it contained all of her troubles. Matthew felt so useless. He was annoyed with himself for allowing the police to leave with nothing gained. All they had done was make matters worse by telling Laura what the Warwickshire police had thought. He put his arm round Laura's shoulders and pulled her closer to him.

She was trembling.

"What were you trying to say to me?" he asked, feeling the whisky burn its way down his throat.

"When?" Laura replied, hesitantly.

"When you were informing us all that your clients were more important than your life," Matthew told her.

He didn't want to hurt her but her reluctance to let the police look at her files had to have more of an explanation than simple confidentiality. He was sure that if any of her clients were in a similar situation, they would not have hesitated.

Laura moved away from his arms as she sat forward on the sofa, her back to him. She looked so fragile. She had gone upstairs and changed while he poured the drinks and had reappeared in her silk pyjamas, explaining that they made her feel normal.

"I saw Emily again on Friday morning," Laura said, quietly.

Matthew closed his eyes. "But we agreed –"

"I know, I know … you asked me not to go but I was so close. It seemed silly not to."

She sipped her whisky.

"When you say you saw her," he said slowly, "do you mean at a distance or to speak to?" Matthew wondered why she had felt the need to go against what they had agreed.

She turned her head and looked at him before answering.

"To speak to, I went to her house," she said quietly.

"Laura, I really don't believe this. Why on earth did you do that?"

"As I said, it seemed silly not to." Turning fully round, she looked Matthew straight in the eyes. "I made a mess of things last time. I wanted to be able to tell you that she was happy and that I'd been wrong, that there is a man in her life."

"Why?"

"So that you could forget her and love me instead." The tears came to her eyes immediately. "I … I am fed up with living in her shadow," she sniffed. "I want you for my own. I don't want to share you with anybody."

He took the glass out of Laura's hands and pulled her towards him. It was the first time she had really let her feelings show. He had only ever told her that he loved her once and that had been on Saturday after her admission to hospital.

He was being unbelievably selfish.

She had always hidden from him what she actually felt about Emily and he had been blind to the way he must have been hurting her.

"I don't know what I can say. I told you how I feel but whether that's sufficient to make up for my heartlessness is for you to decide," he said. "I do love you Laura and I have for a very long time. I just haven't been able to say it."

Laura moved her head so that Matthew could kiss her. "And I love you, Matthew, and I'm sorry …"

"There's nothing for you to apologise for. You've been through hell and back so let's have another drink and try, for at least tonight, to push what's happened to the back of our minds." He kissed her again. "Nobody can hurt us here."

"There is something else I need to tell you, Matthew."

Laura sat up, wincing as she twisted her body so that she could face him.

"Can't it wait?"

"No." Laura took hold of his hands, looking down at his fingers in hers. "I did see Emily but this time I told her who I was."

Her eyes remained down as she waited for his response.

"You told her that you were with me … living with me?" he said, hoping his disbelief wasn't obvious.

Laura nodded. "Yes. Don't be angry, but I had to. I had to tell her."

Matthew shook his head. "How on earth did she react?"

He regretted his question straightaway. How Emily had reacted should not have been his concern. He should have been more concerned about why Laura felt the need to tell her in the first place.

Laura lifted her head and he could see in her eyes the hurt she was feeling. "She was silent," she said. "She just stared at me. I could tell nothing from her expression. She scared me, and I take some scaring. Her silence said more than any words could ever have told me. She sat in the chair opposite me and simply looked intently at me, expressionless and silent."

"What did you do?"

"Other than feeling scared, you mean? I've never, in all my time in the police and since, I've never had anyone look at me the way she did. The coldness and remoteness of her glare almost made me wither in front of her. It was so, so frightening."

Matthew did not want his thoughts to show in anything he said or did but he simply could not believe what Laura was describing. Emily was one of the gentlest, most selfless people he had ever met. As a mother, she would have given her life for her daughter but, other than that, she was incapable of inflicting physical pain on a fly. He did not have to ask why Laura had felt the need to tell her what she had … he was to blame. He had failed Laura and, to try to give herself a little security, she had gone to the source of his insecurity. She hadn't gone there to tell Emily to back off because he was Laura's now. She simply wanted to feel more confident in herself, so she attacked the cause of her pain before it engulfed them both.

Because he had been so blind, it actually went further than that.

She was trying to tell him why she had been so reluctant for the police to look at her files. If they had seen the files, then Emily, for what would have been obvious reasons to the police, would immediately come under suspicion. When Laura told the police she had been to see Emily and why, what could be more of a motive than a jealous ex-wife being told by her ex-husband's very attractive lover to back off?

The police would not have needed any further evidence.

They would have had a field day, although, in Matthew's considered opinion, they would have been so very wrong.

"You think it was Emily, don't you?" he asked very hesitantly, praying that Laura would say, no.

Laura did not have to answer; her eyes told him exactly how she felt.

"You knew it wasn't an accident, didn't you?" he said.

Laura nodded almost imperceptibly.

"But there are so many things that don't add up, Laura," he said. "Why, after nearly six years, would Emily react like that? Why would she try to kill you? I just cannot believe she would do such a thing."

"I've been turning everything over and over in my mind and, for it to happen when it did, only a matter of hours after leaving her,"

Laura said, "I just can't come up with any other explanation. There is nobody else it could be, Matthew. I'm sorry but that's the way I feel."

"Did you actually see her?" he asked, desperation creeping into his voice.

"No, but … but the driver was female. I saw her as I hit the windscreen."

He heard but he didn't want to understand. "No, you're wrong. She couldn't, she wouldn't," he said. "That letter, that's not possible. You don't live with somebody for years and not know them, for Christ's sake."

Laura still had his hands in hers and he felt her grip tighten as she said, "You knew her so well that you foresaw the affair she was having, did you? You knew her so well that, from the time Sarah was born, you knew she wasn't your daughter, did you? You may have thought you knew her, Matthew, but …"

He shook his head. "No, Laura, she's not a murderer. She couldn't run somebody down in cold blood, fully intending to kill them. She may have deceived me but not –"

"It was Emily, Matthew. I know it was her."

Chapter Ten

As dawn was breaking, Matthew woke up in a sweat.

They had gone to bed after consuming the best part of a full bottle of whisky between them. He had drunk because he could not and would not accept that Emily was capable of murder. Laura had matched him glass for glass because she could not, and would not, accept that he didn't believe what she was telling him. Inexorably they had reached the point where the argument had become so verbally vicious that they both ended up in tears.

Once the accusations began to fly, they said things that they would both regret for a very long time. Laura accused Matthew of exploiting her physically and being ultimately responsible for near encounter with death. He accused her of using sex to trap him into the relationship, and deliberately setting out to hurt Emily unnecessarily because he was unable to give Laura what she wanted.

As the tears arrived, so did the realisation that they were simply using each other to try to rid them of the fear that had been there since the 'accident' in Warwick, and even more so since the threatening letter arrived.

Eventually commonsense assumed precedence over alcohol induced nastiness and they went to bed promising that they did not mean what each had said to the other: come the morning, they would reconfirm their promises and try to forget how horrible the experience had been. As a means of reconciliation, they tried to make love, each in need of the physical as well as mental release, but Laura's bruising was such that everything they tried was uncomfortable for her. In the end, they accepted it was not going to happen and settled for drifting off into a troubled sleep in each other's arms.

The dawn chorus was disturbingly loud and Matthew lay and listened to it while he tried to bring some logical thoughts out of his addled mind. He threw back the quilt to try to cool his body. If he remembered correctly, just before they went to bed he eventually got Laura to accept that there was no proof that Emily was responsible for the attack on her and that it was all to do with association of thoughts. She may have seen a female driving the car that hit her, but she agreed it could have been anyone. Emily's reaction to seeing Laura again, and then hearing that Laura was living with him, had played on Laura's mind and she could well have been thinking about it as she was run down. He reminded her how frightened she was by Emily's reaction.

Closing his eyes, he remembered earlier Laura repeating the six words Emily had used after the lengthy period of silence. "I think you'd better leave." At the front door, Laura had tried to apologise but Emily had glared at her. "Just go."

Quizzing Laura he said, "Why, Laura, why? Why go there in the first place?" He was incapable of accepting, let alone explaining, her behaviour.

"I've already told you," she sneered, "but that wouldn't mean anything to you, would it? You have no idea what it's been like living here for the last twelve months without knowing how the man I share a bed with feels about me. You've never been able to be honest with yourself, let alone me."

"Laura, I've told you –"

She laughed at him. "What? You've told me that you love me? It took something pretty fucking dramatic to drag that out of you."

Matthew reached for her hand but she snatched it away. "Don't try and get round me, Matthew. Be honest with me for a change. What do I mean to you other than a good shag? Have you really given me, and the way I feel, any thought at all?"

"I think …"

"It's too late to think, it's a pity you didn't think before all of this happened. If you had shown me, told me that you loved me before now, none of this would have happened. I wouldn't have felt the need to go anywhere near that bloody house and your fucking ex-wife ever again."

She downed the remaining whisky in her glass and reached for the bottle. He didn't try to stop her.

"You're being a little unfair, Laura," he said. " If you remember, it wasn't me that started this relationship. You made it pretty obvious what you wanted from the outset and if I hadn't responded you –"

"Are you trying to tell me that I trapped you into this relationship? If you are, then you are so bloody far away from the truth – "

"You want the truth?" he spat at her. "I'll tell you what the truth is."

By this time, he was standing by the fireplace, gesticulating with his glass and spilling its contents. "That first night you so conveniently seem to have forgotten, it was pretty bloody obvious what you were after. From the moment I saw you in the pub, the outcome was apparent."

"And you were more than willing to give it to me. Don't you dare try to blame it all on me. If I was so transparent, you could have made me only too aware that you weren't interested."

"You are joking, aren't you?" he said.

"I didn't use my body to trap you. What we did happened because we both wanted it, and if you care to delve into your long-term memory banks, you'll discover that it was you who kissed me first."

"This is getting stupid and you're being petty." He said, draining the contents of his glass.

"No, it isn't and no I'm not. You just accused me of fucking trapping you and I'm trying to point out that I fucking didn't." Through the alcoholic haze, Matthew could hear what they were saying – Laura rarely swore – and how ludicrous it was becoming but there seemed to be a divide between sensibility and insensitivity. "It isn't always the man's prerogative, you know."

"And what to do you mean by that?"

"We women have our needs as well, you know," Laura said through clenched teeth.

"What the hell are you on about?"

"Sex! Men think they should always be in control."

Matthew shook his head in total confusion. "Laura, what precisely are you getting at?"

That is the way things went for at least another half an hour. It got worse before it got better. Laura's insecurity with their relationship manifested itself into her need to use sex to control what and when things happened. She felt by being dominant physically, she would keep him. At the same time, she told herself it should not have to be that way. They were living on a knife-edge, neither being honest with the other and it took a very serious incident to make them realise just how close they were to falling apart.

Eventually, when they had run out of insults, they just stopped and looked at each other. Laura was already in tears, and Matthew wasn't far behind her.

They reached a point where further argument would have been even more irrational because they had gone in a complete circle but, fortunately, they both saw sense at the same time. They were suddenly in each other's arms, apologising and saying it wasn't too late.

Matthew shook his head: in all the time he had been married to Emily, he couldn't remember any argument that came close to the previous evening with Laura. He didn't think he was capable of being so horrible even when his mood was alcohol induced.

Laura was now lying on her side, her back to him, her breathing telling him that she was in a deep sleep. It was when he placed his hand on her neck and ran his fingers down the warmth of her skin and over her bruises, that he realised it wasn't just the dawn chorus that had woken him.

He had been dreaming about Patrick, Laura's ex-husband. He saw Laura cowering naked in a corner as her husband lashed out her with his foot.

It was Laura's scream that that woke him.

Having no idea what Patrick looked like didn't stop Matthew now imagining him behind the wheel of the car that hit Laura.

Staring at the bedroom ceiling, he wondered why such an obvious thought hadn't been there before?

Why hadn't she thought of him?

Patrick Schofield had physically abused Laura during their marriage and had threatened further violence since they had separated. Could he have found out she was now living with Matthew and had carried out his threat? It was as feasible and probable as Laura's belief that it could have been Emily.

In fact, in Matthew's mind, it was more feasible and more probable, because Emily hadn't threatened anybody.

Laura turned over next to him but she didn't wake up.

There was a smile on her lips. He adjusted the duvet so that he could see her body. The bruising around her neck, breasts and ribs was a deep purple surrounded by an eclipse of reds and pinks. Her left thigh, which had taken the initial impact, looked incredibly sore and it really was a miracle that the bone had not been shattered.

Could somebody who had once confessed their love for Laura be so sadistic as to try and kill her in broad daylight? Why, after so long, would he suddenly have felt so insanely jealous that he wanted revenge? Then again, why not? It happened all the time – whole families wiped out by some insane individual who previously had led what was to all intents and purposes, a normal life.

Maybe he wasn't right. Perhaps he was clutching at straws in an attempt to rid Laura of the belief that Emily was the driver of the car that hit her. Surely, if Laura thought it might have been Patrick, she would have told the police. She did not owe him anything, but his name hadn't come up in any discussion, not even during the mud-slinging last night. Yes, she had told Matthew about the threats but that had been so long ago.

Somebody was responsible and had deliberately driven at Laura with the sole purpose of killing her.

Matthew got out of bed and went to the bathroom. The image he saw in the mirror was testimony to the previous few days. He felt as awful as he looked. He shaved to try to purge himself of the feeling and, when that didn't work, he had a freezing cold shower but the images kept on returning.

It was a lovely morning so he got dressed having decided he needed to get some fresh air. After standing by the front door for a while, he eventually walked along Southbank and into town. It was a slow walk, and if asked he could not have told anyone whether there were many others about. He was in a daze, his surroundings irrelevant to his thoughts. On reaching the High Street, he turned right and carried on walking. He eventually joined the real world when he realised he was in the small supermarket on the corner of the High Street with the Croydon Road. We wandered aimlessly round the shop but then stopped and picked up a daily paper. As he queued to pay for the paper, he suddenly broke out into another sweat and he felt very giddy. He had to lean against the counter to stop himself from falling over.

He had left Laura by herself, not even bothering to double-lock the front door and without checking to see whether there were any unusual cars parked nearby ... or strangers in the area.

The girl behind the counter gave Matthew a funny look and began to speak, but another customer to Matthew's left asked her a question and she used this distraction to cover her confusion as to what to do about Matthew.

Putting the paper on the counter and mouthing 'Sorry' to the girl, he left shop and sprinted the half-mile back to the cottage, swearing under his breath at his stupidity.

As he neared the front door, he stopped.

Was this the way it had to be?

Were they going to have to look over their shoulders everywhere they went because there was some psychopath waiting to pick his or her moment to have another attempt? The police had nothing to go on. Sergeant Carter had taken the letter with her for forensic testing but he knew that it would be to no avail. They would be no nearer the truth. Were they destined to spend weeks, months, even years, wondering when whoever it was would strike again?

Laura was coming out of the cloakroom as he let himself into the cottage and she appeared not to reciprocate his concern. After staring at her for a few seconds, and without saying a word, he took her in his arms and held her as tightly as her injuries would allow.

"I'm so sorry, Matthew,' she whispered. "I said some horrible things last night. I'm so sorry."

"We both said things we didn't mean," he told her. "We had nobody else to listen to how we felt. It was bound to happen."

She put her head on his shoulder. "I didn't mean what I said."

"And neither did I. We've got it – whatever it was – out of our systems, let's put it behind us."

"I'm so frightened."

"I won't let anything else happen to you. I will be by your side until the police catch whoever it is and lock them up."

He hoped he sounded more confident than he felt.

Laura lifted her head and looked at him.

Her dishevelled hair, her eyes sore from crying and the awful bruise on the side of her face – resembling a grotesque birthmark – told him how low she really was, but looking at her in that state also told him exactly how he felt.

"I love you, Laura, and nobody is going to succeed in hurting you again. I've loved you from the moment I walked into The Grasshopper."

The tears came to her eyes immediately. "Thank you. I'm ... I'm afraid I can go one better than that. I ... I have loved you since you walked into my office," she said softly.

The police called a couple of days later and their news was as Matthew expected. The letter Laura received revealed nothing for them to even start following up. They were able to tell which papers and magazines the script had come from and, in some cases, even the date of publication but it was useless information. They had been in contact with the Warwickshire police and following the call, they went to Warwick to speak to the police authorities there, but they had nothing new either. The eyewitnesses were not witnesses at all. It had all happened so quickly nothing of any import came out of the statements taken. It was not just a question of reaching a dead end; the authorities had not even found the right road to go down in the first place.

Matthew raised the subject of protection but, once again and as was to be expected, the police did not have the resources. They advised Matthew and Laura to be ultra-vigilant and report anything that might be suspicious but, other than that, the police could not help them any further.

As the weeks passed, Matthew and Laura slowly regained their confidence and adopted a routine that paid due consideration to the need to be ultra careful. One of them needed to work because they did not have the immediate capital to fall back on but, fortunately, Laura was able to bring some of the outstanding cases on her books to an early close. Taking Matthew's advice, Laura advised her other clients to take their problems elsewhere because she had decided to shut down her business due to ill health, making sure they all had a full refund.

She did not want to close her business down but understood why it had to happen.

It had not taken much persuasion from Matthew because the enthusiasm for further investigation had left her anyway. Laura only had three months remaining on the lease for her offices, so she was able to cancel it with little difficulty. Janie Poole, Laura's receptionist, took the news badly but the promise of a very good reference and a few thousand pounds in severance pay went some way to appeasing her.

Laura began accompanying Matthew on his lecturing trips. She either stayed in the hotel room reading or watching television or, when the weather permitted, wandering the hotel grounds if they were large enough. She had not only lost her enthusiasm for private investigation, she had also withdrawn into herself.

The change had started shortly after the row they had a few weeks ago. Although she was fine with Matthew, she spent many hours just sitting and thinking, and when they were out together, it was obvious she was very suspicious of strangers – constantly looking around her. She had become an inhibited and distrustful woman, whereas before she had been so gregarious and daring. The social functions that went with Matthew's work would previously have been a great attraction, but now her reluctance to attend was quite noticeable. They talked about how she felt and Laura was ceaselessly apologising for the change in her. Matthew tried to tell her that, after what she had been through, he was surprised how well she was doing.

A couple of months after Laura came out of hospital, it looked as though she had turned the corner on the road to getting back to normal. Nothing else had happened, the police had checked twice and when told all was well, they tended to agree with Matthew – the letter had been from some freak. Laura was more cautious and still clung to Matthew whenever they were out but the smile and laughter he missed so much was there every now and again. Because of this improvement, they decided to go on holiday. She told him that on their return she intended getting a job, which was also progress, but he could see from the way she flinched whenever the phone rang, or there was a knock at the door, that she was still living on her nerves. Her suggestion about a job was more to do with her need to internalise her feelings and build up her own confidence than a commitment to him. A holiday would do them both good.

The decision to go somewhere reasonably exotic was mutual and after scouring various brochures, Laura settled on Penang, a holiday island off the west coast of Malaysia. She chose not to remember – or had genuinely forgotten – that Emily and Matthew had honeymooned in Malaysia but it had been on the east coast rather than the west. He did feel a twinge of remorse when Laura declared that was where she wanted to go.

Matthew splashed out on a suite in the Golden Sands hotel which was situated among half-a-dozen other first-class hotels on the north coast of the island, a short drive from the regional capital, George Town.

All aspects of the journey went smoothly, and in less than a day after getting in the taxi in Westerham, they were walking through the front doors of the Golden Sands Hotel.

Although it was humid, the sun was beating down out of a clear azure sky. Laura seemed to relax the moment they stepped out of the taxi when a smiling bellboy collected their luggage, escorted them to the reception desk and waited to see them to their suite. Check-in was effortless, their suite of rooms idyllic and the view out over the hotel grounds to the Indian Ocean, spectacular.

After Matthew gave him a thirty-dollar tip, the young bellboy suggested if there was anything else they wanted during their stay – and he emphasised *anything* – he would arrange for whatever it was to happen.

Laura was already on the spacious balcony admiring the view.

Chapter Eleven

The first few days of the holiday were heavenly.

Laura started to come out of herself more and more and even suggested that they experimented with some of the less touristy restaurants in the area. If they really wanted to taste the local cuisine, they ought to go where the locals go. The hotel restaurants, of which there were two – one inside and one al fresco – offered security and excellent food, but Laura had always been adventurous, therefore it was with great relief Matthew agreed to her suggestion.

There was also another sign that she was slowly returning to normal. Back in the cottage, and before incidents took a turn for the worse, Laura always dressed so that she could emphasise her excellent figure. Even in joggers and T-shirt, she managed to look sensual – bare feet and midriff, and no bra!

"We are both in our thirties, well I am and you were," she often said. "We are both young and healthy, well I am and you were. There will come a time when either I come out of the other side of the menopause feeling indifferent towards sex or you will lose interest in me. So let's make hay while the sun shines."

He never complained about her openness, indeed, like any sane man, he could not have been luckier, but when he suggested that hopefully they had a good few years to go before old-age set in, he was asked whether he knew how they would feel a few years down the line, let alone in twenty or thirty years' time.

Laura's logic ensured that their physical relationship went from strength to strength, albeit being a touch risqué on occasions. However, her concern about the future became reality a lot earlier than both of them would have expected.

When she came out of hospital, she had changed.

She started wearing nightdresses to bed rather than nothing or one of his old pyjama jackets. She very rarely came out of the bathroom without being dressed for bed and their lovemaking, once she was well enough, became a routine and conventional whereas before it had been, more often than not, spontaneous and adventuress. Whenever he tried to discuss the change in her, she would refuse to talk about it because, in her opinion, there was nothing to discuss.

On the second night of their holiday, he was standing on the balcony with an ice-cold gin and tonic in his hand as he looked out over the twin pools seven floors below, when Laura came up behind him and put her arms round his waist.

"I'm sorry for being such a selfish bitch," she said.

He turned round to face her. She was looking up at him with expectation in her eyes. The bruising on her face had at last disappeared and her complexion was once again nearly flawless.

"As I've told you so many times before, there's no need to apologise," he said.

She took the almost-empty glass from him.

"It doesn't matter what you say, I have still been a bitch."

She reached up and kissed him before leading him to one of the chairs by the small table at the end of the balcony. He sat down and she straddled his legs.

Looking up at her face and watching the telltale signs he knew so well, he said, "Welcome back."

"It's good to be back," she replied huskily.

After welcoming her back, each evening, once they had eaten, they would go down to the beach and stroll along the shoreline in the wet sand until they found a spot that was completely private and then they would strip off for a skinny-dip before making love lying with their legs in the lapping water. They said very little, but it was obvious in the way they clung to each other as they walked back to the hotel, just how they both felt.

It was during the first week, and on the fifth day of their holiday, that Matthew asked Laura to marry him.

It was an option that he thought about often enough but because of his experience with Emily, he just as quickly put it to the back of his mind.

Now everything seemed to be right.

He really did need to move on.

They were at the far end of the beautifully designed lagoon swimming pool, with its large rocks, palms trees and bushes decorating its edges, and small ornamental islands within the pool's perimeter. It was more like a jungle watering hole than one of the hotel's swimming pools.

Matthew was resting by a set of steps in the deepest part of the pool where he had temporarily lost sight of Laura who had been swimming round the pool's edge. All of a sudden, he felt her hands on his legs as she slowly surfaced in front of him, rubbing her body against his. Putting her arms round his neck, she kissed him.

"You are insatiable," he told her.

"And you love it," she said. "You wouldn't want me to be any other way."

"I'm going to have to make an honest woman of you," he said, smiling.

"But not tonight, eh?" she said, not understanding what he meant. Her expression changed when she saw the intensity in Matthew's eyes. She cocked her head to one side and frowned. "What?"

"Will you marry me?" he said quietly.

Her eyes shot open. "What?" she said again..

"I asked you to marry me," he repeated.

After a few seconds, during which Laura's eyes searched his, she said, "How could any girl refuse?" before adding quickly, "not that I'm saying, yes, especially when the proposal comes from somebody who is not able to escape." She smiled. "You're supposed to go down on one knee."

"That's a bit difficult at the moment."

"Then you'll just have to wait for my answer until you do."

They were in high spirits as they walked hand-in-hand from the hotel towards a small restaurant they found a couple of days ago. The food was magnificent but cheap, the atmosphere very local, and the lighting subdued.

Matthew had not asked Laura to marry him on impulse because he had known for some time that it was something he wanted, no matter how often he tried to dismiss the idea. After she was injured, he saw a different side to her character. She wasn't as strong and self-confident as she would like people to believe.

They had discussed children previously but always in the

context of other people's. Matthew was devastated when he lost Sarah because he had always wanted children, a need he put down to having such an early happy childhood himself. He had hoped that Emily and he would have been able to give Sarah a brother. He was still old-fashioned enough to want to be married to the mother of his children, but that wasn't the only reason he had asked Laura to marry him: she had shown him how vulnerable she could be and he wanted to protect her ... permanently.

Never being able to admit to himself, let alone to Laura, how he felt about her was now, in his mind, put right, so they could look to the future in a different way ... as husband and wife. She had almost been killed, which brought home to him just how fragile life really could be – no-one knows what is going to happen tomorrow, next week, next month, next year. It is all guesswork and, more often than not, wrong.

Earlier when they were having a shower together, Matthew attempted to re-enact his proposal by going down on one knee. Aided by a strong gin and tonic, he thought the spray coming from the various wall jets added a certain mood to his second attempt but Laura waved her hand dismissively.

"No," she said, "now is not the right time, Matthew. A lady likes to be wooed and the timing and place has to be right. If you think the fact that we are both naked and my hair is dripping ... no, I'm sorry."

"As the lady wishes," he said.

"That's the first time you've called me a lady," Laura told him, smiling, as she stepped out of the shower.

Matthew thought it was marvellous to have her back, so he accepted her banter and decided that his timing was a little misplaced.

Sitting in the restaurant and attempting to eat noodle starters with Malaysian chopsticks made them both convulse with laughter. Neither of them was used to chopsticks with hinges. Their lightheartedness was so welcome.

"So," asked Laura, lowering her head to the bowl in front of her at the same time trying to be delicate where delicateness was impossible, "what made you ask me to marry you?"

"I think you're being a little presumptuous, Madam. What makes you think that, having tried twice and spurned twice, I am inclined to ask you a third time?"

"I'm not suggesting you ask me a third time," Laura said, her eyes flashing. "I'm merely enquiring why you asked me the first time, that's all."

She picked up her wine glass and took a rather unladylike gulp.

They were both well on their way to being tipsy.

"You were embarrassing me."

"I was what?"

"There were people around. It was the only way I thought you'd start acting properly."

Laura dropped her chopsticks into the bowl. "That's a pretty lame excuse. Do you walk round – perhaps I should say swim – with your eyes closed? We were only doing what many others do in that pool on a regular basis. Why do you think it was designed that way?"

"I thought it was for esoteric, no, I mean aesthetic, reasons." Matthew was trying not to slur his words but he wasn't being very successful.

The restaurant was quite busy, with a good mixture of what appeared to be locals and tourists. From the glances the latter were receiving from the former, the tourists were a definite source of amusement. The music was loud, the lighting subdued and five or six waitresses ensured that the alcohol flowed. No sooner was a glass nearly empty than one of the girls appeared at the table to top it up or ask if another bottle was required. By the time Laura and Matthew were about to start their main course, they were already halfway through their second bottle of a very passable house white wine.

They ordered fish as their main course although, when it arrived, Laura eyed it with apprehension. The fish was a whole grouper, supposedly tasting similar to a bass – an elderly couple on the table next to theirs had informed them – but neither of them had expected it to be as large as it was. Their table was circular and about four feet in diameter; the fish seemed only a foot or so shorter.

"We'll call it Gary, Gary the Grouper," Laura said, her eyes out on stalks. "I've never seen anything quite like it. It's enormous!"

"Beats the local chippy," Matthew commented.

"I could do with a few chips," she said, cutting daintily and somewhat hesitantly through the crisp skin. The meat underneath was off-white and, from the generous portion Laura put on top of the rice on Matthew's plate, beautifully cooked.

Somehow, they managed to eat their way through Gary so, as they left the restaurant they were feeling very full and very tipsy. They wrapped their arms round each other, doing their best to escort and support the other back to the hotel.

Laura was wearing heels that she had coped with on the way to the restaurant but, after fifty yards into the return trip, she gave up and took her shoes off, squealing every few steps as she trod on a piece of gravel or other sharp objects.

She gave Matthew her shoes to carry and hitched up the hem of her dress, peering down at her feet so that she could try to see where she was going. Giggling and squealing accompanied each step, and after refusing Matthew's offer of a piggyback, they made it unsteadily back to the hotel. Once through the main doors they tried to act with modesty as they crossed the foyer towards the lifts.

"Mr Lyan, Mr Lyan!"

Matthew had already pressed the button for the lift when Ho came up to them.

"Mr Lyan, Mr Lyan, there a letter for you."

Ho handed Matthew the envelope.

"Thank you, Ho," he said absent-mindedly as he eyed the address typed on the front of the envelope. He reached in his pocket and took out a handful of coins. "Thank you again, Ho."

As he thanked the bellboy a second time, Matthew felt the hairs on the back of his neck start to prickle. There was something very familiar about the typed address. He had given his contact address to a few people, suggesting that they e-mail him if they needed anything. However, that was all irrelevant because the address on the envelope was to Laura Stanhope c/o Matthew Ryan – *well done, Ho*, Matthew thought.

As well as their full names, the envelope had the postal address of the hotel typed neatly on the front and, as he turned it over, he knew he would find nothing on the back.

"What is it?" Laura asked from inside the lift, her right index finger pressing hard against the doors-open button.

"Just a letter," Matthew told her, hoping that she wouldn't see that he was lying. He had sobered up quickly but he sincerely hoped that she hadn't.

Fortunately, Laura seemed to lose interest immediately and, as the lift rose up to their floor, and swaying slightly, she gave herself a bleary-eyed assessment in the mirror on one wall of the lift. Matthew's mind was on the letter that he had pushed into his back pocket.

Once back in their room, Laura made a beeline for the bathroom, so Matthew went out onto the balcony, the letter burning a hole in his pocket. After he made sure Laura was going to be more than a couple of minutes, he withdrew the letter and, once he had inspected the envelope again, slit it open with his finger before withdrawing the single sheet of paper.

Fucking BitCH

TiMe MAy haVe paSSed BUt mY wiSHinG yOu fucKing DEad hAsn't. yoU prObaBly thINk I'Ve goNE AWay bUt tHis iS To FuCKing reMInd yoU i haVEn't yOu fuCkIng CoW. IF I cAn fiND yOu iN MaLAYa, I CaN fUcKiNg fINd yOu aNYwHere. tHe pOLicE havEN't bEEn muCh helP, haVe tHEy? You'rE FuCKiNg paTHEtic, So patheTIC yOu wILl be dEAd By tHe enD oF tHe yEAr. ALL Fucking SHRiveLLed AnD Dead. NO fuKinG USE tO Anyone. KeEP loOKing oVer yoUR shoulder, BiTcH, I'M oUt tHEre FucKing wATChing yoU.

I AM YoUr FuckinG desTINy

Matthew read the letter twice before he heard Laura coming out of the bathroom. Secreting the envelope in his back pocket again, he turned and rested his arms on the balcony rail, trying to be nonchalant as he looked down at the few people who were still swimming and lounging round the pools.

The sick and perverted author of this second letter would not have needed to step foot out of the UK to find out where they were. Having used a travel agent to book their holiday – information on where they were was readily available. They were dealing with logic, and the problem with logic was you needed to see beyond what seemed rational, and get into the mind of somebody who might think very differently.

"Are you staying out there all night?" Laura asked.

He thought Laura would join him on the balcony but from her question he realised that was not her intention.

"It's not exactly late," he suggested, walking back into the bedroom.

Laura had moved one of the chairs from the small dining table into the middle of the room. She was sitting on it, her legs crossed, a glass of red wine in her hand and she was completely naked.

She looked at him, a wicked smile on her face.

"Now you can ask me properly?"

An hour or so later, they were lying on top of the bed, sipping glasses of champagne. The continuous intake of alcohol was having little effect on Matthew but Laura appeared oblivious to what was really going on.

They had closed the balcony door, turned up the air-conditioning, switched off the lights and left the curtains open so that the glow from the full moon bathed the room.

"And I'd promised myself I'd never get married again," Laura said, breaking a few seconds of silence. She was trying unsuccessfully to hide a smile but Matthew could see that she was stealing furtive glances in his direction.

He decided that playing along with her was the best thing to do. She would have to know the truth soon enough.

"Well, thank you for that," he commented, turning to look at her. "If you must know I'd promised myself that too."

Her face and body had become a phosphorescent sheen in the moonlight. She had already succeeded in acquiring a very reasonable tan whereas Matthew was lagging behind.

Laura was resting the stem of her champagne flute on her

stomach, one knee raised so that the light caught the contrasting paleness of her inner thigh. There were discernible lines left from her bikini pants below her navel and at the tops of her legs. She looked extremely sensual and, although it was only a matter of minutes since they had come out of the shower after making love, Matthew could feel the desire returning.

"But forgetting about me, that's exactly what a man wants to hear after he's asked somebody to marry him."

She nudged his leg with her foot. "Somebody? I said yes, what more do you want?"

"A little more enthusiasm," he teased.

"I thought I'd shown you that as well." This time she rubbed the sole of her foot against his shin.

"You did, but a man needs further proof."

He was trying to be jovial but the contents of the letter were once again foremost in his mind.

"I think I'm managing that without even touching you," she suggested looking down at him.

Chapter Twelve

Matthew and Laura arrived back in the UK as scheduled, a week later. Believing it to be for all the right reasons, he had managed to keep from Laura until the penultimate day the content of the only communication they had received while on holiday. He had intended not saying anything until they were back in Westerham, but events overtook him.

They had spent the day in George Town having taken the cable car to the Chinese Temple to look at the turtles. They had also gone to the Orchid Gardens and marvelled at the colours. It had been a lovely day and not, surprisingly, too humid.

After returning to their room to enjoy a drink on the balcony before dinner, Laura, who had been very quiet for the last part of the afternoon, chose that moment to ask the question, "Are you going to tell me?"

He knew straight away what she was referring to and had been rehearsing in his mind what he was going to say. Keeping the content of the letter from her had been over-protective, but his logic told him that there wasn't a need for both of them to worry any more than they had to … not yet.

He took a sip of his drink. "The letter?" he said.

"What else? Ever since you received it, your mind has been elsewhere. Except when you asked me to marry you, that is." Allowing a knowing smile to cross her lips, she adjusted her feet on the railings so that she could turn and look at Matthew. "It was another threat, wasn't it?" Her voice was calm but her fingers were fidgeting.

He put his hand on hers. "Nothing is going to happen, Laura."

"I don't know how you can say that," she said nervously. "Where is the letter?"

Without answering, he went into the bedroom to recover the envelope from where he had hidden it in the wardrobe. The paper felt hot in his fingers.

How could somebody be so cruel?

He had searched the wording, the choice of capitals or lowercase, the swearing, everything, for a clue but there was nothing. The smudged franking meant the postmark was difficult to make out on the envelope. He doubted whether it would have revealed anything even if it were clear. The police would have to see it and maybe, because it was the second threat, it might generate a little more activity.

Laura looked at him apprehensively as he went back onto the balcony and handed her the envelope. Her eyes stayed on his as she slowly withdrew the single sheet of paper. She read it once before turning the envelope over in her hand so that she could see the address. She placed both envelope and paper on the table next to her before reaching for her drink.

She looked up at Matthew, her face now expressionless. "Thank you for trying to protect me, but if something is addressed to me I am the one who should open it."

"I'm sorry, I ..."

"There's no need to be, Matthew. As I said earlier, I've known for a while you've been hiding something from me. I'd guessed what it was." Laura lifted the glass to her lips. "The police will have to be told."

"Of course, I was going to see them on Friday."

"*We* will go to see them on Friday."

"Of course, *we* will go."

Laura reached for the piece of paper. "Who is it, Matthew? I know you can't answer that but it has to be somebody one of us knows If you don't think it's Emily, then who?"

He sat down and took her hand in his, knowing he was going to have to admit his worst fear. "If it's not one of your clients, then my suspect list is pretty short," he said.

Laura frowned. "What do you mean? Do you think you know who it is?"

Matthew lifted her hand to his lips and kissed her fingers.

"No, I don't know who it is but simple deductions suggest that it could only be one of two people."

"Who?"

"Patrick or Emily."

Laura looked genuinely surprised. "*Patrick* or Emily?" she repeated. "Why Patrick?"

Matthew kept Laura's hand in his. "Emily because of what you believe you saw and Patrick ... I've kept my thoughts to myself since the first letter arrived, if there had been another one –"

"Well, there has now, so why Patrick?"

"I saw little point in discussing it with you before. But now, isn't it obvious, he abused you physically and then made verbal threats after you'd separated." He shrugged. "I think we should have given his name to the police straight away."

Laura folded the piece of paper and placed it carefully back in the envelope before saying anything.

"Patrick may have treated me badly," she said slowly, "but even when he was being violent, he never called me a bitch ... I know that's a very tenuous argument but why would he do that now and what have I done to him for him to want me dead?" Laura spoke as though they were discussing what to have for dinner rather than a second threat to her life. Her composure worried him. "And," she added quickly, lifting her hand in anticipation of Matthew saying something further, "you're overlooking one thing."

"What's that?" he asked. The real question he wanted to ask was how she could stay so calm.

"It's a simple word again and it wasn't used the first time but, on this occasion, it was." She looked down at the envelope before fixing Matthew with a satisfied expression. "How many men would call a woman a *cow*? As well as not calling me a bitch, Patrick certainly never called me a cow."

Thrown by her question Matthew hesitated. He thought he had read the letter so often that he could repeat it word for word, but he hadn't spotted the word *cow* or, if he had, it hadn't registered. Surely it couldn't be as simple as that?

Laura handed him the envelope and he took out the piece of paper – *you probably think I've gone away but this is to fucking remind you that I haven't, you fucking cow* – before Matthew had only seen the word bitch not cow.

"See what I mean?" Emily asked.

He took a deep breath.

"It's a possibility," he admitted reluctantly.

"Possibility? Matthew, women call other women cows, men don't use the word. Have you ever called a woman a cow?"

"No," he said. "Well, not that I can remember, but it seems ..."

"It is a woman. I'd stake my life on it." Laura realised what she had said the moment the words were out, but the initial shock was quickly replaced with a smile when she added, "… not that I intend doing so."

"But you told me Patrick had said that if he couldn't have you then nobody else would. Surely a threat like that is more relevant than the choice of a word?"

Laura actually smiled. "It's not Patrick," she said. "I'm telling you it's a woman."

Matthew was dozing but the thump of the aircraft's wheels touching down on the runway woke him with a jolt. For a moment, he didn't know where he was. Laura's hand was in his and she squeezed his fingers.

As he had dozed his mind had been in a whirl. Being back in England brought with it the added reality of their situation. Regardless of the baseless way in which she had arrived at her explanation, Laura's conclusion had generated the inevitable, but unacceptable, deduction. She had tried to convince Matthew once already that Emily had been driving the car in Warwick and, although she admitted recognition might have been because of recent association, the more they discussed it the more he joined her in believing it could have been Emily.

Everything inside him rebelled against the thought but the more Laura asked him about Emily, the less he realised he actually knew her. Nothing had happened until Laura – and she admitted it had been a gross error of judgement – had gone to see Emily the second time and told her about her relationship with Matthew. Laura's attempted murder happened within an hour of meeting with Emily … that was too much of a coincidence.

They would give the police the second letter but it was unlikely they would learn anything more from it, unless, incredibly, the use of a simple word was a serious pointer towards the sex of the perpetrator. They knew nothing about Emily – but he now realised he should have mentioned her straight away – so they didn't know what had occurred immediately before Laura had been injured, and that he had employed Laura to find Emily all those years ago.

The police might or might not agree that the use of the word *cow* narrowed the field down to it possibly being a female but, if they were supplied them with a name and an address, they would have little choice but to follow up such information.

It still wasn't what he wanted but nor did he want Laura to be constantly in fear of her life. If it turned out that Emily was innocent, they would be back to square one, almost. He would never forgive himself for suspecting Emily and he would never forgive Laura for planting the suspicion in his mind in the first place. Not only would the investigation be going nowhere, he would have to think long and hard about his own future.

Was he being unfair? Would Laura try to lay the blame on Emily deliberately? The answer had to be, no she wouldn't. He *was* being unreasonable. He was in love with Laura and he had asked her to marry him.

No matter how he tried to suppress his feelings for Emily he couldn't really believe that she was capable of doing such a thing nor could he accept how he felt about her would go away once Laura and he were married. Moreover, what if it turned out that Emily did try to kill Laura, and was the author of the threats? She would go to prison and that is something he couldn't live with, knowing he had put her there. Laura would sense how he felt and their relationship would suffer … it might even end.

He would be living with a lie … he was living with a lie.

"Can we go straight to the police station, please?" Laura asked beside him, snapping him back to the present. He realised he was only a couple of miles from Exit 5 off the M25 for Westerham … he had been driving in a trance for the last ten miles.

"I thought we'd agreed to wait until tomorrow," he said.

"We did but why not today? Why wait another night?"

"Because I have to make a decision and I want it to be the right one," he explained.

A few seconds passed before Laura spoke. "Do we have any choice? It's too much of a coincidence, Matthew."

"Don't let's go through all that again but…"

"You will never forgive yourself or me? Is that what you were going to say?"

"No, I'm not saying that but if we tell the police about Emily we must also tell them about your ex-husband."

Moving into the outside lane to overtake a stream of articulated lorries, Matthew glanced in his door and rear view mirrors and saw a dark-blue VW Golf move out about fifty yards behind them. He frowned, his eyes still on the rear view mirror as he deliberately slowed down slightly to see if the VW closed the gap or maintained the distance between them.

Was he becoming paranoid?

He was halfway through overtaking the lorries and the VW was still keeping its distance so he slowed down a little more. He could see the queue of cars forming behind the VW but he wanted to see who was driving it.

The driver of the VW became impatient and flashed the car's headlights in frustration. With that simple action, Matthew realised he was being stupid and, yes, paranoid but he felt he had good reason. He accelerated past the lorries and pulled into the middle lane. The driver of the VW – a man – shook his head as he went by.

Matthew was aware Laura had been watching him but had remained silent. She had leant forward and glanced in her door mirror a couple of times to see what he was up to and as the VW sped by, she too watched the driver intently.

"He could have been anybody," she said quietly.

"He was anybody," Matthew said. "Laura, I know this is going to sound stupid, and if there was a connection you would have already mentioned it, but what sort of car does Emily drive?"

She thought for a moment. "When she took and collected Sarah from school, I think I told you, she was in a Renault Clio, why?"

"The police said that some witnesses identified the car that hit you as a dark-blue VW Golf..."

"Yes, I know." He glanced sideways at her and she had screwed up her eyes, trying to work out what he was getting at. "That's why you just caused a traffic jam about four miles back," she said.

"If it was Emily and it was a Golf, where would she have got it from? There was so little time between you leaving her house and the accident. The attack can't have been pre-meditated because she didn't know who you were during your first visit. Surely nobody would confuse a ... what colour was her Clio?"

"I did tell you that as well, it was red."

"So she went from a Red Clio to a dark-blue VW Golf?"

Laura thought for a moment.

"It's not a stupid question, Matthew, and, yes, I have given it some thought and, no, I don't have an answer. But if it was Emily, then there has to be one. Can I suggest we leave it to the police rather than look for reasons not to tell them?"

"I just want to be sure before ..."

"If we were sure, we wouldn't have waited until now, would we? If it wasn't Emily, they will find that out pretty quickly and she'll be off the hook."

Laura was staring straight through the windscreen at the traffic.

She sounded frustrated.

"I still can't believe ..."

"Then let the police prove you right." Matthew heard her deep intake of breath as she tried to control her temper. "Look, Matthew, I want you to answer me a question now," she said slowly. "Do you want this threat on my life hanging over me to come to an end or do you want Emily to be protected from a few simple questions from the police? From where I'm sitting, I'm not too sure what your answer is going to be."

"You shouldn't have to ask."

"No, I shouldn't"

They got to Sevenoaks Police Station at just after two o'clock in the afternoon, asked for Sergeant Carter and were ushered into an interview room while they waited. Fortunately, Sergeant Carter was on duty and in the station. On this occasion, she had PC Peter Richards with her.

"How can we help, Mr Ryan?" Sergeant Carter asked as they both took a seat at the table. "Good, I see you have a drink".

Matthew handed Sergeant Carter the second threatening letter. She studied Laura and Matthew for a few seconds before taking the single sheet of paper out of the envelope and reading it. As before, she held the piece of paper by the corner, having handled the envelope similarly. Once read, she placed both paper and envelope on the table in front of PC Richards.

"It arrived at the hotel in Penang," Matthew said.

They had told Sergeant Carter that they were going on holiday and where to. There had been no contact while they were away.

"From the way it's been put together, there's little doubt that it's from the same person. But there is a difference." She looked at Laura. "You will have spotted it."

"*Cow*," Laura volunteered. "The word *cow* is used."

Sergeant Carter turned to PC Richards who was frowning and re-reading the piece of paper. "And what does that tell you, PC Richards?"

"I hadn't noticed it, Sergeant, I'm sorry." He looked embarrassed.

"No, most men wouldn't and, even if they did, they might not realise its significance. Our culprit has made her first mistake," she said with a rueful smile, "and if she has made one, she will make others."

PC Richards was looking confused.

"Evidently the majority of men wouldn't call a woman a cow," Matthew informed him, feeling he needed to be involved. "Bitch, slut, slapper but, evidently, a man never calls a woman a cow."

Matthew was surprised how quickly Sergeant Carter noticed the author had used that one simple word and, without qualification, she came to the same conclusion as Laura.

"I wouldn't say never, Mr Ryan, but I'd put a month's salary on the fact that we are dealing with a woman. So what does that tell us?"

"I think we can go one better than that, Sergeant," Matthew said. Laura put her hand on his and squeezed. "We think it might be my ex-wife."

"Your ex-wife," Sergeant Carter repeated slowly. "You were married and you didn't think to tell me the last time we met?" She let her question hang in the air for a second. "And what makes you think it might be your ex-wife?"

After apologising for the oversight, Laura and Matthew spent the next ten minutes telling Sergeant Carter and a somewhat self-conscious PC Richards what had happened. Matthew, rather unwillingly, told them about his marriage and the divorce, including its cause.

"And where does your ex-wife live, Mr Ryan?"

"Leamington Spa," he told her.

"Number 14 Craven Gardens, Leamington Spa, to be precise," Laura added at his shoulder.

"Thank you," Sergeant Carter said as she ran her finger down the notes she had taken. "We'll certainly investigate your suspicions."

"You will be discreet, won't you?" Matthew asked.

Sergeant Carter looked up and there was an audible sigh from Laura. "It won't be us, Mr Ryan. This information will go to the Warwickshire police and they will conduct their own enquiries. The hit-and-run happened on their patch and, as your ex-wife also lives on their patch, it will be over to them. They may well ask to see you."

"Can't you ask them to be discreet?" Matthew asked again.

Sergeant Carter frowned. "Do I take it that you're not sure you're pointing the finger in the right direction?"

"No, it's not that. If it's not Emily, and yes I still have my doubts, I just don't want her …"

"I understand, Mr Ryan and I will pass your wishes on to the Warwickshire police. However, from what you have both told me I think there is a distinct likelihood that your ex-wife …." She paused. "If there is any likelihood at all that she is involved, she will be arrested and taken into custody for questioning. You do understand, don't you?"

Matthew felt he had gone about the admission in entirely the wrong way and Laura's silence suggested she felt the same. It wasn't until they had left the police station in Argyle Street and were heading for the town centre – they had parked in the Bligh's Meadow car park – that she spoke.

"What bloody game do you think you were playing in there?" she threw at him as they turned away from the police station and headed for the car park.

The pavement wasn't crowded.

As soon as he'd told the police about Emily he had expected Laura to tell them about her ex-husband as well, but she hadn't and he didn't think it was his place to do so. Ironically he was about to ask Laura the exact question she had just asked him.

He looked at the people who were close by and on the opposite side of the road. He wasn't looking to see if there was anybody who appeared suspicious – as he had done before – but for some very strange he thought Emily might be waiting for them to leave the station. His guilt had really overpowered him. He shook his head both in reaction to Laura's question and in judgement of his own thought processes.

"Well, are you going to answer me?" Laura was walking on his inside, and she normally hooked her hand into the crook of his arm or they held hands. She had done neither.

"Not now, Laura. Not in the middle of the street," he said.

Laura stopped walking.

He took another couple of paces before turning round to look at her. The way she felt was evident in her eyes and she was on the point of crying.

"Have … have you any idea," she asked, her bottom lip shaking, "what you are doing to me? Having a death threat against me is bad enough, but it's nothing compared with the mental torture you're putting me through."

Matthew reached for her hands and she let him take them. Passers-by were looking at them, some embarrassed, some inquisitive.

"Laura, I don't know what's going on in this head of mine and saying sorry isn't enough for what I am doing to you, but …"

"No buts, Matthew. There mustn't be any more buts. If you need to say but, it means that it's going to carry on, and I can't live with that." She lowered her head. "When that phone rings, I need to know that you will share my delight when we are told she's been caught. I will need to see the relief in your eyes when I no longer have a threat against me. What I do not want to see is your delight and relief when they tell you it's not her."

Matthew put his hand under Laura's chin and lifted her head. "But it is –"

She wrenched his hand away, pushed past him and started running down the street.

Matthew mumbled, "Idiot, idiot, fucking idiot," under his breath as he ran after her.

They now had everyone's attention.

Laura was about ten yards in front of him when he knocked into a little old lady who had been carrying a bundle of shopping bags, the contents of which were scattered all over the pavement. He automatically stopped running and looked round. The woman, who must have been in her eighties, was trying to bend down to pick up her purchases.

Matthew went back to help her.

In so doing he lost sight of Laura.

Chapter Thirteen

He was frantic.

Not only because his stupidity had generated the situation, but also because Laura was out there on her own. Since receiving the first threatening letter, and other than when she stayed in the hotel while he was lecturing, he hadn't been more than a few feet from her but now, because of his foolishness, she was exposed, vulnerable and therefore at risk.

As he desperately searched every shop doorway and turned every corner praying that he would see her, he recalled another exchange they had after he had showed Laura the second letter and she had suggested he was being over-protective towards her.

"You seem to forget I was a policewoman," she reminded him suddenly as she stepped from the shower. They hadn't spoken about the latest threat for a couple of hours but it had obviously been on their minds.

"But you're not one now," he told her.

"I'm referring to my training, Matthew, so stop being deliberately obtuse. I'm still capable of taking care of myself."

He looked her up and down with a smile on his lips. "I must admit you are built for hand-to-hand combat. Just look at that six-pack!"

Laura padded into the bedroom from the bathroom, rubbing her hair with a towel. "That's not what I am saying," she informed him standing a few feet away. "I was trained to be observant and I might be small but I am quite capable of inflicting serious injury on any attacker."

"That's why you went to pieces when you got the first letter, is it?" Matthew asked her.

Laura stepped a little closer to him, and he could see his comment had hurt her. "I didn't go to pieces, as you put it. I was shocked, that's all," she said.

Her eyes suddenly narrowed, and before he knew it, she hooked her right foot behind his legs. In what seemed like one movement, she upended him so that he was lying on the floor face down, with his right arm in a painful arm-lock half way up his back. Laura was sitting on top of him, doing her best to force his right hand up to the back his head.

"Okay, Okay," he said through clenched teeth. The pain she was inflicting was almost unbearable. "I believe you!"

Laura released the pressure on his arm but still held it in a lock.

She bent forward, put her mouth next to his right ear and whispered, "Lightweight, you were so easy."

Now he was frantically looking for her in what had become the equivalent of a rabbit warren. He rushed back to the car park, but when she wasn't waiting by the car he took his mobile phone from his pocket. When they were together they normally only kept Matthew's phone on, but he prayed that on this occasion she had forgotten to turn hers off.

She hadn't.

In frustration, he closed his phone and started jogging down the pedestrian shopping area, looking in every shop and alleyway, hoping that he would catch a glimpse of her. He was attracting attention but he could not have cared less. He had to find her, not only to know that she was safe but also to apologise. He'd been a bloody fool.

After another fruitless twenty minutes of searching, he went back to the car in anticipation that, if she wasn't already there, that's where she would look for him. He thought about going back to the police station but that would have achieved very little other than antagonising Laura even more. After trying her mobile phone again without success, he settled down to wait for as long as it would take.

He watched other cars come and go.

He saw a couple of teenagers who appeared to be up to no good but one of them spotted him watching them and, after nudging his 'accomplice' and nodding in Matthew's direction, they moved on. Matthew turned on the radio and turned it off just as quickly.

After what seemed an eternity but was in fact just under an hour, he saw her. She was walking slowly towards the car from Café Rouge on the corner – had she been in there all the time, watching him?

He got out of the car and started walking towards her. She stopped when she saw him but then she continued towards the car.

"Don't ever do that to me again," he said admonishingly.

Laura stopped just out of arm's reach and he thought it best to give her whatever space she needed.

Her eyes were on fire but she still looked so damned attractive.

This morning they had gone to the cottage to change before going to the police station. She had put on a pink sleeveless top and a pair of white calf-length cotton trousers. They had joked about it being too cold in the UK for her to wear summer clothes. Just before leaving Penang she had her hair done so it was now a little shorter, showed her ears, and it was lighter in colour.

Her sunglasses were on the top of her head and the tan she had quickly acquired so quickly while on holiday was very evident. She just stood a few feet away from Matthew and looked at him.

"I'm so sorry, Laura," he said and she responded by raising her eyebrows. "I know my behaviour has been unforgivable but I promise you, I will never do it again."

Laura let a slight smile cross her lips. "Why do I put up with you? Why do I even bother?"

"Because I need looking after?" he ventured.

As she stepped towards him and he took her in his arms, she said, "You need more than that. I do understand, though. That's why I agreed to become Mrs Ryan."

Matthew was booked to go to Edinburgh for four days after the weekend. Because of the second threatening letter and the way he felt he had let Laura down, he insisted, and she agreed, that she should go with him.

Other than telling him to stop apologising, she said they didn't need to analyse – again – why he literally pleaded with the police to go carefully when they investigated Emily … because she understood. He knew where he had gone wrong and where he had been going wrong for so long. Laura had become incredibly relaxed about the whole affair to the point where Matthew's internalised guilt became even more acute. His guilt also stopped him from asking why Laura's ex-husband hadn't been mentioned.

During the weekend, Laura busied herself about the cottage,

tidying here, dusting there, while he did what he could to bring the garden back to some resemblance of order. He had some preparation to do for his lectures the following week, but that could wait. After a while, Laura joined him in the garden and together they made it look quite respectable.

Late on the Saturday morning they were pruning the roses over by the wall bordering the narrow road that led into town, when Bruce Townsend, their nearest neighbour, strolled by.

While they were in Malaysia, Matthew had asked Bruce to water the essentials in the garden and after giving him a key, to do the same in the house. Although Bruce was trustworthy and had helped them out so many times before – as they had helped him – recent events made Matthew a little wary. However, Laura persuaded him he was being over-cautious and they needed to get on with their lives.

Bruce stopped when he saw them.

"Welcome back," he said. "How was the sun?"

Bruce knew nothing about what was going on, nobody did other than the two of them and the police. He was aware that Laura's injuries had been because of a road traffic accident but no more than that.

Laura joined Matthew by the wall. "It was great thanks, Bruce. It feels quite chilly here this morning."

"We had our summer last Wednesday while you were away," he told them, laughing.

"We were just going to take a break for a coffee. Do you fancy one?" Matthew asked him.

"I was popping into the town to get a few things for Elizabeth but, tell you what, I'll go home and get your key and then, yes, I'll have a coffee with you."

Bruce was in his mid-fifties and looked it. He was short and had a slightly chubby body. His thinning grey hair and the way he dressed, suggested he was still living in the 1950s, but he always had a smile on his face although he had no reason to be happy. He had spent the last five years looking after his wife who tragically suffered with multiple sclerosis. Elizabeth was eight or nine years younger than him, and she was his second wife. His first wife had died a few days before her fortieth birthday after an all too short battle with cancer.

Laura had told Matthew on numerous occasions that Bruce was one of the world's lovely men, always adding that there had to be a few somewhere.

Whenever they saw him in town – or on the few occasions they went to church – Bruce was always being sociable as he stopped and talked to his many friends and acquaintances. At church, though, Matthew had noticed that Bruce always stayed behind so that he could move to a front pew where he knelt down, bowed his head and prayed.

There was no need to guess what he was praying for.

As Laura had said, Bruce was a lovely man, lovely but also so unlucky.

On his return with their keys, they sat at the breakfast bar drinking their coffees and recounting what they had done in Penang. Bruce had been there a couple of times. He had served nearly twenty years in the army and had completed tours in Hong Kong and Brunei. He and Veronica, his first wife, had fallen in love with Malaysia and had taken many opportunities to explore every square inch of the country, but their favourite place was the Cameron Highlands.

At one stage, when Matthew and Laura were telling him about the Orchid Gardens and turtles on the heights above George Town, Bruce's eyes had begun to water.

"That's where Veronica and I went on the last day of our last proper holiday," he reflected. "We were given the bad news only months later. Life can be so unfair."

Matthew gave Bruce a few moments with his memories, pleasurable and sad, before asking, "How's Elizabeth?"

"Wonderful," he replied, suddenly cheerful again. "She's an absolute angel, such strength."

"I must pop over and see her soon," Laura volunteered.

"She would like that," Bruce told her.

After another few minutes, Bruce got up to leave but, when he reached the front door, he hesitated.

"Ah, yes," he said. "I knew there was something I wanted to mention. I think my short-term memory is on the way out," he said, smiling. "Now what was it? There, it's gone again. No it hasn't.

Only joking."

Laura and Matthew stood patiently, waiting to hear what he had to say. Bruce enjoyed a good story and most of the ones he told were against him.

"When did you go?" he asked. "It was the Thursday, wasn't it?"

"Yes," Matthew replied.

Laura's hand slipped into his and as she squeezed his fingers, Matthew guessed she was thinking the same thing: whatever Bruce was going to tell them and unbeknown to him, was related to what happened in Warwick and the subsequent threats.

"So it was the Friday, the day after you went. I came to have a look at the garden to plan my watering strategy. I was over by the garage when a car pulled up down the road and sat there for a few minutes. Then this woman got out. She stayed by the car, smoking a cigarette and looking at your cottage. It was a bit unnerving really. I kept an eye on her, but as soon as she'd finished smoking, she got back in the car, did a three-point turn and drove away."

"You didn't recognise her?" Laura asked, her grip on Matthew's hand tightening slightly.

"No, can't say I did, but I hope you don't mind, I went into the house and double-checked that everything was secure. One of the top windows in your bedroom wasn't fully closed, so I closed it."

"Thank you," Matthew said, "that was my fault." He thought he had checked but clearly he had overlooked that window. He called himself a few names under his breath.

"I'm not sure she saw me but, if she did," Bruce went on, "she didn't indicate as much."

"What did she look like?" Laura asked before Matthew could.

"Not that easy to say. She was about fifty yards away and she was wearing sunglasses. She also stayed on the other side of her car for most of the time, looking over its roof towards the cottage."

They had moved a few feet so that they were now outside under the pergola that framed the front door.

"Can you show us where she stopped?" Matthew asked.

"Of course I can," Bruce said. They all trooped towards the garage and Bruce pointed up the lane. "There," he said "that's where she parked."

"And it was definitely this cottage she was looking at? She

wasn't just admiring the view?"

Bruce shrugged. "I suppose she could have been. It was a lovely day, precursor to that summer I mentioned," he smiled again. "No, I would say she was looking at your cottage."

"So you can't describe her?" Laura asked at Matthew's shoulder, but then she added quickly, "It's just that I didn't tell all my close friends we were away and it may have been one of them paying an impromptu visit."

"So why didn't she come to the cottage?" Bruce said politely. He looked at Matthew and frowned. "Have I opened a can of worms here? I don't want to worry you unnecessarily."

"Not at all Bruce, but you can't be too careful nowadays, can you? What about the car?"

"Easy," he replied. "I had one once, if you remember, but I had to get a bigger one so that Elizabeth could get in and out more easily."

Matthew hoped his impatience wasn't showing. "So what was it?"

"VW," he said. "A VW Golf. Dark colour, probably dark-blue or it could have been black. Oh, that reminds me, one thing I did notice about her was that she had black hair, jet black it was, quite a striking feature. I think she had a very pretty face too but, as I said, she was fifty yards away and wearing sunglasses so she could have been as ugly as sin."

Matthew felt a shiver run down his spine. "Can you remember roughly what time it was on the Friday, Bruce?" he asked.

"I can be more precise than that, Matthew. I came here straight after giving Elizabeth her eleven o'clock medication so it would have been four or five minutes later."

"You couldn't see if there was anyone else in the car?" Laura then asked.

"Not from here, but she didn't behave as though there was." He paused. "Let me think. No, I would say there wasn't. When she was turning the car round I got a good look in the windows and I would say there wasn't."

"And she didn't see you?"

"As I said, if she did she didn't behave as such, not even a wave or a smile. I would have thought if she had seen me she would have come over." Bruce moved towards the gate. "Anyway, I must be getting into town or Elizabeth will be wondering where I am."

"Yes, sorry to have delayed you and thanks again for looking after the garden."

"And the plants inside," Laura added.

"My pleasure, what are neighbours for? It's a lovely cottage and an absolute picture at this time of the year. I'm sure whoever she was just happened to see it and stopped to admire your handiwork while enjoying a cigarette."

Matthew wanted to tell him there was probably a far more sinister explanation. He knew he was clutching at straws, yet again, but first he had to discuss his suspicions with Laura and she wasn't going to like what he had to say but if it was going to help track down the woman who was hell-bent on murdering her, then he was sure he could make her see sense.

He hoped he could make her see sense.

Chapter Fourteen

It had been staring him in the face, so why hadn't he thought of it before.

As he and Laura went back into the cottage he was kicking himself. He hadn't simply ignored the blindingly obvious, he hadn't even thought of it. It was the second time his blindness had interrupted his thought processes. In many ways, deciding that they were dealing with somebody whose mind was unhinged, even a psychopath, gave him added satisfaction. He was sure the police would be able to track the mystery woman – Francesca – from the ferry down with relative ease. She had already made any number of mistakes but then again they could have been deliberate.

"So what do you make of that little episode?" he asked Laura before telling her what he thought. Laura was making them both another coffee.

"Not a lot," Laura shrugged. "As Bruce said, it was probably somebody who just stopped to admire the cottage. For all we know she was looking for a property in the area and liked the look of where we live. It is pretty idyllic." She put the mugs on the breakfast bar. "You obviously made more of it than I did."

"You could say that. Before I phone the police, which we must do as soon as possible, I just want to run what I to am going tell them by you."

"Go ahead," she said expectantly, reaching for her cigarettes.

She had cut down considerably while they had been away, but Matthew now knew when she would reach for the packet, and more often than not it was when they were about to discuss the threats against her.

"Francesca," he said

"Francesca?" Laura repeated, frowning.

"The mystery woman on the ferry."

Laura screwed up her eyes. "Yes, what about her?"

"I think that's who Bruce saw looking at the cottage."

Laura thought for a moment or two, taking a couple of very deep draws on her cigarette. "What makes you think that and why would somebody who tried to kill herself months ago want me dead?" she said.

"Think back to what you said when I told you about it."

Laura stubbed out the cigarette and picked up her coffee. She was watching Matthew very closely. "Remind me," she said.

"Your explanation was that she was attention seeking, that she had no intention of committing suicide. You said that she was simply playing a game and I was a source for her amusement and that I'd played straight into her hands by giving her the attention she wanted." Matthew took a sip of his coffee, his enthusiasm obvious in his movements ... it could help the case against Emily. "Then, when she was through with me, she discarded me. That's why she didn't stop as we'd arranged, that's what you said."

"Okay," Laura said patiently, "but that doesn't explain why she would want me dead."

"I was coming to that. Let's look a little deeper into her psyche, and I know this is going to sound ridiculous, but you also said that the most logical explanations often turn out to be no explanation at all."

"Not always but what I also meant was that sometimes the most logical explanation is overlooked."

"Exactly!" Matthew said. "Before I carry on, answer me one question: when we, and more importantly you, were racking your brains to try and think of somebody, anybody, who could hate you so much they would be willing to run you down in broad daylight, in front of hundreds of witnesses, did Francesca ever enter your mind?"

Laura reached for another cigarette.

He could tell from her expression that she was beginning to understand his logic.

"No, but ..."

"Just 'no' will do for the moment. Neither did I because I had forgotten all about the incident, well almost, but the moment Bruce mentioned that he thought the woman he saw had jet black hair, it all came back to me."

Laura shook her head. "But that was ages ago, and why me?"

"Because we live together and, for all Francesca knows we are husband and wife."

"You didn't mention me to her, did you?"

"No," he said.

"And you didn't tell her where you lived?"

"No."

"Sorry, in that case you've lost me."

"When I went out onto the deck, I thought I was alone. I've no idea whether she was out there at first or whether she came out after me," Matthew insisted.

"Surely you would have seen her come out if she hadn't already been there?"

"Maybe, but there was another door just a little further along from where I was standing, she could quite as easily have come through that."

"All right, go on," Laura said, shaking her head.

"Bear with me when I describe the next bit. I know it sounds ridiculous but hear me out." He drained the dregs of his coffee. "I don't know how to put it, but let's say we are dealing with somebody who is seriously mentally disturbed. Let's say that outwardly she appears quite normal, and for most of the time she is, but inside her brain there is something that triggers very weird behaviour, psychotic behaviour. Let's say …"

"There are a lot of 'let's says', and normally they are a bit like 'if onlys'."

"All right, but bear with me for a little longer. We agree her behaviour was weird to say the least?" Laura nodded. "Okay, let's say" – Laura looked amused – "on that particular day and that particular time, I was the trigger. I was the one who operated the switch that took her from normality to fantasy. She saw in me something she wanted and used the suicide bit to attract my attention …"

"Some chat-up line." Laura was still amused.

"I fell for it, didn't I? I went to help her. How more intimate can you be than saving somebody's life? We were total strangers but within minutes I had put my arm round her and was comforting her. In this thinking-on-my-feet version of events, she lapped it up. It was exactly what she wanted."

"Okay, thinking ahead a bit, why, if you were what she wanted, and from your description of events she had you hooked, did she not stop and wait for you?"

"I'll let that remark about being hooked pass for the moment." He was thinking aloud but he was trying to rationalise things in his own mind before going to the police. He was concerned that he had, no they had, already sent them on one wild goose chase and he didn't want to do the same thing again.

"Obviously I don't know –" he started to say.

"But let's say –" Laura said interrupting him.

"Laura, I am trying to be rational, and although you seem to think it's all very amusing, it's actually pretty damn serious."

"All right, all right," she said, holding up her hands, "but I do think you are allowing your limited knowledge of human psychology and your vivid imagination to become a little intertwined, but go on."

He felt a little stupid and began to think that maybe he was allowing his imagination to run away with him. He was surprised by Laura's attitude but he wasn't going to allow it to stop him in mid flow. He had to get out what he was thinking and, if at the end, it was all too fantastic to take to the police, then so be it.

"Maybe by leaving me at Dover she thought that I would remain intrigued by her," he said. "I had told her that the reason for meeting once on dry land was for me to see that she had calmed down and would not try again."

"You had no control over her. If she wanted to top herself, she would try again without asking you," Laura pointed out.

"That's what she said." Matthew was losing his train of thought and Laura's attitude wasn't helping.

"Are you trying to tell me that this female you met in the most intriguing of circumstances decided that you were the man she wanted and that, before committing herself to a long term relationship, she would suss you out and get rid of the opposition?"

"Yes."

Laura lit a third cigarette. "And it's taken a year … it's not only bizarre but it's also too improbable to even consider as a possibility."

Matthew stood up and went over to the kitchen window.

"It's as much a possibility as thinking that Emily could be responsible," he muttered to himself.

"I'm sorry, I didn't hear you," he heard Laura say.

He turned round. "I said it's as much a possibility as thinking Emily could be responsible."

Laura's expression changed from being amused to being accusatory. "So that's what this is all about. Let's find an alternative, by any means possible, to get Emily off the hook. Some woman takes a liking to this cottage and, just because she's got black hair and drives a dark-coloured VW Golf, she's the lunatic you met on the ferry and the one who tried to murder me in Warwick."

Matthew folded his arms defensively. "She wasn't driving a VW when I met her, remember? But yes, it could be her."

"I think you said her car was an Audi."

"It was but she could have changed it," he said.

"I agree, let's phone Sergeant Carter."

"You what?" Matthew said not believing what Laura had said.

"I said, I agree." Laura got off her stool and went over to him. She put her arms round his neck and kissed him. "I'm sorry if I seemed to be making light of what you were saying but I must admit it had never entered my head as a possibility, but the more I think about it, the more credible it becomes."

"So why the subterfuge?" he asked.

"It wasn't subterfuge. It was my defence mechanism. I should have connected the two incidents myself and I'm bloody annoyed that I didn't."

"So you really think it's a possibility?"

"I think it's more than a possibility. Other than your obvious loyalty towards Emily, there were other things that didn't add up. She had no idea I was going to be in Warwick after I'd seen her and she didn't have time to follow me. Whoever was responsible for the hit and run had been tailing me for God knows how long. Where did Emily get the VW? Why was –"

"Are you telling me that you haven't thought it was Emily all along?"

Laura's arms were still around Matthew's neck, but she pulled away slightly so that she could see him properly. She nodded. "Yes, Matthew, I have to admit my motives for suspecting her were driven by jealousy and not because I really thought she was responsible."

He moved away from her. "I can't believe that you would do such a thing."

"Matthew, I've lived with you for over a year and, in that time, I've watched you and seen you crucify yourself over the break-up of your marriage. If it had been your fault, I could have lived with it, but knowing the way she treated you, it was too much. That's why I went to see her the second time. I know it was a mistake now but I thought if you knew she knew about me, it would help you exorcise her from your mind ... and from your heart. All I did was make matters worse. I'm sorry."

"You do realise that we could be accused of wasting the police's time."

"No, Matthew, that won't happen. We never said that we definitely thought it was Emily. We just had our suspicions. All they will have been doing is following up a lead. I've known all along that they will not find anything." Laura stopped when she saw the expression on his face. "It was only when I compared just now what I had done because of my jealousy of Emily with what this Francesca may have done because of hers with me, that I came to my senses. I have been insanely jealous for months. I'm not proud of it but it's the way I've been." The tears welled up in her eyes and she started to cry. "I'm ... I'm so sorry. I love you so much I couldn't stand even thinking that part of you was with somebody else."

Matthew took her in his arms and held her tightly.

He didn't know what to say. She was right. He had been unable to let go. Even after so many years, he had allowed his feelings for what used to be to get in the way of what he really wanted.

It wasn't Laura's fault.

He had chastised himself often enough for treating her so badly and now it really in the open. Laura was giving him everything that was within her power to give, and he had repaid her with insensitivity and disregard of her true feelings.

He had driven Laura to blame Emily.

She had set out to expunge any emotional attachment he still had for his ex-wife by making him believe that she was capable of murder.

He had forced her into taking such a drastic step.

Chapter Fifteen

"In view of what you have told us already, Mr Ryan, I think it a little early to take your former wife off the suspect list. Anyway, the details were passed to the Warwickshire police yesterday and, for all we know, they may have already been to see her," Sergeant Carter informed Laura and Matthew as they sat a little awkwardly in the same interview room as before. "However, we will certainly also follow up this second woman. You say her name is Francesca but you don't know her last name, is that right?" she asked.

"Yes, I'm sorry, but –" Matthew started to say.

"And the car she was driving was an Audi with the registration number FRA 1 N?"

"Yes."

"She should be reasonably easy to locate. Even if she's sold the car, whether it was with the registration plate or not, the DVLA will be able to come up with an address. Once we know her details, we'll also be able to discover whether she bought a dark coloured VW Golf. May I ask why you didn't think of her as a possibility before?"

"That was my fault," admitted Matthew. "I thought it too fantastic to be given a second thought, but then when our neighbour saw that woman taking more than just a passing interest in our cottage the day after we left for Malaysia, it made me rethink, especially when the description – the little we had to go on that is – seemed to fit her. It may come to nothing but –"

"We'll decide that, Mr Ryan." It was a mild rebuke. "There's nothing else you want to tell me about or anybody else you want adding to the list?" This time there was a hint of sarcasm as Sergeant Carter let her eyes move from Matthew to Laura and back again.

"No, Sergeant, and I apologise again for perhaps wasting your time earlier." Matthew said, hoping once again that Laura would mention her ex-husband … she didn't.

"As I said, we don't know if time has been wasted yet, Mr Ryan. In a situation like this every lead is worth following up. The CID will have taken up the case in the Midlands. As soon as they have anything, good or bad, they will be in touch with me and I will inform you."

"Thank you."

"You must continue to be vigilant, of course."

"Of course we will."

It was while they were in Edinburgh that Laura took a call from Sergeant Carter on Matthew's mobile.

They drove up on the Monday and were due back the following Friday. Over the four days, Matthew was giving a series of lectures as well as overseeing some practical team building exercises for the various levels of management of a large corporation just outside the city. Laura accompanied him for the first couple of days but became bored and decided, on the condition that she was extra cautious, she would explore the city. The weather was exceptionally good and, under normal circumstances, it wouldn't have been a problem but, for obvious reasons, Matthew was not at all happy. However, once Laura got the bit between her teeth about something, it would have taken more than a simple death threat to dissuade her.

He arrived back at the hotel at just after six o'clock in the evening and Laura was already there having had a guided tour of the castle. Freshly showered, she hadn't bothered to put on any clothes and she was lying on the bed on her front thumbing through a magazine.

Standing at the door to the room Matthew looked down at her and thought that she was a very welcome sight, especially after dealing with twenty ultra-keen, energetic, argumentative and pompous young managers all day.

"It's a good job I wasn't room service," he commented, closing the door.

Laura rolled onto her side and rested her head on one hand.

"If you were, then you just had a cheap thrill. They need to put air-conditioning in these hotels. After experiencing that one in Penang, I would say it's a must," Laura said.

"Anything to report?" Matthew asked as he put his laptop and box of tricks on the floor. She was right – the room was stuffy, even with the windows open.

"I was going to wait until you've fixed yourself a drink but, yes, there has been a call."

"Who from?" he said, taking off his suit jacket and undoing his tie with great relief. It had been a hot, gruelling day, although he had been in air-conditioning for a lot of the time.

Laura swung her legs off the bed and went over to the small fridge by the wardrobe.

"I'll get the drinks. What would you like? Gin and tonic?" she asked.

"Yes, please. Who was the call from?"

He discarded his shoes, socks and trousers. He was looking forward to a cool shower but the gin and tonic was going to come first.

"Sergeant Carter." Laura said the name as though she received a phone call from the Kent police two or three times a day.

Matthew stopped what he was doing and waited for the detail. However, Laura busied herself at the fridge preparing the drinks without saying anything. There was something incongruous about seeing his naked fiancée rummaging around in the drinks fridge.

"Laura, are you going to tell me what was said?"

"In a minute, let me do this first."

She handed Matthew his drink before going back over to the bed.

"Well?" Matthew asked as he sat next to her, feeling the cool liquid having the desired effect.

"Emily is definitely off the hook."

He looked sideways at Laura and was about to ask why she hadn't told him the moment he walked into the room, or even contacted him earlier but then thought it wouldn't be the most acceptable question to ask straight away.

He had left her with a number that she could contact him on, as well as having the option of leaving a message on his mobile, which he always switched off when he was lecturing or facilitating. This morning he had forgotten to take his mobile with him.

Despite the not-unexpected news, he had made a promise to himself – and therefore to Laura – that there were going to be no repeats of what had happened before. Although he was bursting to know the details, he was going to let her tell it at her own pace and in her own way. Laura had her reasons and he knew from bitter experience what they were.

"I see," he said as calmly as he could.

"On the day I visited her and after I left, she went in the opposite direction to me. She went to have lunch with some friends in Kenilworth. She was there at the time of the accident, has witnesses and, no, she'd never had, and nor did she have access to, a VW Golf."

"It's as we thought, then," Matthew said, hoping he sounded relaxed but inside, his heart was thumping with relief.

Laura closed the magazine.

"And now you can make love to me, please." She put her drink on the bedside table and lay back on the bed, her arms above her head.

"You've had your shower. I haven't had mine," Matthew told her, putting his glass next to hers.

"So? I can have another and whether you've had one or not doesn't matter now … I want you to make love to me."

He thought he understood why Laura needed him straightaway after telling him about the call. She needed to claim him. Perhaps she did know exactly how he felt.

Uncharacteristically, Laura stayed on her back, kept her arms above her head, closed her eyes and lay perfectly still. Matthew took the hint and did everything he could to please her.

Afterwards, as they lay in each other's arms, she suddenly said, "There was something else. Emily wants to see us both."

Laura's spoke slowly and he heard each word but for whatever reason he didn't fully accept what she had said.

Emily wants to see us both?

Why would Emily want to see them?

He would have thought they were the last people on earth Emily would have wanted to see. Was now the wrong time to ask if there was anything else? If he did ask, the excitement in his voice would definitely tell Laura how he was really feeling.

He took a deep breath and tried to stay calm.

"I didn't expect that," he said quietly.

"Neither did I," Laura said.

"Did she tell the police why she wanted to see us?"

"No."

When he next spoke to Sergeant Carter, she was bound to ask whether they had been to Leamington Spa. Whether her question would have been out of professional concern or female inquisitiveness didn't matter but because she had passed on the message she would want to know.

They found an Italian restaurant in the Old Town on the Royal Mile not far from the castle, and had a passable but simple meal. The city was thronging with tourists and the restaurant they were in was no different to anywhere else. There seemed to be an abundance of Japanese tourists chattering away and taking photographs.

It was a warm and humid evening but, unlike the hotel, the restaurant was air-conditioned. Laura had dressed simply with a loose linen wrap-around skirt and a revealing halter-top. Matthew didn't know whether the subdued lighting in the restaurant enhanced her tan, but as he sat opposite her feeling proud that she was with him, her tan seemed darker and more even. She was glancing around, taking in the various nationalities and languages in their vicinity. She was eating slowly, cutting her food into small pieces before putting each morsel into her mouth.

As he looked at her she shivered. "Are you cold?" he asked, grateful that such a small reaction gave him reason to speak.

Since she'd told him about the phone call and even after making love, Laura had been quiet and initially he found it a little unnerving but, then, trying to think beyond his own needs, he put it down to what Sergeant Carter had said and especially to the fact that Emily had intimated that she wanted to see them. If the possibility of a meeting were on his mind, it would certainly be on Laura's. They needed to discuss what they should do, but only when she was ready.

Slowly she lifted her head so she was looking directly at him. His question seemed to take a while to reach her.

"No, Matthew, I'm not cold. I think maybe somebody just walked over my grave."

It was a cliché but Matthew saw a far deeper meaning in Laura's eyes. "How's your food?"

"Fine, thanks."

She put her knife and fork down on her plate, having eaten only half of spaghetti carbonara. Although he had guessed what was wrong with he thought it best if he let her tell him in her own time. If would give him more time to think about what he was going to say.

"What did you do today?" he asked instead.

"Checking up on me? Trying to find out if I took any risks?" A narrowing of her eyes accompanied her words. "As I've told you so many times before, I'm quite capable of looking after myself," she added a little more softly.

"Laura, it was a genuine question and one that anyone would have asked had they been separated from each other all day."

He finished his meal and looked around for the waiter, in need of another drink.

"Was it? Oh, I am sorry! I did an open-top bus tour and then a bit of window shopping, bought this top and skirt, and generally had a lazy day."

"I wish I could have been with you," he said, biding his time. She was building up to what she really wanted to say. "The group I had today were particularly argumentative and searching."

"I thought that's what you liked," she said, her eyes wandering.

Matthew got the waiter's attention so he ordered a beer for himself and a sparkling water for Laura, which in itself was unusual. Only one glass of red wine while they were out for a meal wasn't normal either.

They both declined the proffered sweet menus.

"It is, but today I could have done without it," he said.

"Oh, why was that?" she asked.

"I suppose my own enthusiasm wasn't what it normally is. I just wanted to get the facts across without having them questioned all the time," he told her.

"Mustn't question facts, must we?"

The beer arrived, and Matthew took a long drink before saying, "All right, Laura, this has gone far enough. I know today's news was greeted with mixed emotions but I thought we'd agreed that, on further analysis, it was very unlikely that Emily had anything to do with the attack on you and what has happened subsequently.

You'd already suggested that you knew it wasn't her."

"Is that the way you spoke to your students today?" Laura reached for her cigarettes but then changed her mind. "If it was, I'm not surprised they were argumentative."

He took a deep breath determined to stay in control.

"Laura, can we go back a couple of hours and start again please? I fully appreciate that we will have received the news about Emily with mixed emotions but there is no need for it to cause friction between us."

"I'm afraid I don't know what you are talking about. What do you mean mixed emotions? As you said, 'on further analysis' we had agreed that Emily was off the hook, so why should the fact that Sergeant Carter merely confirmed what we already thought cause friction?"

She sat back in her chair with her glass in her hand and narrowed eyes. She was deliberately taunting him for some reason and he didn't like it.

"Well, something has upset you. When I left you this morning you were fine, but ever since I got in this evening, you've been, I don't know, different. You have hardly said a word and now it's pretty bloody obvious that you are hell bent on having an argument about something." Matthew placed his beer glass gently on the table. "Nothing has happened to warrant this atmosphere between us, unless there is something you are not telling me."

"And what do you think I'm not telling you?"

"If I knew the answer to that, I wouldn't ask would I?" he said between clenched teeth. He'd raised his voice and he was aware people at the tables close to them were watching him.

Laura, on the other hand, ignored what was going on around them and just looked at him, her eyes no longer narrowed and she was smiling.

"Wonderful," she said. "At last there is a hint of animation. I've been waiting for that all evening."

He shook his head, the sudden change in direction confusing him. "I'm sorry but once again female logic has surpassed itself by throwing the male of the species into total puzzlement," he said.

"Fantastic! We really are getting back to normal."

"Laura," he said, shaking his head, "getting a word out of you since I got back to the room this evening has been like getting blood out of a stone. You do all you can to generate an argument and now, suddenly, you're all smiles. Any man would be puzzled."

"I wasn't deliberately trying to cause an argument. You were in suspended animation and needed to be shocked back into reality," she said.

He shook his head. "If you think you're giving me an adequate explanation for your behaviour over the last few hours, you're sadly mistaken. I'm more confused now than I was before."

"All right," Laura said leaning forward, "let's go back an hour or two as you suggest. Who were you making love to earlier?"

"I don't think ..." Matthew glanced sideways at the couple nearest to them.

"What don't you think ... this is not the time or place? You wanted to talk, so let's talk. I admit that I did what I did deliberately. Have you ever known me lie back and think of England before? Have you –?"

"Laura! I really think if we are going to have this conversation, it ought to be in private."

This time Laura did look at the middle-aged well-dressed couple on the next table. Giving them both the sweetest of smiles she said, "This is a private conversation, but if you would like to know more, then please feel free to join us."

"I am sorry," the man said in accented English.

"I wondered if you wanted to join us," Laura repeated.

"And why would we be wanting to do that?" the man asked. Matthew thought his accent was probably German.

"As I said, so that it would be easier to hear what we are saying," Laura said sweetly.

"We have no wish to hear what you are saying," the man said.

"Good," Laura told him. "I'm pleased that's settled."

"Laura, I think –" Matthew started to say.

"You are a very rude young woman," the woman on the other table said.

"No, I'm not," Laura said, "but it is rude to eavesdrop on other people's conversations."

The woman looked confused. "Eavesdrop?" she said to her husband.

"*Lauschen!*" the man said to her.

"Ah, *lauschen*," the woman repeated before smiling at Laura. "Young lady what you are saying is of no interest to me or my husband, but if you think we were listening to you, then we apologise. Sitting so close such misunderstandings can happen."

Matthew covered his mouth with his hand to hide a sudden smile.

"In that case it is I who should apologise," Laura said. "I'm sorry for misunderstanding your intentions."

The man nodded, also smiling. "Enjoy your evening," he said.

"And you yours," Laura replied.

"What was that all about?" Matthew asked as Laura turned back to face him.

"Just … oh, it doesn't matter." She paused. "So, Matthew, an answer to my question, please. I have admitted what I did was contrived but it wasn't a trap. I wanted to see how you would react."

He was still surprised and just a little embarrassed by the way Laura had spoken to the German couple. "That was unnecessary," he told her, indicating the couple with his eyes.

Laura shrugged. "People shouldn't listen in to other people's private conversations."

"They said they weren't and, even if they were, we aren't in a private place."

Laura caught the waiter's attention and ordered coffee and a couple of brandies.

"So when you're out for a meal, you should only talk about what you're happy for others to hear, is that what you are saying? If that were the case, life would be very, very boring."

"That's not what I am saying but private and intimate shouldn't be confused in a situation like this."

"There's a difference, is there? All right, if you would prefer it, let's talk in veiled speech: it might make it more interesting. As I said, thinking of England isn't a normal pastime I employ in such situations, and you also know that I am not a missionary sort of person, therefore I do not normally partake in any positions such people adopt, unless I'm tired, that is."

Although confused, Matthew was still unable to hide a smile.

"If this is leading to what I think, I'm surprised you can be so flippant. At the time I didn't read any more into what we did other than that you wanted security, confirmation of how I felt about you, because under the circumstances you were vulnerable."

"That's an interesting point," Laura said before pausing while the waiter put the brandy glasses and coffee cups on the table. "Didn't you think that by exposing my vulnerability – I've never heard it called that before – I was trying to tell you something more than just that there was a need for me to feel secure?"

"I'd have preferred it if we'd talked and then, you know, done what we did in our normal way."

"You're missing my point, Matthew. Although we'd talked about it and, yes, perhaps I did know it wasn't Emily from the outset, Sergeant Carter's call wasn't exactly what I wanted to hear and especially the bit about your ex-wife wanting to see us." Laura hadn't referred to Emily as his ex-wife before, previously she had called her by her name. "I did what I did because I wanted to see how you would react."

"And I obviously failed the test."

"I don't know, did you?"

"If I told you I enjoyed every moment, I'm not sure you would believe me," he said as he reached for his brandy.

"I'm pleased you enjoyed it. I'd be worried if you hadn't, but who was I?"

"You," he answered honestly, spreading his hands.

"Was I?"

Matthew rubbed his forehead. "Laura, can we stop evading the issue? You had just told me about Sergeant Carter's message that included Emily's request to see us. It did surprise me just a bit because it was the last thing I was expecting ... that either of us was expecting. As soon as you'd told me what had been said you asked me to ..." He looked across at the Germans who now appeared to be taking more interest in another couple on their other side "... make love to you. Not only did you ask me to make love to you, you also just lay there looking at the ceiling. You don't do that but I thought it was what you wanted. You are being just a little unfair. You are reading more into what we did than actually happened. You asked me to make love to you, so that is what I did.

If what you are really asking is whether, because of what you'd told me, for some bizarre reason I imagined that you were Emily, the answer is no. Regardless of what has happened recently, I actually thought that you believed in me more than that."

Laura thought for a moment, her brandy glass cupped in both hands. "All right, why do you think Emily wants to see us?"

This sudden change of tack wasn't unusual for Laura but, under the circumstances, Matthew was relieved. Although what he had said was the truth, he didn't know whether it had been accepted.

He found her use of something as important as sex to make a point rather strange. Her behaviour had changed yet again. Ever since they received the second threatening letter while in Penang, her mood swings had become extreme. His reactions hadn't helped but it wasn't all down to him. He could understand it if she had gone to pieces and locked herself away but, if anything, the opposite applied.

At times her complacency was worrying, ably demonstrated by her insistence on going shopping alone in Edinburgh. There was still a death threat against her, the police were involved, and now that Emily was no longer a suspect, they were almost back to square one. The police would be trying to find Francesca, but that was probably a long shot, and there was still Laura's ex-husband but ...

Shrugging Matthew said, "Why does she want to see us? Oh, her reasons would be nothing out of the ordinary, I suppose. Maybe she just wants an explanation as to why her ex-husband and his lover thought she was capable of murder."

After attracting the waiter's attention, he asked for the bill.

Laura suddenly seemed to lose some of her buoyancy. Her shoulders slumped and she gave him a sheepish look.

Another mood swing, he thought.

This time she had gone from being the assertive mistress who had used sex in an attempt to demonstrate how she thought he was thinking, to the weak female who needed a hug and reassurance. He didn't like the way he was thinking because he was still very much in love with Laura.

"And do you think we ought to go and see her?"

"I don't know. I haven't seen her for six years and, if we were ever to meet again, I would have liked it to be under different circumstances."

"And what would these different circumstances be?"

This time he shook his head. "Please don't start that again. There was no hidden agenda in what I said."

Laura folded her napkin and straightened out the edges. "I wasn't starting anything again. It's just that you've got to understand where I am …"

The waiter appeared with the bill and Laura never finished her sentence.

Matthew did understand where she was coming from, and he wanted them both to go back there in one piece. Most of the time they were together, they were able to act as they always had done but, on other occasions, he became extremely worried. They seemed to adopt opposite stances, talked in riddles and could rarely see the other's point of view but, most importantly, they didn't appear to want to do anything about it.

The warped mind that had put the threatening letters together had not shown her hand again, not in the open, but in a way she was succeeding in another area. She was driving a wedge into his and Laura's relationship. They could both see what was happening to them but they seemed incapable of doing anything about it.

However, Matthew was determined that not only was he going to keep Laura out of harm's way, he was also going to make sure they came out of it all with an even closer bond than they already had.

Chapter Sixteen

Matthew and Laura returned from Edinburgh without having discussed the Emily situation any further. Regardless, he had decided that they wouldn't gain anything if they did go to see Emily, in fact there was more to lose. He would not be able to look at Emily without ... he couldn't go there. The future was more to do with moving on with their lives, not living in the past.

Having thought about how they could move forward and how the threats and resultant tension that existed between him and Laura could be managed, he wanted to make amends and take the conclusions he'd drawn to Sergeant Carter and discuss them face-to-face ... but without Laura being there. Something needed doing because he was becoming increasingly worried about Laura's mental state.

He managed to do so the following week.

With only a couple of days lecturing on the Wednesday and Thursday, both in London, the opportunity presented itself without any planning. When Laura woke on the Monday morning feeling as though she was coming down with something, he grasped the chance. It was deceitful, he knew, but he believed it was for the right reasons and had to be – short and long term – beneficial. He would tell Laura everything that had been said when he got back.

Sergeant Carter was able to see him at eleven o'clock. Matthew left Laura in bed and made sure the cottage was secure, including setting the alarm for all the windows and doors downstairs. He left a note at the top of the stairs telling Laura about the alarm being set.

"I thought I might see you sometime this week," Sergeant Carter told him as they went through to the canteen for a cup of coffee.

It was an informal visit.

She was off-duty but she had needed to go to the station to collect something she had forgotten. She was dressed in a dark suit, the skirt of which fell below her knees, as that afternoon she was going to an aunt's funeral in Canterbury.

Seeing her for the first time out of uniform, Matthew was a little surprised as to how it changed the way she appeared. In uniform, Sergeant Carter was an imposing character who did things strictly by the book, but even going to the canteen for a social coffee was indicative of the softening of her nature brought about, probably, by a simple change of clothes, albeit in readiness for a funeral.

As part of his repertoire, Matthew gave a lecture on *the Power of a Uniform in a Democratic Society*, and he had to smile as they walked into the canteen, noticing that even the way she walked had changed. He made a mental note to add a few simple changes to his lecture.

"I was up in Edinburgh when you called," he told her as they joined the self-service queue.

"Tea or coffee?" she asked.

"Coffee, please."

"Yes, Miss Stanhope told me."

"I must have gone off in a daze that morning because for the first time I left my mobile behind."

Sergeant Carter smiled. "That's why I came to the station this morning, to collect my mobile."

They took their coffees to a table in the far corner of the canteen and sat down facing each other.

"I suppose you want to know some more details of how things went in Leamington Spa?" Sergeant Carter suggested as she added a couple of sweeteners to her drink.

"Well, yes, if you're able to tell me anything else, that is."

"I'm not sure what Miss Stanhope has already told you. When you rang the station earlier and asked to see me, I thought she would be with you."

"No, she's come down with a bug of some sort and I left her at home. I didn't like leaving her on her own under the circumstances, but we've got to get on with our lives."

Matthew didn't like lying, but he wasn't too sure that if he told Sergeant Carter the truth she would understand. Laura wasn't feeling well so even if they had planned to come together, she wouldn't have made it, so perhaps it wasn't really a lie.

Sergeant Carter looked at him for a few seconds before saying, "Mr Ryan, I've been in the police for more years than I care to remember and I worked in the Met in London before coming down here on promotion. The reason I mention that is because if you're going to meet weirdoes, then London is the place to do it." A wry smile appeared on her face. "In all my time, though, I've never come across a case like this before. People are threatening other people every day, and sometimes the threats come to something, but this one is different. Assuming there is a direct connection, whoever it is took a great risk in attempting to run down Miss Stanhope in Warwick. It was either done out of sheer frustration coupled with determination, or it was a spur of the moment opportunistic act." She screwed up her face as she drank some of her coffee. "Sorry about that." She indicated Matthew's cup. "Not exactly Egon Ronay, is it?"

It certainly wasn't the best Matthew had ever tasted. "It's fine, thank you," he said.

"Liar," she said with a smile. "As I was saying, frustration or opportunism, I don't know which. It could have even been a combination of them both. The threats, though, haven't followed the normal pattern. My previous experience suggests that if somebody is determined enough then, having failed once to carry out a threat, they will try again at the next and earliest opportunity, but that hasn't happened. If, on the other hand, having failed in an actual attempt, the perpetrator decides to adopt a more psychological form of intimidation, the threats become more frequent. That hasn't happened either. Receiving the second threatening letter when you were on holiday suggested that is exactly what would happen on your return, but nothing. It's strange."

"So where do we go from here?"

"It's difficult to say. Being a go-between with the Warwickshire police is not the most ideal situation to be in, especially when you are both living on my patch. I think I told you the last time we met, that CID are dealing with the case in Warwickshire and they are looking into this Francesca woman you told me about, so I am more of a uniformed liaison officer. But that doesn't stop me having an opinion."

"Which is?"

"Do you mind if I ask you some rather personal questions?"

"Don't the police do that with people all the time?"

Sergeant Carter smiled a genuine smile for the first time and it transformed her face. Her eyes lit up and her smile showed that she had dimples, supposedly indicating gentleness and understanding.

"I suppose we do. Inquisitiveness is part of our nature."

"So what would you like to know?" Matthew asked.

Picking up a plastic spoon and she started twisting it in her fingers. "How long have you and Miss Stanhope been living together?"

"She moved in with me in late May last year."

"And you met because she was the private detective you hired to investigate your former wife?"

"Well, in a way. As I told you, I didn't want my ex-wife investigated exactly. Emily and I had been divorced for over five years. I had stopped in 1998 – at her request I hasten to add – paying her any maintenance and therefore really lost the little contact I did have with her and that was via her solicitors. I was using Miss Stanhope to, well ..." Now he was explaining his reasons to a stranger, Matthew was finding it a little difficult. "I was using Laura to check that Emily was all right."

The spoon stopped turning in Sergeant Carter's fingers and she looked at him. "If you don't mind me saying so, Mr Ryan, that sort of unselfishness must be quite unusual, although I didn't say so at the time because you were with Miss Stanhope. Private Investigators are normally asked to look into relationships for vengeful reasons, not as a result of altruism."

Matthew shrugged, feeling slightly embarrassed. "It was the way I felt."

"At the time or do you still feel that way? I'm sorry Mr Ryan," she added quickly, "that was perhaps too personal."

"That was very perceptive of you," he said.

"Maybe, but also it was too personal."

"It's all right, you just threw me a bit for a second . Look, as this visit isn't official in the true sense of the word, can we drop the formalities. My name is Matthew ... but you already know that."

"Gill Phillips and Pete Richards told me you like things to be less formal," Sergeant Carter said, smiling. "Wendy," she told him, reaching across the table to shake hands.

She had quite large hands but her touch was light, not what he had expected.

As she took her hand away she glanced at her watch.

"Sorry, am I taking up too much of your time?" he asked.

"No, not at all, I have to go to a funeral this afternoon and I've taken the day off. I only popped into to get my mobile …"

"Then the last thing you want is to be talking to me."

"Part of the job, Mr … I mean, Matthew. We're never off duty really and I've got the time. Would you like another cup of poison?"

"No thanks."

"I don't blame you." Wendy picked up the spoon again. "As you told me before we sat down, you're really here to find out what happened in Leamington Spa with your ex-wife." Matthew nodded. "That's one of the reasons why I asked about Laura Stanhope. When you came to see me to suggest we might like to look into the possibility that your former wife might have been behind the hit-and-run on Laura, would I be right in saying that Laura was keener than you to follow up the suggestion?"

Matthew didn't want to make Laura out to be vindictive but he remembered Wendy Carter implying as much at the time. "I think, for obvious reasons, I was a little reluctant to follow through with what we'd discussed, but Laura, because of her police background, thought it would be better to have the possibility looked into and dismissed rather than allowing any doubts to linger."

"I see and she thought it was all because of the second visit to your former wife –"

"Can we give her a name too? It's Emily."

"Emily what? What's her surname?" Wendy narrowed her eyes as she asked her question.

"You know, I don't know. When Laura first went up there, she told me she didn't think there was a man in Emily's life." The fact that Emily had been wearing the engagement ring Matthew had given her flashed into his mind. "And I don't know whether she's changed her name. She could have reverted to her maiden name which was Sterling."

"No, Matthew, your former wife still goes by the name of Emily Ryan and your daughter is Sarah Ryan."

Although he had thought about what had happened on so many

occasions, hearing somebody else say their names was upsetting, and to hear Sarah referred to as his daughter after so long, even more so.

All Laura had managed to find out was that she didn't think Emily had a man in her life. If Emily had remarried, she would either have taken her husband's name or reverted to her maiden name. The obvious conclusions were there to be drawn and Matthew drew them. Either Sarah's father had taken them on, but only temporarily, or nothing had come out of the relationship.

Had Emily really been alone since they separated?

"I see," was all Matthew could say. He thought about telling Wendy Carter that Sarah wasn't his daughter but decided it wasn't relevant, and anyway it was all in the past.

Wendy was looking at him doubtfully. "You didn't know?"

"What, that Emily was still using my name?"

"Yes."

"No, I had no idea."

Nevertheless, it did suggest that Laura had maybe been looking for a reason to go back to see Emily a second time. He didn't exactly know why he thought that because when she first went to see Emily she had gone in her professional capacity. He was surprised she hadn't told him but ... perhaps when she discovered that Emily still used his name she was already looking to the future. No, it would have been too soon ... but what other reason could there have been? So was Laura's second visit purely personal?

He sensed that Wendy could see his confusion.

"What exactly did Laura tell you?" she asked her expression remaining unchanged.

"That Emily had been investigated and she was in Kenilworth having lunch with friends at the time of the attack. Also," he added warily, "you told her Emily wanted to see us."

"I suppose that is accurate to a point," Wendy suggested as she stared at Matthew, "but there was more to it than that."

He frowned, wanting to know the rest but just a little apprehensive about asking. "What ...?" He was just about to pose the question when his mobile rang. "Excuse me." He took the phone out of his pocket and checked the number. It was the cottage phone in Westerham. He pressed the accept button. "Laura?"

"Matthew, there's somebody outside," Laura said in a hushed voice.

He looked across at Wendy and she was frowning. "What do you mean?"

"I mean there's somebody outside and they are trying to get in."

"What, in broad daylight?"

"I fully appreciate it's broad daylight but I don't go deaf when the sun comes up. There is somebody trying to get in. Where are you?"

"I'm still in Sevenoaks." He hadn't told Laura he was going to the police station. "More importantly, where are you?"

"I'm in the bedroom."

"Lock the bedroom door and put a chair under the knob. I'll be with you in twenty minutes. The alarm is on downstairs so don't leave the bedroom."

"Twenty minutes?" Laura sounded very frightened.

"Hang on." Matthew covered the mouthpiece and looked at Wendy. "It's Laura. She thinks somebody is trying to get into the cottage. Is there a police car in the area? She's terrified."

"Wait here, I'll go and see," she said a little hesitantly.

"Thanks," Matthew said. He lifted his mobile back to his ear. "Laura, I'll be with you as quickly as I can. Have you phoned the police?"

"No. Can you do it for me?"

"Yes, I'll ring them straightaway."

Why was he lying? Why couldn't he tell her he was there already?

He saw Wendy coming back into the canteen.

"I'll ring them now and get straight back to you," he said. "Have you locked the bedroom door?"

"Yes, and I've put a chair against it."

"I'll ring you back in a couple of minutes."

"All right and Matthew ... I love you."

He thought it strange that she felt the need to declare her love at that particular moment. She must have been scared witless. "And I love you, Laura. You'll be all right. I'll ring you in a couple of minutes."

Wendy reached the table just as he was pressing the disconnect button. "There's a car not far away in Limpsfield Chart. It'll be there in five to ten minutes."

"Thanks, Wendy. I must go." Matthew stood up.

"I'll come with you to your car," she said as she reached for her bag that was hanging over the back of her chair.

They left the canteen and headed for the car park.

"Was there anything you were going to tell me that can't wait?" Matthew asked as they went through the swing doors at the front of the station. He felt frustrated but appreciated Laura's safety was paramount.

"No, but I think we need to talk again, and alone," Wendy said.

Matthew stopped. "What do you mean?"

Wendy shook her head slightly. "Sorry, I didn't mean that to sound the way it did. There are certain things about the threats on Laura's life that I'd prefer I told you alone. It would be best if Laura didn't know just yet. I don't want to frighten her."

"Now you've got me really worried."

They had reached Matthew's car.

"I didn't mean to," Wendy said, looking at him. "I'm back on duty on Friday – give me a ring. Use my mobile."

She handed him a card. Without looking at it, Matthew put it in his pocket. "Thanks," he said, undoing the car door. "Just tell me one thing. You mentioned Francesca earlier. Has anybody come up with anything?"

"That's one of the things I wanted to talk about," Wendy told him.

"I'll ring you on Friday," he said.

"Sorry I can't come with you to see that Laura's all right," Wendy said as he started to close the door.

"That's all right and thank you for giving me so much of your time on your day off. I hope the funeral goes as well as can be expected."

Wendy smiled and nodded. "She was rich and I was her favourite niece. Does that sound awful?"

"Not at all," he said returning her smile, "just truthful."

"The truth is out there for us all," Wendy added, the smile disappearing.

"I hope you are right," Matthew said as he selected first gear.

Chapter Seventeen

There was a police Volvo V70 parked in front of the garage.

It had taken Matthew twenty minutes to get to Westerham from Sevenoaks. He rushed to the front door and let himself in. Laura was in the kitchen with two police officers – both male – drinking tea. The police officers stood up as Matthew entered.

"Hello, darling," Laura said, staying at the kitchen table. She was dressed in her cotton dressing gown and he could see that she was wearing one of his pyjama jackets underneath. "This is Police Constable Chalmers," she told Matthew, indicating the older of the two police officers. He was nearly six and half feet tall, and almost as broad as he was tall. His complexion was very dark, and Matthew noticed that he had extremely hairy arms. Incongruously, Matthew found himself likening him to a bear. "And this is Police Constable …"

"Hetherington," the younger, shorter and slimmer police officer said as Laura hesitated over his name.

Matthew shook both their hands. "Please sit down." Laura was looking remarkably calm. "Did you discover anything?"

"No, Sir," said the bear in a deep voice. "We either frightened whoever it was away or they were gone by the time we got here."

"And they got here very quickly," Laura added from behind the bear.

"Were there any signs of anybody trying to force their way in?"

"No," the bear told Matthew.

PC Hetherington was sipping his tea, his eyes wide open: Matthew decided either he was undergoing his probationary period or he was in awe of his partner.

"We did notice the window in the cloakroom had been forced at some stage," the bear continued, "but your wife told us it was you a couple of months ago when you locked yourselves out." He looked at Matthew for conformation.

"Yes," Matthew said, agreeing with what Laura had told them. There wasn't any point in adding that Laura wasn't his wife. "I've had the door locks changed since."

"May I suggest you have some put on the windows as well, Sir?

If you can get in, so can anybody else whether the house is alarmed or not."

"I've been meaning to," Matthew told him. "You know about the circumstances regarding my wife?"

Laura's eyebrows shot up and she smiled at him. She had obviously calmed down considerably since she phoned earlier.

"We have a little of the background, Sir. The control room gave us some of the detail. It must be very worrying for you both." His demeanour didn't mirror his concern.

"It is," Matthew agreed.

"Well, if anything else happens, you must contact us straightaway." The bear reached for his cap, which was the signal for PC Hetherington to finish the rest of his tea.

"We will."

"Right, we'll be on our way, then." The police officers stood up and Matthew stood with them.

"Thanks for getting here so quickly," he said.

"That's all right," the bear said. "It gave young PC Hetherington his first experience of driving to an emergency."

PC Hetherington looked as though he was none too keen on being patronised.

After going with the police to their car and putting his own car in the garage, Matthew went back into the kitchen.

"So what happened?" he asked Laura.

"It was weird," she said. "I'd been reading but must have dropped off. Something woke me up with a start, I didn't know what it was at first but then I heard this rattling. I'm sure somebody was trying the front door and then they moved round to the back."

"You didn't see anybody?" Matthew sat down and poured himself a cup of tea from the dregs in the teapot.

"Do you want me to make some fresh?" Laura asked.

"No, this'll do. Did you see anybody?"

"Not really, I was upstairs on the landing. I was looking at the note you left me when I thought I saw a shadow at the front door. Whoever it was had moved round to the back when I phoned you."

"It could have been an opportunist burglar who thought we were both out," he said.

Laura wasn't convinced. "I suppose it could have been but I was so scared."

"Yes, I'm sorry, I should have been here."

"You can't be with me every minute of the day."

"Maybe not, but I could have been today," he said.

"Did you get done what you needed in town?"

"I was on my way to the publishers when you rang."

One of the things he'd wanted to do while in Sevenoaks was to have a new brochure designed and printed. The draft was still on the back seat of his car.

"Oh," Laura said, sounding surprised. "You sounded as though you were inside somewhere. I could hear voices."

"I was," Matthew said quickly, wondering why he was about to lie again. "I stopped off for a coffee."

"But you were talking to somebody."

"No, I moved outside so that I could hear you better." He had no idea why the lies were coming so easily. For some reason, having promised himself he would tell her everything on his return, he thought it would be better if for the time being he kept his visit to the police station to himself. Once he had spoken to Wendy Carter again he would then decide whether to come clean.

"Bit of a coincidence they'd heard about me from Sergeant Carter," Laura said.

"Sergeant Carter?" Matthew asked, suddenly wary.

"Yes, when the police arrived they told me that they were aware of our situation as they called it. When I asked who'd told them they said it'd been Sergeant Carter."

Matthew hesitated for a split second. "She's dealing with the case," he said, shrugging, "and I suppose they come from the same station," he suggested.

"Possibly," Laura said, frowning at the same time.

"You're looking much better," he suggested, changing the subject.

"I know. I felt lousy when I woke up this morning but I must admit I feel a lot brighter now. It must have been the adrenalin rush."

She looked at Matthew for a few seconds without saying anything further before taking the used mugs over to the sink.

The kitchen window looked out over the back of garden, which was private enough for Laura to sunbathe topless when the temperature was right. The back door was at one end of the hallway and led out of the house just beyond the kitchen window, so that too was private. The front door, at the other end of the hall, was quite close to the narrow road that led into Westerham. On the other side of the road was the stream, but the rose bushes and the hedge bordering the garden were quite high and both hid it from view. The double garage, which was an old workshop, was detached from the house and stood at an angle between the front door and the front gate, from where some of the garden was on view. However, anyone snooping around the cottage could have done so quite easily, even in broad daylight. Matthew decided to take the bear's advice and get locks fitted to the windows.

"Did you say you're working on Wednesday and Thursday this week?" Laura asked, turning away from the sink.

"Yes, in London and you are coming with me."

"I hadn't planned to. I wanted to start stripping the paper in the study. We've been meaning to redecorate it for months," she said moving across the kitchen. Standing in front of Matthew she undid the tie on her dressing gown.

"But after this morning's experience, Laura, I think it would be best ...' He stopped when Laura let the dressing gown fall from her shoulders onto the floor.

"You must be feeling better," he said as she sat astride him.

The kitchen chair creaked under the extra weight.

"There's only one way to find out," she said lowering her lips onto his and reaching down to undo his belt.

For a few minutes they were both lost in their own world.

There were no threats or potential intruders to distract them from what they were doing. Laura had the ability to change his mood ... their moods. The worry caused by what had happened that morning, the concerns that Wendy Carter had raised but didn't have the time to explain, and the general feeling of vulnerability and exposure generated by both, disappeared as Laura moved slowly, her arms round his neck, her lips on his.

The disagreement they'd had in Edinburgh was now history.

"I ... think ... this ... chair ... is ... going ... to ... break,"

Laura said, her eyes screwed up, her head thrown back.

Matthew smiled because he was still wearing his collar and tie.

"Let it, it can be replaced," he said.

"But ... oh, God!"

The front doorbell rang.

"There's ..." Laura let out a very dull moan and Matthew felt her body relax against him.

The doorbell rang again.

"I'll get it," he told her, putting his hands on her hips and lifting.

"No, you haven't ..."

"Later."

It was Bruce Townsend.

"Sorry I rang and rang, Matthew," Bruce apologised as Matthew opened the door, "but I saw the police car, and after the incident the other day I just wanted to check all was okay."

"Sorry it took so long to get to the door. We were upstairs."

Matthew didn't know why he felt the need to provide an explanation. He smiled to himself as he wondered how straight-laced Bruce would react if he told him precisely what he and Laura had been doing.

"The police?" Bruce said again.

Matthew wasn't sure where Laura had gone so he wasn't too keen on inviting Bruce into the cottage. He thought about inventing an explanation that wouldn't generate too much concern, but he didn't know what Bruce had seen.

"I was in Sevenoaks and, as Laura didn't feel too well first thing this morning, she was still in bed. She thought she heard somebody snooping round the house so she called me and I called the police."

"Oh, I see. Was there anybody?" Bruce asked.

"Not when the police got here."

"I shouldn't think so. You could hear them a mile away. I often wonder why they give so much notice. How's Laura?" he asked peering round Matthew into the cottage.

"She's fine thanks, Bruce. She's gone back to bed."

"Oh, right. Do you think there was any connection?"

"Between today and what you saw while we were away?"

"Yes."

Matthew shrugged. "There might be, but we don't know."

"I would say there could be, Matthew," Bruce said, consumed by sudden enthusiasm.

"Why?"

"The police car came past me at a rate of knots as I was coming down the road from town. Not by the stream, I went the other way. Saw them stop by your cottage and just as I did, I noticed a VW Golf parked in front of the Wilson's at the top of the road." He carried on in a rush. "I was sure it was the same one and there was nobody in it, so I took its number this time." He reached in his pocket and took out a piece of paper. "I thought you might want it." He handed Matthew the piece of paper.

"R 756 GNV," Matthew read.

"It was the same model and colour," Bruce added.

"Well thanks for that, Bruce. I'll pass it on to the police."

"Probably nothing but you can't be too safe, can you?"

"No."

"Right, I'll be off. Give Laura my best wishes. It must have worried her, you not being there when it happened."

"Yes, it did."

With another glance into the cottage, Bruce waved his hand and walked down the path towards the gate.

"Thanks again, Bruce," Matthew called after him. Bruce stopped at the gate and gave another wave.

After closing the front door he looked at the piece of paper.

"What's that?" Laura asked from the kitchen doorway, her dressing gown hanging open.

"Bruce, he came to enquire about the police car and he thinks he saw that Golf again, parked up the road by the Wilson's house. He gave me its registration number," Matthew told her, walking back down the hall.

"What are you going to do?"

"Nothing with this at the moment, but I've got other ideas for you. We've got a little bit of unfinished business to attend to."

Laura smiled as she backed towards the kitchen table, shedding the dressing gown.

"Do you realise you forgot to do up your zip?" she added as she lifted her bottom onto the table. "You also forgot to tuck your shirt in at the back."

"That was all your fault," he said smiling down at her.
"Everything seems to be my fault," she said, pouting.
"You have you ways of making up for it," he said.
"I do, don't I?" she said.

Chapter Eighteen

Laura changed her mind and went to London with Matthew.

When he was working, she spent most of her time getting lost in the shopping crowds on Oxford, Regent and Bond Streets. She promised that she would keep looking over her shoulder, but deep down he knew she would feel secure; the anonymity of multi-cultural hordes providing what she needed. Laura had also reminded him of her training: in Warwick, the attack was unexpected, now she was prepared.

On their return from London on the Thursday evening, a reminder in the form of a third threatening letter was lying on the front door mat. It was very similar to the others and Laura seemed to treat it as though it was a bit of junk mail, reading it and putting it to one side, commenting only that the police would need to see it.

It was after they had eaten and had gone into the conservatory that Matthew picked the envelope up to reread its contents.

fUcKIng BitCH

It started again

THiS Is jUSt aNOtHEr reMinder tHAt yOu wILl be FUckIng dEAd By tHe enD oF tHe yEAr. KeEP on loOKing oVer yoUR shoulder, BiTcH, I'M still oUt tHEre FuCking wATChing yoU.

I AM YoUr fUcKiNg desTINy

"There's no mention that she came anywhere near the house," he said, sitting down next to Laura on the wicker two-seater. "I would have thought if she had been to the cottage, she would have said so to show how clever she is." He put the letter on the coffee table in front of them. "And she didn't use the word 'cow' this time."

Laura was smoking a cigarette and holding a gin and tonic.

She smirked. "As time passes, I'm beginning to think we really are dealing with a crank. Maybe there isn't a connection between what happened in Warwick and those letters," she said, the contempt she felt obvious in her eyes.

"What makes you say that?"

She shrugged. "I don't know but what I do know is that I'm now more annoyed than frightened. If the threats are for real, she has had every opportunity to have another go. We have been careful but regardless there have been times when the threat could have been carried out, but nothing has happened."

"So does that mean you're not taking what you heard on Monday seriously? You know, the intruder?"

"It could have been my imagination," she said. "As I told you, I was dozing and I could have been dreaming. Maybe I imagined the noises and, when I woke up, I thought they were for real."

"Possibly, but I still don't think we should become too complacent."

They had drunk a bottle of wine with their pasta and Matthew had to admit he was also feeling surprisingly relaxed. "You've got a hairdresser's appointment tomorrow, haven't you?" he asked.

Laura nodded. "I changed from Sally in Westerham to a place in Sevenoaks. Sally was having difficulty in making ends meet and decided to go back to Canterbury. Her parents live there."

"I'll take you in and drop you off, and then I'll go to the police with this latest threat and talk to Wen … er, Sergeant Carter, if she's there." He stole a glance at Laura but she didn't seem to have picked up on the fact that he was on the point of using Sergeant Carter's first name. It was an innocent mistake to make but one that could be so easily misinterpreted, and then he could have some explaining to do.

Stubbing out her cigarette, Laura said, "Fine. She may have something to tell us about Francesca-whatever-her-name-is."

"Possibly."

Laura didn't appear overly concerned about him seeing Wendy Carter on his own, which seemed to suggest that at least one of the concerns emanating from the previous Monday's meeting was unfounded.

Matthew rang the station straight after dropping Laura off at the hairdressers but was told that Sergeant Carter wasn't there. She had taken the rest of the week off. He swore under his breath but then he remembered he had her business card. He took it out of his wallet and rang her mobile.

Wendy Carter answered on the second ring. "Hello, Wendy Carter," she said.

"Wendy, it's Matthew Ryan. We agreed to meet again but when I rang the station they told me you –"

"Yes," she said, interrupting. "I took an extra few days off but didn't let you know because I knew you had my mobile number."

"There's been another letter," Matthew told her, stepping out of the way of a group of teenagers who were taking up nearly the whole pavement.

"Is it the same as the others?"

"Yes, well, if not the same it's very similar."

"Have you got it with you?"

"Yes, and I put it in a plastic bag."

He had taken one of the bags out of the drawer in the kitchen where Laura hoarded every conceivable size and shaped bag they got from all of their supermarket visits.

"All right," Wendy said matter-of-factly, "where are you?"

"I've just dropped Laura off at the hairdressers in the High Street. I'm parked in the Bligh's Meadow car park."

"Where are you now?"

"Just walking past Woolworths in the High Street."

"Okay, down the High Street from where you are, back towards the car park, there's a pub called The Oak Tree. I'll meet you in there in about fifteen minutes."

"See you there."

Matthew found the pub, ordered a coffee and took it to a corner table where he thought they would be able to have a bit of privacy. There weren't many people in the pub at that time anyway.

When Wendy arrived, he didn't recognise her at first. She had done something different to her hair and applied some make-up. As with the previous time he met her, the transformation from the severe uniformed official to an attractive young woman was significant. The faded blue jeans – the legs of which seemed to go on forever – exaggerated her height. On top, she was wearing a yellow shirt with pockets, raised seams, and rolled-up sleeves to just below her elbows. The make-up round her brown eyes contrasted beautifully with her black eyebrows.

"Hello, Matthew," she said, sitting next to him on the wooden settle.

"Hello," he said, "I didn't recognise you when you first came in." They both smiled. "How did the funeral go?"

"As all funerals go. Relatives who haven't seen each other for years ask why it takes somebody to die for everyone to get together. They make promises that they'll all meet up again under happier circumstances, each knowing that they never will, until the next funeral, that is." She looked up and smiled at the barmaid who brought her the coffee she'd ordered on entering the pub. "Thank you."

"What about weddings and Christenings? You're too young to be a cynic," Matthew told her.

"The truth isn't cynicism," she said. "How long have we got?" She saw Matthew frown, so she added, "… before you have to pick Laura up from the hairdressers?"

"I agreed to meet her in the Café Rouge at one o'clock."

Wendy looked at her watch. "We've got a couple of hours, then."

Matthew nodded, wondering why they needed so long.

"If it's all right by you, when we've drunk our coffees I would like to go somewhere a little more private because I want to talk to you completely off the record. Somebody I know might see us here." Matthew was just about to agree when she said, "In theory, I shouldn't take any evidence from you while I'm off duty, but I won't tell if you won't."

"Fine by," he said as he reached into his jacket pocket for the plastic bag.

Wendy put her hand on his arm. "Not here, later," she said.

Her fingers stayed against his arm for a few seconds and there was something quite intimate about her touch. He wondered whether he felt that way because up to that point she was officialdom, and by touching his arm it lowered a barrier – which ought to have remained between them – but only slightly.

"I gather nothing was found when the patrol car went to your house on Monday?" she asked, withdrawing her hand, but her eyes were still on his.

She was sitting very close to him on the settle and her thigh was touching his. He could smell the fragrance of her perfume. He decided he was being stupid but he couldn't help but ask himself if there was a hidden agenda in their meeting that was only known to Wendy Carter.

"No," he said. "The police car got there very quickly but the two police officers saw nobody suspicious and found nothing which suggested they had been an intruder in the garden."

"I see," Wendy said. "That's a pity: I was hoping that they would find something. We really are very short of anything to go on at the moment."

"What about Francesca, the woman from the ferry? You implied on Monday that you had something to tell me."

A few seconds passed during which Wendy searched his eyes for something but then said, "Yes, I have."

"And?"

"She was found dead in early June this year, having committed suicide," she told him.

Matthew didn't know how he should feel. Wendy's news was a shock but he wasn't sure why. On the one hand he believed he had – regardless of Laura's theories – saved Francesca's life on the ferry but on the other hand, if Francesca had committed suicide in June then ... he and Laura had been completely off the mark. After it was proven that Emily could not have been anywhere near Warwick when Laura was so nearly killed, Francesca – in their minds – had become their prime suspect.

"How?" Matthew asked quietly.

"It wasn't very nice, actually, not that any suicide is nice in reality."

"What did she do?"

"She hung herself and it was days before she was found," Wendy said.

Matthew frowned, not knowing why he had formulated his next

question in his mind. "Isn't that unusual for a woman?" he asked. "Hanging, I mean."

"It is. Grown women, unlike teenage girls, tend to go for an overdose or they slash their wrists, but Francesca Middleton-Smythe chose to hang herself."

"Francesca Middleton-Smythe," he repeated. "I didn't see anything in the papers."

"You wouldn't have done unless you were looking. Evidently it was in a couple of the Nationals but buried in among the usual trivia." Wendy reached into her shoulder bag for a tissue and she dabbed at the end of her nose. "Touch of hay fever. Sorry."

"Are you able to tell me anymore?" Matthew asked.

"You want all the gory details do you?" Wendy said, a flicker of a smile appearing at the corners of her mouth.

"Well, no, but after the incident on the ferry in March, I suppose I feel as though I am slightly responsible."

"Don't be," Wendy said. "Before you met her on the boat she had tried suicide once before in Germany but it was put down to a cry for help. Then, after you saved her life, she tried on two more occasions, and the second attempt resulted in her being sectioned and held in a psychiatric secure unit for a month or so. If she hadn't been released so quickly having been told that her mental state was a temporary blip, a simple aberration, she would probably be alive today."

"Was she just mentally disturbed or did she have cause?"

"Mentally disturbed is very polite, isn't it?" Wendy said. "But then you're that sort of person, aren't you? Was she a 'nutter' you mean?"

Matthew nodded and smiled, remembering quite vividly every second of his encounter with Francesca on the ferry from Calais.

"Yes," he said. "That's what I mean."

"Not originally, no. From what the Devon police found out and passed on to Warwickshire, she was married to an army officer. They had a little girl, Rebecca I think her name was. She was only five when she died of leukaemia in 1999. After Rebecca's funeral in the UK – she and her husband were in Germany at the time – Francesca stayed with her parents for quite a while. She was depressed and justifiably, and that would explain why she took an overdose. Her husband had gone back to Germany to continue with his tour. She rejoined her husband in late 1999 but, from what the police files say, some of which reached the papers, she never got over her daughter's death.

"When you met her on the boat, she had walked out on her husband. She had discovered that when he went back to Germany on his own, he'd started or continued an affair with one of the British teachers over there. I think it was in a place called Gütersloh. Anyway, it was too much for her. She didn't bother to pack anything: she just got in her car and drove. The suicide attempt you stopped was never reported –"

"I knew I should have done something about it at the time," Matthew said.

"Don't punish yourself, Matthew. You did more than most people would have done under the circumstances. A lot of people would have just walked away."

"But I should have reported it."

"What, and got involved?"

"I don't know," he said.

"She went back to her parents. Her father was, and still is as far as I know, a farmer down in Somerset. As I said, Francesca tried to commit suicide on two more occasions, both with overdoses. After the second attempt, she was committed and then released in May this year when she went back to her parents. She went missing on 1st June, her wedding anniversary, which also happened to be her thirty-second birthday. She was found, as I said, on 10th June." Wendy finished her coffee.

"Another?" Matthew asked.

"No, thanks, but let me finish telling you about Francesca and then we'll make a move."

"All right. Why did it take so long to find her?"

"When she went missing," Wendy said, "every inch of her father's farm was searched, and his immediate neighbours' farms, but the search wasn't wide enough. Finding her in a remote and almost derelict barn about fifty miles away in Devon wasn't what was expected. The land had come on the market and a prospective buyer was checking out what was on offer. He just happened to choose the right or, in his case, the wrong barn to go into. It hadn't been used for about twenty years. The roof had rotted and partly collapsed, the slates had blown off in various gales and inside it was full of two-foot high weeds and the odd rusting farm implement. That's where Francesca was found."

"You certainly got all the detail," Matthew said.

"The Devon police faxed me the full report."

"You said she'd hanged herself."

"That was the Coroner's verdict, yes. She killed herself while the balance of her mind was disturbed." Wendy said, but her tone suggested she wasn't convinced.

"You make it sound as though there were other possibilities," he suggested.

"Yes, you could say that. Evidently, there was some doubt initially. When they found her she was hanging from one of the remaining roof supports in the barn. She'd used the sort of rope you can buy in any hardware store and one of those multi-coloured collapsible boxes people have for storing things in the boot of their cars to stand on. Her feet were only just off the ground."

"So why were the police suspicious and are you sure you don't want another coffee, or even a drink?"

"No, honestly, I've nearly finished."

A few more people were beginning to drift into the pub and Matthew was pleased Wendy had suggested they go somewhere else. It had been at the back of his mind that if she felt she could tell him about Francesca's suicide over a cup of coffee, what else was there to tell.

"It was never established how Francesca had got to the barn," Wendy continued. "Her car was found parked in a multi-storey car park in Totnes, about fifteen miles away."

"She may have walked," Matthew suggested.

"What, fifteen miles just to commit suicide? Why didn't she choose something closer to home and simply drive there?"

Matthew shook his head. "I've no idea."

"Nor had anybody else … and then there were the mutilations. It appeared as though they were self-inflicted but there was an element of doubt."

"Mutilations?"

The barmaid had begun to look in their direction, and Matthew guessed it was because they had already made one cup of coffee last half an hour.

"One of the reasons why she was committed before she attempted suicide for the second time was because she had started mutilating herself. She was cutting her arms, legs and abdomen, not deeply, but sufficiently badly to leave scars. She was careful and hid what she was doing from her parents. When discovered she was completely naked, which is unusual on its own. Very few people who commit suicide take all their clothes off before doing whatever they have planned for themselves. Her clothes were found neatly folded in one corner of the barn. There was also evidence that she'd conducted self-mutilation before hanging herself. Her legs and thighs had deep lacerations and there was one very particularly deep wound across her abdomen about midway between her navel and the tops of her thighs. The cuts on her arms and legs were almost exactly as she'd done before, but the deeper wound, if self-inflicted, would have taken a lot of courage."

An image of Francesca hanging by her neck, her body mutilated, rushed into Matthew's mind, and he closed his eyes for a few seconds.

"So does suicide!" he said.

"Agreed, but with suicide people intend killing themselves, normally as painlessly as possible. The wound to her lower abdomen wasn't deep enough to kill her but she would have been in a lot of pain."

"Was a knife found?"

"Yes, a Stanley-knife by her clothes and there was a trail of blood from there to where she chose to hang herself, only about ten feet away, but there was still a trail."

"Fingerprints?"

"That's another thing. There was none on the knife and there were no gloves found at the scene. Her fingerprints should have been on the knife."

"So she drove to Totnes," Matthew said, "and walked fifteen miles from there to this barn where she took off all her clothes, mutilated herself with a Stanley-knife, but left no fingerprints, and hung herself from a beam on the opposite side of the barn, to be found by a property speculator ten days later?"

"In a nutshell, yes."

"Right, well, what can I say?"

He closed his eyes and shook his head, trying to rid himself of the image Wendy's description had created.

"There's not a lot –" Wendy was interrupted by the barmaid.

She reached for their empty coffee cups and asked, "Finished?" rather abruptly.

"Yes, thank you," Wendy told her, smiling sweetly.

"Anything else?" the barmaid – a rather plump young woman – enquired, again brusquely.

"No, thank you," Matthew said, "we're just leaving."

"Oh," the barmaid said and turned away.

"I must just pop to the loo before we go," Wendy advised Matthew. "I won't be a second."

As he watched Wendy retreating across the bar, Matthew's thoughts were understandably confused. The news was shocking but it asked more questions than it answered. He and Laura had had a doubtful short list of two – well three if Laura's ex-husband were included, but he had still not been mentioned to the police – and now there wasn't even a short list. Emily was no longer a suspect and Wendy's description of what had happened to Francesca and when, meant she couldn't have sent the third threatening letter. So it was now very unlikely she sent the first two letters or had anything to do with what happened to Laura in Warwick, and nor had she been watching the cottage from behind a dark-coloured VW Golf.

He closed his eyes and thought again about when he met Francesca on the ferry. Maybe, just maybe, if he had reported what had happened to her, she might still be alive today. If the authorities had known that she had attempted to throw herself from a cross-channel ferry, they would have reacted differently. Life is full of *if onlys* – Laura had reminded him often enough – and he was going to have to live with what he had been told. He could visualise the scene in the barn as though he had been there, but this time it was accompanied by another unanswered question which he asked Wendy as they were making their way across to the Bligh's Meadow car park.

"You implied that there was some doubt initially whether

Francesca had committed suicide," he said.

"I suppose I did, yes," Wendy said, opening her bag to look for her keys.

"So are you saying that murder wasn't discounted?"

Matthew looked across the top of the car at Wendy but she didn't make eye contact.

"Well?" he asked.

"Yes," she said, unlocking the door of her nearly new Vauxhall Vectra. "An open verdict was expected."

"That means that the cause of death isn't known, doesn't it?"

"Yes," Wendy said now looking at him

"So why wasn't the verdict left open rather than it being one of suicide?"

Wendy dipped down into the car without answering.

Once seated Matthew said, "So?"

"It appears the verdict was based on the lack of motive," Wendy said, putting the key in the ignition. "Although there were a number of unanswered questions, her history of suicide attempts and self-mutilation all pointed towards suicide on this occasion as well. Her parents said that they had become increasingly worried about her since she had been released from hospital." Wendy put both hands on the steering wheel and sighed. "Evidently she suffered from severe bouts of depression and was on any number of pills to try and improve her self-esteem. Her husband hadn't wanted to know before she was admitted to hospital, and although her parents told the police that she had forgiven him and wanted to go back to him, he wasn't interested. He had started divorce proceedings using desertion as the grounds. According to her parents, Francesca was devastated especially when she could have cited her husband's adultery as just cause for her to divorce him."

Wendy started the car and took the north exit from the car park out onto the Pembroke Road..

"Do you think things could have been different if I'd reported what had happened?"

Wendy looked across at him. "You're not going to start punishing yourself, are you? No, things would not have been different and I'm not just saying that. She was one very mixed-up lady, with good reason, and adding one attempt to the list would not have stopped what ultimately happened."

At the junction with the London Road, Wendy indicated right.

"Where are we going?"

"You don't feel threatened, do you? Sorry, I shouldn't have said that under the circumstances."

Matthew smiled. "Not unless you're putting yourself on the suspect list?" he said.

"What suspect list?" Wendy asked.

"My thoughts exactly," he said.

"There's a wildlife reserve not far from here ... have you been there?"

"Not that I know of."

"Oh, all right but as it's such a nice day, I thought we could go for a walk." Wendy checked her watch again. "It's only just over a mile and we've still got more than an hour. Don't read anything into this, but I do think it's important that I speak to you off the record and in total privacy."

"I would be lying if I said I wasn't slightly intrigued by what we are doing ... but going back to what you said about there not being a motive for any other person's involvement in Francesca's death, what about her husband?"

"Not a possibility. He was on exercise in Kenya from early April to the end of June. He didn't even come back for her funeral."

"All this was on her file?"

"We have to be extremely comprehensive and particularly careful about what is recorded. Even the most irrelevant points of detail can mean something when related to other matters and, historically, we have to be able to do exactly what I did with Francesca's file. Although a verdict is reached, we have to be able to reopen such files at any stage."

"Are you suggesting that might happen in Francesca's case?"

"No ... Fuck!" Wendy swerved as the driver of a car coming the opposite way misjudged the distance he needed to overtake. With a bit of expert driving, Wendy avoided what could have been a nasty accident. "Sorry about that," she said.

"No need to apologise. I should be thanking you," he said taking a deep breath and feeling the adrenalin rush.

"No, I meant for swearing."

"Swearing was quite appropriate under the circumstances."

"If I'd got his number, I'd call the station and get him stopped," she said.

"Can you do that?"

"All the time," she said, looking at Matthew and smiling. "Be warned. Nearly there."

Soon after joining the Bradbourne Vale Road, Wendy indicated left, turned off the main road and drove for a few hundred yards before going over a cattle grid into a car park in which there were only four other cars. She switched off the engine and peered out of the windscreen.

"The weather's holding and it's quite warm. Fancy a stroll?" she asked, opening her door.

"That's why we are here."

Matthew got out of the car and Wendy operated the central locking system from her side. "Let's go that way," she suggested, pointing at a track leading off through some trees towards a lake.

"No,' Matthew said. "I've never been here before."

"It's been open for quite a while and can get quite crowded but I like to come here when I need to think."

Wendy had left her shoulder bag in the car. She was walking by Matthew's side with her thumbs tucked into her pockets.

"And what is there for you to think about today?" he asked as he took off his lightweight jacket and put it over his shoulder.

"Not yet, Matthew. There's somewhere we can sit down just along here. There's only room for a couple of people, so it's quite private."

They strolled in silence for about another hundred yards before the main path turned away from the water. Wendy went in front of Matthew, leading the way down a narrower overgrown path through some shrubs and bushes that, after about ten yards, came to a very small stony beach. There was about a foot's drop down onto the stones. In the middle of this secluded spot, there was an ideally placed log.

"This used to be used by fishermen who couldn't be bothered to get a permit; it's now used by the police, namely me, to think."

Wendy sat down on the log before motioning for Matthew to sit next to her.

"It's a lovely spot," he commented.

For a while, they both looked out over the lake without saying anything. A couple of people were walking on the other side, but where they were sitting meant they were completely on their own. Matthew thought the situation rather incongruous, but no doubt Wendy would tell him why they were there when she was ready. He didn't have to wait long.

"What I am going to say is completely off the record, Matthew," she said, "that's why we are here. I shouldn't be here and neither should you. The investigation into the threats against Laura –"

Matthew interrupted. "Sorry to stop you straightaway, but from what you've just said I have a feeling I'm not going to like what you are going to say."

"No, I don't think you are, so do you want me to carry on?"

"We've come all this way and it would be a pity to waste the time so yes, I do want to hear what you have to tell me."

"As I was saying," Wendy said. "The investigation into the threats against Laura is not being conducted by the Kent police, and as a result this meeting would not be condoned in any way shape or form by my superiors. Even if we did have ownership of the investigation, the CID would be looking after it and, once again, my superiors would not agree with what I am doing. In fact, they would forbid it."

Wendy stretched her legs in front of her so that she could kick off her shoes.

"In that case," he said, still looking down at her feet, "before you say any more, are *you* sure *you* want to go on? I want to hear what you have to say but I wouldn't want to get you into trouble."

She thought for a moment. "Yes, I do want to. I hope my reasons will become apparent and acceptable as I tell you what I think you ought to know."

"I'll shut up and listen."

She turned towards Matthew and smiled, the backs of her fingers brushing against his arm. "You're a lovely man Matthew, but I don't think you know what's going on under your own nose."

"What do you mean?" he said, his brow furrowing.

"I thought you were going to shut up and listen," she said.

"Sorry."

"I started to ask you on Monday but I thought it the wrong time and place. I wanted to do some more digging and I also wanted to make sure, when we did meet, I was absolutely sure of my facts."

"As I said in the car, this all sounds intriguing."

"Matthew, shut up and listen, please. This is hard enough as it is. I first got to hear about you when I read the report submitted after you were told about Laura's accident. Later I saw Richards and Phillips in the canteen and commented that although their report was straightforward, they had put it together well. She is young and they are both relatively inexperienced, so they need all the encouragement they can get. The Police Service has so much red tape to contend with nowadays it can become very, very frustrating and we are losing quite a few youngsters because they spend more time filling in forms and writing reports than interfacing with the public, which was the reason why they joined in the first place. It's important, therefore, to give encouragement whenever possible, even when you don't believe in the system yourself. You made quite an impression on Richards and Phillips. They wished every person they came across was like you, but I had to point out that if they were, they would be out of a job –"

"I'm not as –"

"Matthew!"

"Sorry."

"They were particularly pleased when you asked for their first names. They knew it was against procedures when dealing formally with the public but they thought, under the circumstances, it would be all right. I did point out to them that it wasn't but I didn't give them a real ticking off. I was on duty when your call came in to say that you, or rather Laura, had received a threatening letter. Officially, I wasn't the one who should have come out to you but as soon as I heard the name I asked the duty inspector if I could take the call. I wanted to meet the lovely Saint Matthew in person."

Wendy bent down, picked up a stone, and threw it towards the water. A dog bounded through the bushes from behind them and followed the stone into the water.

"Charlie! Charlie!" a man shouted from behind them. "Where are you, Charlie?"

By this time, Charlie – a King Charles spaniel – was twenty yards out in the water, yapping and looking for a stone that he thought should have floated.

The man, still calling, also appeared out of the bushes.

"Oh, I'm sorry," he said, as he spotted Wendy and Matthew. "Saw Charlie come this way and …"

The man was probably in his mid-sixties and had an upright posture. His neatly trimmed hair was almost white as was his military-style moustache. He was wearing a check shirt with a cravat, cavalry twills and robust sparkling, although now slightly dusty, brown brogues.

"Sorry," he said again. "Charlie, come here, you little devil."

Charlie ignored his owner and continued yapping and swimming in circles searching for the stone.

"Know what to do," the man said. He bent down and picked up a stick that he threw towards the dog. Unfortunately, he was a little more accurate than he intended and it landed on the dog's head. The yapping became a yelp as Charlie disappeared under water, which brought an "Oops!" from the man.

Fortunately, Charlie recovered, grabbed the stick in his mouth and struck out for the shore. Once back on dry land, with the stick still in his mouth, Charlie shook himself, spraying Wendy and Matthew with a fine shower of dog smelling water. This occasioned another "Oops" from the man.

"So sorry," he added. "Come on, Charlie, let's leave these nice people alone."

Charlie dropped the stick in front of Matthew before looking up at him expectantly. The man produced a lead and fastened it onto Charlie's collar, muttering, "So sorry," again.

Then, with a final "So sorry," the man and Charlie, pulling against the lead, disappeared back into the bushes.

Wendy and Matthew burst out laughing.

"I'll give you an odds-on bet what he used to do for a living," Wendy suggested.

"Your bet's not accepted. Do you realise that neither of us said a word to either man or dog?"

"What was there to say? Anyway, he will be in deep water himself if he's caught. Dogs aren't allowed in this reserve."

Instinctively Matthew put his hand on Wendy's and squeezed.

She gently took her hand away. "Don't let's complicate things more than they already are," she said.

"I'm sorry," Matthew said. "I shouldn't have done that."

"You sound like our departing Colonel Blimp," she replied, making light of the matter.

Matthew didn't think Wendy had arranged the meeting for any other reason than to tell him what she'd yet to relate, but he'd acted as though they knew each other more than they did..

"No, I really am sorry. That shouldn't have happened."

"Maybe not but you only touched and squeezed my hand, so let's not get things out of proportion. Let's pretend it didn't happen at all and get on with the real reason we are here." Whether consciously or not, she moved a few inches further along the log. "As I was saying, I wanted to meet Saint Matthew. You were and are exactly as Gill Richards and Peter Phillips described you, but that's all I'm going to say. There's nothing worse than a man with an over-inflated ego."

"I'm still sorry," he said.

"Don't be," she said before pausing for a few seconds. "Matthew, I have to admit that when I first met her, I didn't take to Laura … I'm sorry to say that but I didn't. There was something about her that … how can I put it? She unnerved me. You know, the way you instinctively feel about somebody when you first meet them?" – her question was rhetorical – "I'm sorry, Matthew, but I didn't take to her at all." Wendy paused again but Matthew didn't interrupt. "Anyway, that apart, I was intrigued when one of you – it must have been you because I remember the look in her eyes when it was mentioned – told me she had been in the police force. I logged that away and whether it was out of bitchiness or not, I decided to carry out a few of my own investigations. I asked you on Monday what you knew about the reasons why she left the police but I didn't give you a real opportunity to answer. Can I ask that same question again?"

Matthew thought for a moment and frowned when he concluded that he genuinely didn't know, or thought he didn't know why she had left the police. As far as Wendy not taking to Laura, that was nothing new and it was something he and Laura had discussed. Her explanation was that other women immediately saw her as a threat.

"I'm not sure, Wendy," he said. "I know while serving she was studying for a law degree via the Open University and, in contrast, she was married to a man who got a certain satisfaction out of beating her up. They –"

"I knew she was married," Wendy said, "but ... no, you finish what you were going to say"

"Well ... they were divorced about eighteen months ago," he said while kicking himself for the slip up, but then he thought that maybe it was opportune. Laura's ex-husband hadn't been mentioned to the police, but now Emily and Francesca were no longer suspects, perhaps he ought to be.

"I think I'd assumed," he said, "Laura left the police so that she could have a clean break from some very unhappy memories and also to make use of her degree. A combination of her experience in the police and her degree lead her to set up her own investigating business."

"Although I knew she was married, from a professional point of view I could ask you why this ex-husband hasn't been mentioned before," Wendy said, "but we won't go there at the moment." She paused before asking, "So you base what you think were the reasons for Laura leaving the police on assumptions rather than fact?"

"You sound like a policewoman."

"I am a policewoman and a damn good one at that."

"I'll come quietly."

"That remains to be seen," she said, looking straight at Matthew, before adding, "So she has never said, nor even eluded to the fact, that she was asked to leave or, putting it a little more officially, invited to resign?"

"No," Matthew said very warily, shocked by the suggestion and its real meaning. "You can't be serious?"

"I'm afraid I am, Matthew, deadly serious."

"Why, for God's sake?" he asked.

"Why am I telling you or why was she asked to resign?"

"Both I suppose."

He could feel his heart thumping heavily in his chest. His mind was already telling him things he didn't understand and not sure he really wanted to know where this was leading.

"Before I say any more, I have to point out that nothing was ever proven one way or the other," Wendy said.

Matthew thought for a moment.

"I don't know you that well, Wendy, but I don't think you would be deliberately malicious, not under the circumstances, even if you didn't take to Laura when you first met her. She may have left the police under a cloud and not told me for her own reasons, but she is still faced with these threats against her life and she needs me to stand by her. We've been together too long for me to even think of deserting her now."

"I'm not suggesting you do desert her, as you put it, but if you'd prefer not to know what I discovered, you only have to tell me to stop," Wendy said. "We'll forget we ever came here and we'll go back to our formal public/police relationship."

"I think we've already gone too far for that to ever happen, don't you?" he said, and he meant it.

"Are you telling me you really want to know what I found out?" Wendy asked.

"Yes, I suppose I am."

Wendy moved on the log slightly so that she was facing him.

"Matthew, Laura was asked to resign from the Surrey Police Service because she made a number of allegedly false accusations against senior members of the force. She claimed that one Inspector raped her, that another sexually harassed her and that a female sergeant propositioned her while they were both on duty. Due to the lack of enforceable evidence, none of her accusations came to anything. She left the claim of rape until two months after it supposedly happened, the sexual harassment couldn't have happened when she said it did and the female sergeant was, and as far as I know still is, very happily married with two young children." Wendy paused. "I'm sorry, Matthew, but my informant with the Surrey lot believes that Laura … that Laura is a compulsive liar."

Wendy waited for some reaction from him, but other than looking at her in total disbelief, he couldn't say anything. He wasn't just stunned he was mortified by what he had been told.

When he didn't say anything Wendy added, "As I implied, none of what I've said was proven either way but Laura's position in the police became untenable. In other words, nobody would willingly team up with her. She was asked to resign and, after telling the world she was going to sue for unfair dismissal, she eventually went as quietly as a lamb, leaving everybody to draw their own conclusions."

Matthew sat in silence. He looked over the lake as the words 'compulsive liar' whirled round and round in his mind – Laura wasn't being accused of simply lying, she was being called a compulsive liar. It was like an illness. It was like a drug. One set of lies create more lies and, without them, the liar has difficulty in surviving.

They are sick and thrive on lying because, to them, lies are the truth and the truth is a lie. Life is one big lie. Everything they do could be a lie; everything they say could be a lie. It didn't matter if Wendy's informant had got the description wrong, he or she could just as easily have said Laura was a pathological liar, or a sociopath.

They were just labels.

The bottom line was that Laura might not be what she seemed.

According to Wendy Carter, Laura was a proven liar.

Why else would she resign without seeking advice or going to a tribunal? Surely if she believed the accusations she had made were the truth then she wouldn't have left the police without putting up a damn good fight. It was in her nature so her actions – or lack of them – seemed contradictory.

His mind was racing as he tried to remember things that Laura had said which later proved to be wrong but there was nothing. If she were a compulsive liar then how had she lived with him for so long without him detecting something in her behaviour that might have warned him?

"There's ... there's no chance that your informant may have got it wrong?" he asked quietly, not wanting to hear Wendy's answer but wishing she was going to say something in Laura's defence.

"I'm sorry, Matthew," she said, "I know the guy who told me what had happened very well, and he was with the Surrey Police

Service when Laura was with them. He served in the same station for a while. Nobody but nobody who was there at the time has a good word to say about her. I think you, and maybe the rest of us, have been well and truly deceived."

Initially he didn't connect the two events but suddenly out of his very confused mind came the realisation that maybe there was something that would suggest Laura had lied to him and to the police.

"So," he said hesitantly, "are you saying that these threats to her life are also lies? Are you saying she's making them up, that she is the author of the threats against her?"

Wendy looked at him and he could see in her eyes an understanding of what he must be going through. "I don't know for sure but …" she said slowly. "But I … I would say so, yes, they could be lies."

"But I've seen them, you've seen them," Matthew said, reaching into his jacket pocket before passing a crumpled plastic bag to Wendy. "And there's the latest one."

Wendy took the bag but didn't even look at it before putting it in her own pocket. "I think, and Matthew this is currently just an opinion not a fact, but I think you are right, Laura may be the author of her own threatening letters."

He shook his head in disbelief as he pondered the ramifications of what Wendy had just said. He had been deceived; they had all been deceived. Other words rushed into his mind: swindled, conned, tricked, double-crossed, duped. but none of the words was adequate enough to describe how he felt.

But why?

Why would she do it?

Was there truth in anything Laura had told him?

How does somebody who gets their kicks out of lying become a private investigator? People pay good money – lots of good money – for the truth. Then again, maybe the truth isn't what some people want to hear; maybe lies are more acceptable … maybe Laura was selective; perhaps she told the truth when it suited her. She couldn't have been lying to him all time. He hadn't been looking for lies but surely if she had been lying then he would have known.

Had she lied to him about Emily?

Everything that had happened since he first met Laura in her office over a year ago rushed round in his mind. Had she been lying from the outset? If what Wendy had told him was true, there was no telling what he could believe and what he couldn't ... but why would Laura want to lie in the first place?

It was equally inconceivable, but could Wendy be lying?

She was an experienced police officer; she had no reason to lie. If he could say that about Wendy whom he hardly knew, why was he so ready to believe that Laura – the woman he had asked to marry him – was a liar? Was there anything he could pinpoint that would give him even a modicum of proof either way? From the very beginning their relationship had been built on trust. Why would she deliberately introduce falsified death threats into their lives when everything else to that point had been so normal?

"Have you told the Warwickshire police what you have just told me?" he said, his apprehension evident.

"No, not yet," Wendy said.

"Thank God. I –"

"Let me qualify the reason," Wendy said, interrupting him.

"Yes, sorry."

"Because she was asked to resign it meant she was considered no longer suitable for police service, but she did resign and so there was no disciplinary action taken against her. As I said, nothing was proven either way although opinions were formed and expressed."

"But if you think the threatening letters ..."

"Yes, I'm afraid I am duty bound to tell my superiors what I now know, and they will tell their opposite numbers up in the Midlands. What they do with the information is up to them, but I think they will find it difficult to prove, once again, that the evidence – the threatening letters – is false. Laura, if indeed it is her, has been very careful. At the moment there is no proof she put those threatening letters together and the Warwickshire Police won't be able to prosecute for wasting police time without the evidence."

Matthew slumped forward, his head in his hands.

"Fuck!" he said, "Fuck! Fuck! Fuck!"

He felt Wendy's arm go round his shoulders. He wanted to bury his head against her.

Why?

Why, if Wendy's suspicions were true, why did Laura need to lie?

He felt so stupid, so utterly humiliated.

"What ... what about Warwick?" he asked, lifting his head. "Surely she didn't lie about what happened there?"

It was a glimmer of hope.

"No, of course that happened. I don't think she would have deliberately walked in front of a moving car," Wendy said. "But once again, and this is only my opinion, I think she may have used the fact that the police thought it was deliberate. In reality it was probably some misguided youngster who temporarily lost control of a powerful car which resulted in it looking like a deliberate act."

"So, what you are saying is that she manufactured all three of the letters. She posted the second threatening letter so that it would arrive at the hotel in Penang, and then on our return when we all thought things had gone quiet, she posted the third letter. Is that right?"

"They are all possibilities, yes," Wendy said.

"And when I was with you and I got that worrying phone call from Laura, in actual fact there was nobody prowling around outside the cottage and trying to get in. She fabricated the entire situation and lied."

"Yes, I am sorry, but that is what I think."

"But why? Why would she do such a thing?"

"That I don't know."

"It's all so incredible, if you weren't sitting there and telling me all of this I would think I was dreaming, but ..." Matthew stopped and said, "Hang on a minute, the first letter, that arrived while she was in hospital in Sevenoaks. How could she have put that together?"

Wendy smiled ruefully. "I don't know, Matthew, but maybe, just maybe the accident in Warwick was coincidental. Maybe she'd actually planned for something else to happen."

Matthew shook his head. "I really can't get my brain to accept what you've told me," he said. "Even before she was injured – and she could so easily have been killed – you are suggesting that from the day she moved in with me we have been living a lie, her lies?"

"No, I'm not saying that at all Matthew. Something may have triggered her behaviour. It could be that up to that point – whatever it might have been – she was perfectly normal."

"What the hell am I going to do?"

"I don't know," Wendy said. "But I had to tell you before I told anybody else, officially that is. If you found out that the Warwickshire police were dropping their investigations due to the lack of evidence, you could have carried on living with a compulsive liar without knowing. I hope you don't think it wrong and unprofessional of me, but I had to do what I thought was for the best."

"No. I understand why you told me," he said. "And I respect the fact that you are stepping outside officialdom to do so ... I just hope you won't get into trouble."

"Not unless you tell somebody," she said, smiling ruefully.

"No fear of that," he told her. He shook his head as he said, "Do you know what I do for a living, Wendy?"

"No, Matthew, but I'd like you to tell me."

"I advise other people how to behave, how to manage their lives. I am a continuous improvement consultant. I lecture people on how to improve their management techniques. I am supposed to understand human behaviour. It's a fucking farce, isn't it?"

"Come here."

Wendy pulled Matthew towards her and he buried his face against her neck and shoulder, inhaling her smell, wallowing in the temporary security it gave him.

He knew he was being weak.

Was Laura really a compulsive liar?

Chapter Nineteen

"Tell me one last thing before you drop me off, Wendy," Matthew said as they approached Sevenoaks twenty minutes later. After such a serious disclosure, he needed the time to take on board the detail and its possible aftermath: Wendy recognised his need.

"If I can," she replied, as they approached Pembroke Road.

"When you phoned me in Edinburgh and spoke to Laura instead, what did you tell her about what Emily had said after she'd been seen by the police?"

"I was waiting for you to ask, but you had to ask before I could tell you. I think I've ruined your day, and perhaps your life, enough in the last couple of hours."

Wendy stopped at the traffic lights, and looked at Matthew. "She was understandably livid at being accused of deliberately running somebody down," she said. "Her exact words were ... are you sure you want to hear this?"

"Yes, I may as well know all of it."

"She said, 'Tell that bastard ex-husband of mine and that lying slut of a female he's living with that they can both rot in hell'."

Matthew needed a couple of seconds for the words to be absorbed. If he had been Emily, he would have said exactly the same thing. "Those were the precise words you told Laura on the phone last week when we were in Edinburgh?" he asked.

"Yes, Matthew, those were the exact words." Wendy said turning left into Pembroke Road. "I'll drop you in Bligh's Meadow, if that's all right."

"Yes, that's fine, thank you" he said.

"Laura knew you were coming to see me, didn't she?" Wendy said as she took the right filter for the entrance to the car park.

"Yes, she did, but she won't know what you found out about her On the other hand she will know that it is likely you will have told me the truth about Emily?"

Wendy waited until she had parked in the first available slot, and switched off the engine before replying.

"Compulsive liars believe their lies are the truth. It's an illness, Matthew, but I'm sure in your line of work you know far more about it than I do about such things. Laura feels perfectly safe with the version of the events she has given you because that is what she believes really happened. What I told her your ex-wife had actually said will be, in her mind, a pack of lies."

Wendy moved the sun visor down and checked her appearance in the mirror.

"I suppose there could be no law degree," Matthew suggested. "And there were no beatings from her husband and maybe there wasn't even a husband."

Wendy closed the visor and nodded. "There was a husband but no record of reported abuse, not everything in her life will be a lie. If it were, she simply couldn't exist."

Matthew fell silent, trying to think of some way he could just walk away from his own existence but with little hope of finding a new one.

In the last couple of hours his world had fallen apart.

Again.

The supposed threats had been bad enough, but to find out they were part of some devious web of intrigue, a concerted effort by Laura to create a situation where she would be the only one to gain – but gain what? What did she hope to achieve from her lies? Did she do it because she craved attention?

He remembered some years ago listening to a lecture by an visiting American who talked about something called Histrionic Personality Disorder, a condition whereby a person acts in an excessively emotional and dramatic manner, including obsession with physical appearance, extreme extroversion, and inappropriate sexually seductive behaviour just to get attention. There was also the Münchausen syndrome, but that was to do with feigning disease, illness or psychological disorders to gain attention ... but why was he thinking like that, why was he trying to find a label to pin on Laura?

He checked his watch; they had agreed to meet in Café Rouge at two o'clock for a late lunch. He had ten minutes.

"Wendy, thank you for taking me into your confidence, I didn't like what you had to say but I appreciate why you told me. At least I know where I stand. It's what I'm going to do about it that worries me now."

"I understand." Wendy reached over the handbrake and put her fingers against Matthew's leg.

"I'm sorry for what happened at the lake."

"Don't be silly, I've just done the same, we're both tactile people that's all." Wendy's fingers left his leg and went to his chin, turning Matthew's face towards her, she leant over and brushed her lips against his. "There you go," she said, "now I've made it much worse." Her smile disappeared. "Knowing what I had to tell you and the effect it would have, other complications like this, if there are to be any, will have to wait." She looked deeply into his eyes. "What I have done today would be considered very unprofessional by some, and others would go so far as to classify it as misconduct. I would say I did it because you had a right to know before people outside your life who don't know you, attempt to influence it. I have not broken any rules because I am a woman first and a –"

"There's no need to justify to me what you've done, Wendy. All I can say is thank you once again for being honest and the risks you took to tell me."

"There's no need. If there's to be another time when perhaps we can talk about something else then … as I said, I'm a woman first."

"I would like that," he said.

Matthew reached for the door release.

"What are you going to do?" Wendy asked.

He stopped and faced her. "Do you know, I haven't the faintest idea."

As Matthew pushed the door open and got out of the car, Wendy said, "You've got my mobile number and I've got yours. If you need me as a friend, ring me."

"And if I need you officially?" he asked, leaning back into the car.

"You'll find me at the station," she said. "Ask for Sergeant Carter," she added smiling.

"Thanks again."

Matthew closed the door, took a deep breath and walked across the car park towards Café Rouge.

But what was he really walking towards?

Laura was already in the café when he got there.

There was a cup of coffee in front of her and two or three plastic shopping bags were hanging from the back of her chair. As Matthew walked across the café, he had to admit that she looked stunning. Her hair was shorter than he'd seen it before and beautifully cut, it divided evenly either side of her forehead so that it framed her large blue-green eyes and her small ears were now on full view.

His heart suddenly went out to her.

Why, he thought, as he crossed the final few feet to the table, *does somebody who has your looks, your mind and your body, and who could have anything she wanted, live in a world of lies?*

He felt compassion for her and for himself because he was the one who was going to have to shatter that world. If everything was true, she not only needed professional help but also handling very carefully. Getting her the right sort of help would take time. There were hidden and unknown depths to cope with before anything else could even start to happen.

"Hello, Matthew! What do you think?" Laura asked, lifting her hands to her hair.

He bent down and kissed her. "I think it looks fantastic but why the change?"

He sat down.

"I've ordered the *croquettes d'églefin*, is that okay? We both loved their fishcakes the last time we were in here," she said.

"Yes, that's fine."

"I thought that with everything that's going on, I needed to inject some fresh ideas into our lives, so I decided my hair should come first, you always say I've got pretty ears. We're also going to start taking more exercise and eating out more," she told him with great enthusiasm. "Anyway, that's enough about me and my ideas, how did you get on with Sergeant Carter? Was it her you saw?"

Matthew nodded. "Yes. Actually she'd been off for a few days, had to go to a family funeral."

"And what did she say?"

The waiter arrived, asked Matthew what he would like to drink and told them their *croquettes* would be about ten minutes. Matthew ordered a beer.

"What did she say?" Laura repeated her question when the

waiter had moved away.

Laura looked at him over the top of her coffee cup.

"There's not a lot she could say," he said. "The latest threat was really no different to the others. She said she would send it to the Warwickshire police and see what they made of it."

He looked round the restaurant so that he didn't have to make eye contact. He hadn't had time to decide what he should do so he felt that by behaving normally would give him that time ... but he had no idea how much time he was going to need.

"What about the other things? The attempted break-in and the VW Bruce saw?"

Matthew closed his eyes but hopefully not so that she noticed. He'd put the piece of paper Bruce had given him, together with the number of the car he'd seen, in with the latest letter. After what he'd been told, mentioning it to Wendy Carter hadn't even crossed his mind.

"Oh," he said, thinking quickly, "she thought it unlikely that there would be a connection between the two but they would look into it anyway."

It was Laura's turn to shake her head. "I would agree with her, as I said, I probably dreamt it all anyway. They won't arrest me for wasting police time, will they?"

Matthew wanted to shout at her.

He wanted to scream at her, "Stop it! Stop it! Stop it! Come out of this fantasy world and let me help you," but instead he said, "No, it was too real for you or for me to ignore. You were obviously scared witless when you phoned me."

Was he only helping her by playing along with her lies? If that's what they were. He couldn't just barge in, call her a liar and tell her to get the hell out of his life.

"She didn't say anything else?" Her eyes narrowed slightly as she asked her question.

"What about?" he said, delaying his answer so that he could think. The need to be on his guard, to come up with a plan ... to come up with anything, was all happening too quickly.

"I don't know," Laura said, a note of irritation creeping into her voice. "Did she have any more news of ... I don't know, Francesca whatever-her-name is, for example?"

"They can't find her," Matthew lied.

"So it could still be her?"

"It's a possibility," he said.

"They're useless aren't they? The police, they're useless?"

"You should know."

Laura's eyes widened. "Why?"

"Well you were one of them."

"Oh, I see." She relaxed. "Yes, I suppose in saying that I'm saying I was useless as well, with emphasis on *was*." She smiled. "But I have other talents, don't I?"

Matthew felt her toes rubbing against his calf.

His beer and the meals arrived.

"You certainly do," he said as the waiter withdrew from the table.

"And," Laura suggested, picking up a chip with her fingers and nibbling at it, "we'll try one of them out as soon as we get back to the cottage."

"If you insist," he said, attempting a smile but it was a weak effort.

She had changed the subject and ordinarily he would have put it down to Laura being Laura, but now he was suspicious of every word she said.

"Why should I have to insist? Since when have you ever resisted my advances?" she asked, pouting.

Since I found out about what you really are, Matthew thought. "Because I know resistance is futile," he replied, smiling.

"Correct! So what else did you do this morning? I literally got out of the salon only a few minutes ago. I was going to ring you earlier but didn't want to interrupt anything."

"I went to the publishers after the police station," he lied again.

The draft brochure was still in the boot of his car.

"And afterwards I went for a walk round town," he added.

"You must have been bored silly."

"No, not at all," he said. He was tempted to add: "*The last thing I was, was bored.*"

"Matthew, what's wrong? You haven't eaten anything yet and you seem miles away. Is there something you're not telling me?"

"No, no, I suppose I'm just a little tired. I didn't sleep too well last night."

"You're not coming down with something, are you? You haven't got what I had on Monday?"

Laura drained her coffee cup.

Something about the way she was looking at him suggested she knew he had discovered rather more than he was letting on. Whether it was the truth or a lie depended on who was saying what. However, he might be looking for something he thought ought to be there but wasn't. It was as though she was on the other side of a very thin piece of glass. He could see every feature: her lips, her dimples, her eyes, and yet he knew if he reached out to try to touch her and get into her mind, his attempt would fail.

"No, I don't think so. It's just tiredness," he said.

To show willing, he picked up his fork and started eating, although his stomach was rebelling against any intake of food.

"Come on, cheer up," she said smiling, but there was still that look in her eyes.

"As I said, I'm just a bit tired."

"Is everything the same for next week? The last three days, I think you said."

"Yes. It's Birmingham on Wednesday and Thursday, and then Stafford on Friday."

"What is it this time?"

"It's an IT Company, they call themselves Prospects for All, and their headquarters is in Birmingham. They want to restructure and they've asked me to look at their ideas and, if I agree with them, how best the restructuring should be implemented."

"So you haven't got any lecturing to do this time?"

"No, well not until Friday. In Stafford it's a construction company who want me to give the standard package to middle management. We'll travel up there after I've finished in Birmingham on Thursday."

Laura rarely asked what he actually did at the various seminars he ran, so he wondered what had generated the interest. Was he really now going to question everything she now said and asked?

The answer was probably, yes.

"Stafford doesn't sound very exciting."

"I'm sure you'll find something to do. I should be finished by four at the latest."

"Anything's better than sitting at home on my own."

Although he had reacted differently when he was with Wendy Carter, Matthew wasn't yet ready to believe everything he had been told but it would be necessary at some stage to broach the subject ... when the time came he would have to do it with sensitivity and support. If there was any truth in the accusations, Laura might deny everything but it was what she would do after the denials that really worried him.

He didn't want to set any traps but – if it came to that – that is what he might have to do ... a simple test that he hoped she passed with flying colours. How often do you read about the bullying of loyal individuals by the very organisation to which they showed such devotion and just because they told the truth? For this very reason, he was willing to fight for Laura and, in so doing, give her the benefit of the doubt.

He was aware he could be in denial himself and she could be guilty as charged but believing in her for now was the better option. Treating her as though he didn't believe what he'd been told may just mean they could find a way out of whatever might exist, and once outside looking in it could be that the least amount of long term harm was done.

During the drive back to Westerham, he decided that although he was grateful to Wendy Carter for doing what she thought best, the weight of the responsibility now placed well and truly on his shoulders was enormous. There was actually no proof that Laura had produced the threatening letters, nor that she had made up the attempted break-in the previous Monday, and that the hit-and-run in Warwick hadn't been deliberate – although she had never said it was.

Similarly, there was no proof that the accusations Laura had made against the Surrey police weren't true ... Wendy had reiterated that. Maybe to reduce the mud slinging, the hierarchy in the Surrey police had closed ranks and finally managed to drum her out of the service. All those accused were senior enough to be able to do what was necessary to cover their own backs and at the same time ensure that the source of the problem went away quietly.

He accepted that Laura had lied to him about what Wendy Carter had said to her in Edinburgh – that was a fact – although she may have had her reasons. So maybe that was where he should start. There was also her law degree: its validity would be easy to check. Whether she had a degree or not was minor compared with the other things.

Wendy hadn't said when she was going to tell her superiors about what she had discovered but, as it was Friday, it probably wouldn't be until the following Monday. It could be a few days or maybe even weeks before the Warwickshire police decided what they would do next. If there wasn't any proof, placing their investigations on hold or closing the file were theoretically, their only options. It would also depend on what priority they had given the case. There hadn't been any progress because, other than discovering proof that Laura was her own worst enemy and needed professional psychiatric help, what else could they conclude? If she had a psychiatric problem, she needed psychiatric help, not prosecution or further persecution.

Regardless, whatever Laura was or wasn't, she was sitting in the car next to him, her feet up on the dashboard, her skirt having fallen almost to the tops of her thighs, taking in the scenery.

And she was smiling.

She looked gorgeous and it was impossible to believe that she could be the author of malicious lies and intimidation.

The weather had improved after lunch.

When Wendy and Matthew had been by the lake it had been warm enough but it had looked slightly threatening to the west. Now the sky was almost cloudless and, if the weather report on the radio playing quietly in the background was anything to go by, they were in for a good few days and especially a good weekend.

Matthew rather wished the future in other areas appeared as promising. In the short term, he could behave as though nothing had happened.

The long term could be a different matter.

He prayed that wouldn't be the case.

"You were very quiet during the drive home," Laura told him as she led the way to the front door of the cottage. He was behind her carrying her purchases. "Are you still feeling tired and bit groggy?"

Before Matthew could answer, she put the key in the lock, opened the door and skipped down the hall to turn the house alarm off.

Taking Laura's purchases into the kitchen, he put them on the breakfast bar before flicking on the kettle for a cup of tea. Before they went out he had deliberately left the morning's post on the table at the far end of the kitchen, but he did have a quick look at the five or six envelopes to see if there was anything important. Of course, one of the things he looked for then was another threatening letter, but that was before they went out so he hadn't known what he was going to be told by Wendy Carter. Now, with so many possibilities playing on his mind, he looked across at the envelopes with greater scepticism. He went over and checked the envelopes again. The letters all looked official and none addressed to Laura.

As he played with one of the envelopes between his fingers, he wondered which word processor Laura would have used to type the envelopes and where she was when she laboriously cut out and stuck the individual letters on the paper. Because each threat would have taken a long time to put together, it must have been while he was away. He shook his head: it couldn't be her – there would have been some evidence, he just didn't believe it.

The first letter continued to nag away at his mind. How on earth, when she was in hospital, had she managed to post the letter for it to arrive so soon after the accident? Wendy had suggested that the accident was a coincidence and Laura having posted the first letter the previous week, had planned something else to happen.

It all seemed so incredible and with no explanation as to why she would need to do anything like that in the first place.

Then again, maybe out of necessity he was once again clutching at straws, looking for anything that might suggest Laura was completely innocent. After all, it was what he really wanted.

He was still shaking his head in disbelief when Laura came into the kitchen.

"Anything for me?" she enquired, reaching up into the cupboard for a couple of mugs.

"No, it's the usual junk mail and bills."

When Laura stopped work, she also stopped paying her contribution into their joint account and Matthew was picking up all of the bills again. However, work had been quite lucrative and they were out of the financial sticky patch he thought they were in a few months ago.

"Will you make the tea? I want to try on some of the clothes I bought and show them to you." Without waiting for an answer, Laura grabbed the bags from the breakfast bar and disappeared.

Matthew made the tea and opened some of the envelopes.

Half way through, he stopped and looked out of the window.

Could anything be more normal?

A couple return from town and while the man made the tea and checked the mail, the woman goes upstairs to put on, and show off, something she had bought.

It was all so normal. He shook his head again.

Perhaps it would be better if he didn't do or say anything? He ought to dismiss everything he had been told.

Other than the threatening letters, there really had been nothing else. Nobody had been hurt other than Laura herself. When Wendy had told him what she believed had happened, his immediate thoughts were about what a fool he'd been and how he'd been deceived. He had thought about his own humiliation and given no thought at all as to why Laura had felt the need for the attention.

She hadn't done him any harm. In fact, the opposite applied. She had taken his boring life, turned it upside down and gently lowered him back to the sort of existence he'd never experienced before. She had been patient in every respect. All right, there was the odd argument brought about mainly because of his attitude towards Emily, but that had all been his fault. In many ways, Laura had been the one who had suffered because of him. Could that be the reason why she might have gone to such extremes to seek attention.

Had he really been that blind?

Maybe, when she left the Surrey police, she didn't go through with the unfair dismissal claim because she knew she would be fighting against the system, a system she knew she couldn't beat?

He sipped his tea thoughtfully.

A small cough alerted him to the fact that Laura was leaning against the doorjamb.

"Well?" she said.

Her unblinking dark eyes stared at him as she let a wicked grin creep onto her lips. As she posed with one arm extended towards the ceiling and a long-stemmed red rose between her teeth, she tilted her head slightly to one side and moved her leg so that one knee appeared from the folds of the sheer red full-length negligee she was wearing.

"Well?" she repeated. "Are you going to close your mouth and tell me what you think?"

"Are you trying to give me a heart attack?" he said as all thoughts of what he might be living with disappeared.

"Not yet," Laura said, "not until we've discussed further life insurance." She dropped her arm and added, "It's satin and lace. Aren't you going to say whether you like it? I'm beginning to feel a little stupid. It is only mid-afternoon."

"You look ... well, extremely sexy and fabulous are the only words I can think of."

"I told you things were going to change and this, after my hair, is the first of them."

"So who makes the next move?" Matthew asked.

"I've done my bit, so I suppose it's up to you. You know me. Personally I couldn't care less whether it's the middle of the afternoon or not!"

Moving across the kitchen towards her, Matthew decided his meeting with Sergeant Wendy Carter hadn't happened.

Chapter Twenty

About an hour later, they were sitting opposite each other in the conservatory drinking champagne rather than the stale tea Matthew had made earlier.

"That was something else," he told Laura, meaning every word. "You must be the most amazingly sensual woman on this earth."

After showering, Laura had dried and brushed her hair and it was exactly as it had been when he had met her in the café. She was wearing the white bathrobe she had brought back from Penang and although it was too big for her, she looked sensational.

Her expression was one of utter contentment.

"What's with the *must be*?" she said, smiling. "It's remarkable what a bit of imagination can do, isn't it?" she commented, as she lifted the champagne flute to her lips, the wicked look still in her eyes.

If for whatever reason, he had resisted the earlier temptation, he would have unnecessarily hurt her feelings and not satisfied his own desires. He hadn't known how he was going to feel when she finally collapsed on top of him but the feeling of love that exuded from every pore was more than he'd hoped for. She was his and she had every right to expect him to protect her from the outside world, and that is what he would do.

Nothing was ever proven: they had been Wendy's words.

Looking up at Laura, he wondered why he had listened to let alone accepted the lies about her. In his own mind, he had overreacted to Laura's supposed guilt.

None of her accusers had been living with her for over a year, so how could they know her and what she was capable of doing?

They were the liars, not Laura.

Matthew finished his fourth glass of champagne and reached for the nearly empty bottle from the ice bucket.

"It's only just after five o'clock, I think Bruce would say we are decadent and probably even immoral," Laura said as she leant forward so that Matthew could refill her glass.

"I hope he wasn't peering in through the window doing his

neighbourly bit, thinking we were out." Matthew could feel the champagne whirling and whooshing round in his mind.

"I think there's more to Bruce than meets the eye. I think he fancies me." The look was back in her eyes.

"Most men fancy you," he told her.

"I'm quite happy with you, thank you. You are tall, dark and handsome – well, five feet eleven-ish, dark-ish and handsome-ish. What more could a girl ask for? I've always wanted to see you with a moustache or even a beard. Would you grow one for me?"

Matthew smiled. He did have a beard when he and Emily first met. Why he ever grew it in the first place was beyond him, maybe he was going through a personality crisis, or just a simple phase.

The beard lasted three months. He could still remember Emily's exact words. "You either take that excuse for a hedgehog off your face or I intend withdrawing all overseas aid and imposing sanctions." He had gone straight to the bathroom and shaved it off.

"I don't think it would suit me," he told Laura.

"How do know until you've grown one?"

Lifting the nearly burnt out cigarette from the ashtray to her lips, she squeezed her eyes closed and puckered her nose when she realised she was sucking on the burning filter.

Matthew smiled again ... she looked like a little girl, a little innocent girl.

"I had one once and I was told it didn't suit me," he said.

Laura stubbed out the burning filter in the ashtray. "Oh," she said, rubbing her fingers together to get rid of some ash. "Who told you it didn't suit you. Was it Emily?"

"Yes, she said it looked like a hedgehog." It was the first time Emily's name had been mentioned when he hadn't detected resentment in Laura's expression.

It was progress, but Laura's next question put him immediately back on his guard. "What did Sergeant Carter tell you about Emily?"

He thought for a moment before saying, "She told me about Emily having lunch in Kenilworth and that she had lots of witnesses." He had to think quickly, her question was leading him away from the direction he'd decided was right.

"I told you that," Laura said a little too sharply. "No, I mean about Emily wanting to see us."

Matthew maintained eye contact, trying to read something, anything, into Laura's expression. He wanted to know the reason behind her question: if he told her the truth, would she call Wendy Carter a liar?

On the other hand, would she admit that she had lied? He was going backwards but Laura had asked the question.

Closing his eyes, he said slowly, "She told me that Emily had said, 'Tell that bastard ex-husband of mine and that lying slut of a female he's living with that they can both rot in hell'."

He took a deep breath and opened his eyes. Laura held his gaze for a few seconds before she lowered her head and looked straight into her champagne glass.

"The cow!" she said between clenched teeth.

"Why did you tell me that Emily wanted to see us?" Matthew asked. He'd drunk too much champagne and it wasn't the right time but it was Laura who was forcing the pace, not him.

"Because I knew you wouldn't go," Laura said softly, her fingers now playing with a loose thread on her dressing gown.

"I'm sorry I didn't catch all of that." He had heard exactly what she had said but he wanted Laura to repeat it because it was what he really wanted to hear.

Lifting her head, she repeated what she had said, "*Because I knew you wouldn't go.*" Tears were forming in her eyes.

"I'm sorry, Laura but why, when it appears that Emily wants us both in hell, do you tell me she wants to see us? It's the complete opposite."

"I've ... I've just said, *because ... I ... knew ... you ... wouldn't ... go.*" She spaced the words out and said them as though she was speaking to a child.

"And ... I ... don't ... understand," Matthew said slowly and, he hoped, quietly.

Laura lit another cigarette and went back to worrying the loose thread. "I didn't know what to tell you. I knew the truth would be very painful for you ..."

"But it would have been the truth, wouldn't it?"

"Let me finish," Laura said irritably. "I knew the truth would be very painful for you, so I ... I thought it would better to make you think she'd forgiven you."

"But what if I'd decided to go?"

"I thought I would have sufficient influence over you to be able to persuade you not to go. Nothing would have been gained by seeing her, but you would have still thought she had forgiven you." Laura stubbed the cigarette out, her annoyance obvious. "Why didn't that cow of a policewoman have the sense to understand?"

Because she was telling me for a different reason, he thought. *She was telling me as an example of the way you can lie, Laura.*

Matthew closed his eyes. He needed to think.

If Wendy was right, he would have expected Laura to deny that she had ever been told anything about *bastard husbands*, *sluts* and *rotting in hell*. Surely, he should have expected but not wanted an immediate denial?

No, what Laura had said was considerate and, yes, she may well have been able to persuade him not to go and see Emily. The temptation would have been very strong but there was nothing to gain. A simple apology would have been inadequate when balanced with the trauma – because that's what it would have been – of seeing Emily and perhaps Sarah again, and it would have put his relationship with Laura back God knows how many months … it could even have resulted in them breaking up completely.

On the other hand, was Laura being devious, coming up with an explanation that she'd had a week to think about? She knew that Wendy Carter would tell him what Emily had really said. Is that why Laura had been quite happy for him to see Wendy on his own?

That had surprised him at the time.

If the two women had faced each other, one saying one thing, the other refuting it, it would have been more difficult, if not impossible, to explain to him why she had lied to him in the first place.

He looked across at Laura. She was still fiddling with her robe and the loose thread was now a couple of inches long.

With her head bowed, she was waiting for his verdict.

Did he believe her or was she being deceitful?

The new negligee, and what had gone with it, was it all part of her ruse? Had she deliberately set out to seduce him away from the truth she believed he now knew?

His thoughts still asked the same question: why? Why would she want to do such a thing?

Since meeting in Café Rouge, she hadn't mentioned Emily and, under the circumstances, he would have thought she would have been very eager to find out what he'd been told. The details about lunch in Kenilworth had been the truth. Why had Emily called her a lying slut, why not just a slut? What else had she said? Was he back to where he was hours ago?

"If you decided to make up your own version of what Sergeant Carter had told you" – he couldn't use the word 'lie' – "solely for my benefit, then thank you. But I think you would agree now it would have been better to tell me what Emily had really said." He couldn't bring himself to use the word 'truth' either. "You knew I'd find out from Sergeant Carter."

"I told you. I didn't want you to be hurt."

"I know but I would have been able to handle it."

Laura looked up. The tears were rolling down her cheeks but he wondered if they were the tears of a naughty little girl who had lied.

"I'm sorry, but …"

Matthew went across to her and took her in his arms. "You did it for me and I'm grateful, but we don't know what may happen next. Since you were knocked down, there have been three letters, each threatening your life, and they haven't gone away. There's still somebody out there threatening you. We must not forget that and we must keep everything else in perspective."

There, Matthew thought, *you have your chance to come clean. I have given you the opportunity to tell me the truth, to get it all out in the open. Whatever your reasons were for doing it, we will find a way to solve what's troubling you.*

When Laura didn't say anything, he wanted to take her by the shoulders and plead with her to tell him the truth, the whole truth. She lifted her head slowly, so he bent forward and kissed away the tears on her cheeks.

Suddenly her whole face broke into a knowing smile. She moved one hand up towards his neck, slipped it inside his dressing gown and gently moved the tips of her fingers across his chest as

she bent forward and kissed him.
    Did he have his answer?

Chapter Twenty-One

On the Saturday morning, Laura and Matthew went to the supermarket in Oxted before going into the town for a wander. They walked hand-in-hand round the shops, not talking about anything of consequence and enjoying the warm weather.

Anybody looking at them would think they were like countless other working couples, doing at weekends what others were able to do during the week.

They spent the afternoon tending the garden but Laura left him to it at about four o'clock because she wanted to prepare an extra-special meal for that evening and she needed the time.

Earlier when Bruce was on another trip to the local shops, he stopped by for a brief chat but he made no mention of seeing his rogue VW Golf again.

"I think he only goes to the shops for a break from Elizabeth," Laura commented after he had left and he was out of earshot.

"That's a little unfair," Matthew said. "He idolises the very ground she walks on."

"That would be a little difficult when she can't walk."

Matthew shot a look at Laura. She was deadheading some geraniums by the birdbath and seemed unconcerned by what she had said.

He decided to leave it.

When they had stopped off for a morning coffee in Oxted, and during the session in the garden, Matthew caught Laura watching him a couple of times, her eyes narrowed and suspicious. In the coffee shop when he looked at her, she smiled, but in the garden, she looked away quickly and got on with what she was doing. She was either trying to work out what he knew and what he didn't know or he was becoming increasingly obsessed with the situation, believing her every action and every word, had a hidden meaning or message.

Later, Laura, having already laid out the conservatory for dinner, told Matthew that she wanted to eat quite late because it was going to be by candlelight. Once he came in from the garden, he was banished from the kitchen so that he didn't get in the way.

He decided that before having a shower he would change and go for a walk. There wasn't even a hint from Laura that he shouldn't leave her in the cottage on her own, and neither did she complain when he left the back door open deliberately to allow the breeze into the house, nor when he opened a few of the windows for the same reason.

After turning right out of Southbank, Matthew instinctively crossed the road and took the footpath to the churchyard and to the church itself. He assumed the church would be closed – as it often was for 'security reasons' – but on this occasion it was open. He had never been a regular churchgoer but he had gone with Laura a few times because she felt they ought to cleanse their souls – of what, he now wondered – every now and again.

There were a few other people in the church, but he found a pew on the far side from the door where he could sit down with reasonable privacy. After sitting down, and a little hesitantly, he clasped his hands together and bowed his head. He really didn't know whether he believed in God or not but he felt he had good cause to ask Him to guide him through whatever lay ahead for him and Laura. Maybe he was in a minefield that manifested itself out of a cauldron of ignorance, but regardless, he did want there to be a way out for both of them, and together.

Leaving the church ten minutes later, he retraced his steps. When he reached the High Street, he stood at the junction opposite Whitworth's, an excellent antique furniture emporium and thought about which way he should go. He had about an hour. Seeing people to his left sitting outside The Grasshopper enjoying a drink, he decided to go and have a cold pint of lager himself.

After walking into the pub, the first person he saw was Brian Smith, their doctor. He was standing at the bar with a man Matthew didn't recognise and they appeared to be deep in conversation. Matthew thought he would leave them to it but, just as he was about to go towards the other end of the bar, Brian saw him and waved him over.

"Good evening, Matthew," Brian greeted him, patting him on the shoulder. "Laura not with you?" he asked, looking towards the door.

"No, she's at home preparing dinner. I've been sent out. Can I get you another drink?"

"No, no," Brian said hurriedly. "Seeing you in here on your own is such a rarity I think I ought to buy you one. What will it be?"

"A lager, please."

The man with Brian was looking a little uncomfortable so Matthew held out his hand. "Matthew Ryan," he said, "one of Brian's many happy patients."

"Oh, I'm sorry, that was very rude of me," Brian said, turning round. "Matthew this is Peter Chilcott. He and his wife are down from Warwickshire for the weekend."

Peter and Matthew shook hands.

Taller than Brian but a little shorter than Matthew, Peter had a slim build but with very muscular arms. His tanned face, arms and balding head suggested he had been on holiday recently, and his hair – the little he had – was light brown, flecked with grey: Matthew put his age at around fifty. He had a very happy, lived-in face and Matthew's initial impressions were very favourable.

"Look, why don't you two go out the front and see if there's a table. It's getting a bit crowded at the bar," Brian suggested. "I'll bring the drinks out. Another bitter, Peter?"

"Please," Peter said his eyes still on Matthew. He raised his eyebrows a little and smiled.

"A great organiser, our Brian," he told Matthew as they went out through the door. "It must be because he's a doctor."

"Could be," Matthew agreed. "Look, there's a table."

A group of youngsters were vacating a picnic table at the far end of the strip of grass, so they made a beeline for it.

"So, you're from Warwickshire," Matthew said after they sat down. "Have you known Brian long?"

"About fifteen years. Before coming to Westerham, he was in general practice in Alcester. We met playing golf and we got on. When our wives met, they liked each other and the four of us have been friends ever since." He finished the dregs of his pint and watched a couple of speeding motorcyclists being noisily anti-social as they headed out on the Sevenoaks road. "When I say we met playing golf, it was quite amusing actually. Do you play yourself?"

"I do when I can. I've played a couple of times with Brian but recently time has been against me."

Peter nodded. "It's much the same for me. Have you played the Stratford-on-Avon course?"

Matthew smiled. "I've not only played the course but I lived in Stratford until about six or seven years ago."

"Good Lord!" Peter said, surprised. "Whereabouts?"

"On the Chipping Norton road, about a quarter of a mile from the river."

Peter shook his head. "We could have been near neighbours. My house is on the same side of river but a good deal closer to it, almost in the bloody thing. It's along the ..." Peter stopped as Brian walked tentatively towards them carrying three dripping pints of beer.

"Sorry, Brian," Matthew said. "I should have come to help you."

"No problemo," Brian replied, plonking the pints in front of them and sitting down next to Matthew and opposite Peter.

"I was just going to tell Matthew how we first met, Brian. Do you want to tell it?"

"No, no," Brian replied, starting to laugh. "You tell it far better than I do."

Peter took a sip of his pint. "We were playing in a monthly medal, fifteen years ago – when we were about your age – and I'd already played the short tenth. Do you remember the tenth, par three, most of which is a sort of trench?" It was the hole where Matthew almost had a hole-in-one but, not wanting to interrupt Peter's story, he just nodded. "I'd already played it and was on the eleventh, all steamed up because the round was going pretty well.

"I was at the top of my back swing when matie here," he indicated Brian, "bellowed, and I mean bellowed, the loudest 'Fore!' you've ever heard on any golf course anywhere, from the tenth. I was committed to the swing, cocked it up and put the ball out of bounds over the hedge to the right. Bloody fuming, I was.

"Anyway, the two guys I was playing with and I all heard a 'thunk', but because the others had been watching me, none of us saw the trajectory of Brian's ball. We agreed it must have landed pretty close but, on my say so, and because I was still fuming about being put off my shot – my third shot was centre fairway by the way – we marched off the tee without even suggesting where Brian's ball might be but, in fairness, we didn't bloody know anyway.

"After I'd played my fourth, pin high and then one putt for a five – escaping with just the one shot dropped – I looked back and Brian here was attacking the hedge by the tee with what look like a spade."

"It was my three-wood, actually," Brian said, giggling.

Smiling to himself, Matthew assumed Brian and Peter were already on their fourth of fifth pint.

"Anyway, didn't think any more about it. Continued to have a good round, submitted my card – a three over par seventy-five, I think –"

"What do you mean, you think?" Brian said, interrupting. "You know bloody well it was and you won the medal as a result, so stop being so bloody modest." He was already halfway through his pint and Matthew had hardly started his. "Peter knows every game he has ever played and what he scored ever since he took up golf," Brian added, looking at Matthew.

"All right, I won on that occasion. Anyway –"

"Won on that occasion?" Brian said, interrupting again. "You always bloody win." He turned to Matthew. "He plays off three point one and he's still a bandit!"

"All right, Brian, let me finish my story," Peter said. Matthew was beginning to change his opinion of Peter. "As I said, I didn't think any more about it. When I got home, I emptied out my bag because it needed a good clean but when I upended it to get out the, you know, the bits and pieces that get in there without any explanation –"

"Detritus," Brian said.

"If you say so, Brian, anyway this bloody ball fell out with everything else. It was an Ultra. Now, I don't play with Ultras, so it couldn't have been mine" – Matthew was really changing his opinion of Peter – "but it had three red dots on it. I thought back to the incident on the eleventh tee.

"Anyhow, I kept the ball in my bag and the next time I saw Brian in the clubhouse – I knew him by sight only then – I asked him about it and, bugger me if it wasn't his ball! The 'thunk' we all heard was the ball going straight into the top of my bag. It must have gone down the slot I used for my driver because my driver was in my hands. What are the chances of something like that happening?"

Peter and Brian convulsed with laughter and Matthew managed a broad smile, wondering how often the story had been told and whether it had become embellished over the years.

"And we've been friends ever since," Peter finished off by saying, once he had his laughter under control.

"Good story, eh, Matthew?" Brian asked.

"Yes, very good," Matthew replied with faked enthusiasm.

Actually, it was a good story – as golfing stories go – but he kept on thinking back to Laura, and why couldn't he be leading a normal existence like Brian and Peter. He assumed Brian and Peter's wives were doing exactly what Laura was doing, but for him it was different.

By coincidence, Brian looked at his watch and said, "Must be going shortly because we'll be in real trouble if we're late. How's Laura?"

"She's fully recovered, thanks. She's back to normal," Matthew told him.

"Laura, Matthew's partner," Brian said turning towards Peter, "was injured in a hit-and-run a couple of months ago. It was in your neck of the woods, actually, Warwick, wasn't it, Matthew?"

"Yes, that's right."

"Oh, whereabouts?" Peter asked.

"She was crossing the road by the Town Hall. The car didn't stop," Matthew said, not wanting to give any further details.

"She's a beautiful looking girl," Brian said. "It would have been an absolute tragedy if Matthew had lost her."

Matthew allowed a quizzical smile to cross his lips as he nodded solemnly. He'd never put Brian down as being sexist but he wondered if Laura was anything but a 'beautiful looking' girl, he would have described her differently.

"Look," Brian said, interrupting Matthew's thoughts, "we really must go." He swung one leg over the bench and then hesitated. "Peter and I are playing golf tomorrow morning and we were playing with Philip Atkinson, but he phoned just before we left the house and cried off, wife ill or something. Fancy joining us?"

"No, I don't –"

"Oh, go on, Matthew," Peter said, sounding genuinely enthusiastic about the idea. "It'll give us the chance to get better acquainted."

"Maggie and Sophie might be coming to caddie. They fancy the walk. You know what'll happen: they will walk and we'll pull our own damn trolleys. Why not bring Laura? She might be a good distraction for Peter and we could be in with a chance of beating him."

"Sounds a nice idea, but …"

"You're not doing anything else, are you? Got nothing else planned?"

"Well no, but I …"

"That's settled, then. Bit of an early start, though. Tee time's booked for ten to nine. We'll see you there and have a spot of lunch afterwards maybe," Brian said as they both stood up. "And tell Laura to wear the tightest trousers she can find. An unfair advantage, I know, but not one that should be overlooked, nor proven, should that become necessary."

Brian winked at Matthew.

"All right, but I can make no promises about Laura being there," Matthew told them.

They all shook hands.

"See you tomorrow," Brian said with a further wink.

"Yes, see you tomorrow." Matthew replied, reluctantly.

"And why won't you be put off by this bottom in tight trousers?" Matthew heard Peter ask Brian as they walked away.

"I've seen more of Laura Stanhope in real life than you will in your dreams," Brian replied, probably thinking that Matthew hadn't heard his comment.

Matthew resumed his seat.

He thought that Brian's remark was not only out of character but also unprofessional. He was Laura's GP, for God's sake. He wondered how many other women he saw professionally and bragged about to his friends. Watching them walk away, Matthew decided he'd not only changed his opinion of Peter, but also of Brian.

Laura had wanted to make an impact, and she certainly did that.

The dress she wore for dinner that evening was another of her purchases. It was a long, light yellowy-green, shiny creation that seemed to shimmer as she walked. It had very thin shoulder straps and the material dipped tantalisingly between her breasts. The back was also low and there was a split in the material on her left thigh that went on forever.

With this creation – as she called it – she wore stiletto slip-on gold sandals that looked totally impractical but added to the allure of the dress. She wore no jewellery other than the engagement ring Matthew had bought her the day after he proposed.

They had gone into George Town by taxi from their hotel and spent hours going round every jewellers' shop they could find before she chose something she wanted – a single but large diamond that, in the UK, would have cost triple what Matthew paid for it.

Now, moving round the conservatory the flickering lights caught the diamond every now and again and it sparkled, acting as a reminder that Laura was after all his fiancée and he must always remember that when his mind began to wander towards more negative thoughts.

The candles on the table – with a couple of others placed strategically on the windowsills in the conservatory – created a very romantic setting. Laura put Russell Watson and Andrea Bocelli on random on the CD player and set about entertaining Matthew.

He wasn't allowed to do anything other than opening the wine.

During the first course, which was her own homemade pâté, and the second – veal in a white wine and herb sauce with new potatoes, asparagus and fresh-minted garden peas – Laura continued with her entertainment. She told Matthew stories about her childhood and teenage years that she had never told him before.

Previously she had mentioned that her brother was in Australia and also that she had a younger sister but she hadn't talked very much before about the times they were all together. Matthew had never met Laura's parents, whom she had only mentioned in passing. He thought there might have been some sort of family rift

After living with Laura for so long he could, or even should, have expected to meet her parents at least, but the meeting didn't happen and as time passed, it had become less important to him. Recent revelations had obviously introduced doubts where doubts had not previously existed.

Laura did phone her mother quite regularly, but Matthew had never heard her talking to her father and, on any number of occasions, before she had given up her business, she had gone alone to visit her parents in Nottingham. Whenever she returned and Matthew asked after them, all she said was, "Fine thanks," or "Yes, they're okay, thanks." Her visits suggested that a family dispute was less likely but there was still the question of her relationship with her father.

Sometimes when Laura had accompanied him to seminars, and they had been within easy driving distance of Nottingham, he had again raised the possibility of both of them going to see her parents once he had finished lecturing. Without using the exact words, he'd been told to back off. At the time he'd been slightly affronted as no explanation accompanied the refusal, but now he questioned why he had never been allowed near the rest of her family.

Matthew's parents – he was an only child – died in a car crash in the north of Scotland when he was at university. His mother's sister – Aunt Annie – had assumed the motherly role but, after Emily and he were married, it was almost as though the aunt handed over total responsibility for him to Emily and got on with her own life, which quite sadly didn't seem to include him any longer. After a couple of years he got a letter to say Aunt Annie had emigrated to Canada and, only a year after that, a further letter from a complete stranger, telling him that his aunt had died.

Matthew's father had also been an only child and therefore, other than distant relatives who didn't know what he was doing and he didn't know who they were, let alone what they were doing, he had nobody.

When Laura began to tell Matthew a previously unrelated story about her childhood, he wondered whether she was asking him to share the moment with her, or if there was some other, more sinister, ulterior motive. Regardless and to begin with, she communicated an air of innocence, naivety and virtuousness that temporarily blew away any suspicions he may have.

"I remember once when I was fourteen," Laura said, putting her knife and fork down on an empty plate after enjoying her own cooking, "going to the Lake District with mummy and daddy, Simon and Lisa on holiday. I was a little bitch in those days, so bloody precocious." She looked at Matthew and there was a gleam in her eyes. "And don't you dare say 'no change there then'."

"I wasn't going to," Matthew said, smiling.

"Good. Anyway, I thought everybody owed me a favour and if somebody had something I didn't have and I wanted it, I played merry hell until I got it. If I didn't get it, I would sulk for days. If we went out to eat and Lisa or Simon seemed to have one more chip on their plates than me, I would go into a strop.

"In the Lake District, we were staying somewhere near Grasmere, I think. We had gone out for a meal and I was being a right little Madam. Daddy asked me what I wanted to eat and I chose one of the most expensive meals on the menu, I didn't know what it was but I chose it because of the price. Of course, goodie-two-shoes Lisa and grown-up Simon were being the idyllic children, but not out-of-control Laura. I remember daddy asking why I wanted the sea bass. He pointed out I had never wanted fish before. I remember what happened next word for word:

'Because I like it,' I said.

'How do you know you like it if you've never had it before?' daddy asked patiently.

'How do you know I've never had it?' I said defiantly.

'Because your mother buys the food for the house and cooks it, and I buy it when we are out, that's how. Your mother doesn't buy and cook sea bass and I've never bought you sea bass when we've been out, so I ask you again, how do you know you like it?' he said."

Laura looked at Matthew and smiled.

"My father hated to argue and he always tried to reason with me, which was the last thing he should have done. What I needed was hard discipline not negotiation, and understanding. I didn't let up, because I said:

"'Cos.'

'What sort of answer is that, 'cos?' daddy said.

'It's my answer,' I said.

'Choose something else,' daddy told me.

'I want sea bass,' I persisted.

'You're not having sea bass,' daddy said.

"Mummy kept very quiet. She was more concerned about what other people who were sitting near us were thinking. Lisa glared at me and Simon, like Mummy, was becoming increasingly embarrassed. I think I told my entire family that I hated them before I stormed out of the restaurant. I didn't know where I was but one of the first people I saw was a policeman. I stopped and told him I was being abused and what was he going to do about it?" Seeing Matthew's shocked reaction, Laura said, "Well, I was, in a way. The policeman took me to the police station because I wouldn't tell him where I lived. I didn't know where I lived, we were on holiday. How was I supposed to know where the hotel was?

"I was told to take a seat in reception and the policeman brought me a drink of orange. I remember to this day, it was in a plastic cup and tasted of anything but orange. After about ten minutes, a woman police constable took me into a side room. She started asking me questions about the abuse I was suffering. I panicked because I realised that I had gone too far and things were getting serious. She wouldn't have it when I told her I'd maybe overstated what I really meant – I couldn't say I'd been joking – and that I'd simply had a row with my father. She kept on asking me where daddy had touched me, how long he had been touching me for and whether he'd done anything more than just touch me.

"She asked me if Mummy knew what he was doing. What she was suggesting daddy had done to me made me feel sick. When she wouldn't let up, I became quite frightened. Eventually, though, she started to believe me and her whole attitude changed. She gave me a right telling off.

"As we were leaving the room where I'd been questioned, daddy was in the reception area looking frantic. There was nothing the police could do other than be annoyed with me, but the way they looked at daddy, and each other, suggested they didn't believe nothing had happened.

"Daddy, though, was all right in the police station in front of everyone and he was sort of all right as he frog-marched me back to the hotel – I never did get a meal that night – but once we were inside the room, he changed. He really lost his temper with me and threatened to beat me to within an inch of my life. When I shouted at him that none of it would have happened if he'd let me have the sea bass, he suddenly calmed down and just glared at me.

"Simon was in his own room, but Lisa and I had an adjoining room to my parents. Daddy shouted for Lisa and told her to go and get Simon, which she did. He just held onto the top of my arms so I couldn't move. When Lisa got back with Simon, daddy told them to sit on the bed. Mummy was in the bathroom taking an awfully long time over something.

'Now my girl," daddy said. 'I'm going to teach you a lesson I should have taught you a lot of years ago. I want Simon and Lisa here as witnesses just in case your warped little mind' – those were the exact words he used, Matthew – 'just in case your warped little mind tries to make more of what I'm going to do to you than is actually going to happen.'

"I was terrified. I had never seen that look in his eyes before. I wanted to ask why mummy wasn't needed as a witness but I knew that would make him even angrier. I couldn't hear a sound from the bathroom so I assumed she was listening at the door. Daddy pulled the chair from over by the wall – it was a sort of dining room chair – and sat on it, still holding my arms. I was wearing a skirt and I suddenly realised what was going to happen. He was far too strong for me, so I started to scream.

'Don't you dare,' he sneered at me, clamping one hand over my mouth. 'You make one more sound and it'll be ten times worse.'

"He turned me round, lifted the back of my skirt *and* pulled my pants down over my bottom right in front of Simon. Before I could struggle again, I was pinned over his knee and he slapped my bottom so hard and for so long it went from hurting to being numb. It was more than the pain, the humiliation I felt in front of Simon and Lisa was awful. I was fourteen, for God's sake, and being treated like an eight-year old.

"I looked over at Simon and Lisa. Simon was leaning back on

the bed, smiling, looking at my bottom with everything on display, and I mean everything, and Lisa just sat there with her mouth and eyes wide open. I'm sure mummy had opened the bathroom door a little so she could see, but as my head was only a foot from the carpet, I couldn't twist it enough to be sure.

"I started to scream again at one stage but an extra hard slap quickly shut me up. It seemed to go on for hours but it was probably only for a few minutes. When the slapping finally stopped, and before letting me go, daddy pulled my pants up and my skirt down. He then stood me in front of him, ignoring my tears.

"I was mortified. He held the tops of my arms, but gently this time, and said, *'Now young lady, learn your lesson. Either you start behaving and stop bringing disgrace on this family or I will have to consider further and more drastic action. I will never lift a finger to you again, that I promise. You might be fourteen but you are not too old to go into care. Do you want me to throw you out of this family?'*

"When I didn't answer, the grip on my arms became tighter. *'Answer me, Laura,'* daddy said in a controlled voice.

"I thought I'd done nothing to warrant being threatened with being taken into care, and I knew he would never let such a thing happen, but it was still more to do with the embarrassment of what he'd done in front of the others.

'No Daddy,' I said.

'Then, learn your lesson,' were his final words on the matter.

"From that day onwards, Matthew," Laura said, looking at him properly for the first time since she started her story, "other than the odd temper tantrum, I was as good as gold. Ordering sea bass because it was the most expensive item on the menu changed my life. I will never, ever forget it. It was the humiliation and my father telling me I had a warped mind that really hurt. As I lay in bed that evening, my bottom still smarting, and Lisa not having said a word to me, I swore that I would never suffer any form of humiliation ever again, not from anybody. Patrick tried, but I never let him humiliate me in public, ever."

Laura fell silent and lowered her eyes.

As she began her story, Matthew wondered about her reasons

for going into such detail, and especially after such an enjoyable evening. Was it because by confessing to what sort of child she was, and in a roundabout way, she was trying to explain? Did she suspect Matthew had been told a lot more than he was telling her?

Had her father recognised in her, at such an early age, the woman she would eventually grow into? There must have been more to what happened than Laura had described for her father to say she had a warped mind.

The story was one thing but during the telling, her voice and demeanour raised other concerns.

She had sounded so childlike, so vulnerable.

Had the humiliation she suffered then and at other times, festered and grown inside her over the years so that now she lived in her own world? Had the short-term benefits from her father's beating actually set the seeds for longer-term changes that had taken over her life?

There were so many questions but so few, if any, answers.

"Wow!" Matthew said. "That was some story."

Laura looked up, her eyes slightly narrowed. He thought she was judging whether he was being serious or perhaps making fun of her.

"Fourteen, Matthew, I was fourteen," she said

Matthew reached across the table and put his hand on hers.

She was shaking.

"It must have been awful."

"It was."

Next she said something that under normal circumstances would have been regarded as rather strange but after what he had been told it began to answer some of his questions.

"Perhaps now you understand," she said.

"I think I am beginning to understand, Laura," Matthew told her.

Chapter Twenty-Two

After Laura had cleared away the plates and dishes from the main course, she asked whether Matthew minded if she had a cigarette before she served the pudding. She always asked and he never minded. She lit the cigarette and sat back in her chair.

She looked at him and smiled.

Her mood had changed.

"I saw Brian Smith when I was in the village earlier," he said.

Westerham was a small town but some of its inhabitants always liked to refer to it as the village.

"Oh, how is he?" Laura asked a little hesitantly, but her voice was back to normal.

"Fine," Matthew told her. "I popped into The Grasshopper for a pint and he was in there with a friend of his who is down for the weekend."

"That was nice for you," she said, exhaling a stream of smoke.

She was looking at him intently, but he didn't think it was Brian Smith she wanted to talk about. "That's another story," Matthew said, smiling. "But the reason for mentioning it is that he asked me to play golf tomorrow morning."

"I hope you said yes. It's so long since you played. I've felt quite guilty."

"Why would my not playing golf make you feel guilty?"

Matthew topped up their wine glasses.

"Well, I feel this thing that's been going on with me, you know, it's meant that you've felt the need to be near me as much as possible," she said. "It would be good for you to get out and have a little male company for a change."

Laura picked up her wine glass.

"Well that won't happen tomorrow because they asked if you would go as well." He saw Laura's eyebrows go up in surprise, so he said quickly, "Their wives will be there. They want to go for the walk."

"I've never walked round a golf course in my life," Laura said, stubbing out her cigarette in the ashtray. "I wouldn't know what to do."

"There's nothing to do. Just look pretty."

"Pretty?"

"Wait and see, but for once I'll choose what you wear."

"This sounds intriguing. Why?"

"Do you want to come?"

"Well after what you've said, how can I refuse?" Laura still looked surprised. "But don't I have to stand in particular places and not talk and things?"

"I thought you'd never been round a golf course before?"

"I haven't but I know women who have."

Sitting opposite him she looked so innocent and beguiling. The story about her father had come from the heart and he was so sure she was trying to explain ... but explain what?

"That really is a gorgeous dress," Matthew told her. "It must have cost a fortune."

Laura looked down. "I admit it wasn't cheap but I took one look at it and fell in love." She lifted her head slowly, her eyes now smiling as she said, "A little like the effect you had on me when we first met."

"Thank you. You didn't do too badly yourself," he said as he wondered if now was the time to see if Laura was really committed to their relationship. If she was, it might help or even suggest how he should handle what he'd been told. "So, if we are in that sort of mood, what about setting a date? Let me make an honest woman of you."

Laura's eyes misted over.

She didn't blink but neither did she break eye contact.

"There's no rush, is there?" she said softly ... not the answer he wanted.

Right up to the time Wendy Carter had felt it necessary to tell him about the alleged reasons why Laura had left the Surrey Police Service, he had looked forward to the day he and Laura would get married. She was still young as she had a few years to go before she reached the big four zero. They hadn't really discussed children but Laura had never alluded to not wanting any. He wanted them to become a proper family before it was too late. If more than one child came along even better, but regardless, he wanted one, two or more children to have a youngish mother.Chauvinistic or not, he thought it more important for a mother to be able to relate to children, especially daughters, and therefore age mattered.

Matthew hadn't told Wendy Carter that he and Laura were engaged, although knowing how observant women can be with such matters she may have noticed that Laura was wearing a ring when they went to the police station after returning from Malaysia. He hadn't seen the need to tell her when he and Wendy last met, it would have merely added to his humiliation.

He had obviously given the engagement some thought since his lone meeting with Wendy. Laura had readily agreed to marry him – well after two or three attempts – but until she gave him real cause to question the reason why she was with him – which in her defence she hadn't – he saw little point worrying for the sake of it. Looking at Laura now a strange analogy came into his mind: if reports suggested that a pet poodle had savaged a child, it is unlikely people would believe it, but if true, there had to be provocation.

Laura looked so innocent and defenceless he just could not accept that she was guilty of anything, but why did she say there was no rush? He needed an answer.

"Is there really any reason why we should delay getting married?" he asked. "We've been living together for nearly eighteen months, we both know the other's little foibles, we're compatible, we like the same things and thanks to you, our sex life is fantastic. So why wait?"

Laura lit another cigarette.

"I've told you often enough about the way Patrick treated me and I've gone into a certain amount of detail but I've never told you everything. Before we married, he was every woman's dream of what a future husband should be like. He was caring, understanding and tender, and he made me feel as though I was what he'd always looked for in a wife.

"After we were married, he changed overnight and made my life hell. He took away my confidence and made me feel totally inadequate." She inhaled deeply on her cigarette. "I told you about the incident with my father, I suppose, to try and make you understand how my childhood affected me psychologically. But after we got married, Patrick broke me into little pieces. He was like Prince Charming when we were in other people's company but at home, he was a monster.

"When you and I met, I had only just started to put the pieces back together again but I saw in you somebody who would help me get my life in order. All right, you could argue that I was in a strange sort of business for someone who lacked social awareness and confidence. I was more than capable, as are many people, of presenting one face to the outside world and at the same time being a total mess inside. You have done more for me since I moved in with you – and that was one hell of decision on both our parts – than I could have wished for, you've treated me like the person I really want to be. And then when the accident happened, you were there for me ..."

"What else –?"

"No, Matthew, I've got to give you my reasons for not wanting to rush things. Please let me finish."

"I'm sorry."

"Then the threats started. Again, while maybe on the outside I seem to be coping quite well, on the inside I was terrified, and I am still terrified. When we were in Edinburgh you'll never know how I felt when I went out on my own, but I had to. I had to prove to you that I had the courage to face up to what was going on.

"Other than the letters, there has been nothing, I know, and maybe it is some weirdo who is doing it to me, to us, but we could be wrong. It could be someone who is biding her time, just waiting for the right set of circumstances.

"If the letters hadn't started – and after you asked me to marry you – you would have been really shocked by the speed with which I wanted to get that wedding ring on my finger."

Laura stubbed out the cigarette before lighting another one straightaway.

"Yes, we do know each other's faults, not that either of us have that many. We are compatible, we do like the same things and, yes, our sex life is fantastic, but there is still this cloud hanging over us. Before the first letter arrived, I thought I had just stepped off the pavement at the wrong time. I had reached the stage, thanks mainly to you, where I was almost back together again.

"I admit I was ready and so looking forward to changing my name to Ryan, even before you asked me to marry you, but then my world, our world, was shattered. Not only was I back to being in pieces but this time I'd taken you with me. I am finding that very difficult to live with. Until whoever it might be is found, I won't be ready, Matthew. I'm sorry, I know it sounds stupid, but that is the way I feel."

Being thrown into a yet another quandary didn't surprise him. If he believed Laura, then everything she said was understandable and largely acceptable. If he believed Wendy Carter and Laura was the author of the threatening letters, then he wasn't even back to square one, he was now further back than he'd ever been.

If she had come up with any other reason other than the letters, he would have been able to accept whatever she said. He would have been willing to wait. He would have found a way to bring Laura out of wherever she was. However, that wasn't the case and, once again, he didn't know what to do or say because he didn't know what to believe.

So what did he say?

"I understand."

"I knew you would," Laura said, her eyes telling him the same thing. "I will promise you here and now, Matthew Ryan, that within one month of the letters stopping because whoever it is has been caught and locked up, I will become Mrs Laura Ryan and I keep my promises."

"I can't ask more of you than that," he said.

Laura smiled and cocked her head.

"And, now, for my final offering this evening," she said, interrupting his thoughts and standing up. "I have prepared for your gastronomic delight, wait for it, spotted dick and custard."

She bowed slightly before heading for the kitchen.

"So," Laura said, as they enjoyed a particularly good coffee she wanted to try, "two things. The first is I want you to run through the basic etiquette I must observe on the golf course tomorrow because I don't want to look like a silly girl in front of Maggie and whatever the other woman's name is … "

"Sophie."

"Sophie. And what's his name?"

"Peter."

"Peter ... I'll be able to cope with Peter. He'll be just like every other man, all eyes and dreams," – Matthew almost interrupted to ask her what she meant by *able to cope* but she held up her hand to stop him – "but before we go into all that boring stuff, this dress ..."

"What about your dress?"

"You said you liked it?" she said as she moved her chair away from the table and then sat down again. She crossed her legs with the inevitable effect as the material fell away from her thigh.

"I do, I think it's absolutely gorgeous."

Standing up, she moved the chair out of the way.

"Well, I said the spotted dick was your final offering ... did you like it, by the way?"

"Yes, I did, it was lovely," Matthew said.

"Good. Well it wasn't quite your final offering. If my timing is right ..." she said as she bent down and turned up the music on the CD before selecting a particular track – "the piece of music I've chosen, *The Flower Duet*, lasts approximately four minutes. I am going to take exactly that amount of time, and I've been practising while you were out, to remove this dress and you will note, for your added delight, that I am not wearing anything underneath. When I am naked, and this is your side of the bargain, you also have the same four minutes to be ready to accept me. I felt randy enough doing it on my own, so God knows how I'll feel doing it in front of you. Do you understand the rules?

"I think so," Matthew answered, smiling and shaking his head. "You've planned ever minute detail for this evening, haven't you?"

Laura's expression became serious. "Except for what we've just discussed but don't let's go there again ... not yet." She was silent for a few seconds. "But, yes, everything else," she said, her face lighting up again, "has been planned in detail. However the success of this finale is rather dependent on you, so you'd better come up with the goods, if you see what I mean."

"I think I understand."

She put her hands on her hips and pouted. "There you go again: you think, you think, you think. Well, it doesn't make any difference, because if what I am going to do fails to have the desired effect, I'm going to trade you in for a new model because you will have failed your daily MOT test."

"On what grounds?" he asked, playing along with her. Her enthusiasm where sex was concerned was as usual, infectious.

"I think we would put it down to a broken cylinder." She put her hand over her mouth and giggled. "I thought that was rather good."

"It was very good."

"Thank you but now you must shut up. You're playing for time."

She bent over the CD player again, checked she had what she wanted, and pressed play. As the music started, she moved back into the middle of the conservatory and sat on the chair, facing Matthew. Her eyes narrowed slightly, and there was a permanent smile on her lips and in her eyes. She moved the hem of the dress so that her legs were almost completely uncovered. She kicked off her shoes and then began to gyrate slowly on the chair, with just the tips of her toes touching the floor. One hand moved slowly to her right shoulder and she equally slowly moved the thin strap until it hung loosely by her arm.

The material fell away.

She carried on moving as *The Flower Duet* played, she bared one of her breasts and then the other. As the music neared the end, she stood up and the laws of gravity took over as the dress shimmered to the floor.

Previously she had done some particularly provocative things, but the combination of music, candlelight and her absolute sensuality guaranteed his readiness.

Without saying a thing, she floated across the conservatory, sat astride him and, within seconds, they were kissing and making love.

'Incredible' was an inadequate word to describe how she made Matthew feel but 'unthinkable' was exactly the word he needed to describe what Wendy Carter would have had him believe.

They were all wrong.

Laura had to be the victim.

They reached the Golf Club at just before eight thirty the next morning. The car park was already quite full, which wasn't surprising for a Sunday morning.

Laura, her eyes wide open, looked around apprehensively. Matthew had asked her to go with him before on any number of occasions, but she had always declined, saying that it was part of his independence so she would be intruding.

At first, he gave up arguing and then, he gave up asking.

"So," Laura had said earlier that morning, "you were going to select what I should wear. The forecast is good, so what do you suggest?" She was standing naked in front of her wardrobe, surveying her vast array of clothing.

Matthew was still in bed, enjoying a cup of tea. "I didn't mean literally but there are certain things you can't wear."

She turned round, holding a pair of jeans in front of her.

"Those for a start," he said.

"What, jeans?"

"Yes, I'm sorry, they're banned. According to golf clubs, jeans are the cause of all unacceptable and deviant behaviour and, if you wore those, you would obviously not have the intelligence to understand the rules and the etiquette. They are the devil's clothing, and it's the same with short shorts, short socks with long shorts and collarless shirts. All indicate a form of barbarism."

He placed the cup back in its saucer with a superior air.

"That's utter rubbish," commented Laura, still holding the jeans in front of her.

"It is, isn't it, but rules are rules, and if you break them you are pilloried naked by the 18th hole and people can chip golf balls at you."

Laura's expression suggested she wasn't too sure whether he was being serious or not. "Right," she said, returning the jeans to the wardrobe. "I'm not sure …"

"What about those white ones, you know, the ones that sit on your hips and come mid-way down your calves."

She searched along the extended row of trousers and extracted a hanger. "These?" she asked.

He nodded. "I think so."

"But these are neither long shorts nor trousers. I don't want people chipping golf balls at me."

Matthew thought she was actually being serious. "It's different for ladies because golf clubs are generally, and wrongly, still a man's domain and therefore highly chauvinistic. The shorter the shorts and the tighter the trousers the women wear the better."

"You're joking. Have you seen some of the sights on television among the women golfers? And as for the men, golf seems to be an excuse to wear the most garish and unsightly clothing, clothing they wouldn't be seen dead in anywhere else."

"You're learning very quickly," Matthew said, smiling.

Laura looked at the trousers again, frowning. "But these are very tight," she informed him, "and I don't normally wear pants with them because they show the lines."

Matthew smiled again, really enjoying what was happening. "Can you walk in them?"

"Of course I can."

"Can you wear sensible shoes for a five or six mile hike?"

"Yes, and ones that actually go with these."

"They're perfect."

Whether Laura would approve, he didn't know but he was going to show her off because he had a feeling that Peter Chilcott was going to get right up his nose.

"What about a top?"

"I'll leave that to you."

She ran her finger along the rail and extracted two sleeveless blouses, holding them up for his approval. "Which one?"

Matthew screwed up his face. "Not sure," he said, "I like them both. The yellowy-green one, it's almost the same colour as that dress you wore for a while last night."

Laura wrinkled her nose and put out her tongue. "Do I have to wear a bra?"

"You never wear a bra."

"I do ... sometimes."

"I didn't know you had any."

"Of course I've got bras, well two, I think."

"You prefer to go without."

She shrugged, looking down at herself. "My boobs are too small and a bra is uncomfortable."

"Then don't wear one. Oh, and take a pullover or something,

just in case."

Laura slowly opened her door and looked around the car park.

Matthew's five-year old BMW 525 Estate was an acceptable model for the golf club, or so one of the more pompous members had told him. It was a good job he loved golf because he had never come across such arrogance anywhere else except in some of the better hotels.

He was in a good mood.

Laura had seen to that and he was ready for the day's challenge.

While he was extracting his clubs from the boot of the car, another car tooted behind him. He turned round and this very large, metallic maroon Mercedes 600 SEL glided past with Peter waving from the driver's seat and Brian leaning forward and waving from the passenger's seat. He couldn't see Maggie, but he assumed the woman he could see was Sophie as she sat in the back looking regal and superior. He thought she might lift her white-gloved hand and wave too, but she didn't oblige.

The car drifted on and stopped twenty yards away.

Because Brian was on the Golf Club's committee in some capacity or another, he had a reserved space next to the clubhouse.

"Who, or should I say what, was that?" Laura asked, having joined Matthew after standing by the wall so that she could survey the course and have a cigarette.

The clubhouse, an austere looking building with windows that seemed to frown down on players on the eighteenth green, was quite high up and at least five holes were visible from the car park and the clubhouse windows.

"That was the opposition," Matthew told her.

"What a car!"

"Did you like it?"

"No, it stank of posturing. It wasn't Brian's car, was it?" Laura asked and Matthew shook his head. "In that case, I bet this Peter is a real poseur. What does he do?"

"Do you know, I never got round to asking him yesterday. No doubt we will be told in graphic detail at some stage or another, if we are lucky enough for it to be restricted to a stage, that is."

Matthew and Laura made their way to the first tee and hung

back with the others for the introductions.

While dressing that morning, Laura had given him the once over and her seal of approval for his dark-blue trousers with a sober maroon shirt. Brian was wearing tartan trousers and a green shirt – Laura's expression as she gave him a peck on the cheek suggested his attire was just acceptable but Peter, in his yellow shirt and bright red trousers, meant that she had to cover her mouth with her hand to suppress a laugh. Neither would she have missed the leer as he looked her up and down.

Maggie, Brian's wife, whom both Laura and Matthew had met before on a number of occasions, was a lovely woman, and a genuine Christian. She and Brian were regular churchgoers, but Maggie was also a pillar of the local community. She was on a number of committees and, before meeting her, Matthew had expected her to be rather haughty and permanently clad in a tweed suit and brogues. But she was the opposite: a diminutive and shy woman, who was very quiet and unassuming, and would do anything for anybody.

Sophie – and Matthew decided she didn't look anything like a *Sophie* – on the other hand, was the opposite. Peter had implied the day before that Maggie and Sophie were firm friends, but Matthew couldn't see why. Whereas Maggie was wearing sensible slacks and a matching floral blouse, Sophie – a large lady with permed-grey hair tied back with a green scarf – was wearing the same as Peter but in reverse.

As they walked towards the first tee, Matthew saw a couple of other golfers nudging each other and smiling.

Sophie greeted Laura with a forced smile and, as expected, a regal handshake. Matthew thought for a moment that Laura, who seemed to have the devil in her, was going to curtsey, but fortunately, she refrained. However she did whisper, "Have I got to be with that for four hours?" as she rejoined Matthew.

When walking away from the 1st Tee, Brian came up close to Matthew and said, "Well done, Matthew. Laura looks fantastic, so we're in with a chance."

Laura stayed with Matthew for the first eight holes, and every now again made some comment or other to him about either Peter or Sophie. Having said she hadn't been on a golf course before, she took very little time to work out where to stand and what not to do when shots were being taken. Such etiquette appeared patronising, but it is a well-known fact that a thrush singing five miles away is more than likely to be the reason for a bad shot than the golfer himself.

By the ninth hole, Matthew realised two things.

The first was that the happenings of the previous months, and more importantly Friday morning, hadn't entered his mind at all, and the second was that Peter wasn't the hotshot golfer Matthew had been told he was. Either the sight of Laura's bottom was having the desired effect or he was just having an off-day but, regardless, as they approached the tenth tee, Peter and Matthew were level pegging and Brian was a couple of points behind.

By then, Laura had started walking with Maggie who seemed, understandably, more interested in the flora and fauna than the golf. They were never very far away from the actual players, but they were in deep conversation and, every now and again, Laura would giggle at something Maggie said, which suggested that Maggie, shy or not, was keeping her well entertained.

Just under two hours later and as they all stood on the eighteenth tee, Peter had moved ahead of Matthew by one point, who in turn was still just two points ahead of Brian.

The eighteenth hole, besides being a good closing hole, was very picturesque. It was a long downhill Par 4 with a slight dogleg to the left, and a narrow fairway. Rhododendron bushes and other shrubs acted as boundaries and the green, bordered on two sides by water, had a narrow the entrance guarded by an array of bunkers.

Their first shots were close together on the fairway but then, as Peter selected a club for his second shot, Laura, by design or not, played her own masterstroke. As Peter pulled what looked like a six-iron from his bag, the cover from one of his woods fell to the ground. Laura was closest to him so she automatically bent down to pick up the cover. The front of her top fell away and Peter's eyes went out on stalks. He glanced quickly in Sophie's direction and then back at Laura, who handed the cover to him with a sweet and innocent smile.

It was obvious from the way he addressed his ball that Peter was flustered and, fortunately for Brian, but more so for Matthew, he proceeded to over hit his shot. It was with great satisfaction that the other two saw the plop as Peter's ball disappeared into the water beyond the green. Brian's was a magnificent shot to within a couple of feet of the pin for a birdie, and Matthew's rolled onto the green for an eventual par.

As they shook hands, with Brian unable to contain his delight, they agreed that Matthew had won with thirty-eight points, Brian had come second with thirty-seven points and Peter, who failed to score on the last hole, was third with thirty-six points. Matthew was silently pleased with himself, whereas Peter was seething.

Peter and Sophie struck out for the clubhouse before the rest of them. Brian with Maggie standing by his side turned to Laura and Matthew and said, "That was masterful. As I said to you yesterday, nothing can be proven."

"I don't think Laura meant it," Matthew commented, looking at Laura.

"Meant or not, it was the clincher," Brian retorted.

"What are you two on about?" Laura asked in all innocence.

"I'll explain," offered Maggie, a delightful sparkle in her eye. "I'll show Laura where the powder room is." She took Laura's arm and they wandered off towards the clubhouse like long lost friends.

It was over lunch that things came to a head. Brian wouldn't let drop the fact that Peter had lost and, at every opportunity, needled him.

"When was the last time you did that?" Brian asked Peter, a broad grin on his face.

"What?" Peter enquired, pretending not to understand.

"Put your ball in the water and come third out of three?"

"And it wouldn't have happened today if young Laura here hadn't flashed her titties at me deliberately," he boomed. "She's been wiggling her bum and rubbing against me all morning."

Matthew was prepared to laugh off his comments but he could see Laura bristling immediately.

"I did no such thing," she said, a definite barb in her voice.

"Huh!" Peter said, leaning back in his chair. "I suppose you're going to try and tell me you didn't know what you were doing."

Sophie was looking daggers at Laura, Maggie had bowed her

head and Brian was as shocked as Matthew was.

"I do not," Laura said through clenched teeth, "go around flashing my titties, as you so politely called them, at anybody. Even if I did, you would be the last in the queue."

"You little hussy," Sophie piped in. "We all saw what you were up to."

"Sophie, I think ..." Matthew started to say.

"No, Matthew," Laura said, "I would like Sophie to explain why, after knowing me for just a few hours, she feels she has the right to call me a little hussy." When Sophie didn't answer immediately, Laura added: "Well?"

Brian said, "I think we all ought to calm down. I was only pulling your leg, Peter."

"I'm still waiting," Laura said.

The table fell silent and all eyes were on Sophie, including a few of the men who were on adjoining tables.

"Well ..." she blustered, "well ... the way you're dressed for a start. Ladies simply do not wear such things when they're on the golf course."

"Are you saying I'm not a lady?" Laura leaned even further forward, her body language demonstrating her aggression.

"No, I'm not saying that," said Sophie, some of the bluster gone. "I'm simply saying, well ..."

"That my trousers are too tight?"

"Well, yes, that and other things."

"What other things?"

It was Peter's turn to try to calm things down. "Sophie, it was just a bit of fun. Let's leave it," he said.

"No, I don't want to leave it," argued Laura. Matthew glared at her but it didn't stop her. "If Sophie's got something to say," Laura continued, "let her say it. What other things? Perhaps you can tell me when I'm supposed to have brushed against your husband. I spent most of the time talking to Maggie and was well away from him."

Remembering that he was a club official, Brian looked about him. Matthew guessed that being party to a scene in front of other members would not augur well when he was up for election again. Maggie still had her head bowed, but Matthew thought he detected a smile on her face. Peter was trying to make himself as small as possible and Matthew had begun to enjoy the fight Laura was putting up against a pretty overbearing opponent. Laura, who was half Sophie's size, was really putting her on the spot.

"I'm not going to take back what I said," Sophie said haughtily. "You were … you were flaunting your body at my husband."

"Flaunting?" Laura repeated quietly. "Are you telling me that I am an exhibitionist?"

"Why else would you not wear any undergarments?"

Matthew nearly burst out laughing, but when he saw Laura's face, the inclination disappeared immediately.

"Undergarments?" Laura repeated loudly. "If you mean a bra and pants, say so and I'll tell you why. Unlike you, I have a small body and don't need half a ton of support. Because my breasts are small and firm rather than large, shapeless and floppy, I feel more comfortable not wearing a bra, but if your husband gets a kick out of looking down the front of my top, that really isn't my problem, is it? Perhaps you ought to ask yourself why he needs to. I am wearing pants, if you must know, and no doubt what I am going to say next will turn your husband on even further, but you have probably never heard of a thong either, have you? I do not flaunt my body at anybody other than Matthew, and even if I did, it wouldn't be to kinky old men."

Sophie sat with her mouth open, Brian was hiding his behind his hand, Peter had joined Maggie lowering his head, and Matthew felt like applauding.

"And now, Matthew, I would like to go home," Laura said as she stood up, her chair scraping on the tiled floor.

"What about lunch?" Brian asked. "We've ordered."

"Stuff your lunch, Brian," Laura said. "I'm sorry, this is not your fault, but I am not going to sit here and be humiliated by a woman who has about as much dress sense as an elephant, albeit she resembles one."

With that, Laura stormed out of the bar.

Matthew stood up without feeling the need to apologise to either of the Chilcotts. "There are good losers and bad losers," he said, looking at Peter and Sophie, "but I object as much as Laura to what you have implied." He turned to the others. "Brian, Maggie, I'm sorry that what could have been a thoroughly enjoyable day has been ruined for us all by your friends. I will ring you later."

As he followed Laura out of the bar, he heard Sophie say, "I've never been so insulted in all my life."

To which he heard Brian say, "That surprises me."

Laura was waiting by the car, leaning against the bonnet with her arms folded and looking like thunder.

"I'm so sorry, Laura. That was entirely my fault. I should never …"

"Just take me home, Matthew." She was almost in tears. "Take me home and don't ever ask me to come to this fucking place ever again."

The short trip home was in silence and, after going into the cottage, Laura ran straight upstairs and slammed the bedroom door, making it rather obvious that Matthew needn't follow her.

Chapter Twenty-Three

When Laura hadn't emerged after an hour, Matthew decided he ought to try and pacify her. He made a couple of mugs of tea and was just about to go upstairs when the phone rang. Putting both mugs in one hand, he picked up the receiver.

"Hello."

"Matthew, it's Brian," and he sounded very serious.

"Look, I really am sorry about what happened today but the Chilcotts truly did go too far. It was all supposed to be a bit of fun," Matthew said, as he felt the hot mugs beginning to burn his fingers. "Hang on a second, Brian ..."

He put the mugs on the telephone table but the contents of one mug slopped over the book in which Laura kept addresses and telephone numbers.

"Shit!" he mouthed. He took out his handkerchief and attempted to mop the mess up, but only managed to nudge the other mug causing further spillage. "Look, Brian," he said into the mouthpiece, "can I call you back? I've just managed –"

"No, Matthew. I'd prefer to say what I've got to say straightaway." Brian was still very serious and Matthew suddenly became worried. "The incident in the clubhouse," Brian continued, "was unfortunate, and Peter and Sophie were entirely to blame, and I've told them so."

"So ..."

"It's a little more serious than that, I'm afraid."

"More serious? Why? What do you mean?" Matthew asked.

"Somebody – and we have a pretty shrewd idea who – scraped a coin or a key or something pretty sharp all the way down the side of Peter's car."

"Oh, shit!" was all Matthew could say.

"There are a lot of expensive cars in that car park, Matthew, and none of the others was touched. Peter's car was singled out and I'm afraid it looks very much as though Laura might have done it."

"Laura? No, she can't have. She was waiting by my car when I got to her."

"Having passed Peter's to get to yours," Brian said.

"Maybe but that doesn't mean she did it ... she wouldn't ... so why Laura? It could just as well have been me. I was pretty annoyed too, you know."

"You wouldn't do such a thing," Brian said.

"And Laura would, is that what you're saying?"

"The police are here now," Brian said, ignoring Matthew's question.

"The police? What on earth –?"

"Peter's Mercedes is brand new, Matthew, and the scratch is deep and runs from the rear to the front wing. You're talking about a lot of damage and considerable expense to repair it."

"But why the police?" Matthew asked.

"It was a criminal act, it's criminal damage, Matthew. I'm sorry, but I thought I'd better let you know that Peter has given them your details."

"My details?"

"Yes," Brian said. "Your details."

Laura was lying on top of the bed when Matthew went into the room. She had taken off all her clothes except her thong. Looking up at him, she intertwined her fingers before lifting her arms and putting her hands behind her head.

She smiled.

"Did you hear the phone ring?" he asked her.

"Of course I did, it rang in here as well but I thought, as you were downstairs, you would answer it. It was bound to be for you." She patted the bed next to her. "Why don't you come and sit down? I feel ..."

Matthew stayed at the end of the bed. "Do you want to know who it was?" he asked.

"Only if you sit down," she said sulkily.

"It was Brian and he was still at the golf club."

"So?" Laura shrugged, her hands still behind her head.

"He was phoning to say the police had been called," Matthew said as he rested his hands on the footboard.

His grip tightened as Laura's smile broadened, and without any sign of knowing what Matthew was alluding to, she asked, "Has there been a murder or something?"

"No, Laura nothing like that but what has happened isn't a laughing matter."

Bending one knee, Laura moved her other leg towards the edge of the bed. "All right, I'll stop laughing but will you stop being evasive and get to the point. What did Brian say had happened?" She lowered her arms and rested her hands on her stomach.

"I think you can tell me that," Matthew said.

"Me?" Laura feigned surprise as she moved her leg a little further across the bed, her hand moving over her hip and onto the top of her thigh.

"Laura, will … will you stop that and be honest with me?" he pleaded.

"Stop what?" she said looking down at herself. "Oh that! I am being honest with you." She smiled again as her fingers began stroking the inside of her thigh.

"What did you do to Peter Chilcott's car?"

Laura frowned and her fingers stopped moving.

"*What did I do to Peter Chilcott's car?*" she repeated slowly. "I didn't do anything to it," she said. "But I remember saying it was posturing and he was a poseur." Her fingers moved higher and started stroking again.

"Did you damage it in any way?" Matthew asked, keeping his eyes on hers.

Suddenly Laura sat up with her back against the headboard. She reached for a pillow and placed it across her lap. "Damage it? Why would I do anything like that?" she said, pouting.

"It could have been because of what he and his wife said to you."

Matthew's hands were still on the footboard and he felt a trickle of perspiration run down his back. He didn't think he'd misjudged her this time because the guilt was written all over her face..

"Oh, that! A pair of fucking silly old farts … I said what I had to say, gave as good as I got, you heard me."

"I did. Where did you go when you left the clubhouse?"

She frowned. "Back to our car, of course…. you saw me."

"I saw you at the car," he said, "but I didn't see you walking to it."

"Matthew, are you accusing me of doing something to the

Chilcotts' car?" she asked as she clasped her hands on top of the pillow.

"I'm not accusing you of anything. I'm simply asking you whether ... did you go anywhere near their car when you left the clubhouse?"

"I saw it, of course I saw it – it's not the sort of car you miss – but I didn't go anywhere near it other than to get to your car," she said.

"Are you sure?"

"Of course I'm sure. Matthew what's –"

"Then I suggest you put some clothes on and come downstairs, I've a feeling the police will be here in a few minutes," he said before turning to leave the room.

"The police?" Laura repeated from behind him. "Why are they coming here?"

"Because," Matthew said, turning round again, "I think Peter Chilcott has accused you of damaging his car."

"Me? Damaging his car?"

"Will you stop repeating everything I say? Now get dressed and come downstairs."

Matthew left the room.

He felt he had been talking to his teenage daughter rather than his fiancée, never having seen Laura like that before. If she hadn't done anything to the Chilcotts' car then why had she looked so guilty?

After collecting the mugs from the telephone table, he went into the kitchen to pour the tea away.

The doorbell rang five minutes later.

"Good afternoon, Sir," a police officer said as Matthew opened the door.

Another police officer stood just behind the first one. Regardless of their recent dealings with the police, Matthew didn't recognise either of the two officers.

"Good afternoon, constable," Matthew said and was going to add, "I think I know why you are here," but he didn't.

"Sir, I'm PC Leadbetter and this is PC Hall, we are investigating some damage that was done at the local golf club this afternoon and we think you may be able to help with our enquiries."

"You'd better come in."

Matthew stood back but they hesitated. "After you, Sir."

Leading the way into the living room, Matthew wondered where Laura was. "Please sit down and tell me how I can help?" he said.

"Not you, Sir." PC Leadbetter took a notebook from his pocket and flipped it open. "We would like to speak to a …" he said as he looked down at his book, "a … a Miss Laura Stanhope. We have got the right address, haven't we, Sir?"

"Yes," Matthew said, feigning surprise. "May I ask why you want to speak to her?"

"As we said, Sir, there's been some damage at the golf club and we think Miss Stanhope …"

Laura walked into the room. The police officers looked in her direction.

"You want to speak to me?" she asked.

"Are you Miss Laura Stanhope?" PC Leadbetter asked.

"Yes."

On entering the room both officers had remained standing and were still wearing their hats. They were of a similar age – mid to late thirties – and were of a similar build.

"Were you at the Westerham golf club between thirteen hundred hours and fourteen hundred hours today, Madam?" PC Leadbetter asked.

"If you mean was I at the golf club between one and two o'clock, then, yes, of course I was," Laura told them. She had put on exactly the same clothes she'd worn earlier that day. "Why?" she asked crossing the room and sitting on the sofa, smiling as she asked her question.

"A Mr …" – he referred to his notebook again – "… a Mr Peter Chilcott had his car damaged and he gave us your name as the possible perpetrator."

"*Perpetrator?*" Laura repeated, still with an amused look on her face. "What sort of word is that? This is because of his damn wife, isn't it?"

"We don't know about that, Madam. What we do know is that he thinks you were the one who might have damaged his car."

PC Hall was looking around the room, either disinterested in proceedings or looking for some vital clues in the pictures on the walls.

"Then he has got his wires crossed, hasn't he?" Laura said as the smile disappeared. "And, actually, I object to him sending you here asking questions." Laura hadn't taken her eyes off the police officer since she walked in the room.

"He didn't send us, Madam. As I said, we are following up on our enquiries," PC Leadbetter said.

"So you've been to see, or are going to see, some other likely – what did you call them? – some other likely perpetrators are you?"

"No, Madam, because yours was the only name Mr Chilcott gave us."

"Oh, was it? So, this Mr Chilcott is actually saying – no accusing me – of damaging his car, is he?"

The police officer ignored Laura's question. "Did you and the Chilcotts have an argument, Madam?"

"They said some pretty nasty things about me, yes," Laura said, "They humiliated me in front of my fiancé and my friends, and now they are humiliating me again by sending you here."

"As I said, Madam, Mr Chilcott did not send us here …"

"All right, you are just following up on your enquiries."

Matthew wanted to tell her to stop being antagonistic, but before he could Laura said, "So what am I supposed to have done to Mr Chilcott's car?"

"It was scratched rather badly, all the way down one side, Madam."

Laura shrugged. "You might be surprised to hear I am actually very sorry that car has been damaged because it is, or should I say was, rather beautiful."

PC Leadbetter did look surprised. "Oh!" he said.

"And," Laura said leaning forward slightly, "they may have said some pretty horrible things to me, but do I look like the sort of person who would go around scratching people's cars out of revenge?"

"Well, no …"

"There you are, then. Mr Chilcott and his bitch of a wife gave me good reason to do them damage, but as for their car, no, Constable, I am afraid you are wasting your time."

"So you're saying you did not do it?"

"I most certainly am … but," she then added as PC Leadbetter started to speak, "if Mr Chilcott persists with unproven accusations, he might discover that I have one or two of my own."

Matthew jerked his head round and stared down at Laura as he wondered what she was going to say.

"I'm sorry, Madam, what do you mean?" PC Hall asked, speaking for the first time.

"I mean nothing at this stage," Laura said. "All I am saying is that Mr Chilcott needs to be careful as to who he points his finger at because he could find himself being accused himself of doing something pretty damn serious."

Both police officers frowned and exchanged looks.

"And you, Sir?" PC Leadbetter asked, turning to Matthew. "Were you with Miss Stanhope when she left the clubhouse?"

"No, not with her," Matthew said and saw Laura's eyes dart in his direction, "but because she left the clubhouse so quickly I left soon after her. As I stood up to leave, I did see her crossing the car park."

"And could you see Mr Chilcott's car after you'd stood up?"

Matthew thought very quickly. He remembered that he could see the car but he hadn't seen Laura. "Yes," he said.

"And did you see Miss Stanhope go anywhere near it?"

"No, other than to pass it to get to my car."

"What, she physically had to pass Mr Chilcott's car to get your car?" PC Hall asked.

"Constable, Mr Chilcott's car was in a reserved space directly outside the clubhouse. Anybody leaving the clubhouse would have had to pass it to get to any other car in the car park," Matthew said, patiently.

"I see, Sir, and …"

"Yes, Miss Stanhope passed it, as I did a few seconds later."

"Thank you, Sir and Madam."

The two police officers moved towards the door.

"We will be asking at the clubhouse if there were any witnesses, but if you say Miss Stanhope didn't go anywhere near the car other than to pass it like anybody else would have had to do, Sir, it's unlikely anybody else will be aware that any damage has been done to the car."

"Excuse me, Officer," Laura said standing up and putting her hands on her hips, "Miss bloody Stanhope says she didn't damage Mr Chilcott's fucking car. That should be good enough."

"Of course, Madam," PC Leadbetter said, his face expressionless. "Are you sure there's nothing further you want to add to what you implied earlier?" he asked.

"And what did I imply earlier?" Laura said, her hands still on her hips.

"That Mr Chilcott might have done something inappropriate to you," he said.

Laura looked genuinely shocked. "Did I imply that? I don't think I said anything that should have led you to draw a conclusion like that." She turned to face Matthew. "Did I Matthew?" she asked.

Matthew shook his and said, "No, you didn't."

PC Leadbetter took a deep breath. "Thank you for your help, Madam. We'll see ourselves out, Sir."

"You didn't have to lie for me," Laura insisted after they heard the front door close. "I didn't do it, so nobody can prove I did."

"Then I didn't lie for you, did I?" Matthew said. "But are you, Laura?"

Matthew poured himself a whisky from the decanter on the dresser. After quickly swallowing the contents of the glass, he poured himself another.

"What do you mean? Am I what?" she asked. "Am I sure I didn't do it or am I sure they can't prove it?"

"I don't know," he said as he turned to face her.

He held the glass in front of him and rested against the dresser. He knew that she would see the accusation in his eyes, but that's how it had to be if he was going to get the truth out of her.

"Don't I get one of those?" she asked.

Matthew poured Laura a whisky and handed it to her.

"You have to admit it looks pretty suspicious," he said.

"What exactly are you implying?" Laura asked, sitting on the sofa her eyes on fire.

"Laura, I'm not implying anything. All I'm saying is that when you left the table you were pretty fired up and, after what you told me last night," he added quickly holding up his hand, "you had every reason to be the way you were, I …"

"It was you who told me to wear those damn trousers."

Matthew frowned. "The trousers have nothing to do with it. Peter was a bad loser and his wife was even worse. They were going to blame anything and everyone but themselves. The point is, you were very angry and you could have done it without knowing."

"Don't talk such fucking rubbish, Matthew!" Laura shouted. "If I'd run a key or a coin down the side of a fucking brand new Mercedes, I would have remembered." She drank her whisky in one gulp and stood up. "It's the fact you don't believe me that's really getting to me."

"And what was that other thing about?" he asked.

"What other thing?"

"You told the police that Peter Chilcott needed to be careful who he was accusing of damaging his car because you might have some accusations of your own. What was that all about?"

"Well … well," Laura said. "I was annoyed and he did … he did try to …"

"He did try to what?" Matthew asked.

"Well … on the … I don't know … on the hole where he hit his ball into the woods and I thought … I thought I knew where it had gone …"

"The thirteenth?"

"It doesn't matter what hole it was … he touched me … he …"

"Peter Chilcott touched you? What do you mean he touched you?"

"Well … his hand, his fingers, brushed against, touched my bottom. He … before you and Brian came to help find his ball, he touched me …"

"What, he touched your bottom deliberately?" Matthew asked.

"He said it wasn't deliberate and he apologised but …"

"So it could have been an accident?"

"No, he did it deliberately," Laura said, her eyes dropping to her whisky glass.

"Are you sure?"

"Yes, he'd been leering at me all day and he ..."

"Why didn't you tell me about this before?"

"I couldn't prove it, there was no one else there when he touched me," Laura said, her head still bowed.

"Well, I think –"

"And he can't prove I damaged his car, can he?" she said as she looked up at Matthew. "And as I didn't do it, there never will be any proof."

Matthew had drunk too much whisky too quickly and it hit him like a door banging in a gale. He had to put a hand onto the dresser to stop himself from swaying. Laura was watching him, her eyes unblinking. Perhaps now was the time – perhaps now was the time when he could find out what had really been going on, and what was really behind all of this.

"It's not only what happened to that car, Laura, is it ...?" He paused as he began to have second thoughts about what he knew he had to say, but then he rushed on. "It's the threatening letters as well. Was that you? Did you put them together? Did you send those letters to yourself for some reason?"

If he hadn't been watching her he wouldn't have believed what she did next. It was almost as though it happened in slow motion.

After drawing back her arm she threw the whisky glass at him.

He moved his head quickly but still felt the glass touch his cheek as it flew passed him. The glass shattered against the wall behind him. He was so startled he didn't react as Laura launched herself across the gap between them, her fingers like claws and her arms flailing.

"You bastard, you fucking bastard," she shouted. "I thought you believed in me." He felt her spittle on his face.

Matthew managed to get hold of her wrists as she attempted to drag her nails down his cheeks. She started kicking out at him: the wildness in her eye unbelievable. Because she wasn't wearing any shoes, the first blow she landed on his leg hurt her more than it hurt him, but then she brought her knee up with such force that, although she missed her intended target, she gave him a dead leg. Even though his leg gave way, he managed to hang onto to her wrists. Incongruously, the mock fight they had in the hotel in Penang flashed through his mind so he knew how good she was, but this time she was like a wild animal.

Suddenly the strength and will to fight left her. She went limp as Matthew continued to hold her wrist, if he let her go she would fall to the floor. She slumped against him, her sobs shaking his body as well as hers. He wrapped his arms round her and hugged her, kissing the top of her head.

"It'll be all right," he said. "We'll get you some help, find out what's causing all of this and …"

"I … I didn't do … do any of those things."

"No, of course you didn't. But you need help Laura …"

"Why … why do I need help if I … I haven't done anything?" She pulled her head away from Matthew and looked up. "Go … go on, answer me. If I … I haven't done anything, why … why do I need help?"

Matthew moved his hands from her shoulders to the sides of her face, his thumbs wiping away her tears.

She was a little girl again.

He moved his fingers over her eyebrows, down the sides of her nose, over her lips. She was his little girl and he had to protect her. Matthew bent down and brushed his lips against hers and she responded by putting her arms round his neck and kissing him back.

"You … you have to believe me, Laura. Everything will turn out all right," Matthew said, her hair soft against his face, her smell playing havoc with his thoughts.

"There … there are a lot of evil people out there, Matthew."

"Of course there are, that is why I need to take care of you?" he said.

The next thing Laura said sent shivers down his spine.

"Will you, Daddy?"

Chapter Twenty-Four

Matthew picked Laura up in his arms.

He carried her over to the sofa where he could hold her as tightly as he dared. Her head rested on his chest until she eventually fell asleep with her thumb in her mouth.

In just forty-eight hours their world had collapsed and he really, really did not know what to do. Although he had thought about it, he hadn't been able to admit to himself that Laura really did need professional psychiatric help. Each time he had thought about the possibility before he had recoiled and asked himself why he didn't trust his own judgement as to who Laura really was, and his own ability to deal with the situation.

What was now staring him in the face hadn't even been a possibility. He had allowed his own conceit, his own belief that the way he was handling the situation was the only way. Others wouldn't understand.

Until meeting Wendy Carter on Friday, he firmly believed everything Laura told him. There had been no reason to doubt her. Saturday had been mentally exhausting but, externally, perfectly normal. Saturday evening had been so wonderful and, as they had gone to bed, walking up the stairs with their arms round each other, he honestly believed that Wendy Carter and her cohorts had got it all wrong, maybe not deliberately but mere interpretation can so easily lead to inaccurate conclusions.

The system had been too big for Laura to fight by herself.

He had honestly believed he was engaged to a loving, caring and thoughtful woman with whom he wanted to spend the rest of his life. Often, as he'd held her in his arms in bed, staring at the curtain moving slightly in the breeze and listening to her breathing becoming steadier and steadier as she fell asleep, the slight twitching from her body as her mind adjusted to unconsciousness, he didn't believe that he could be any happier.

On each of these occasions Laura had replaced the irreplaceable.

Now she was asleep once again, exhausted by her mental anguish, the same twitches, the same steady breathing, but rather than being a sensual fully-grown woman, she had regressed into a little girl in a woman's body who needed help.

The truth was now known and all because a bloody arrogant golfer couldn't stand losing.

Laura had needed loving.

Her body had needed loving and her mind had needed loving too but it had needed a different kind of love. Her mind needed understanding.

As two people who are so close adjust to the other's little eccentricities, she had needed Matthew to adjust. For so long he succeeded without knowing there was a need for adjustment in the first place. He had no idea that she was ill and had been for such a long time. Laura hadn't said or done anything that would have led him to believe she was ill, so very ill.

Some sort of trigger must have caused her to regress. The row in the golf club had brought it all out into the open, but it had started with the first letter and nothing he could pinpoint might be the cause.

He had only ever considered that Laura's injuries had resulted from a deliberate act, an act that could have ended in her death. Wendy Carter had suggested that Laura had used it as an opportunistic replacement for what she had really planned.

So what had she really planned? Whatever it was, it could still have been the trigger ... albeit self-induced.

The trauma of being flung over the roof of a car and thrown like a rag doll onto the road would have affected anybody. Had she banged her head harder than anybody suspected? Was there latent damage that hadn't been detected? The withdrawal into herself had been temporary as she attempted to cope with the experience. She hadn't felt the need to lock herself away for hours and she hadn't asked for professional counselling. She had shown a resilience that had amazed him. Her experience in Warwick hadn't weakened her: it had given her added strength to deal with the aftermath.

Laura's head moved slightly against his chest and, with the palm of his hand, Matthew stroked her hair gently. She had dribbled, a small damp patch appearing on the front of his shirt next to her lips. He wiped the corner of her mouth with his finger.

Had she felt so insecure that she had needed to gain his attention by manufacturing the threatening letters? That possibility had crossed his mind soon after Wendy Carter had told him her version of the truth. He thought he had been giving Laura all she needed but, until she had almost died, he had never told her he loved her. He'd never given her the security of those few words.

Words?

That's all they were, but without them ... just maybe.

Saying he loved her would have shown support for her feelings, her actions and the little things that she needed: the little things that matter and that make the bigger things happen automatically. He had loved her but he had never told her he loved her until after the accident. After what had happened with Emily, Matthew had been scared to declare his love. Three simple words, could they have prevented all of this?

Was it that easy?

Perhaps his obsession with the past had been the real cause.

Had he been so soaked up in his own self-pity that he couldn't see what was happening in front of him? He'd found an irreplaceable, delicate and beautiful porcelain vase, but didn't realise that by handling it roughly he might just break it.

Laura had told him that she was in pieces before they met. Outwardly, she was able to present herself as an efficient, capable and robust businesswoman, but inside she was hurting and in tatters. She let Matthew help her put those pieces back together again, to rebuild her self-esteem and her own beliefs. Together they found the right pieces and carefully glued them back in place, but all the time he was chipping away at her very foundations, until finally she collapsed into herself again, and all because he was unable to say three simple words.

Why had Laura called him 'Daddy'?

Why, when he had driven her to the depths she hadn't experienced for so long, had she called him 'Daddy'? Why, when she needed help like she'd never needed it before, did she call him 'Daddy'?

When trying to analyse and therefore understand the importance of the story about the sea bass immediately after she related the experience all he saw in front of him was a beautiful young woman who had done everything she could to give him an idyllic evening.

Was the link to her father a lot deeper and a lot more serious than he wanted to consider? Was what had happened to her at last coming to the surface and she was finding the experience unmanageable? If her father – and maybe others – had abused her and she had internalised the experience, allowing it to fester for so many years, perhaps he could begin to understand what was happening.

Laura had described how her mother had cowered in the bathroom when her father had beaten her in front of her brother and sister, because of what had happened during and after the sea bass incident. Perhaps her mother had known that Laura's father abused her but she was too scared to report the matter.

Maybe Matthew now had an explanation as to why he had never met Laura's parents, let alone her siblings.

Perhaps they all knew.

Laura stirred and her hand reached up to Matthew's shoulder.

He felt her head move, followed by a sleepy, "My mouth tastes awful." She gazed up at him, her eyes suggesting she didn't have the faintest idea where she was. "How long have I been asleep?" she asked, running her tongue over her lips.

"About an hour," he told her, smoothing her hair.

"I didn't dream about that visit from the police, did I?" she said sitting up.

"No, I'm afraid they were for real." Matthew moved his hands onto her face, running his knuckles down her cheek. "You're beautiful when you've just woken up."

Laura stretched and yawned. "Only when I wake up? Wow, I feel as though I've been asleep for a week."

"No, just an hour," he told her.

"I didn't do that to Peter Chilcott's car. You do believe me, don't you?" she said.

Her voice was normal, no sign of the childlike intonation that had frightened him so much before she fell asleep.

"Of course, I do. It was just a silly misunderstanding."

Laura smiled and tapped his bottom lip with her forefinger. "Are you humouring me, or even patronising me?"

"I wouldn't dream of it," he said.

"Good." Laura leant forward and kissed him. "Right I must go and clean my teeth. My mouth is all yucky."

"All right," he said, taking his arm from around her shoulders.

"What time is it?" Laura asked as she got to the door.

Matthew checked his watch. "A little after five."

"Are you hungry yet? We didn't have any lunch."

"No, not particularly. We could –"

"No, neither am I," Laura said. "Shall we pop through to The Grasshopper later and have a bar snack?"

"Good idea, that's exactly what I was going to suggest."

The Grasshopper didn't concern him: if Peter and Brian were in there they would just have to face the music. The fact that Laura hadn't mentioned Matthew's accusation that she was the author of her own threatening letters did concern him. She had either logged it away or she genuinely couldn't remember because she had already been acting very strangely.

"I'm going to have a long soak before we go out," Laura shouted from upstairs. "Are you going to join me?"

"Shortly," he shouted back, "I've got a couple of things I want to do first."

"Don't be long."

When Laura had been asleep, and question after question had whirled round in his mind, he had thought about Patrick Schofield, her ex-husband. There was still no proof that Laura had done any of the things for which she stood accused: no proof that the rape, sexual harassment and lesbian propositioning hadn't happened: no proof that the Surrey police hadn't closed ranks and forced her to retire: no proof that she had been the author of the letters and finally, no proof that she had damaged Peter Chilcott's car. The regression to a childlike voice had been frightening, but it hadn't happened before. As soon as she woke up she was back to normal.

So did he actually have sufficient undeniable facts to ask for help? No he didn't. He only had his and other people's suspicions.

If he were able to find something tangible, maybe they could progress. Although previously he had dismissed her relationship with her ex-husband as being unfortunate but inconsequential, perhaps now he was a source of information. If Laura had written her own threatening letters – for whatever reason – then the ex-husband might be able to provide a few answers. He would have to chose the right time and place because he wouldn't want to cause a scene.

However, he wasn't going to give up on Laura.

She needed his help more now than at any other time.

Going upstairs as quietly as he could, he listened at the bathroom door. He could hear the bath water running and Laura was humming a tune to herself, seemingly oblivious to what was happening around her. He went into the bedroom and round to her side of the bed. As well as the address book by the phone, he knew she kept another book in her bedside drawer. He had seen her looking at it one evening a few months ago, and when she became aware that he was in the room, she'd snapped it shut and looked at him guiltily.

"What's that?" he asked her, more because she probably expected him to ask rather than out of genuine interest.

"My little black book," she said, putting it back in the drawer.

"And what's in your little black book?" Matthew asked, rummaging through his side of the wardrobe for something to wear.

They were going to the theatre.

"Little black book things," she replied before changing the subject.

He had forgotten all about the incident until the seeds of his idea came back to him. Opening the drawer, he couldn't see the book at first. There were scraps of paper, emery boards, a couple of old novels and her contraceptive pills, along with countless other items.

Trying not to disturb anything, he felt under the novels and touched what he thought must be the book. It was an address book, so he went through to the 'Ss', and looked for Schofield.

It was there.

One address in Fulham in London had been crossed out and another address written underneath. It was an address in Solihull, near Birmingham, and it gave a telephone number. He had no idea how recent the amendment was. Going to his bedside drawer, he extracted a piece of paper and a pencil. He made a note of the address and telephone number before replacing Laura's little black book exactly as he'd found it. He was tempted to scan the rest of the page, but even under such circumstances, Laura deserved some privacy.

"What took you so long?" she asked when he opened the bathroom door five minutes later.

She was lying back in the middle of the bath, her whole body covered by soapsuds, her smiling face just above the surface of the water and as pretty as ever.

Matthew put the open bottle of cold white wine and two glasses next to her. "It's only been a few minutes," he told her, stepping into the bath after she'd moved over to make room for him.

"What have you been doing?"

"On an impulse I tried to ring Brian," he lied, "to tell him that we were pretty upset that Peter had blamed you for the damage to his car."

"And? What do you mean you tried?" Laura wiggled her bottom so that she could sit up and pour the wine.

"There was no reply."

"Do you think the police have arrested him for being slanderous about me?" Laura asked, handing Matthew a glass of wine.

"I doubt it."

"Yes, so do I."

Over the next two days, Matthew enjoyed slipping back into a reasonable, albeit contrived, routine. He realised that seeing Patrick Schofield without Laura being aware was not going to be easy, but his determination was still there. Popping into Sevenoaks was one thing but Solihull generated a completely different scenario. Obviously going to Birmingham next Tuesday night presented an ideal opportunity, but unless he was able to sneak through to Solihull during the day, the chance wouldn't be there. He didn't particularly want to do any sneaking anywhere but he did need something to work with.

Unexpectedly, Laura provided him with the opportunity to do what he had planned. He had popped out for a couple of odds and ends on the Monday and, when he got back, there had been a phone call.

"Daddy's not well," Laura told him, looking very concerned. "He's had a slight stroke and although the doctor thinks he'll make a full recovery, mum is worried and wants me to go and see him."

The mention of her father and the worry his situation immediately generated in her, made Matthew wonder whether his earlier assumption that her father could be the source of Laura's behaviour, was purely speculative.

"Then of course you must go," he said. "Why don't I take you there tomorrow before going through to Birmingham and then you can give me a call when you want collecting? I'll be free in the evenings and we are due in Stafford on Friday. It's not a million miles away."

Laura broke eye contact and said, "I'd prefer to be independent, Matthew, then I won't feel that you're waiting for a call all the time."

He shrugged. "If that's what you'd prefer. What about …?"

"The threats? It's been ages since the accident, Matthew. I really do think it was some crank who picked up on what happened from the paper. I'll be careful, though."

"I'll still be worried," he said.

"I'll get a hired car. Can we afford it?"

"Of course we can," he said.

"I'll do that tomorrow morning and leave at the same time as you. I'll let mum know later."

Matthew had got used to being cut out of any suggestion of conversation to do with her parents, but her behaviour the day before, after the police had been, was still obviously foremost in his mind. He couldn't help thinking that there was more to this visit to Nottingham than he was being told, but why would she make up some story about her father having a stroke?

It was all a bit of a coincidence for the call to arrive while he was conveniently in the village doing some shopping. He was trying to second-guess her but he believed it was for the right reasons.

When Laura went to the loo a couple of minutes later, he checked the phone for the last call but the caller had withheld their number, but the time was right. Perhaps he was being overly suspicious, she hadn't said whether she had phoned her mother or whether her mother had phoned her, but he would have thought, if her father had had a stroke, it would have been Laura's mother who had made the call.

They both left the following day at just after three.

Laura hired a Ford Focus for four days and Matthew kept it in his rear view mirror as they went clockwise round the M25. At the M40 junction he peeled off and with much flashing of lights and waving, they said good-bye to each other.

Once he was on his own, it felt strange.

Normally he would have been thinking about the work that was ahead of him but recent events dictated his thought processes; his concentration easily guided away from work and onto Laura.

After booking into the hotel in the centre of Birmingham and checking with Laura on her mobile that she'd arrived safely, he called the number he had copied from her black book.

The phone was answered on the third ring.

"Hello. Julie Schofield."

Matthew hadn't expected a woman to answer, so he was temporarily stuck for words. He didn't know that Laura's ex-husband had remarried, and to some extent if he assumed the woman who answered the phone was his wife, then Patrick Schofield's credibility had just gone up a notch or two.

The woman had to say 'Hello' again before he responded.

"Good evening, Mrs Schofield. I'm sorry to disturb you but is it possible I could speak with your husband?"

"Patrick?"

"If that's at all possible, yes please."

"I'm afraid he's not home yet. He will be in about seven if you'd like to ring back."

Her voice was refined but not posh.

"Yes, I'll do that. I'll leave it until about eight to be on the safe side."

"If you could leave it until later in that case, because I'm planning the meal for eight," the woman said.

"Would nine o'clock be all right?"

"Yes, we'll be finished by then."

"Thank —"

"Who shall I say called?"

"My name is Matthew Ryan but your husband doesn't know me."

A few seconds of silence followed before Julie Schofield asked, "Can I tell him what it's about, Mr Ryan?"

"It's personal but nothing to worry about."

Matthew decided he couldn't really tell her that he wanted to ask him about his ex-wife.

"Sounds intriguing, Mr Ryan," Julie Schofield said, her voice softening for some inexplicable reason. "I'll tell him you'll call back. Must go, the baby is crying. 'Bye."

"'Bye," Matthew said to the dialling tone.

He had dinner in the hotel and a generous whisky in the bar, and phoned Patrick Schofield's number from his room at exactly nine o'clock.

"Schofield," a deep male voice said.

Matthew thought Patrick Schofield sounded tired but expectant. He also wondered what conclusions his wife had drawn and relayed to him.

"Mr Schofield, my name is Matthew Ryan and ..."

"Yes, my wife said you'd rung. How can I help you Mr Ryan?" Patrick Schofield asked pleasantly.

"It's a bit delicate actually," Matthew said and took a deep breath. "I would like to ask you a few questions about your ex-wife, Laura Stanhope."

"Laura?" Patrick Schofield repeated quietly and just a little suspiciously. "But ... wait a minute..." Matthew heard a door closing and the phone being picked up again. "Why do you want to talk to me about Laura? Are you the police?"

"No, I'm not the police," Matthew said, wondering whether what he had planned to say was right after all. If he were too evasive, he thought Patrick Schofield would hang up but if he told him the truth, he might still lose him. "Laura lives with me, Mr Schofield, and has done so for quite a while. I'm very worried about her. I'm worried about her safety but more importantly I'm worried about her sanity."

There was an audible gasp at the other end of the phone

followed by a few seconds silence.

"I thought …" Patrick Schofield started to say but changed to, "I think … yes, all right. Where are you?"

"I'm staying at the Holiday Inn in Birmingham."

"Is it the one in the centre?"

"Yes," Matthew said.

"How long are you there for?" Patrick asked.

"I'm there tonight and tomorrow night. I go home the following day."

"Under the circumstances," Patrick said, "I would have suggested that I come to you, but I'm on the road again tomorrow." Further silence. "Look, are you free tomorrow evening?"

"I could make myself free," Matthew said.

There had been a suggestion that Matthew and a couple of the senior managers from *Prospects for All* go out to dinner, but there were no firm arrangements. For Matthew this was far more important.

"Can you come here?" Patrick asked.

"I certainly can," he said, hoping his sudden enthusiasm wasn't too apparent.

Matthew was very surprised by Patrick Schofield's almost immediate agreement to a meeting and even more so at being invited to the house.

"But are you sure, Mr Schofield? I don't want to intrude," Matthew said as he tried to picture him as he spoke.

He had quite a deep but soft voice and he spoke very distinctly. He certainly didn't sound like a violent man and especially not one who would abuse a woman: but what do wife-beaters sound like?

"Mr Ryan, I am more than willing to discuss Laura with you," Patrick Schofield replied, but the way he said Laura's name suggested he was actually not too keen on the proposal. "Hang on a minute again, will you?"

Matthew heard the door being opened followed by mumbled voices in the background.

"Mr Ryan?" Patrick Schofield said after a short while.

"I'm still here."

"I'll be home about half six tomorrow evening. Would you be able to get here for seven?"

"Yes, but are you sure?"

"If I wasn't sure, Mr Ryan, I wouldn't be suggesting it. I don't necessarily relish the thought of talking about Laura but circumstances suggest you call is timely."

Matthew wanted to ask what he meant by his last remark and about his current wife: would she mind the discussion taking place or was she due to be out?

Patrick seemed to read Matthew's thoughts because he said, "Julie's throwing together a curry or something tomorrow for supper. She can cook for three as easily for two and that is on her suggestion."

Shocked by the offer of such hospitality, it was his turn to be silent. He had expected, if Patrick Schofield had agreed to a meeting at all, for it to take place in the hotel or a pub somewhere, anywhere but in his own home.

"That's very kind of you," Matthew said and he was going to add, "Are you sure?" but, after the previous minor rebuke, he didn't.

"I would like to say it's my pleasure but unfortunately I don't think it's going to be particularly pleasurable for either of us or for Julie," Patrick said.

"I thought that might be the case. Mr Schofield. You don't know me, I could be any Tom, Dick or Harry, but may I ask what I said that made you decide to invite me to your home and so readily?" Matthew asked.

"Three things, Mr Ryan, two of which you didn't say," Patrick said without any hesitation. "The first is that Julie and I have an eleven-month old baby and neither of us like leaving him with a sitter unless we really have to; second Julie was in the Surrey police with Laura and knew her pretty well, in fact she introduced her to me; and third, you said you were worried about Laura's sanity. Will that do you?"

"Yes, thank you."

"I'll give you the address. It's ..."

"I already have it." Matthew read it out to him. "I just need to know roughly how to find you."

"How did you get this number and the address in the first place, Mr Ryan?"

"From Laura. Well, not strictly from Laura, from a personal address book she keeps."

"I see. I think I might know the book you mean."

Matthew got tremendous reassurance from those few words. They were sharing an intimacy about Laura that under normal circumstances he might have objected to, but he actually felt the reverse.

"Where do you live with Laura?" Patrick asked.

"I have a cottage in Westerham, in Kent."

"And that is where Laura is now, while you're away, that is? I am assuming you're in Birmingham on business, or have you come just to see me?"

"No, you're right, on business primarily, but to answer your question, no, Laura's not there. She's in Nottingham visiting her parents."

This time there were more than a few moments of silence, so Matthew said, "Are you still there?"

"Yes, I'm still here. I don't want to add to your worries, Mr Ryan, but Laura's parents died years ago. Her father died suddenly of a heart attack in 1990 and her mother committed suicide a few months later. Supposedly she was extremely distraught after her husband's death and her suicide was put down to a broken heart but I have my own opinion."

Laura's parents were dead and had been long before he and Laura met. So why had she lied? Why had she needed to make him think they were still living? More importantly, if she wasn't in Nottingham with her parents, where was she and what was she doing?

"Then ..." Matthew started to say but changed his mind. "What about her brother Simon in Australia and her sister, Lisa?"

"Oh, Simon and Lisa, her brother and sister, she's told you about them, has she?"

Matthew could sense that Patrick Schofield was smiling, but not because he was amused. "Yes," he said tentatively.

"They don't exist, Mr Ryan. A bit like most of the world that Laura Stanhope lives in, it simply doesn't exist. Laura was an only child."

Chapter Twenty-Five

Matthew found the Schofields' address without s problem..

It was a detached house on the edge of a well-to-do estate in Solihull. There was a V Registered Mk10 Jaguar parked outside a double garage at right angles to the main house, with two individual green doors.

As they lived at the end of a cul-de-sac, Matthew assumed they liked a little peace and quiet, but his apprehension over-shadowed any normal thoughts or opinions.

A bit like most of the world that Laura Stanhope lives in, it doesn't exist, Patrick Schofield had said. Those words made Matthew's situation – their situation – far worse than his imagination had previously allowed ... if the words had been true.

If Laura's parents were dead, to whom had she been speaking on the phone? Matthew had heard her talking to her mother and there had been two-way conversations, hadn't there? Where had she gone when she had supposedly been visiting her parents?

Why invent a brother and sister?

The front door opened a matter of seconds after he rang the bell, interrupting his thoughts.

A tall, very elegant, woman smiled nervously at him and her brow creased as she asked, "Mr Ryan?"

"Yes," he told her.

Mrs Julie Schofield was not what he had expected.

As well as being tall and very elegant, Julie Schofield also had the blackest skin he had ever seen. A high forehead and very short hair complemented a statuesque face from which he could not take his eyes. She had a long straight nose, high cheekbones and large eyes, the irises of which were the same colour as her skin. As she smiled a greeting, she presented very even and white teeth between full lips to which she had applied a pink gloss.

She had to be the most beautiful woman he had ever seen.

He felt he ought to bow in her presence.

Opening the door further, Julie Schofield stood back,.

"Please come in, Mr Ryan, Patrick was a little later than he'd hoped and he's having a shower. He asked me to apologise and to say that he'd be down in a few minutes."

Her voice was like silk and, as she led the way through the hall, she glided rather than walked.

She was wearing dark-blue cotton flared trousers, the bottoms of which rested on small bare feet. Her toenails were the same pink as her fingernails and lips. On top, she wore a white collarless cotton shirt with three-quarter length sleeves.

Julie Schofield led Matthew through the kitchen – where the aroma of curry and herbs filled the room – and into what he presumed was a day room. It wasn't a conservatory and it wasn't a dining room. Whatever its name, in the centre there was a small glass-topped dining table set for three people. Beyond this table were a two-seater rattan sofa and a couple of rattan chairs. Two large windows looked out over a well-stocked walled-garden.

Julie gestured with a slender long-fingered hand towards one of the chairs. "Please sit down, Mr Ryan. Can I get you a drink? Gin and tonic? You look like the sort of man who would enjoy a gin and tonic."

"Please," Matthew replied. "That's very kind of you."

Julie smiled and headed back towards the kitchen.

Impeccably decorated, on most surfaces there were what looked like reminders from the Schofields' travels: oriental drapes, middle-eastern rugs, hats and carved figures positioned at various critical points made the room what it was – magnificent. There were strategically placed healthy looking plants, the flowers of which contrasted exactly with the other decorations. It was a beautiful and tastefully decorated room.

Matthew heard voices in the kitchen and Patrick Schofield walked into the room holding two cut-glass tumblers.

"Mr Ryan," he said, handing Matthew one of the tumblers. "I'm sorry I wasn't here to greet you earlier but, as Julie explained, I was a little later than expected."

After taking the tumbler from his host, Matthew held out his hand.

Patrick, like Julie, was not what he had expected.

He was very tall – probably two or even three inches taller than Matthew – and had thick wavy dark hair that flopped over his forehead in a very boyish sort of way. His skin was tanned and swarthy. The yellow short-sleeved shirt and neatly pressed cream chinos made him appear fully relaxed and yet well dressed. His handshake was firm.

"My name is Matthew. Considering what we are going to talk about, perhaps we should dispense with unnecessary formalities."

As he spoke, Matthew thought back to the comment Wendy Carter made about him needing to be informal to be relaxed. He didn't think the need for informality would have applied to where he now was, but the Schofields were certainly not what he expected, so why should his behaviour necessarily suggest the need for formality?

"I quite agree, and it's Patrick," Patrick said, smiling understandingly. "And I'm sorry if I forced the issue a bit on the phone."

He motioned towards the chair and Matthew sat down again. Patrick perched on the edge of the sofa.

"Julie says that dinner will be about thirty minutes," Patrick said. "She'll join us again in a little while."

"I'm sorry to have contacted you in the way I did, but I needed to know something about Laura's past and you were –"

"I'm sorry to interrupt, Matthew, but your call was not unexpected. It could have happened at any time and come from any source. When I say your call, I don't mean you specifically." Patrick held his tumbler in both hands and stared down at the clear liquid. He looked up slowly, his blue-grey eyes appearing to reach into Matthew's mind. "But, in some ways, I'm relieved it is you who has contacted me because it could so easily have been the police, a solicitor or even worse."

There was some chinking and the sounds of general movement coming from the kitchen.

"I know this is going to seem a little strange, and you can tell me to mind my own business, but can we start with you and Julie?" Patrick raised his eyebrows in surprise. "I don't want to inadvertently put my foot in it, especially as neither of you are what I expected. It's a most unusual reason to come and see you, and I don't want to make a mess of things before we start."

A rueful smile crossed Patrick's lips. "Not what you expected?" he repeated. "I suppose you were expecting to see a wife-beating philanderer or even a prominent member of the criminal fraternity?"

Matthew returned his smile. "I don't think I knew what to expect," but he wanted to say, "Yes, that's exactly what I was expecting."

Patrick pursed his lips and nodded. "Well, I suppose that is one thing that goes in my favour," Patrick said and Matthew frowned. "You have to believe me when I tell you that when I wasn't beating her, I was," he paused and looked over his shoulder towards the kitchen, "sleeping with every other woman I could find."

This time his smile was genuine as he held up his hand.

"I wasn't, I hasten to add, but I'd be surprised if that's not what you'd been told. I am very aware of what she was telling everybody on top of what she accused me of to my face. No doubt you've been told that I also walked off with all of her money?"

"No, there's been no mention of that," Matthew said.

"Well, she will be building up to tell you, she's probably saving it for the right moment." He paused. "You asked about Julie," he said, becoming serious again. "I suppose she ought to be in here really if we are going to talk about her. She has her own story to tell you so, for no other reason than that, would you mind if we waited until then?"

"Fine, I'm sorry … "

"Fifteen minutes," the cry came from the kitchen, "and could you open the wine, Patrick?"

"Okay, J," Patrick shouted back. "I'll do the wine in a sec," but then he said more quietly, "How long have you and Laura been together?"

"Nearly eighteen months," Matthew told him. "And, until recently, everything has been fine." He felt the need, even then, to jump to Laura's defence.

"And what's happened recently that resulted in you contacting me?" Patrick took a sip of his gin and tonic, screwing up his eyes as he swallowed.

After a deep breath Matthew said, "An attempted suicide on a cross-channel ferry, a hit-and run, threatening letters, a presumptuous police woman and a scratched Mercedes 600 SEL."

Patrick's eyes opened wide. "There's a connection?"

Matthew nodded slowly. "I'm afraid there is."

"You'd better tell me."

"Like you," Matthew said, "don't you think it ought to wait until your wife is with us?"

"Of course," Patrick replied holding up his hand. "I'll fix the wine. Would you like another gin and tonic?"

"I'd better not."

Matthew's host disappeared into the kitchen and he could hear Patrick and Julie talking.

They sat down to eat a few minutes later and Julie explained that in the glass dish in front of him was a mixture of melon, grapes, peach and apricot, with a liberal topping of Cointreau and cinnamon.

"This really is very kind of you both," Matthew told them, raising his eyebrows when he realised just how liberal Julie had been with the Cointreau.

"If we have something to discuss, it may as well be in as pleasant an atmosphere as possible," Julie said, looking at Matthew as though she had known him for years rather than just minutes.

"But you've gone to so much trouble," Matthew said.

"We were having curry anyway and this took minutes to put together." Julie picked up a piece of melon on her spoon and popped it in her mouth. "Now stop being so polite and tell us what has brought you here."

Matthew looked at Patrick and he nodded slightly. "I find it quite incredible that I'm here at all," Matthew started by saying, "but I have to find out the truth. Regardless of why I'm here, I still feel guilty. I feel I've broken a trust."

"You mustn't," Patrick told him. "If guilt, loyalty and trust really were that important, Laura would never have placed you in the position where you need to find out the truth in the first place. I only hope we can give you the answers you need."

"Thanks for that but," Matthew said, shrugging, "she has this hold on me." He looked at Julie. "I was saying earlier that an attempted suicide on a cross-channel ferry, a hit-and run, threatening letters, a presumptuous policewoman and a scratched

Mercedes 600 SEL are the real reasons I am here."

"They all sound intriguing. Which would you like to start with?" Julie asked.

"Darling," Patrick chipped in, "I did rather imply that …"

"That's all right, I'm quite happy doing it this way round," Matthew told him. "It's only recently that I started to have my doubts but they appear to stem from an incident on a P&O cross-channel ferry back in March this year."

Julie and Patrick Schofield listened intently. At one point Julie asked Matthew to pause while she went and checked on the rice.

"It'll be about five minutes," she told them, resuming her seat. "Please go on, Matthew."

Matthew told them everything about the ferry, what had happened afterwards, and not once did he stop and wonder why. As he moved on to the quiet period between the ferry and the hit-and-run, he did say the connection was tenuous, but he was sure there was one. When he described how the first threatening letter had arrived, Patrick nodded and exchanged looks with Julie but said nothing. Matthew had reached the heart-to-heart he had with Wendy Carter when Julie apologised and said that if she didn't attend to the rice it would be over-cooked.

She served the second course and the aroma of the curry filled the room.

"I'm sure I know Wendy Carter," Julie suggested, resuming her seat. "Is she tall, slim, dark hair with a slightly prominent nose?"

"Yes," Matthew replied, nodding. "That's a pretty accurate description."

"Then I do know her. I'm sure she came and gave us a lecture on females and their acceptance in the police force, when we were in training,.."

"Darling," Patrick said, putting his hand on hers, "can we let Matthew finish?"

"Yes, I'm sorry, Matthew. You were saying."

Matthew explained that even after the initial doubts planted in his mind by Wendy Carter, he found that he was making excuses for Laura, looking for ways to try to prove that she wasn't the liar that he'd been told she was. That was when something as minor as a scratched car had made him realise that although there was no proof, there were also no excuses. He knew that Laura had been responsible for the damage to Peter Chilcott's car and she had known that he knew but she continued denying any involvement.

The curry was magnificent, bordering on being mind-blowingly hot. However, the accompanying sauces, fruits, nuts and garlic Naan bread seemed to placate the explosion that went with every mouthful. It was an experience and very difficult to try to be serious at the same time. It crossed Matthew's mind that if Julie and Patrick ate like that every night, they must save pounds on restaurant bills.

He decided that Julie Schofield was one very talented woman.

"Do you mind if I ask how you met Laura?" Patrick said.

He'd tackled the curry with style and certainly gave no indication that it was as hot as Matthew had found it.

"Of course you can," Matthew said and went on to explain about his separation and then divorce from Emily. When he added that he always had the need to know Emily and Sarah were all right, Julie stopped eating and looked at him.

"Are you serious?"

"I'm afraid I am." Matthew told her, feeling slightly embarrassed under her scrutiny.

Matthew had come to see Patrick Schofield to find out what he needed to know about Laura, but he found that he was telling them more about himself than he had told anybody else since Emily and he had separated.

"But she'd done the dirty on you," Julie said. "She was the one who was having the affair and she'd even passed off a little girl she had by her lover as yours. Why should you have a conscience?" She saw Matthew's reaction. "Oh, I'm sorry, Matthew!" She reached across the table and put her hand on his arm. "I shouldn't have said it like that."

Matthew smiled at her. "That's all right. You've every right to think that way but it wasn't a conscience," he said, putting his fork down on an empty plate, his mouth on fire. "That, Julie," he added with difficulty, "was the most fantastic curry I've ever tasted."

Frowning Julie asked, "Was it too hot for you? Would you like some sugar or a glass of milk?"

"No, no," Matthew told her, not wanting to offend. "It was simply perfect."

"Well, thank you," Julie said, smiling and appearing to be pleased with his intended compliment. "We'll have a short break before seconds." She dabbed at her mouth with her napkin, peering at Matthew as she did so. "But you were saying ... I'm sorry I interrupted you."

"No, not at all Julie ... Emily may have, as you put it, done the dirty on me, but that did not alter how I felt about her. I just wanted to know – "

"Sorry to interrupt you again, Matthew, but did Laura know how you felt about your ex-wife from the outset?" Patrick asked.

"Yes, I'm afraid my feelings were ever present so it would have been obvious from the moment I first met her in her office. Why?"

Matthew felt he knew the answer to his question and he wasn't disappointed.

"I think the nail has just been hit well and truly on the head," Patrick suggested. "And it was only weeks after you met that Laura moved in with you?"

"Again, yes. I know it sounds pretty unprofessional but that's exactly what happened," Matthew said.

"I think, if you don't mind, Matthew, now would be the right time to hear what Julie has to tell you," Patrick said as he reached behind him and took some small cigars out of the drawer in the dresser.

Matthew was just a little surprised when Julie accepted and lit one of the cigars before saying, "Laura and I met when I joined her in Guildford after I'd finished training. In fact, she was my mentor for a while. I took to her straightaway. She was exactly what I wanted to be: dedicated, professional, and yet able to leave it all behind her when off duty. In other words, as well as being highly professional, she could party as well. She was also welcoming and very, very helpful, telling me who to trust and who to avoid. In the police, being female was bad enough when joining a new station, but to be female and black, well," Julie said, spreading her hands, "need I say more?"

"Probably not," Matthew said.

What he didn't understand was why somebody who was as

beautiful as Julie Schofield had wanted to join the police in the first place. She could have chosen any number of professions, most of which would have been far more lucrative and one hell of a lot safer.

"I would say, of course not," Julie explained, her eyes flashing as she corrected him, "but that's another story. Laura was brilliant though. I don't have to tell you that she's one very attractive female and all the men were drooling over her, but she seemed to spurn all their advances.

"I was in a relationship when I met Laura. Paul, my boyfriend, was also in the police but he was with the Met. He was the one who talked me into joining and suggested the Surrey police. He said they needed shaking up because their ethnic recruitment figures were way behind the rest of the country. He thought I'd enjoy the challenge. I have to add that Paul was white … but I'm getting away from the point again. It was through Paul that I introduced Laura to Patrick. We were at a party at Paul's flat in Bayswater and he was celebrating his thirtieth. There were loads of people there. I knew Patrick in passing because he and Paul had met at the local squash club, and I'd seen him once or twice when I went through to collect Paul."

Julie stopped as Patrick began to speak.

"I'd taken my fiancée to the party," Patrick said, picking up from where Julie had paused, "and I'm going to cut a long story very short," he explained steeling a glance at Julie who reacted by sticking her tongue out. "Kate, my fiancée, and I had a blazing row. She accused me of flirting with Laura when in fact the reverse applied. Kate, a little the worse for drink, stormed out of the party and, by the time I reached the street having realised what she was doing, I was just in time to see her disappearing in a taxi. The previous couple of weeks had been – how can I put it? – a little argumentative, so I let her go and went back to the party."

Patrick took a gulp of wine and lit another small cigar.

"Suffice to say, I had too much to drink," he said, "and, I hope you don't mind me saying this, I finished up in bed with Laura. The following morning we laughed it off, as neither of us could remember very much about how we'd got there, let alone what we'd done. About two months later, after there had been zero contact between us, she phoned me at the office. I am sure if I had been able to remember anything about it, if anything did happen – and Laura assured me it had – it would have been quite an experience. Once again I hope you don't mind me saying that, but there's little point in, well, pretending such things didn't happen between Laura and me."

Matthew shook his head. "Of course I don't mind. If I did, I wouldn't be here," he said.

"She'd got Patrick's number from Paul," Julie interjected, "because Laura had told me after that night she and Patrick had made some arrangement or other. I assumed that Patrick and Kate had finished and Laura was now on the scene."

"But that wasn't the case," Patrick carried on. "This out-of-the-blue phone call was to tell me that she was pregnant and what was I going to do about it? Evidently she didn't agree with abortion." Patrick spread his hands. "Kate and I were sort of back on speaking terms by then. It had taken that long to convince her that I was the innocent party. Suddenly the innocent party discovered he was going to be a father. What would you have done?" he asked, looking at Matthew but not wanting an answer.

Matthew hadn't noticed the baby alarm but there was suddenly a whimper, followed by rustling from behind the vase of lilies on the dresser.

"Joe's stirring," Julie said. "You two carry on, I know what Patrick's going to tell you next. I'll just go and check on him."

"Other than emigrating, there wasn't a lot I could do," Patrick continued once Julie had left the room. "To put things pretty bluntly, I ditched Kate and did the honourable thing. There was no way I could walk away from that kind of responsibility." He saw Matthew's surprise. "Chivalry isn't dead, you know," he said, smiling, "but perhaps stupidity goes hand-in-hand with it on occasions."

"You married Laura because she said she was pregnant and you were the father?" Matthew asked.

"In a nutshell, yep, that's exactly what I did. We got married six weeks after she told me. As Julie said, Laura is a good looking woman, as you well know, and I must admit I'd liked what I'd heard about her as well, other than the bit about her being pregnant, that is. We married in a registry office. My parents refused to attend because they idolised Kate and threatened to disown me, and Laura told me that her parents couldn't be there because they were in Australia visiting her brother. I knew nothing about the truth and the fictitious sister Lisa at this stage. At the wedding were Paul and Julie, a couple of other friends, and that was it. You could say it was a quiet affair. Footloose one minute, other than trying to keep Kate on-side, the next minute I'm married and going to be a father."

Matthew could hear Julie moving around in the room above them. "So what happened?" he said, finding Patrick's story as intriguing as his own.

"What happened?" Patrick repeated. "I'll tell you what bloody happened. We went to the Seychelles for a week on honeymoon. That was all the time either of us could afford to take off from work. We were by the hotel pool one day and, as I watched Laura climb out of the water – she was wearing a very skimpy bikini – and considering by then she was supposed to be nearly four months pregnant, I just happened to say she was very lucky she was to still so slim. As cool as a cucumber she lay back on the lounger next to me and said, "That's because I'm not pregnant … you can guess my reaction," Patrick continued.

The way he drew on his cigar left Matthew in no doubt as to what Patrick's reaction would have been.

"She proceeded to bloody well tell me that a week before we were married her period started, but she felt we couldn't cancel the wedding. She had meant to tell me but didn't know how to go about it because she wanted to be pregnant and felt very down when she discovered that she wasn't. I felt completely and utterly trapped. Although I'd been engaged to Kate, I'd had no intention of being married for years. Suddenly, not only was I married, but also I was married to a woman I didn't love. I didn't even bother to check I was being told the truth because, then, I didn't know what I know now."

Julie came back into the room.

"Where have you got to?" she asked.

In her arms, she had a very sleepy chocolate coloured little boy, his head resting against her shoulder, a dummy in his mouth and a pair of big brown eyes that were staring at Matthew.

Matthew smiled at him and he immediately turned his head away.

"I've just discovered that Laura isn't pregnant," Patrick told her. "Matthew meet Joe ... Joe this is Matthew!"

"Hello, Joe," Matthew said to the back of the child's head.

"The turning point," Julie commented, sitting down and arranging Joe on her lap so that he had little choice but to look at Matthew. "But before you hear the rest of what we have to say, can I get you some more curry, Matthew?"

"What I had was absolutely superb but I won't have any more, thank you. Isn't he gorgeous?" Matthew said, smiling.

"I'm pleased you liked it and, as for him," she said, looking down at Joe, "he's eleven months' worth of trouble. Patrick, what about you, more?"

"No thanks, darling."

"I won't either," Julie said, reaching for the wine bottle with her spare hand. Patrick beat her to it and topped up their glasses. "The pudding is cold, so we can wait for that. Can I pinch another of your cigars?" Julie said, reaching into the tin by Patrick's hand and putting the small cigar by her plate. "I'll save it until this bundle of fun goes back upstairs. Are you sure you don't want one?" she asked Matthew.

"No, thanks," Matthew replied, wishing he did smoke. He wanted to hear the rest of what Patrick had to say..

He obliged a few seconds later.

"Things went downhill from there. She used every trick in the book to try and keep me but, fortunately," he said, reaching across the table and putting his hand on Julie's arm, "none of them worked."

His eyes switched back to Matthew.

"Don't misunderstand me, when I say she used every trick in the book, it wasn't exactly trickery, it was more like prostitution." When he saw Matthew's reaction, he said hurriedly, "I'm sorry, Matthew, but I see little point in holding back the punches. You came here for the truth and it would be wrong not to give it to you."

"I understand, but ..."

"Are you telling me she hasn't used the same technique on you when she has wanted something or was trying to worm her way out of whatever? She's got a fantastic body, and she knows how to use it, but, by Christ, does she know it … but I have to apologise again for being rather personal."

Matthew hoped how he felt wasn't too obvious. He didn't think any man would have liked to hear another man describing the woman he lived with – the woman he thought he loved – in such a way, even if they had been married. He thought back to only four days earlier when he had gone to the bedroom to accuse her of damaging Peter Chilcott's car and the way she tried to move him away from what he was saying.

Now he thought about it, there were other occasions as well – at the time, they seemed so innocent – but, in a flash, many now had explanations.

He closed his eyes and nodded.

"There's no need to apologise because she has done exactly the same with me."

"I thought she might have," Patrick said, placing his fingers gently against Joe's arm and stroking it, the baby's eyes sparkling as he recognised his father through sleep filled eyes.

"About four months after Laura returned to work, her behaviour changed," Julie said. "She started being very dismissive towards me and she went from being aloof with the men in the station to being downright flirtatious and suggestive. I knew nothing of what was going on with Patrick, of course. He was up in London and, by this time, Paul and I were history. Laura evaded answering any questions about her relationship with Patrick and, as for meeting up with him, she dismissed any such suggestion with a glare. She had told me she had miscarried but also she and Patrick were so in love, it simply didn't matter. As soon as they were ready, they would be trying for another baby. You can see how the change in her behaviour didn't compute with what she was telling me.

"Anyway, the young PCs got short shrift. Laura made a beeline for the Sergeants and the Inspectors. It reached the point where it became extremely embarrassing to be near her. It was almost as though she was a different person to the one I'd considered to be my best friend. Then, out of nowhere, she accused one of the

Inspectors of rape. It simply could not have happened when she said it did but, regardless of him furnishing proof he was elsewhere at the time, she was adamant he had raped her. The time span between when she said it had happened and her reporting it, was put down to the fact that she had been utterly traumatised. Then, while the Inspector was suspended and Internal Investigations were looking into the accusation – the most disliked element of any police force, not by the public but by the police themselves – up pops Laura with further accusations, accusing a male Sergeant of sexual harassment and a female Sergeant of propositioning her. Laura's behaviour became utterly bizarre. Both sergeants were suspended and the station really started to suffer."

Julie passed Joe, who had fallen asleep, carefully to Patrick.

"Take him up, darling, and be careful," she said.

Patrick took Joe and cradled him. "Be careful of what?" he asked standing up.

"Dropping him," Julie told him, a wicked smile on her face.

"Have I ever?"

"Not recently."

Patrick bent down, kissed Julie on top of the head and left the room, Joe a sleeping bundle in his arms. Matthew's mind went back to when he had done exactly the same thing with Sarah.

"He really is gorgeous," Matthew said.

"I hope you're referring to Joe?" Julie asked, her eyes sparkling.

Matthew smiled and shook his head. "As I told Patrick, neither of you are as I expected," he said.

"And Joe?" Julie asked, lighting the cigar.

"I gathered from what you said on the phone that there was a baby in the house, but ..."

"Patrick and I have been married for just over 18 months. I was pregnant with Joe when we got married, and I mean I *was* pregnant, I wasn't doing another Laura on him."

She sipped her wine.

"We met again by sheer coincidence when he was still married to Laura, I mean before the divorce came through. Paul's father died suddenly, and although Paul and I were no more, I had got on very well with his parents. I went to the funeral and so did Patrick, and that was when I found out what had really been going on.

Patrick knew I was very close to Laura, but when I asked him why she'd changed so much, he opened up his heart to me and," she said, shrugging, "the rest is history. I fell in love with him. Actually if I told you the whole truth, I had been in love with him for some time. I'd always thought he was something special, but he was Laura's and I didn't muck around with my best friend's husband, not until they'd separated anyway. After we'd decided we had a future together, I fell pregnant almost straightaway and we got married as soon as possible after his divorce came through, but before Joe was born. I did feel a little embarrassed taking the vows with my tummy bulging under my dress."

"So what exactly was Laura up to? She told me that Patrick had abused her mentally and physically and went into a certain amount of detail but, having met him, I can't see it," Matthew said.

"Patrick couldn't and wouldn't hurt a fly," Julie said, spreading her hands on the table. "And, if anything, the truth was the complete reverse. She was the one who did the abusing. She had conned Patrick into marriage and as soon as he discovered the truth, he wanted out. As I said earlier, she used every trick in the book to keep him. Look at him and look at her. If you were told that he was abusing her, who would you believe?"

"Well," Matthew said hesitantly, "I have to say her, and I did."

"Of course you would and as you say did, and so did everyone else. She even mutilated herself and told the world he had done it."

"So what happened?"

Julie lowered her head and took a few seconds to answer. "Patrick was arrested and charged with actual bodily harm." She looked up.. "Can you believe it?" she said. "That bitch lied so convincingly he finished up in court …" Pausing, she lifted her eyes to the ceiling as they both heard movement above them. "He is the gentlest and most caring man I have ever met and yet he was …" She fell silent again when Patrick coughed as he came through from the kitchen.

He stopped just inside the room and looked at them both.

"Should I go out again?" he asked.

"No, not at all," Matthew said a little too quickly.

"I wasn't found guilty," Patrick said as he sat down and took hold of Julie's hand. "It was Laura's word against mine and, fortunately, I had some pretty good character witnesses, one of whom is right here with us."

"When he says he wasn't found guilty, he actually means that the case was dismissed," Julie said and paused, but then through clenched teeth she said, "She's a vindictive, scheming little cow. If she can't have something, she will do everything she can to make sure nobody else can have it either. She'll also stop at nothing to see somebody she hates suffer."

Matthew saw Patrick squeeze Julie's hand.

"We've been living life on a knife-edge," Patrick said. "It's been too quiet. Perhaps now you will understand why getting your phone call was, in many ways, what we needed."

Matthew shook his head, not fully understanding what he meant. "I'm sorry," he said, "but ..."

"It's easy, really. If you hadn't appeared on the scene when you did, we would still be wondering where she was and what she was planning. She would probably have done whatever she could to destroy the happiness Julie and I have found."

Patrick smiled when he could see that Matthew still didn't understand.

"We now know that you took the heat off us." Patrick said, shrugging. "You became a substitute target. After you phoned yesterday, we had no idea why she had you in her sights, that was not until you told us about your feelings for your first wife."

"Are you saying you have been waiting for, what, over two years, if not longer, for Laura to get some sort of revenge?"

"That's exactly what we are saying," Patrick said.

"God, I'm sorry."

"There's no need for you to apologise. We had guessed somebody like you existed," Julie said. "There had to be somebody who unknowingly had taken the heat off us."

"And you're saying that it's all because of Emily?" Matthew asked, not believing his own question.

"Your mistake was that you let her know you were still in love with your ex-wife," Patrick said slowly.

"And if my perception is right, you still are," Julie added.

Matthew looked at her and nodded.

"You gave her something to corrupt, something for her to gain satisfaction from by destroying it," Julie said.

"She set out to destroy my feelings for a woman I hadn't seen in years? Is that what you're saying?" Matthew asked.

They both nodded. "We're only guessing but, yes, that's what we think," Julie said.

"But why?"

The last eighteen months flashed through his mind in seconds, and he couldn't believe that everything he and Laura had done together had been part of a warped mind that was hell bent on destroying him.

"Men," Julie said, breaking into his thoughts.

"Men?" Matthew repeated.

"She hates men, Matthew. We think she needs to destroy every man she meets who shows any affection towards her."

"I'm sorry to repeat the same question, but why?"

Patrick took his hand from Julie's and lit another small cigar. "I've got no evidence, no proof of what I'm going to say, but I think she did suffer abuse, not from me, but a lot, lot earlier in her life and at the hands of her father."

"What? Her father abused her?"

Was it possible that after Laura had told him about the incident in the restaurant when she had been a young teenager, he had been right all along? If the abuse did happen, only now was the damage manifesting itself into open hatred.

"The evidence was staring me in the face from the start," Julie said. "From the moment she befriended me and the things she talked about, she was a classic case. I think – and please understand this is purely my opinion – that when her father died, her plans were thwarted. I think she'd always harboured the need for ultimate revenge but against him, so when he upped and died, he took with him her freedom. From that moment all men became a substitute target."

"The accusations she made against the people with you were all part of it?" Matthew asked.

"In a way but I'm not a psychiatrist," Julie said. "If I were asked to describe what I understood paranoid schizophrenia to mean, I would say Laura Stanhope."

"The trouble is, Matthew, she's so bloody clever with it."

Patrick said. "She calculates what needs to be done so far in advance. We mere mortals are lost in the present. She craves attention and lies to get it, but at the same time she is planning. Seeking attention is her tactic, her strategy, and her ultimate aim is to destroy any man, as Julie suggested, who simply looks at her in what she considers to be the wrong way."

Matthew shook his head and sighed.

"I can see the mental dilemma you are in," Patrick said. "And I'm sorry if we've just added to it, but you had to know the truth."

"Yes, I did," Matthew said.

"I think a stiff brandy may help," Patrick suggested, and got up from the table.

Describing how he felt as a mental dilemma was an understatement; a psychological nightmare would be more accurate. Having accused himself so often of being blind to the reality, if what he'd been told now was the truth, it wasn't just blindness but also the most serious form of irony. He had asked Laura to marry him and believed it was what she wanted too. Because he had only seen and heard what he wanted to see and hear, he had drawn all the wrong conclusions and Laura hadn't given him any reason to think otherwise.

No matter what Wendy Carter had told him, not once did he consider Laura's words and actions were all part of homophobic plot.

Why would he?

Because Julie and Patrick Schofield were so credible, he realised that not only was Laura hell-bent on ruining his life for whatever reason, but Emily was a possible target too. He had no idea what had really gone on when Laura had been to see her, but he could now hazard a guess. Why else would she want to go back and see her.

Having fallen for all of Laura's trickery and manipulation, he felt such a fool.

He had empathised and sympathised, been there for her whenever she needed him, but all the time he had been digging his own grave.

What was he going to do now? How many times had he asked that question during the last few days? Now, though, the question needed asking for a different reason.

If Laura wasn't in Nottingham, where was she?

Without realising it, Matthew had already drunk half of the brandy Patrick gave him.

"So what do I do now? No," he added quickly, "I can't expect you to answer the impossible. Only I can … but why, when you know what has been going on, haven't you done anything to stop her?"

"Until you rang, we were in the same situation, the same predicament, we have now placed you in," Julie admitted, with a slight tremor in her voice.

Patrick immediately covered her hand with his.

"We assumed, as we said earlier, that the heat was off us temporarily because she had somebody else in her sights," he said. "We prayed that whatever she was doing to whoever it was would keep her away from us. That sounds awfully selfish but I think you will now understand."

"I certainly do, but by coming here I've probably brought her to you," Matthew said.

Patrick smiled ruefully, shrugging at the same time. "They say there's strength in numbers. If she knows where you are then she will know what we have told you. I –"

"If I'd known before what you've told me this evening, I wouldn't have come anywhere near you. I would have kept well away," Matthew said.

Patrick shrugged again. "It doesn't matter. Maybe Julie and I had just stuck our heads in the sand. Laura probably had something planned for us all along and when you came on the scene we were put on hold … for a while." He looked at Matthew, his eyes sad but hopeful. "It's now not a question of what we can do, is it? It's what do *you* do with what we've told you?"

"Wait?"

"Wait? Wait for what?" Patrick said.

"At the moment I haven't the faintest idea," Matthew told him.

Chapter Twenty-Six

Matthew stayed the night.

He wanted to phone for a taxi but the Schofields wouldn't let him. After more alcohol and much heart-searching, he had an understandably fitful night's sleep but, in the morning he felt surprisingly refreshed and ready to do something, although he wasn't too sure what that something ought to be.

Nonetheless, out of the cauldron of bewilderment had come two decisions.

To comply with the first decision was easy. He called Bradbury and Son Ltd – the construction company in Stafford he was due to be with at ten-thirty this morning – and cancelled the tutorial. He told a white lie, explaining that food poisoning prevented him from doing anything. His excuse was accepted and they rearranged the date, although he wondered if he would ever fulfil the commitment.

Doing what went with his second decision was going to be more difficult.

The Schofields' hospitality had been quite extraordinary from the outset. As he lay awake trying to fathom out everything he'd been told, Matthew attempted to generate some lucidity into his thought processes and wondered what he would have done if roles had been reversed.

How would he have reacted if a total stranger – a man – had rung him at home and asked to come and speak to him about Emily? Would he have invited him round for supper with Laura there, fed him and given him his best brandy?

Would he have then tucked this stranger up in their guest room? Probably not.

Matthew would have been inquisitive but not to the point of absurdity. Two people he had never met before had invited him into their home and treated him as though he were a long lost friend, and he had accepted everything they said and did at face value.

Then again, Emily wasn't Laura and didn't have the background and the history that might just have generated sufficient inquisitiveness for him to offer that type of hospitality. For all they knew, he might have been in league with Laura. He might have been party to some devious plan she had concocted.

Minds wander during the night, especially when the brain is saying that sleep really ought to be the alternative.

Matthew wasn't any different.

His mind wandered too.

Why would Laura lie about her parents? Why make up a brother and sister? Why spend nearly eighteen months living with him, making him feel as though he was her answer to all that she had ever wanted, if her aim was to destroy him?

They had been so happy – or so he thought.

Even when the letters started arriving, they had held onto their happiness, albeit Laura had become withdrawn It was their combined strengths that had pulled them through but now he realised it had actually only required one mind – his – because he didn't know what was going on.

Laura had known exactly what was happening. Although he had doubted Wendy Carter's version of events, Julie had said she thought she knew Wendy, but only in passing, and yet they had told identical stories about what happened with Laura when she was in the Surrey police. The stories had to be true. Why would Patrick and Julie Schofield lie, and from such an elaborate standpoint? Nothing had been contrived because there hadn't been time.

So, was it really all over?

Had what he been told now convinced him that the truth had been staring him in the face from the moment Wendy Carter had taken him to the lake near Sevenoaks to try and persuade him that Laura was not to be trusted?

Laura really was the liar they had all accused her of being.

Without knowing the truth, he had fallen in love with her and love can make the smitten so blind. In retrospect, perhaps he had thought he needed to fall in love with her.

When he had looked at Emily – knowing it was for the last time – he swore to himself that he would never fall in love again, he would never let another woman break his heart the way Emily had. However, Laura had succeeded in doing exactly that because he was defenceless against her allure, her charisma, her sense of humour, her everything. He believed he fell in love with her long before the Warwick incident, but he was unable to admit it to himself and therefore to her. How could he, as someone who believed he understood human behaviour, have been so blind to the truth?

What was the truth?

His addled brain – made worse by the brandy Patrick had plied him with – told him to try and call Laura about an hour after he'd gone to bed. After selecting her number on his mobile, he must have stared at it for a couple of minutes before he pressed the call button. The first time it rang twice and the call ended. He tried repeatedly, but each resulted in being put straight through to her voice mail.

Matthew couldn't leave a message.

What could he have said?

Hello, Laura, I'm in your ex-husband's spare bed, and he and his gorgeous new wife have spent the whole evening telling me what a liar and a bitch you are. Perhaps Julie should have used the word 'cow' – in fact he remembered she had – *instead of bitch, that would have been in keeping with your imagination, wouldn't it? They even told me that you want to destroy me. I think we need to talk about that. Call me back when you can to tell me you're not what they say you are. Oh, and rather than destroying me, shall we still get married as we planned?*

If he couldn't leave a message, what the hell did he think he might have said to her if she had answered?

It was shortly after trying to ring Laura that Matthew made his second decision.

Sitting now in the Schofields' kitchen eating a cooked breakfast – something he hadn't had in months – and watching Julie with Joe on her lap holding a bottle to his lips, Matthew knew that he was right.

Patrick had left for work soon after Matthew got up.

With many apologies, and after extracting a promise from Matthew that he would ring within a couple of days, he went to work. He said nothing about the previous evening other than advising Matthew to take care and to watch Laura like a hawk.

Matthew could feel that Julie's eyes were on him as he ate.

Joe was slurping contentedly at the bottle.

"You probably think we're strange," Julie said suddenly.

Matthew looked up and her eyes were wide and questioning. "Strange? Why do you think that?" he said.

"Well it's a bizarre situation, isn't it? If a month, a week, two days ago, somebody had told you that you would be tucking into poached eggs and bacon in Laura's ex-husband's kitchen, with his wife sitting opposite you clutching and feeding his young son, you'd have thought they were crazy. And yet, here you are." Julie took the teat gently from Joe's mouth and looked at him, smiling, and then at the bottle. "That's your lot, young man," she told him, placing the bottle on the table and wiping his mouth with a tissue.

Joe gurgled, looked up at his mother adoringly and smiled at her with his big brown eyes. He was a lovely chocolaty colour, his hair black and curly, and he had his mother's high cheekbones and full lips. He was going to break a few hearts when the time came.

"I can't deny that it's not what I would have expected," Matthew said, "but, in many ways, I'm pleased and just a little relieved that it has happened."

"We share the same feelings but for different reasons," Julie said.

Joe's eyes closed, contented after his breakfast.

"Patrick is not the sort of man who is easily scared but, small though she is, Laura scared the living daylights out of him, but more for my and Joe's sake than his."

Joe's peace was disturbed as Julie lifted him onto her shoulder and started patting his back.

Matthew put the knife and fork down on an empty plate.

"That was delicious, thank you," he said.

"Don't mention it."

His opinion of Julie hadn't changed.

At eight o'clock in the morning, dressed in grey joggers and a yellow cotton top, and with no make-up, she was still the most beautiful woman he had ever seen. Her beauty was mirrored in her character as she gave the impression of being one of life's good people. Matthew decided Patrick was a very lucky man.

"What I can't understand," he said, "is why, over the years, nothing has ever happened, which may have resulted in Laura being investigated. Surely Patrick and I aren't the first men that warranted being targets for her warped mind?"

Julie picked up her mug of coffee. "As I told you last night," she said, "we were the best of friends when I first went to Guildford. Our friendship generated quite a lot of gossip, not for any reason other than we were such a contrast. A tall, black novice and a small, white mentor were the best of friends. I'm sure everybody thought that there had to be something else to it." Julie smiled and shrugged. "Although we were very good friends, Laura kept a lot of her private life private and I didn't like to ask too many questions. When Patrick and Laura got together, there didn't seem to be any need to go into her history. She seemed happy with the present and with what the future held, or so I thought."

"The allegations she made, nothing came out of them at all?" Matthew asked.

"What, the alleged rape and stuff?" He nodded. "No, no charges were ever brought and the Super kept the press at bay. Nothing could be proven either way."

"So why was Laura told to resign?" Matthew drained his coffee cup and Julie immediately refilled it. "Thanks," he said.

Julie screwed up her nose and said, "She wasn't exactly told to resign, but it was pretty obvious that her position in the Surrey force had become untenable. She was offered a transfer but she chose to accept the resignation option."

"I see. Did you lose touch with her afterwards or …"

"Lose touch? That's one of the reasons why Patrick and I have been so worried. She threatened me and not just the once."

"Why? Was it because she knew about you and him getting together?"

"That was exactly why. When Patrick's case was thrown out on the grounds of insufficient and uncorroborated evidence, he and I were already together. Basically she told me to keep looking over my shoulder because one day she would get her revenge."

The shock must have shown on Matthew's face. "Surely you could have done something about that? You were still in the police, weren't you?"

"Yes, I was and, yes, I could but, at the time, I thought Laura had quite enough on her plate," Julie said. "I didn't take her threats too seriously anyway but more recently – and I mean in the last few months – some strange things have been happening. Just little things, harmless things, but none had ready explanations."

"Such as?"

"I received unsigned 'with-sympathy' cards when nothing had happened to warrant them; there were phone calls during the early hours of the morning which went dead when answered and the numbers were always withheld; taxis arrived at the door when we hadn't ordered them – that sort of thing. Nothing too serious, just annoying, but Patrick was convinced it was Laura. Actually, when you rang on Wednesday, that very morning we'd received another card and Patrick said he'd had enough but, when you did ring, we decided to wait to hear what you had to say first. As we told you last night, we were worried but we also chose not to do anything about what we believed she was doing."

"And now?" Matthew asked.

"Patrick and I were talking until the early hours – I hope we didn't keep you awake – and felt that our problems were nothing compared with yours." Julie said as she screwed up her face again. "Sorry, I didn't mean that to sound the way it did."

"Not at all and I took it the way you meant it," Matthew said as he checked his watch. He had to leave if he was going to stick with his second decision. "Julie, you probably know her as well as anybody else, what do you think she's actually capable of? The threats against you, surely of you believed she was capable of carrying them out, you would have done something … or Patrick would?"

Julie hesitated before answering. "That's something Patrick and I've often discussed, and we don't know. She's never, as far as I know, actually done anyone any physical harm, but whether she's capable of it, that's another question," Julie said. "Why, have you decided to confront her?"

"I have little choice, so, yes," Matthew said a little reluctantly. "That's got to happen, and sooner rather than later. If she is going to get the help she needs, somebody has to do something pretty decisive, and it looks very much as though I'm that person. But there's something else I have to do before confronting her."

"What's that?" Julie asked, her eyebrows raised.

"I'm going to see Emily. I've got to go and see Emily to make sure she is safe," Matthew said.

Chapter Twenty-Seven

Having bought an A-Z at the first garage in Leamington Spa, Matthew located Craven Gardens without any trouble. He sat and stared at the black lines in the book, trying to picture what he was going to find. As he left Solihull, his resolve to go and see Emily hadn't weakened but he did question his motives for the decision every yard of the way. If she was at risk then the police would be involved because, after all, they had been to see her. Julie Schofield had been threatened, so why not Emily?

Earlier Julie asked him why he had decided to go to see his ex-wife.

"For the same reason I came to see you," Matthew told her. "I want the truth."

"But what can she tell you? What more is there to know?" Julie said.

"I don't know but I do want to know she is safe."

Julie shrugged and said, "And you'll find that out when you get there."

"I hope so."

Now he wasn't so sure.

It was just after eleven in the morning as he drove out of the garage. There was every chance that his apprehension would become frustration as Emily might be at work or out shopping. Six years was a long time and he had no right to appear suddenly without the courtesy of a phone call, but if Emily was part of Laura's scheming, and therefore at risk, he had to do something about it.

Calling ahead wasn't an option because he didn't have her number to phone, but even if he had, she could say that she didn't want to see him or she could put the phone down without saying anything.

Matthew stopped a couple of times to check the A-Z but eventually he turned into Bubbenhall Road that led to Craven Gardens. It was a typical 1980s English estate, a mixture of three, four and five-bedroomed houses, the communal grass recently cut and the mature trees in full leaf, but with the leaves beginning to turn. It was a sunny day. There were quite a few children out playing and, as he searched for No 14, he tried to picture what Emily would look like.

He knew he wouldn't recognise Sarah.

She could so easily be one of the girls he could see playing on the grassed areas, and some in the road. Seeing the children, he wondered if it was half-term.

Nos. 4 and 6 were on a slight bend and the first thing Matthew saw, beyond a Parcel Force van, was a police car. He automatically braked, stopping in the middle of the road. The police car, a Peugeot 306, was empty as far as he could see, but it was outside No 14. Everything and nothing ran through his mind. He tried to look through the walls of the house and picture who was there and what they were saying.

The driver of another car approaching from behind beeped its horn giving Matthew little choice but to move. He crawled past No. 14, noticing that the police car had masked a red Renault Clio parked with its nose very close to the single garage door.

No. 14 was a detached – probably four-bedroomed – house, and only 'detached' if the term was used loosely. The gap between Emily's house and the neighbours' houses on either side was minimal.

Craven Gardens was a cul-de-sac, so Matthew drove to the end, turned the car round and parked so that he was far enough away but in direct line-of-sight with what he believed was Emily's house.

He waited.

After a number of minutes of irrational thought, he wondered what was he going to do when the police left?

Could he waltz up to the front door and explain that he had been passing, saw the police leaving and wanted to check that everything was all right? It actually wasn't far from the truth, except that he hadn't been just passing. How do you just pass a house that's in a no-through road? If he was going to stick to what he'd decided, he had to tell the truth.

There had been enough lies.

He wanted to know what Laura had said to Emily during both of her visits, if indeed there had been two, because he still didn't really know what to believe.

The front door of No 14 Craven Gardens opened. A female police officer followed by a male officer appeared. Matthew wondered how many curtains up and down the street were twitching.

Then suddenly Emily was there.

He hadn't seen her for over six years but it was like looking at the woman he'd first fallen in love with so long ago.

He closed his eyes in disbelief.

This wasn't the way it was meant to be. He was supposed to be dispassionate; there shouldn't have been any feelings there anymore. So why was his heart pounding in his chest, his ears thumping, and why were tears trying to run from his eyes? Why did he want to rush from the car, take Emily in his arms and tell her that there was nothing to worry about because he was where he always should have been, by her side?

The police car reversed across the road into the drive opposite and then drove away. Emily watched them go and looked up and down the road, her eyes resting for a few seconds on Matthew's car. There must have been somebody else in the house because she said something and looked up and down the road once again, before closing the front door.

Matthew decided if he didn't react straightaway he would find every reason possible to follow the police to the end of the road, and then what – return to Westerham as though nothing had happened? He didn't even know whether Laura would be there. He'd eventually given up trying to contact her on her mobile. He hadn't the faintest idea where she was and who she was with.

But why did he think she would be with anybody?

Another incongruous thought to intermingle with all the others.

He started the engine and slowly moved forward. It was now or never. Parking at the side of the road, he got out of the car and walked up the pathway to the front door, trying not to look at the windows of the house.

He rang the bell and closed his eyes.

The door opened seconds later.

Matthew had never seen the young girl before. She was no more than fifteen, had a pretty but spotty face and was rather plump.

"Yes?" the girl enquired. She had obviously been crying, her eyes were red rimmed and looked very sore. "Can ... can I help you?"

"May I speak to Emily, please?" Matthew asked, his voice catching as he said her name.

"Now is not a good time," the girl said. "Can you come back later?"

"If I go now, I'll probably never come back. It's important, I ..."

Emily appeared behind the girl and her hand flew to her mouth as she recognised him.

She let out a loud gasp. "Matthew!" she muttered behind her hand.

The girl looked behind her and then at Matthew. She overcame her confusion by stepping to one side so that Emily could move closer.

But she didn't move. "What do you want?" she said, with her hand still at her mouth and her eyes wide open in shock.

"To see you," Matthew said.

"Why?"

"To explain," he said.

"Explain what?" Emily asked.

"I'm not too sure."

Slowly Emily lowered her hand. "Why now? The police ..."

"I know. I waited until they'd gone."

Emily frowned. The girl was still standing to one side, her eyes darting from Emily to Matthew as she followed the exchange.

"Why were they ...?"

"What do you want?" Emily asked again, this time her words sounding suspicious.

"To speak with you," he said.

"Why?"

Emily was wearing a business suit, white blouse and black formal shoes. She had also been crying. There was no make-up. Her dishevelled hair and her expression suggested that she was very, very worried about something

"This is very difficult for us both," he suggested. "Can I come in?"

"I don't know."

The girl suddenly found her voice. "Mrs Ryan wants and needs to be left alone," she said authoritatively.

Mrs Ryan?

Why did she say 'Mrs Ryan'? Ryan was the name they had shared. It was their name. Was she still calling herself Mrs Ryan? Laura had told him she was still Emily Ryan, but Laura was a liar, wasn't she?

Emily's face relaxed a little.

"It's all right, Kate," she said, placing a motherly hand on the girl's shoulder. "This is Matthew Ryan and he was my husband."

"Then ..." the girl started to say.

"No, Kate. I know what you are thinking, but no. Mr Ryan would never harm Sarah."

"Sarah?" Matthew exclaimed.

"Sarah's ... Sarah's been abducted," Emily said, her voice catching, the tears returning to her eyes. She turned away and disappeared into the room nearest to her.

The girl, Kate, moved and blocked Matthew's way.

She folded her arms defiantly.

"Emily's right, I wouldn't do anything to harm Sarah."

Kate narrowed her eyes for a few seconds but then she stood to one side. "You'd better come in then," she said.

"Thank you."

He went through the door of the room Emily had disappeared into and she was sitting on the edge of an easy chair, clutching a tissue to her eyes.

She didn't look up.

"What's happened?" he asked, standing just inside the room.

"Kate ... Kate took Sarah to the park ... to the park this morning. Sarah was playing on the swings and Kate went to get her an ice-cream and ... and somebody took her."

"I ... I was only gone for a couple of minutes," Kate said, behind Matthew.

He turned round to look at her and she burst into tears.

"What time did it happen?" he asked quietly but his mind was already racing.

"About two hours ... two hours ago."

"And the police?"

"What about them?"

"What did they have say?"

"They wanted a photograph and things," Kate said, moving further into the room.

"Kate," Emily said, lifting her head, "you go home now. Your mother will be worried."

"But she doesn't know what has happened and I –"

"Please, Kate. Go home now. I'll call you if and when I hear anything," Emily told her.

"But what about …?" Kate started to say, looking at Matthew.

"I'll be perfectly safe," Emily said.

"Are you sure?" Kate said.

"I'm sure."

"Well, all right, but …"

"Kate, please."

Kate left, albeit reluctantly, and Matthew heard the front door slam.

"I am safe with you, aren't I?" Emily asked, looking at him.

"You shouldn't have to ask," he said.

"I know, but why *are* you here?"

"I'm glad I am," he said.

Emily lowered her head and said quietly, "So am I."

Matthew moved slowly across the room until he was a few feet from Emily. "What can I do?"

She lifted her eyes to his and stood up. "Hold me?" she said.

Without waiting for an answer, she walked into his arms and buried her head against his shoulder, her tears quickly soaked his shirt.

"I'm … I'm so worried and frightened for Sarah. You read about such awful things happening and you never believe they could happen to you," Emily said.

They were in the kitchen, drinking their third cup of tea.

Emily had cried but said nothing more.

Matthew had held her as tightly as he dared, feeling the sobs shudder through her body, wanting to talk but knowing that he had no right to expect to be taken into her confidence. He had invaded her life after being away for so long and now she had every right to be suspicious. He had expected her to be not only shocked to see him but also to be told, in no uncertain terms, to go away and never even think about being within a mile of her ever again. What were the words Wendy Carter had used? *Tell that bastard ex-husband of mine and that lying slut of a female he's living with that they can both rot in hell.*

Emily hadn't asked whether Laura was with him.

He thought that might have been her first reaction, her first question, when she saw him. Instead, there had been no mention of Laura, and Emily was sitting across the table from him clutching her cup of tea in both hands. He remembered seeing her sitting like that so many times before.

He couldn't stop looking at her.

Her face was drawn with the agony she felt, but otherwise it hadn't changed. He could see her pulse beating in her neck and he wanted to reach across the table and touch it, not believing that after so long he could feel so strongly about another human being.

"You said Kate left Sarah on the swings in the play-park. Surely there were other children and adults there?" he asked.

Emily nodded, her eyes evading his. "Yes …yes, there were, but they didn't know who Sarah was and who she was with. Anybody could have taken her." She spoke softly and slowly. "Kate thought that, because she'd only be a couple of minutes, Sarah would be safe."

"Why on earth –?"

"Don't, Matthew. We can all be wise after the event …" Emily stopped what she was about to say and, for the first time, made direct eye contact. "I've asked you twice already but I've yet to have an answer. Why are you here and within hours of what's happened to Sarah? It is just a coincidence, isn't it?"

Matthew could see the pleading in her eyes and he wanted to reach for her hand. "If I were to say it is an awful coincidence then only you can decide whether to believe me or not. You told Kate that I wouldn't harm Sarah. You believed what you said then and I'm asking you to believe me now."

Emily thought for a moment. "I do," she said slowly, "but you must understand how it looks."

He nodded. "The reason I'm here, though, is unimportant compared with what you are going through," he said.

"But I want to know." She looked down at her hands holding the cup. "I need to know."

"To apologise."

She lifted her head and screwed up her eyes.

"The police? When they came to see me about ..." Matthew nodded again. "I couldn't believe that you would think that I was capable of trying to kill somebody."

"I didn't."

"Then why ...?"

"It's a very long story, Emily, and one that I hope will be over very soon."

Matthew drank the remainder of his tea, feeling that he could do with something a good deal stronger.

"What was it all about?" Emily asked.

"Laura, the woman who came to see you, was receiving threatening letters and she thought ..."

"That I was sending them?"

"Yes."

"Why would I do something like that?"

"She told me that she'd come to see you to tell you that she was living with me. Your reaction frightened her and –"

"My reaction frightened her? She must ..." Emily stopped but then said, "No, now is not the time to go there."

Things were moving too quickly.

Matthew hadn't rehearsed what he was going to say because he didn't think he was going to get this far. He didn't know what the whole truth was and what it wasn't, and with Emily worrying herself sick about Sarah, now was not the time.

"Can we leave the reason why I'm here and concentrate on Sarah? I saw the police leaving. What are they doing about Sarah?" he asked.

Emily was quiet for a moment or two, her expression suggesting, as he'd already thought, that taking him into her confidence wasn't that easy to accept.

"We only reported her missing an hour ago ... but there's not a lot they can do. Kate was frantic and searched all round the park before she rang me at work and told me what had happened."

"So there's nobody at the park at the moment who Sarah knows? What if she had just wandered off and she has found her way back to the playground? She could be there now wondering where Kate is."

Emily's head dropped. "Because Kate did have the sense to ask some of the other adults there whether they'd seen anything and ..." – the tears had returned to Emily's eyes and her hands were shaking – "and ... and one of the mothers told her that she saw another woman approach Sarah and she seemed to go off quite happily with her."

"What? They gave the impression that Sarah and this woman knew each other?"

"Yes, that's how ... that's how Kate interpreted what she was told."

"And was there a description?"

"Not a very good one," Emily said.

"You told the police?"

"Of course!"

A flash of annoyance crossed Emily's face.

Matthew felt his body shudder although it wasn't cold in the kitchen. "Will you tell me?" he said.

Emily took a deep breath. "The description could fit a million women but the woman who took Sarah was described as being very pretty, small, slim, about thirty, with short light brown hair."

"What was she wearing?"

"A white skirt and blue top."

Matthew felt the hairs on the back of his neck begin to prickle. "Anything else?"

"No, other than they were seen getting into a car."

"I suppose ..."

"It was red and she thought it was a Ford Focus. The woman who had noticed what was happening was pretty sure about the car because she had a Focus herself."

Matthew closed his eyes.

It wasn't even a long shot. The description of both the woman and the car fitted.

Why?

Why would Laura want to abduct Sarah?

But perhaps he already had the answer and it was sitting across the table from him.

He was surprised Emily hadn't made the connection but, then again why should she? Maybe she had. Maybe she really thought that he and Laura were in this together and his arrival was far from being a coincidence.

"And the police?"

Emily looked at the small watch on her wrist. It was the one Matthew had given her as an anniversary present seven years ago.

"They said somebody would be here by one o'clock and whoever it was would stay with me," Emily told him.

"Presumably in case you are contacted?"

"Yes."

"I'm so sorry Emily but Sarah will be all right, I'm sure."

Over the years he had hated being told not to worry by people who hadn't the faintest idea what they were talking about, so what right did he have to say the same to Emily?

"I think it would be best if you weren't still here when the police return," Emily suggested, the tears still in her eyes although she wasn't crying.

"I understand."

"They might think it's a bit suspicious that on the day my daughter disappears her ..." Emily stopped and looked away.

"What were you going to say?"

She shrugged without looking at Matthew. "Well, you have to admit it is a bit of a coincidence, isn't it?"

"Emily, that's exactly what it is, you have to believe me. A stranger might ..."

"Isn't that what we are, Matthew, strangers?"

"I'm not so sure."

He stole a glance at his watch. It was twelve forty-five.

The prickling at the nape of his neck had stopped but what had generated the feeling hadn't gone way. Time was now a key factor, and although it was the last thing he wanted to do, he had to get away and find out whether his imagination was in fact telling him the truth.

If Laura had snatched Sarah, where would she have taken her?

There was one place he could start and that was at the cottage in Westerham. If he waited and told the police about his suspicions, there was every possibility that his arrest would follow and while in custody, the police would to try to find and deal with a woman who was unstable and unpredictable.

He decided he would give himself twenty-four hours and, if he hadn't found Laura and Sarah by then, he wouldn't go to the police, but he would contact Wendy Carter.

At least she had the background and the understanding.

Chapter Twenty-Eight

Matthew drove into Westerham just over two hours later, the M40 and M25 hadn't been too busy at that time of day.

He felt awful about leaving Emily alone.

As he left he saw her standing by the window.

Her arms were folded and she didn't wave ... he wondered what she was thinking.

Not knowing what to read into her body language, he prayed that he would see her again when he would be able to explain his real reason for going to see her. She hadn't asked any more questions – there wasn't time – but she had to know.

He could understand how things must have looked to her. Sarah goes missing and within an hour or so, and after over six years, he turns up on her doorstep. Of course it all looked very suspicious, and in retrospect, he was surprised he was allowed into the house. Maybe telling the police about his visit was the logical next step for her, but he didn't believe that would be the case. Emily still felt something for him – he saw it, he felt it, and she trusted him. When he held her and she put her head on his shoulder, there was compassion from both of them – or was it wishful thinking? He couldn't come up with any reason why she would show such feelings towards him – not after all this time and after what had happened with Laura.

He only hoped there was time to put things right – he needed to find Sarah and return her to her mother.

After leaving Craven Gardens, he parked the car out of sight of Emily's house and rang Laura's mobile but, as he expected, there was no reply. He rang the cottage but the answer-phone clicked in after six rings. He left a message for Laura to contact him as soon as she got the message but he knew there wouldn't be a return call.

He waited.

When he saw the police car turn into Craven Gardens just before one o'clock and he knew Emily was no longer alone, he felt he could leave.

Just before he selected first gear, he wrote down Emily's landline number, which he noted from the phone in the hall.

As he got to the cottage in Westerham, he had convinced himself that there would be no sign of life. If there was and his first guess at where Laura might have taken Sarah proved to be right, it would generate more questions than it answered. If Laura had taken Sarah to punish him and Emily, then the last place she would chose would be Westerham.

His intuition was right which meant his logic was wrong.

Driving down Rysted Lane he could see a couple of the bedroom windows were open and the car Laura had hired was parked to one side of the garage.

He felt himself beginning to panic as he brought the car to an abrupt halt, and stared at the cottage. What was she playing at? Why would she bring Sarah to the cottage?

He took his foot off the brake.

Putting the BMW next to the Focus, he sat for a few minutes, wondering how he should handle the unexpected. Could he be wrong about Laura taking Sarah? Even if she hadn't, he still had to face facts: his relationship with her had changed irrevocably and she would know it.

If Sarah was there, he doubted whether Laura would harm a little six-year old girl but, then again, Sarah wasn't any little six-year old, was she? No, if Sarah was in the cottage with Laura, there had to be another reason.

Suddenly, he realised he had made an assumption that was bordering on the stupid. Laura wouldn't know that he knew Sarah had been abducted, would she? He wasn't due back until late this afternoon so how could she know he'd been to see Emily. Even if she had picked up his messages, he hadn't said anything about where he was.

After getting out of the car, he walked slowly down the path towards the front door. He couldn't see any movement or hear any voices.

It was a lovely afternoon.

There was a slight breeze rustling the leaves in the trees above his head, the birds were singing and – as the wind was from the north – there was the distant background hum of the traffic on the M25.

Other than that, there was nothing.

The front door opened without him having to operate the double lock, which confirmed there was somebody in the cottage. The kitchen was empty, as was the living room and dining room, but as he was passing the bottom of the stairs for the second time, he heard giggling coming from upstairs.

He stopped.

She was there – Sarah was in the cottage.

He took a deep breath, not believing what he was hearing but at the same time relaxing, because he now knew she was safe.

Climbing very slowly up each step one at a time as lightly as he could, he tried to remember which one squeaked and which didn't.

The giggling continued and then Laura's laughter joined Sarah's. He could hear water splashing and the shower running.

He reached the bathroom door and listened.

As he waited, he realised his whole body was shaking.

"Now, young lady," Matthew heard Laura say in a perfectly normal voice, "we must get that hair rinsed, your body dried and then get dressed. Your daddy will be home later."

Dropping to his haunches against the wall, he closed his eyes in total disbelief but also again in total relief.

Sarah really was safe and, so far, unharmed.

He had to let Emily know as quickly as possible, but before he did, he had to hear Sarah speak. He had only ever heard baby gurgles before so he just wanted to hear her voice ... and he certainly wouldn't recognise her. Children change so much in over six years.

There was a lot of explaining to do and not just to Emily, but that could wait.

"What's daddy like?"

It was Sarah.

After she was born he remembered lying awake and imagining her growing up, her first words, her calling him *daddy*, and now, under the most worrying of circumstances, he had just heard her call him *daddy* for the first time. His whole body seemed to tingle with those few simple words.

His elation left him as soon as the truth hit him.

Sarah wasn't referring to him – how could she when she didn't know him? But she *was* asking what he was like, so what had Laura told her?

"Oh, he's tall, with dark wavyish sort of hair. He's got blue-grey eyes, a straight nose, lovely white teeth and dimples. That's where you get yours from …"

"What?" Sarah said.

"Those dimples." Sarah giggled. "They're just like your daddy's."

"Is he kind?"

"Do you mean will he spend lots of money on you?" Laura asked.

There were a few seconds of silence.

"No, but that would be nice," Sarah said and then there was more giggling. "But is he kind?" she asked again.

"He's probably the kindest person I have ever met," Laura told Sarah.

As he heard those few words, Matthew felt himself filling up with confusion. Why would Laura say something like that to a young girl if she was hell bent on destroying him? There had to be another explanation.

"And I'm sure you will love him as much as I love him," he heard Laura say.

Matthew lifted his hands to his face, not believing what he was hearing.

Laura had abducted Sarah for him.

She had taken what she believed was his.

"Now, let's wash those suds off your back and we'll get you dried and dressed. We want you looking your best for your daddy."

The shower splashed and Sarah giggled again.

"And … and mummy doesn't mind?" he heard Sarah ask.

"No, she doesn't mind at all."

Matthew heard Laura lift Sarah out of the bath.

"Your mummy and after such a long time, wanted you to meet your daddy. Of course she doesn't mind."

"But why isn't mummy here?"

"She will be," Laura told her, "but she couldn't get away from work, that's why she asked me to collect you from the park and bring you down here early."

Matthew knew he had to get outside so that he could ring Emily before Laura and Sarah came out of the bathroom. When he went back to the cottage, he had to pretend, for Sarah's sake, that he expected her to be there when he got in from work. She mustn't be frightened and suspect that anything was out of the ordinary.

The explanations would come later but, for now, they must wait.

Once outside, he ran down the path to the car and reversed away from the garage before selecting first gear. He drove slowly up Rysted Lane until he was out of sight of the cottage.

He called the number he'd seen on Emily's phone in the hall.

"Hello," a female voice said after the fourth ring.

"Emily? It's Matthew."

"Matthew, what –?"

"Don't say anything, Emily, just listen. Sarah is safe."

There was an audible gasp. "What –?"

"Emily, please listen. Sarah is safe and well. I can't explain now. Are the police with you?"

"Yes."

"Are they listening to this call?"

Emily hesitated. "Yes, they are."

"Emily, if you ever loved me, you have to trust me. Sarah is safe and she will remain safe. It's all been a terrible misunderstanding. She will be back with you, if not tonight, then tomorrow. Please, please, trust me."

"What –?"

"I must go but please trust me."

After pressing the 'end call' button on his mobile, he looked at it. He knew nothing about the police's ability to trace telephone numbers, especially mobile numbers, other than what he'd seen on television. It didn't really matter whether the number was traced or not, he could have been anywhere, but could they pinpoint the spot from which a call was made?

Did it matter?

He probably had a couple of hours to persuade Laura that Sarah had to go back to her mother. Once Sarah was safe, he would find out the truth. If Laura was trying to destroy him for whatever reason, why did she tell Sarah that she loved him? Why would she take Sarah to the cottage if she didn't want him to find her?

The questions would have to wait.

As he reversed the BMW in next to the Focus for the second time, he beeped the horn. He wanted to make everything appear normal. He didn't know where Laura had been, other than to Leamington Spa, but she didn't know where he'd been either. As far as she was concerned, he was returning home early after three days business in the Midlands. The fact that they hadn't spoken for seventy two hours was irrelevant ... Sarah's safety was critical.

The explanations would come later.

Going to the front door, it opened before he could put the key in the lock.

They were there.

Sarah was at the door with Laura behind her, with her hands resting on the little girl's shoulders. Laura was smiling as she always did when Matthew arrived home after a trip away. She was still wearing the skirt and top the woman in the park had described.

Sarah looked very apprehensive, her hand up to her mouth, her feet shifting nervously. She had her mother's blonde hair, which was still wet from her bath ... and her mother's eyes. The blue shorts and a red T-shirt she was wearing made everything look so normal.

"This is your daddy, he's come home early just for you," Laura said, bending down and speaking into Sarah's ear. "See, he's exactly as I described him."

Perhaps for the first time, Matthew knew what he had to do. He mustn't show anything other than delight at meeting Sarah. If Laura sensed he knew what she had done, he didn't want to second-guess what she might do next. The time for further mistakes was over – he had ignored so many signs and warnings over the preceding months.

"Hello," he said squatting down. "You must be Sarah."

Sarah screwed up her face and pushed her body back against Laura's legs.

"Now, come on, Sarah," Laura said gently, "don't be shy, say hello to your daddy. He's been looking forward to meeting you all day."

As she spoke, Laura looked at Matthew in such a way that suggested there was nothing wrong with what she was doing. She was now living in a parallel world, her own world, but for her it was utterly real.

"Look, I'll show you," Laura said. "I'll kiss daddy hello and then you can do the same."

Laura reached round Sarah, put her hand behind Matthew's neck, and drew his face towards hers. Their lips met and he felt the tip of her tongue brush fleetingly against his.

"There you are. Now you give your daddy a kiss. Bend down, daddy," Laura said.

Sarah, a little reluctantly, put her arms on Matthew's shoulders, closed her eyes and puckered her lips. He kissed her on her forehead.

"Now, that wasn't very good, daddy, was it? You want a proper kiss don't you, Sarah?"

"Yes," Sarah said in a hesitant whisper.

"All right," Matthew said, kissing her as gently as he could.

"There, we've all said hello," Laura said. "Let's go in now and have a cup of tea."

Laura and Sarah led the way but, just inside the door, Sarah stopped, reached up and took Matthew's hand in hers.

"I'll show you the way, Daddy," she said, gaining in confidence. "I've never had a daddy before."

Laura looked over her shoulder and smiled.

A million things were going through Matthew's mind.

Question after question whirled round from every corner of his brain, each new question replaced by the need to know one thing: what had been happening in this little girl's life for the last six years?

I've never had a Daddy before.

"Go and sit at the table with daddy while I make the tea," Laura told Sarah.

Looking down at the young and expectant smiling face as she once again took his hand and led him towards the table, he couldn't spoil this moment for her, he couldn't tell her he wasn't her daddy.

Not now.

She would have to know, but not now.

"What do you like in a sandwich, Sarah?" Laura asked, opening the cupboard by the freezer. "There's jam, marmalade, marmite …"

"Marmite please," Sarah told Laura, but her eyes never left Matthew.

He was faced with a little girl who was staring at him with wide-open eyes, her expectations so obvious, and yet he didn't know what to say. It needed Sarah to take the initiative but her question wasn't quite what he'd anticipated.

"Why don't you and mummy live together?" she asked.

Matthew looked across the kitchen towards Laura. She was spreading butter on a slice of bread but stopped as she waited for him to say something.

"We thought it best if we didn't," he said. "We were making each other unhappy."

Sarah screwed up her little face in confusion. "So why did you get married?"

"We thought –" he started to say.

"There you are, Sarah," Laura said, placing a sandwich in front of her. "Now why don't you ask daddy some different questions? There's no need to know just yet what happened all those years ago. You've only just met."

Laura went back across the kitchen to make the tea as the kettle had just clicked off. "Tell you what," she said, "why don't we ask you the questions. I'll start … Um, let me see, does daddy look as you expected him to look?"

Sarah picked up the sandwich and took a bite, her eyes studying Matthew's face. "Older," she said, innocently, "and taller. When the other girls at school ask me why my daddy never collects me, I tell them that he is abroad with his job – mummy told me to say that – but I've told them he is tall, has dark hair and he is good looking." She took another bite of her sandwich. "I suppose, yes, he does look like what I expected. Why have you never been to see me?" she then asked, the sandwich poised between the plate and her mouth.

"It's not that I didn't want to, Sarah. I just thought it best if I didn't," he said.

"Why?"

"Because I didn't want to upset your mummy," he said.

"But other girls at school whose mummies and daddies no longer live together see their daddies. They go to them for weekends and they say they have lots of fun, but you never even came to see me."

Her little face dropped and she started fiddling with the remains of her sandwich.

Matthew covered Sarah's hand with his.

"I wanted to, Sarah, believe me, but I didn't think it would have been for the best," he told her, but he knew she wouldn't understand.

Laura puts mugs of tea on the table and a glass of orange for Sarah. "You're here now, Sarah, because your mummy and daddy feel you are old enough to understand," she said almost as though she had read his thoughts.

"But mummy should be here too."

"As I told you when you were having your bath, she'll be here later," Laura said, stealing a look at Matthew. "She had to work."

Matthew sensed annoyance creeping into Laura's voice, although her face gave nothing away. She was behaving as though she really did expect him to believe her and was asking him to be part of this world she had created.

She sat down and picked up her mug of tea.

"I need to go to the toilet," Sarah said, pushing her chair away from the table.

"Can you manage on your own?" Laura asked her, moving the orange away from the edge of the table.

"Of course I can," Sarah said. "I have managed for years."

"You know where the bathroom is," Laura said.

"I'll be fine," Sarah informed them both, shrugging as she left the kitchen.

"What's going on?" Matthew asked Laura once Sarah was out of earshot.

Laura looked genuinely surprised. "With Sarah, you mean?"

"Of course I mean Sarah," he said.

"I thought it was time you met her," Laura told him, as though he should have know what her answer would be.

"But do you realise what you've done?"

"Done? I've done nothing. I've merely brought a little girl down to Westerham to meet her father."

Laura was sipping her tea as though they were discussing where they should go shopping. He wanted to ask her where she'd been while he was in Birmingham but something told him to wait. Laura was being cold, almost distant.

"But you can't just take somebody's daughter like that, it's against the law," he said.

"I didn't take somebody's daughter, I brought Sarah to see her father – you."

"But it was without her mother's permission?"

Reminding Laura that he'd told her more than once that Sarah wasn't his daughter would have achieved nothing. She needed help, medical help, but before he could do anything about that, he had to return Sarah to Leamington Spa.

First, though, he had to get Sarah out of the cottage and away from Laura. There was no apparent threat but if he allowed this charade to carry on it was going to be a lot more difficult as each minute passed.

"You heard me tell Sarah just now, her mother will be down later," Laura said.

Matthew wanted to shout at her, take her by the shoulders and shake some sense into her. "Yes, I'm sorry, of course you did," he said.

Laura looked at her watch. "She should be here about eight o'clock, if the traffic isn't too bad."

"Does she plan to stay?" he said, not believing what he was asking.

Laura nodded.

She looked so young and innocent but something had happened to cause her to enter into this fantasy world she had created. After talking to Julie and Patrick, it certainly wasn't what he had expected. He foresaw confrontation, tears, mood swings, regression – he foresaw everything but this.

"For the weekend," Laura said. "She'll take Sarah back with her on Sunday."

"How long ago did you arrange all of this?"

"Oh, about a month or so," Laura said. "We thought it'd be a lovely surprise for you."

Sarah was taking longer than he'd expected. "It really is a lovely surprise," he said, smiling. "I'll just go and check on Sarah." He got up and went to the door. "And then," he said, "I'll take her to the village and get something nice for supper. We haven't got much in, have we?"

Laura turned her head and looked at him, her eyes narrowing slightly. "I went shopping yesterday. It's all unloaded and put away," she said.

"Okay, that's great."

Matthew looked round and saw that Sarah was half way down the stairs. Stepping out of Laura's sight, he lifted a finger to his lips and gestured for Sarah to sit down where she was. She gave him a funny look but did as he asked. Going a little way into the kitchen he said, "So what have you got for this evening?"

Laura was still sitting at the kitchen table. "I bought pizzas. I thought we could heat them up when Emily gets here. Pizza, salad and garlic bread, if that's all right." She smiled for the first time since he'd seen her at the front door.

"Yes, that'll be fine," he said, returning her smile. "I'll be back in a sec."

He almost ran down the hall. He held his finger to his lips, and Sarah frowned. Taking her by the hand he almost yanked her down the remainder of the steps and then towards the front door, grabbing the car keys and his mobile phone as he passed the hall table.

Sarah didn't make a noise until they got to the door, but then she suddenly jerked backwards and screamed.

"Where are you taking her?" Laura asked, standing by the kitchen door.

As soon as Sarah saw Laura, she pulled herself free from Matthew and ran down the hall. Laura put a protective arm round the child and they both looked at him.

"I asked where were you were taking her?" Laura repeated.

Sarah's eyes were wide open, staring at him, terrified.

"Back to where she should be," Matthew said, starting to move down the hall, "with her mother. What you have done –?"

"Don't, Matthew, don't come any closer."

Laura's eyes suddenly became wild and the protective arm round Sarah tightened as her forearm moved up towards Sarah's neck. From behind her she produced a kitchen knife.

"I've told you, Sarah is where she is supposed to be, with her father."

Matthew stopped. "Look, this is stupid," he said as calmly as he could, not taking his eyes from the knife in Laura's hand. "Neither of us want Sarah to be harmed, just let her go and then –"

"What?" Laura screamed at him.

He saw Sarah wince.

"What will you do then? Have me locked up?" She pointed the knife at him. "You think I'm fucking stupid, don't you? I know where you've been. You've been finding out all about me, haven't you? And how were Patrick and the lovely Julie?"

"How do you know …?"

"Because I fucking saw you, didn't I? I told you I'm not stupid. So how are they?"

"They –"

"I don't want to fucking know," Laura spat at him.

She pulled Sarah a little further into the kitchen.

Matthew instinctively moved forward.

"Stop!" Laura shouted.

"I want …" Sarah started to say.

"And you can fucking shut up as well."

Now there were silent tears streaming down Sarah's face.

"So what happens now?" Matthew asked, trying to keep his voice calm.

Inside everything was churning. He had made a gross error of judgement and created a situation that put Sarah's life at risk.

There was supposed to be no risk taking.

Laura looked uncertain. She hadn't planned for this. "I … I don't … I'll tell you what happens, you leave … no … "

"You want me to leave so that I can go for the police?" Matthew spread his hands. "I'm not going anywhere. I'm not leaving Sarah alone with you."

Whimpering had joined Sarah's tears. She really was terrified.

"So, what do you suggest?" Laura said sarcastically. needing time to think.

"I suggest you put that knife down, let Sarah go, and we can talk about this like adults."

Matthew took a step forward.

Laura lowered the knife so that the cutting-edge was against Sarah's throat.

"Talk like adults?" she repeated in a singsong voice. "I told you, if you come any nearer, I'll cut her."

Matthew screwed up his eyes. "Why? Why Laura? Why are you doing this? Why would you want to harm Sarah?"

Laura's mouth opened wide and her top lip curled upwards as she threw her head back and laughed. "You've no fucking idea, have you? You're pathetic. I've done it once so I'm quite capable of doing it again. You've –"

"What do you mean you've done it once? What are you talking about?" Matthew shouted at her.

A satisfied, maniacal expression crossed Laura's face. "I've used a knife. I've used one before and I'll use it again."

"Laura," he said slowly, "what are you talking about?"

"Francesca fucking Middleton-Smythe didn't hang herself," she sneered triumphantly. "I did it. I cut the cow and then made it look like a suicide."

Chapter Twenty-Nine

Matthew could feel the sweat running down his back.

He closed his eyes only wanting to open them again if none of this was happening. It couldn't be happening.

Laura had to be lying.

There was no logical explanation for her wanting to meet Francesca, let alone harming her. She had to be lying, and if she were lying about that, she was lying about what she could do to Sarah ... but if she were lying, how did she know that Francesca was dead, and that she had committed suicide?

Opening his eyes, he stared at Laura.

"All right, Laura," he said quietly this time, trying to keep in control of his voice, "this has gone far enough. You are ill and you need help. Please don't make things worse for yourself. Just give me the knife and let Sarah come to me."

"Why?" Laura spat at him, her eyes narrowing and her grip on the knife tightening. "I've just told you, I murdered that fucking woman and you tell me not to make things worse? How could things be worse?" She moved her arm and jerked Sarah's head up. "This little Madam here is your flesh and blood, there's nothing I would like more ..."

Sarah suddenly slumped, her legs caving in beneath her, her eyes closed. Laura struggled to hold her up but she wasn't strong enough. She went down on her knees in an attempt to support her.

Sarah was like a rag doll in front of her.

Matthew knew he had to act, he could see in Laura's eyes that she didn't know what to do next. The knife was hanging by her side as she tried to pull Sarah upright.

"Wake up, you little bitch, stand up!" Laura shouted at Sarah.

Matthew launched himself into the space between them aiming for Laura's right side. She detected the movement and looked up, lifting the knife as she did. Grabbing for her wrist, he misjudged it, and felt the blade of the knife cutting into his hand ... but somehow, he wrestled the knife from her and threw it into the kitchen.

To defend herself, Laura had to release Sarah who had now

slumped completely to the floor. Matthew could feel the blood pouring out of the cut to his hand,

Suddenly Laura leapt at him over Sarah, her hands and fingers like claws. "You bastard!" she shrieked, spittle covering his face.

She was on top of him, her arms and legs lashing out.

Although small he knew how strong she was, and what she could do. With lips drawn back from her teeth, she tried to bite him. The blood from his hand was getting everywhere and his grip on her wrist was slippery.

"You've fucking abused me for long enough!" Laura shouted as she forced one of her knees between Matthew's legs and tried to jerk it upwards.

The sides of her mouth were frothing and there was madness in her eyes. Taking hold of both of her wrists, he tried to throw her off balance, but it took all his strength to fend off the blows from her hands and feet.

They fell onto the floor.

He managed to get both of his legs round Laura's middle and he squeezed as hard as he could. At first she didn't react but suddenly the strength went out of her and she collapsed on top of him, her screams and profanities replaced by whimpering.

They lay like that for a full minute, both gasping for breath.

Matthew's blood was everywhere.

He thought Laura had passed out but as he started to lift her from him, she made one final attempt to scrabble away but he had the upper hand, he grabbed her again and she gave in straightaway.

Laura was lying on her front, the side of her face against the carpet and he had both of her arms behind her, forcing them up her back.

"It's over," he gasped. "I don't want to hurt you, but if I have to, I will."

He was still out of breath.

The fight hadn't lasted long but Laura had fought like a demented cat. The skill she demonstrated in Penang wasn't there. His mind also flashed back to the struggle he had with Francesca on the cross-channel ferry.

Now Laura was subdued.

He looked around, trying to locate something that he could use to tie her wrists and ankles. The tieback for the hall curtain was hanging loose so, holding her wrists with a bloodied hand, he stretched for it and then fastened her wrists together. His blood covered the back of her T-shirt and her face. To retrieve the other tieback he had to release his grip on her, but she didn't move.

He fastened the cord round her ankles.

During the fight, they had moved away from Sarah.

Matthew looked at the little bundle, praying that Sarah had only fainted. She was lying on her side, facing away from him. Lifting her arm, he felt for a pulse.

It was there and it was strong.

He had to get a dressing on his hand. The cut was deep and it was still bleeding badly.

He picked Sarah up and carried her through to the living room, placing her on the sofa before going back to the kitchen to get the first aid box. As he stepped over Laura, her eyes remained closed but she was breathing steadily. There were bubbles of spittle on her lips.

After bathing and dressing the wound on his hand as best he could, he went to the phone and called Wendy Carter's mobile. He knew he should have dialled 999 but there was still this underlying need to protect Laura as much as he could.

He didn't want to speak to any strangers.

"Wendy Carter," she said in a tired voice.

"Wendy, it's Matthew Ryan."

"Matthew, sorry, I didn't look to see who the call was from. What –?"

"Wendy, please just listen first, and then I'll do whatever you tell me."

He took the phone into the living room and sat down by Sarah. Her eyes were open but there wasn't any reaction when she saw him.

She seemed to be in a trance.

"It's Laura," he said. "There's been a fight and I have had to tie her up for her own safety."

"Why what's happened?" Wendy asked, sounding shocked.

"Wendy, it's a long story and I'd prefer to tell you face-to-face. Can you come as soon as possible?"

"Well ... hang on a minute." Matthew heard some mumbling in the background before she came back on the phone. "Matthew, if I understand you correctly, I can't come unofficially, you realise that?"

"Of course, but can you at least come yourself?"

His hand was beginning to throb and he could see that the blood was already oozing through the bandage. He felt weak and slightly nauseous.

"Yes. We'll be there in about twenty minutes."

"Thanks."

"Matthew, are you all right? You sound as though ..."

"It wasn't very pleasant doing what I had to do," Matthew told her. "A knife was involved."

"A knife!" she repeated. "Are either of you hurt?"

"My hand's cut, that's all."

"Badly?"

"Pretty badly, yes."

"An ambulance will be coming with us."

"I don't think ..."

The trouble was he wasn't thinking.

Somebody ought to check Sarah over.

"Yes, okay." He said.

He deliberately hadn't mentioned Sarah to Wendy because he wanted to be able to explain what had happened when she could see him, when they were face to face.

He needed to keep an eye on both Laura and Sarah before the police arrived but he didn't want them to be in the same room. Sarah was still traumatised and he thought if she saw Laura, it would make matters worse.

He went into the hall.

Laura was as he had left her but her eyes were now open. He knelt down beside her and lifted her in to a sitting position, her back against the wall. She looked at him with a sad smile on her face.

"I suppose you think you've won?" she whispered, her voice sounding very strange.

Matthew got a cushion from the hall chair and put it behind her head.

"There is no winning and losing, Laura. You're ill and you need help," he said, trying to avoid her eyes.

She ignored him. "Did you enjoy the fight? Did it turn you on?" she asked solicitously.

Matthew held up his bandaged hand. "So much so, I did this to make it more realistic," he said, shaking his head as he checked her ankles and wrists to make sure the ties weren't too tight. Her shoes had come off during the fight and her feet were spotted with his blood. He wet a finger and rubbed the spots off.

It suddenly hit him that he had really lost her.

His mind had been in such a turmoil he hadn't given himself time to appreciate the full consequences of what had happened. Laura had to be locked up for her own safety and assessed.

He was still holding her foot in his hand. There was no going back from this because it was all over. He had woken up from the long nightmare he didn't realise he was having until a few days ago.

"Did tying me up –?"

"Stop it, Laura," he said. "It's all over. The police will be here in a minute and then …"

"You think they'll take me away," she said, her lips showing the hate that he now knew had been building up inside her for so long, "so that you can go back to her and that daughter of yours?"

"That will never happen, Laura. You see, you made one fundamental mistake. You forgot I told you that Sarah isn't my daughter. I haven't the faintest idea who –"

"No," Laura said, her eyes narrowing. "You made the mistake. She *is* your daughter. You *are* her father. I don't care what that bitch of an ex-wife told you, she is your daughter, and therefore I didn't make the mistake, you did."

"How can you be so sure?" he asked, knowing Laura was lying.

"I was a private investigator, don't forget, and I have contacts. If she isn't your daughter why wasn't her birth certificate changed after you were divorced."

"I didn't know that was possible."

Laura smiled.

Matthew heard the distant wail of a police siren and from her reaction Laura heard it too.

"Kiss me," she said suddenly.

"What?"

"Kiss me. Just one last kiss, please." She lifted her head from the wall and stared at him with unblinking eyes. "I do love you, I have always loved you and I did want to be Mrs Ryan."

"What do you mean?" he asked.

"I mean you have made another dreadful mistake, but it's too late now. Kiss me, just once more, please."

Matthew was still holding her foot.

He bent forward and their lips touched, gently at first but then her tongue shot into his mouth and memories of what they had done together flooded back. It couldn't have all been a lie, he thought. She had to have some feelings for him. He lifted his hand from her foot and ran his fingers down the side of her face.

He wanted to touch her one last time.

Laura pushed her mouth harder against his.

Suddenly, the pain was excruciating.

Laura had Matthew's bottom lip between her teeth and she was biting as hard as she could. He managed to get his fingers into the corner of her mouth and he forced it open.

"You bitch!" he shouted, lifting his bandaged hand to his lips. It came away with fresh blood on the material.

She sneered.

His blood was on her mouth and it dribbled down towards her chin.

"Don't you mean 'you cow'? Now who will they believe?" she snarled. "When they hear what you did to me and what you've done, you'll be the one who will be taken away. Nobody abuses me and gets away with it."

The police sirens were outside.

Matthew's lip was already swelling up, the taste of blood horrible.

"They will listen to the truth, Laura," he told her with difficulty.

He went into the living room to check on Sarah.

She was still lying on the sofa but with her eyes squeezed closed and her thumb was in her mouth. Matthew brushed a few strands of hair away from her forehead.

"It'll all be over soon," he told her, "and then I'll take you back to your mummy."

Sarah didn't open her eyes but he felt her little body shudder.

The doctor explained that the palm of the hand was one of the most awkward places to anaesthetise and stitch but, although it was painful, Matthew couldn't have cared less. His hand and lip were throbbing and his head was thumping. Just outside the treatment room, two police officers were waiting to take him to the police station.

Laura had kept her promise.

She dredged the accusations she made against him from the depths of her sadistic imagination and the police had little choice but to arrest him. As he got into the ambulance with a police officer either side of him, Wendy Carter told him not to worry and that the truth would prevail.

Matthew did not share her optimism.

A young woman police officer took Sarah away. Laura had even told the police that he had abused Sarah as well, and that he was integral to the plot to snatch her from her mother.

Catching only a fleeting glimpse of her as she was taken through the front door, he prayed that the awful experience would not have any long-term effects on her

Sarah didn't look back and he didn't blame her.

Watching the needle doing its best to join the palm of his hand together, and with his lip feeling as though he had completed ten rounds with a prize-fighter, he felt totally dejected and isolated. He hadn't been told everything, but all he needed to know at that stage was that he'd been accused of rape, physical and mental abuse against Laura and aiding in Sarah's abduction and subsequent abuse.

There was going to be a time for self-recrimination, but right at that moment he was more concerned with self-preservation. As far as he was aware, he hadn't done anything wrong other than offer a home, security and probably the most important of all, love, to an absolute bitch from hell. She may have been pretty and petite but she had become his nightmare. Even when Patrick and Julie had tried to tell him the truth, he had inwardly done everything he could to find excuses and ways of controlling the situation. He had dismissed the obvious and, as a result, he now found himself in police custody.

He had been an absolute fool.

A total idiot.

"That'll be painful for a while," the doctor informed him. "She must have put up one hell of a fight."

The nurse, who was assisting the doctor, took the dish over to a side table.

"I beg your pardon?" Matthew said.

The doctor was packing away his other bits and pieces. He shrugged and the nurse, a woman in her mid-fifties, turned to look at them. "Oh, nothing," the doctor said without making eye contact, "I just thought she must have put up a fight, that's all."

"What exactly are you implying?" Matthew asked him, rolling down the sleeve of his blood-spattered shirt.

"Nothing, mate," the doctor said, holding one hand up defensively.

He was young – probably early thirties – with dark hair and an equally dark complexion, as well as being quite tall and good looking. He had a scar that resembled a duelling scar running from the corner of his left eye and across his cheek so that it almost reached his mouth.

He stopped what he was doing and glared at Matthew.

"All right," he said quite vehemently, glancing towards the door. "I don't like men who go around beating up women."

Matthew slowly slipped on his jacket. "And you have decided that's what I did?" he said.

"Well," the doctor said, this time slightly defensively, "the police out there suggest as much."

Matthew nodded. "I see. The jury has heard the evidence, discussed it and has come up with a guilty verdict, have they?"

The doctor went onto the attack again. "Your type makes me sick if –"

"My type? What exactly is my type, doctor?" Matthew held up his hand. "No, don't bother answering that," he said, "because if you do you might just put your career on the line more than you already have. For your information, *mate*, this," he held up his hand again, "and this," he pointed at his swollen lip, "are as a result of me defending myself while trying to save the life of a little girl who some madwoman had decided was fair game for her sadistic fantasies. If that doesn't conform to the stereotype you get in here, then I apologise. But on this occasion you are way off the mark." Matthew moved towards the door. "I suggest in future you concentrate on what you are paid to do and keep your opinions to yourself."

Matthew opened the door and the police officers stood up.

"I'm all yours," he said to them, slamming the door. "But hopefully not for too long."

It turned out to be longer than he anticipated but he was back at the cottage and scrubbing the carpet in the hall by midnight. Although he felt dead on his feet, he knew that if he went to bed the last thing that would come to him would be sleep.

Wendy Carter had played a major part in his release.

Although questioned, he was surprised when it appeared to be a matter of routine rather than what he had expected. The two interviewing officers repeated the accusations Laura had made but then the senior of the two – a middle-aged woman in civilian clothes – said, "… but we don't believe anything that woman has said." Having gone over his version of events – which is what took the time because he needed to go as far back to the accident in Warwick and the first threatening letter – the police seemed satisfied.

When told he was free to leave, it was with the caveat that he might be required for further questioning. Just as he was about to leave the station, Wendy Carter appeared through a side door and guided him towards a room opposite the main desk. Closing the door, she said, "Well, things certainly reached a head, didn't they?"

"The understatement of the year," Matthew said as he sat down by the open window so that he could breathe in the fresh air. It was late and the air was cool.

The room, which he hadn't been in before, was simply furnished but, as it had a small fridge, a kettle, mugs and various containers on a table, he assumed it was a waiting room rather than one allocated for interrogation.

"So what has happened?" he asked.

He touched his lip. It was still very sore.

"I can't tell you everything," Wendy told him as she checked the kettle to see if there was any water in it, "but I'm afraid Laura has been sectioned."

"So quickly? I'm surprised but what does it actually mean?"

"Basically we can't do anything more with her until the psychiatrists have had their go."

"So who was it …?"

"Sarah. She might be only six or, as she insisted, very nearly seven, but she is one cool little girl …"

"Sarah! Where is she?"

Wendy turned round from plugging in the kettle. "I'm sorry, Matthew, but she's currently in a car on her way home. She was thoroughly checked over and, other than still being a little frightened, she is fine. I spoke to her mother personally and she told me about your visit."

"I decided to go and see her before I knew about Sarah being taken," he said.

"Yes, I know." Wendy selected a couple of mugs, inspecting them for cleanliness. "Coffee or tea?"

"Coffee, please. Black, sweet and strong."

Wendy smiled, spooning coffee granules into the mugs. "As I said, she was one cool little girl. I wouldn't have believed she would recover so quickly after being threatened the way she was, but she corroborated everything that you'd described."

Wendy added water to the coffee and took the mugs over to the table.

"But why has Laura been sectioned? Surely …?"

Wendy sipped her coffee. "Probably because she's mad." She put the mugs on the table. "No, sorry, that wasn't what I meant to say …"

"But it is the truth."

"I can but agree. When interviewed and she sensed that her version of events was being questioned, she went berserk. She attacked the WPC who was with her in the interview room and it took two PCs to restrain her. She was frothing at the mouth and needed cuffing and locking up. The duty doctor was called and he took one look at her and, well, you know the rest."

The coffee was very strong, very sweet and very hot, but it was as good as a shot of whisky, although Matthew did wince as he held the hot rim of the mug against his lip.

What had happened seemed like a lifetime ago, leaving him feeling as though Wendy was talking about a complete stranger, not the woman he had asked to marry him. He was surprised how easily he had managed already to distance himself from reality. He knew the truth would hit him at some stage but, until then, he would manage as best he could.

"She told me that she murdered Francesca Middleton-Smythe," he said.

"It wouldn't surprise me if at some stage she doesn't confess to assassinating JF Kennedy." Wendy reached across the table and her fingers touched Matthew's. "Again, I'm sorry. That was uncalled for but we are checking out the Middleton-Smythe connection. I assume you repeated to her what I told you had happened."

"No, I didn't. I told her that the investigations were ongoing," he said.

"Are you sure?"

"Positive."

"Thanks for that, but she could have found out what happened to her some other way." Wendy changed tack. "How on earth did you manage to stay with her for so long?"

Matthew shook his head. "Up until the last week, there was nothing that made me think she was anything else but normal. It's all happened so quickly." He stared at the coffee. "I can't believe what's happened."

"Believe me when I say I'm sorry it did happen but, as I tried to explain last Friday, it was always on the cards."

Matthew took a deep breath. "So, I'm off the hook, am I?"

"You were never really on it," Wendy said. "I'd briefed my boss as to what was going on and I'll just say that contingencies were already in place. Under the circumstances, your arrest was routine."

"I won't ask what you mean by that, but good," he said solemnly. "What happens next?"

"We'll have to wait for the psychiatrist's report before we know, but thank God it ended the way it did. Things could have been a lot worse."

"You can say that again but, even so, it's a pity they had to happen at all." He finished his coffee. "Well, I'd better go before you change your minds."

Wendy smiled. "I'm not a policewoman twenty-four hours a day, you know. If you need a shoulder then …"

"Thanks." Matthew stood up, the chair scraped on the floor. "I'll need a bit of time."

"Of course, but the offer is still there."

Wendy Carter also stood up.

They started to shake hands, but Wendy changed her mind and put hers on Matthew's shoulders. She kissed him on the cheek before moving her lips to his.

It was a brief, light but very intimate kiss.

"Do I need to apologise this time?" she asked.

"Only if you don't intend kissing me again."

She smiled. "You're a lovely man, Matthew Ryan, but you're also a very gullible one. Please learn from what you've experienced – women can be worse than any man, please don't forget that the next time."

After exchanging a look that meant something only to them, he left, the fresh air hitting him as he walked out of station, but perhaps not out of Wendy Carter's life.

As he got into the waiting taxi, he felt empty, and just a little bewildered.

Chapter Thirty

Matthew had scrubbed the hall carpet until his left arm ached, but no matter how much he tried, he couldn't cleanse his mind of what had happened.

He imagined Laura in some institution somewhere, in a padded cell and probably heavily sedated. During her more lucid moments, he wondered if she felt as lost and lonely as he did.

He couldn't hate her.

Something had happened in her life to twist her mind. If only she had let him try to help rather than use him as a means to an end. She had come very close to achieving her aim and destroying him.

He wondered if he would ever know the real reason she was the way she was.

Was she abused as a child?

And he meant really abused?

After throwing the scrubbing brush at the wall in frustration, he went into the living room. He picked up the whisky decanter and a glass from the sideboard with the full intention of drinking himself into a stupor.

He went into the conservatory because he couldn't go anywhere else in the house. Her things were everywhere, and while one item belonging to her existed, she existed.

Sitting down, he saw her dancing to the *Flower Duet* as she slowly let her dress fall to the floor. Had it all been a charade, a very serious and violent game for which only Laura had known the rules?

The whisky eventually worked and he fell into a troubled sleep.

Something woke him but it took him a few seconds to realise what it was – the phone was ringing.

The sound was piercing and he wondered who it might be.

He didn't want to speak to anybody, there was nothing anybody could say to make him feel better.

He let it ring.

The answer-phone cut in.

"Hello, Matthew," a voice he recognised immediately said. "It's Emily."

He scrambled across the floor listening to her as he raced for the receiver.

"I was told you would probably be at home and I wanted to –"

"Emily? I'm here," he almost shouted, lifting the receiver to his ear and jabbing at the answer-phone.

There were a few seconds silence.

"I wanted to say thank you for what you did and to apologise for thinking …"

"Emily, I don't warrant either. I'm so sorry for placing Sarah in danger. I was so wrapped up in my own self-interests I didn't see what was coming. I'm so sorry. How is Sarah?"

"Very subdued but she's as well as can be expected. She can't stop talking about you and what you did," Emily said.

"Thank God I was able …"

"She also wants to know why she hadn't met you before."

"What do you mean?" he said.

"After such a traumatic experience, one of the first things she asked me when the police brought her home was why I hadn't let her meet her daddy before."

Matthew closed his eyes. "That must have been very difficult, for you especially – " he said quietly.

"I told her we divorced when she was a very little girl and that our lives had taken separate courses that meant we …"

"Emily, I think she's been lied to quite enough, don't you?"

"That wasn't really a lie, but I agree, Matthew, that's why I promised to ring you and ask whether you'd like to come and see your daughter again."

"My … my daughter?"

He didn't think anything could be said that would hit him like a sledgehammer ever again: two words, just two words that meant more to him …

"Your daughter, Matthew," Emily said again.

"But …"

"Can we leave the explanations until we can see each other?"

"But, you … I've always believed she was …"

"At the time I thought it was the right thing to do."

"How can …?"

"Matthew, please, not now. I will tell you everything, but not now."

"It's been a long time."

"Too long," Emily said.

"I'll be with you as soon as I can but hopefully within a few hours," he said as the tears came to his eyes.

"I'll tell Sarah and we'll both be waiting."

Chapter Thirty-One

Before leaving Westerham, Matthew phoned Wendy Carter's mobile.

Although he was allowed to come home without being charged, he didn't want to jeopardise any future investigations, or maybe generate the odd change of heart because of what could be determined as his strange behaviour.

As far as he knew, Laura was in a secure unit somewhere, waiting to be assessed, and at some stage the police would want to take a full statement from him. However, after what had happened, rushing up to see his ex-wife and daughter within hours of his fiancée being sectioned might appear a little peculiar. Things were moving very, very quickly – too quickly? – and his reactions needed to be rational and his actions properly thought through.

That would make a change.

Wendy answered almost immediately.

"Hello, Matthew," she said, sounding as though she was genuinely pleased to hear from him. "You're lucky to have caught me. After yesterday's excitement I've just come off duty and I was about to enjoy an undisturbed long hot bath."

"Sorry, Wendy, but I do need to talk to you. Well, in fact, I need your advice," he said. "Something has come –"

"Talk away. How are you feeling and did you get some sleep?"

"I'm a bit sore but otherwise okay, and what sleep I had was alcohol-induced," he said.

"I wish I could have joined you ... with the alcohol, that is," Wendy told him.

"I can't believe ... No, I don't want to go there at the moment."

"I don't blame you. So what can I do for you?" she asked.

"Yes, sorry, I'm keeping you from your bath but ... but I had a phone call a few minutes ago ... from Emily."

"Ah," Wendy said. "Did you? And what did she want?"

There hadn't been any intentional emphasis when Wendy had said 'What did *she* want?' but Matthew noted a definite change in her tone of voice.

"Well ... for a start she told me that Sarah ... that Sarah is my daughter after all …"

After so long believing the opposite, he couldn't get his head round the words he was using. Laura had told him that Sarah was his daughter but, well, she was a proven liar, wasn't she?

"What? But why did your *ex-wife* tell you …?"

This time there was a definite barb in the way she said *ex-wife*.

"I don't know what's been going on, Wendy, but depending on how you answer my next question, I might find out."

"And what is your next question?" she asked, sounding reluctant, almost as though she knew what was coming.

"Emily wants me to go to Leamington and … I wondered if there were any official reason why I can't go," Matthew said.

"What do you mean?"

"Well, because of the kidnapping and my involvement with Laura, I thought maybe I was … you know, still a suspect, and going to see Emily would appear suspicious," he said, before adding, "and if not suspicious, then perhaps a little strange."

There was an audible sigh at the other end of the phone, followed by a few seconds' silence. "You're putting me on the spot, Matthew," Wendy said. "That's an official question and I am off duty."

"Yes, I'm sorry, but I didn't know …"

"You did call my mobile."

"Yes, I did, but I thought …"

"What do you hope to gain from going to see Emily?" Wendy asked.

"Wendy, I have just discovered that the little girl I helped save yesterday is my daughter, after believing for six years that she was somebody else's. Isn't that reason enough?"

"Yes, I suppose it is, but …" Wendy started to say but stopped.

"So … is there any official reason …?"

"As I told you yesterday, you are off the hook but … no, if it's what you want to do, then there is no official reason why you can't go up there, but I will have to record this phone call on the file when I go in tomorrow."

"I understand, so …"

"Matthew, please remember what I said yesterday. You are a lovely man, but where women are concerned, you don't have a clue. Please, please be careful."

"What are suggesting?"

"I'm not suggesting anything. I'm just asking you to be careful, that's all. It's less than twenty-four hours since ... I don't have to tell you, do I?"

"No and is that a police officer talking or a woman?" Matthew asked.

"I'm a woman first, Matthew, and I know how calculating and devious we can be."

"Tell me about it," he said.

"Just be careful," Wendy said again. "And ring me when you get back."

"I will," he said, before adding, "Wendy, you've been wonderful all the way through this nightmare and I don't think I've ever said thank you."

"As I said, call me when you get back and I might just give you the opportunity to say thank you properly. Just don't rush into anything you might regret ... not again."

"I won't, I just want to see my daughter. Surely you can understand that."

"Yes, Matthew, I can but ... just be careful."

"I will and thank you. 'Bye Wendy."

"'Bye, Matthew and please call me when you get back."

The traffic on the M25 and M40 was heavier than he had expected and it took him over three hours to reach the outskirts of Leamington Spa. He had hurriedly packed an overnight bag and he allowed a rueful smile to cross his lips as he locked the front door of the cottage.

He eventually got away from Westerham at just after two o'clock.

His excitement and anticipation of what awaited him in Leamington Spa counteracted the throbbing in his bandaged hand and the soreness of his still swollen lip. As it was his right hand that had been injured, changing gear wasn't a problem and he was able to rest his injured hand on the steering wheel. He was all too aware that he looked a bit of a mess but the importance of the next few hours supplanted all else.

After leaving the M40 at Junction 13, he took the Banbury Road towards the town. He was driving in a bit of a daze – in fact he was more apprehensive now than when he'd taken Emily's call that morning – so he followed the signs to the town centre, knowing he could find his way to Emily's house from there. He reached the top of the Parade in the town centre, turned right into Clarendon Avenue and then left into Clarendon Street.

Although he had packed an overnight bag, he hadn't thought about how long he would be in the area, and therefore he hadn't given finding somewhere to stay any consideration. Pulling up behind a car that was reversing into a parking space, he noticed The Lansdowne Hotel on the other side of the road. He wasn't far from Craven Gardens, so on impulse he pulled across the road, parked and went into the hotel.

He booked a room for three nights.

It was Saturday and he didn't have any engagements until the following Wednesday, and even they could be postponed if necessary. If he still looked the way he did, it didn't matter whether he was delayed or not, he would cancel anyway.

After looking him up and down, the receptionist in the hotel – a small, plump, middle-aged woman whom he guessed might be the owner – obviously wanted to ask him about his injuries but managed to keep her inquisitiveness to herself. With his right hand bandaged and the swollen lip, he did look as though he'd been in a fight, but nobody seeing him would understand – or perhaps believe – whom he had fought with and why.

As he drove into Craven Gardens ten minutes later, he slowed down to a crawl and then stopped.

He was doing the right thing, wasn't he?

It was a lovely day – the sun was shining and the sky was a clear blue. Would it have made any difference if it was pouring with rain and blowing a howling gale?

No, it wouldn't.

He really wasn't sure whether he had done the right thing in rushing up to Leamington Spa, but when he'd heard Emily say that Sarah was his daughter after all, he knew he couldn't stay away. What he didn't understand was why she had lied to him in the first place.

Did he want an explanation as to why he had missed out on six years of his daughter's life?

Yes, he did, but regardless of what the explanation might be, he didn't feel any bitterness towards Emily? Perhaps he was that naive and gullible man Wendy Carter had described him as being.

After taking a deep breath he selected first gear and drove the remaining fifty or so yards to No 14.

As he got to Emily's house, he glanced to his left.

Sarah was at the window, and when she saw him she waved excitedly before disappearing back into the room.

His daughter waved at him – *his daughter*.

He needn't have had any reservations whatsoever. As he had said to Wendy, Sarah alone was a good enough reason for him to be where he was.

He pulled in behind Emily's Clio but no sooner had he stopped than Sarah was on the opposite side of his car, knocking on the side window and smiling.

The innocence of a six – nearly seven – year old, he thought.

He opened his door and got out of the car.

Sarah rushed towards him from the back of the car and he picked her up with his left arm and whirled her round. Sarah put her arms round his neck and hugged him.

"Hello, Daddy," she said. "I love you."

"Hello, Sarah," he said as he kissed her, as best he could, on the cheek. "And I love you."

Sarah pulled back and looked at him. "I'm sorry that lady hurt you," she said.

Matthew smiled. "It's all right, Sarah. It looks worse than it is."

Emily was at the front door smiling at them both, with her arms folded. Then he saw the tears streaming down her face.

She was wearing jeans and a loose-fitting white top.

When Matthew lowered Sarah to the ground, she immediately took hold of his good hand. "Come on, Daddy," she said. "Mummy's waiting and I'll show you the house."

Reaching the front door Matthew stopped a few feet from Emily. She didn't attempt to hide her tears and he felt himself welling up too. Just being within a few feet of her again was a marvel and he didn't want to break the spell. Sarah's hand was still in his as Emily closed the gap between them. She put her hands on his shoulders and their faces were only inches apart.

"Thank you for coming, and so quickly," she said.

He saw her eyes dart to his swollen lip.

Matthew bent down and lifted Sarah up into the crook of his arm, and then in full view of whoever might be watching, he, Emily and Sarah put their arms round each other and they were all crying.

"I can't believe this is happening," Matthew said as he felt Emily's face next to his.

"It is happening, Daddy," a little voice said.

Emily and Matthew drew apart but still hung on to each other as they looked at Sarah. "It is happening," Sarah said again, looking anxiously from her mother to her father.

"Shall we go inside?" Emily suggested.

With Sarah clutching on to him, he followed Emily towards the kitchen. She turned round to face him, the tears streaming down her face.

"I've dreamed of this day for so long," she said. "And I'm sorry you had to be injured to make this all possible."

"The injuries are superficial," he said. "I couldn't even dream that this day would come because I didn't think it would ever happen."

"Well, it has," Sarah said.

They all laughed through their tears.

"Tell Daddy what you want to do," Emily said to Sarah.

Sarah looked at her father. "I want to go for a McDonalds, please," she said.

"A McDonalds?" Matthew repeated, his surprise evident.

"Yes," Sarah said. "All my friends go to McDonalds with their mummies and daddies, so that's what I want to do. And as it's Saturday afternoon, some of them might be there and I want to show off my daddy."

"Then that's what we will do," Matthew said.

Sarah, very reluctantly, went to bed at just after nine o'clock this evening. The remainder of the afternoon and early evening went as well as circumstances allowed, but was summed up for them all by

Sarah once again when she said, "We're just like a proper family," as she sunk her teeth into a quarter-pounder with cheese.

Conversation that afternoon was difficult because both Matthew and Emily were brimming with questions, and not only about the last six years. However, they were questions that would have to wait, so instead they concentrated on what Sarah had to say, and like any six – nearly seven – year-old girl, she had a lot to say.

Her excitement was very evident.

There were a couple of her school friends in the restaurant, and both Emily and Matthew had to smile when they saw the look Sarah gave them. It was as though she was saying, "See, I told you I had a daddy. Well, here he is."

There were no introductions because it was neither the time nor the place, plus of course none of them knew what the next twenty-four hours were going to bring, let alone the longer term.

So Sarah told Matthew all about her school and her friends, and when she could get a word in, Emily explained that her financial consultancy had gone from strength to strength.

Although there were no embarrassing silences, the explanation that Matthew so wanted would have to wait.

They went for a walk in Jephson Gardens – it was an option Matthew and Emily discussed when Sarah went to the restaurant toilet.

"How is she really?" Matthew asked.

"Subdued," Emily told him. "When the police brought her back yesterday evening, she was understandably very clingy, but this morning it was as though nothing had happened. She will want to talk but only when she is ready. The police told me what a great little girl she is and how she etold them, in detail, what had happened."

"That's why I'm able to be here," he said. "I had no idea that Laura was planning something like that."

"Let's not talk about her, not yet … we will need to talk but not yet … but tell me one thing: that mad woman is locked up, isn't she?"

"Yes, she's been sectioned, and evidently it could take weeks for her to be assessed."

"I'm so sorry for you," Emily said.

Matthew shook his head. "Don't be, I brought it on myself, but as you said, let's not talk about her. What does Sarah want to do when we leave here?"

"Let's ask her when ... here she is," she said smiling as Sarah rejoined them at the table.

It was Sarah's choice to go for an early evening walk.

The play area, from which Laura snatched her just over twenty-four hours earlier, was at the far end of the park. Sarah took Matthew's good hand in one of hers and held her mother's hand as well. She dragged two amazed adults towards the swings as though absolutely nothing had happened ... or was she telling them she did know but they had to move on?

Now Emily and Matthew were alone, and they were sitting either side of the fireplace, facing each other. They were both clutching long glasses of gin and tonic. Because of the circumstances, he hadn't really noticed the room in detail when he'd been there the previous day, but now he could see that, with the odd exception, the ornaments and pictures were the ones he and Emily had shared in their own house before that fateful day.

Because of recent occurrences, he was less confused but he was still puzzled as to what really started his first nightmare.

"So," he said, "I still can't believe I'm sitting here, but –"

"Before we go there," Emily said, interrupting, "what's happening tonight?"

"What do you mean?"

"Well ..."

"Emily, there's no need to worry. I've booked into The Lansdowne on Clarendon Street and I've got a front door key, so there are no time restrictions. This can take as long as is needed. Just tell me when you want me to go, I –"

"In that case, can we just wait and see? I don't know what your circumstances are, Matt. The police told me very little really, but ..."

"We both have an awful lot to tell the other but ..." He stopped and looked at Emily. "Explanations are only necessary if ... I don't know how to say what ..."

"Then let me help," Emily said. "The ... the moment I heard

you walk out of the house all those years ago, I so regretted what had happened. I knew I had made the biggest mistake of my life, and ..."

"By walking out, I made the biggest mistake of my life, too," Matthew said.

"I'm so, so sorry, Matthew, but at the time I thought it was for the best, for all the right reasons, no matter how much it hurt us both."

"I don't understand," he said slowly.

"And there's no reason why you should," she told him. "I want to tell you everything but ... I want to tell you how much I've missed you, how I have longed for you to be sitting where you are now. I ..." The tears were back. "I *was* seeing someone back then," she said, "but it wasn't someone I was involved with, not ... not in that way, and it wasn't a *he*, it was a *she* and she was a psychotherapist." Emily paused but only for a few seconds and Matthew didn't want to interrupt her. "I was suffering from MDD. You'll know what that is."

"I know it stands for Major Depressive Disorder, but I don't know much more about it," Matthew said.

"Initially they thought it was chronic postnatal depression but then they changed their minds. I knew what I was doing to you. I could see it in everything you did and said. I ... I was making all our lives, but mainly your life, so miserable I really didn't know what to do. The psychotherapist told me you should have been with me when I went to see her, but I couldn't take you with me. Don't ask me why, because if I had, none of this might have happened. Even before Sarah was born, I knew something was very wrong. I was so low. I thought it was because of how I looked. Evidently losing your self-esteem during pregnancy is quite common. I felt so useless, helpless and worthless. I thought I could never go back to how I once was. It was as though my whole head was inside out. I was so depressed I was even suicidal. When you were away on business I came so close a couple of times to taking an overdose – I wasn't brave enough to do anything else – but as it turned out, I wasn't brave enough to do that either."

"Emily, I –"

"No, Matt, let me finish. There isn't a lot more to say, and when

I have, you must decide whether there is a way forward for us," Emily said before taking a deep breath. "I know how utterly stupid this is going to sound – and you will have guessed by now – but I invented the man I was supposed to be having an affair with, and also the fact that he was Sarah's father. At the time I had decided the psychotherapist was useless because I wasn't getting anywhere. I certainly wasn't getting any better ... I was actually getting worse. I refused to take the drugs she prescribed for me –"

"You were always reluctant to take even an aspirin when you had a headache," Matthew said.

"I know," Emily said smiling. "I've always hated anything like that. But once again, if I had done as I was told, then who knows ... I was convinced I was ruining your life and the only solution was to let you go your own way –"

"But it wasn't just me, it was Sarah as well," Matthew said.

"Yes, yes, I know. I thought maybe when Sarah was born things would change but they didn't ... they got worse, but not because of her. I can assure you she was never ever in any danger. Early on the psychotherapist wanted to call in social services, but I convinced her that Sarah was not the cause. My despair went far deeper than just postnatal depression ... Sarah was perfectly safe but I hated what I was doing to you, and the state of mind I was in told me the only way out of it all was to let you go."

"But ... I'm sorry, Emily, I knew you were suffering from some sort of depression but if only you had ... if only *I* had –"

"There are so many *if onlys*, Matt. It took me over a year to recover fully but by then it was too late –"

"It would never have been too late," he said.

"It was then, Matthew, because after about nine months I did meet somebody else. We never lived together and the relationship only lasted six months, but in that time he helped to lift me out of whatever I was in. He did what the psychotherapist had been unable to do. But as soon as I was back to normal ... well, let me just say he knew that my heart was somewhere else, and it was ... it was wherever you were."

"So why didn't you even then try and find me?"

"I couldn't. I assumed you had moved on and would be with someone else. You could never have survived on your own,"

Emily said as she let a smile cross her lips. "But I was wrong, wasn't I?"

"Yes, Laura and I didn't ..."

"Let me finish, Matt."

"Sorry."

"As I told you earlier, I ploughed all my energy into being the best mother I could be to Sarah and into the consultancy, but even that didn't work. After five years of being without you I decided that I had to find out where you were and whether you –"

"You're not going to believe this but I did exactly the same thing, and that is why Laura –"

"What do you mean?" Emily asked, frowning.

"I wanted to know how you and Sarah were, so I employed Laura to find out ..."

"You what?"

"Laura was a private investigator and I employed her. I just wanted to know that you and Sarah were all right and happy," Matthew said.

Emily finished her drink before looking straight at Matthew.

"She did find me but there was no mention of you employing her. She told me that she was pregnant and that you were the father, and that you were going to get married. She knew you were still in love with me and she came to warn me off."

"None of that was true," Matthew said, "not then anyway."

"She was so rational, Matt. She told me if I had any ideas of getting back with you –"

"But it had been five years. Why would she ...?"

"I've no idea how she knew that I was trying to find you but after she told me she was pregnant and that you were getting married, well, I didn't bother asking any more questions," Emily said.

"And the second time she came to see you, why –?"

"What second time? There was no second time. The next thing that happened was when the police came to see me about the accident and accused me of running her down deliberately."

"Is that when I became a bastard of an ex-husband and Laura a lying slut?" he asked, smiling ruefully.

"It could have been worse," Emily said.

Matthew shook his head.

Getting his mind round what Laura had done to him was one thing, but trying to understand why Emily had decided that he was better off without her and Sarah was another. Both situations were unbelievable but for totally different reasons.

Both women had suffered mentally and their resultant behaviour had been equally irrational. Emily had lied because she thought she was ruining his life and the best course was to push him away, give him his *freedom.*

But Laura had wanted the opposite.

In a roundabout way, though, Emily was the reason he and Laura were together and his second nightmare had started, although he didn't know it at the time. If his relationship with Emily had simply fallen apart, then he would have understood, but it hadn't.

He shook his head and smiled.

"Did the last six-plus years really happen?" he asked.

"They did and I caused them." Emily said. "The question now is whether you can forgive me or not?"

"I was an idiot," he said, "an idiot because I let you go so easily, and an idiot to let Laura into my life when I did. I left you because it was what I thought you wanted. If only …"

"So, what happens now?" Emily asked.

"I've come back into your lives, yours and Sarah's, but as far as Sarah's concerned it is for the first time because she will have no memories of what … and it would be awful if … you know what I'm trying to say, Emily."

"Yes, I do and I don't want to give you a reason … This woman, Laura Stanhope, as I said, the police only told me so much about what happened, what –?"

"It's over, Emily. By taking Sarah the way she did, she showed what she was really capable of and … well, she's out of my life for good."

"So, after what we have now discussed, there is only one thing to read into why you are here," Emily said. "I will need to tell you a lot more about what I went through but, for now, just knowing –"

"You don't have anybody who …"

"No, not now, and as I said, not for a very long time …"

"So ... what do *you* want... It's been ..."

"I would have thought that was obvious. I ... I want you to be ... I want Sarah to have her father back, back to where he should have been for all this time," Emily said.

"And you and me? I couldn't ..."

Emily allowed a weak smile to cross her lips. "I ... I would be part of the package, if you want me to be," she said.

Standing up, Matthew held out his good arm. Emily stood in front of him and put her hands on his shoulders. They stared into each other's eyes.

"I want to kiss you," she said, "but ..."

"If you're gentle, it won't hurt ..."

They kissed as best they could.

"I was, and have been, a fool," Emily said as they finally parted.

"Emily, I think I may well have been the bigger fool," Matthew said, smiling.

"My name's Em, remember," she said, returning his smile. "You're not going back to the hotel tonight, are you?"

"Not tonight, tomorrow night or ever," Matthew said.

The End

About the Author

Nigel Lampard was a Lieutenant-Colonel in the British Army and after thirty-nine years of active service he retired in 1999. Trained as an ammunition and explosives expert, he travelled the world and was appointed an Order of the British Empire for services to his country.

As a second career he helped British Forces personnel with their transition to civilian life, and finally retired in 2007, when he and his wife Jane moved to Leigh-on-Sea in Essex. Married for over forty years, they have two sons and four grandchildren.

Nigel started writing after a tour in Berlin in the early 1980s – he fell in love with what was then a walled and divided city. After leaving Berlin, the only way he could continue this love was to write about it. By the time he completed the draft for his first novel he was already in love with writing.

Made in the USA
Charleston, SC
14 April 2015